THE AZTEC SECRET

JOE TOPLIFFE

THE AZTEC SECRET

Copyright © 2020 by Joe Topliffe

The following is a work of fiction. The story, characters, setting and events are either products of the author's imagination or are used fictitiously.

ISBN-13: 979-8648553828

ASIN: B08B7K5DJS

No part of this book may be photocopied, reproduced or distributed (electronically or otherwise) without the prior written permission of the author.

PROLOGUE

The sunset cast a dim orange glow that pierced through the trees of the rainforest. Birds chirped as a spider monkey swung from one tree to another, narrowly avoiding the green jays' nest. Thirty feet below, the trampling march of men could be heard. Leading the way was Hernán Cortés. Having been in this strange new land for the best part of two years, he was well versed in the dangers of travelling through these wooded areas in small numbers. Warriors from any number of tribes could ambush and take him prisoner, to be killed later in a sacrificial ceremony. But there was no chance of that now. Cortés was far from alone as he marched on through the trees. He had amassed a small army made up of his loyal Spanish soldiers and the Tlaxcalan tribe, with whom he'd struck a deal to gain their allegiance in the eradication of the Aztec empire.

A lot had happened in his two years in Mesoamerica. He had recruited soldiers from Trinidad and sailed from Cuba five-hundred strong to arrive in these new lands. From there he acquainted himself with the Aztec culture, before destroying it piece by piece, settlement by settlement. His journey from the Yucatan Peninsula, through Tabasco and across the country had been successful; he'd claimed the lands and converted some of the natives to Christianity. But for all his efforts to expand the Spanish empire, he had been labelled a mutineer and a disgrace by the crown for travelling to the new lands against orders. For everything he'd done for his country, this was how they repaid him; by fixating on one insignificant detail and ignoring his vastly outweighing accomplishments. His greatest conquest, the Aztec capital city of Tenochtitlán, still lay ahead of him. It would be a difficult task, but one that would truly be worthy of recognition. If he was able to do this, King Charles V would surely be unable to ignore his achievements any longer.

The city loomed into view as the dying light faded into blackness. He could see the tips of the familiar pyramids, the gentle flicker of flame from the newly lit torches as the emptying streets were being prepped for nightfall. He ceased his progress and turned to address his men. The marching feet stopped abruptly, the forest falling silent. Seeing the mass of soldiers under his command, Cortés took a moment to reflect on the progress he'd made. Looking then to the city of Tenochtitlán, he contemplated his next move. It was not his first visit to the capital, and the memory of fleeing the city after the death of the Aztec ruler, Moctezuma II, was all too fresh. After arriving in Tenochtitlán the first time, he had learned that the Aztec people considered him an emissary of the feathered serpent god Quetzalcoatl. He was taken in by Moctezuma II as a guest. Cortés preyed on their beliefs, using this knowledge to instil a sense of importance about him and his men. He would not be seen as a threat while this belief was held. Perhaps Moctezuma's greatest failure had been in offering gifts of gold to Cortés and his men. In an attempt to appease his strange foreign guests, he had only alerted them to the presence of riches and aggravated their lust for wealth.

Cortés had a plan to learn as much about this culture as possible; to uncover their weaknesses and formulate a plan to take over the city. It was going well, until he had to leave his lieutenant, Pedro de Alvarado, in charge while he saw off the men sent by the Governor of Cuba. Cortés had disobeyed the Governor's orders by setting sail to the new lands, and the Governor sought revenge. In his temporary role as leader while Cortés was away, Alvarado made a crucial mistake, orchestrating a massacre of the citizens who were celebrating the festival of Toxcatl. The revolt that occurred in the aftermath forced his men to flee the city.

He had wanted to fight, to conquer the city and ensure his efforts had not been in vain, but Cortés was a smart man. He had lost a lot of men and knew the odds were stacked heavily against him, so he would need to temporarily retreat to bide his time. The Tlaxcalans had been easily bought on the promise of immunity from sacrifice and control of Tenochtitlán. Cortés didn't care for the rule of the city, for he knew there was more out there for him to see; more for him to conquer. With an allegiance like this and the reinforcements that arrived from Cuba to aid him, his army was strong enough to quash the remnants of Moctezuma II's legacy. The Aztec king that had once welcomed him as a guest was dead, but there were always others ready to take his place.

Now Cortés had returned, and the time for vengeance, the time for a recognition of his successes, was at hand. Looking back to his army, he gave orders to Pedro de Alvarado to distribute among his men. Then he issued commands to his concubine, Doña Marina; a local Nahua woman who had become a personal advisor to him in his journey through this new land. She spoke the local Nahuatl language and had learned Spanish in her time with Cortés. It was much easier relaying messages to the locals now that she had become proficient in his mother tongue. He no longer relied on the intermediate translation provided by the priest Geronimo de Aguilar. Aguilar had made himself useful to Cortés when it was learned he spoke the Chontal Maya language; a language also understood by Doña Marina. Now that commands could be taken directly from Spanish to Nahuatl, they were dispersed to both armies much quicker. With the orders delivered and the tactics set, he was ready to strike.

**

The siege of Tenochtitlán had been long and brutal, but in the end successful. The city was his, and Cortés set about letting the world know of his conquest, including the Spanish King. It was late evening and a fire roared in the room he'd adopted as his private study. He was standing at a table, looking over the map he'd roughly drawn of the new world they were uncovering piece by piece. He felt confident of his conquest of Mexico, but there were lands to the south that were still undiscovered. Suddenly, the door burst open and two Spanish soldiers entered, dragging a prisoner with them. The weary man being dragged along the floor looked as though he'd been plucked from the battlefield, his flesh cut and bruised all over, and there was a wild fury in his bloodshot eyes. He wore the distinctive armour of the higher-ranking Aztec warrior, made from animal hide, leather, and cotton. While the armour had once covered his entire torso, the material had since been cut away above the midriff, revealing the man's injuries.

The Aztec Secret

'What is the meaning of this?' Cortés was outraged by the sudden intrusion.

'We found this man fleeing the city,' the more senior of the Spanish soldiers replied. 'He was part of a larger group that escaped the southern end of the capital.'

The prisoner was thrown onto his knees in front of the soldiers, his hands tightly bound together in front of him. The man looked exhausted; likely using up most of his strength attempting to fight off his captors.

'Why bring him here and not simply kill him?' Cortés asked, visibly annoyed by the soldiers' decision to bother him with this matter. 'Their empire is dead. If they wish to flee, let them. They know what fate awaits if they return. I am not interested in keeping prisoners.' He went back to the map on the table.

'Sir, we believe this group was smuggling gold out of the city.'

This piqued his interest. 'Gold?'

'Yes, and we have word that there are rare gems too.'

Cortés was now staring the prisoner in the eye, suddenly excited by the prospect of greater wealth. A gift of riches to the king would be a fitting accompaniment to the news that they had reclaimed the city and conquered this part of New Spain. The prisoner looked back at him, his eyes clearly displaying his hatred of the man who'd destroyed everything he'd lived for.

'Tell me about these gems.'

'We don't know much, but we have another source who told us there was one more beautiful than any other she'd seen. She said it was a sacred stone; one that was precious to the late king.'

Moctezuma's personal treasure. Cortés thought he'd found the last of it when he'd had the whole city ransacked.

His men were getting sloppy; the victory had given them a reason to relax. Didn't they know there was still work to be done? If this jewel really was as they said, it would make the perfect tribute to the king.

'There's one other thing,' the soldier added.

'Yes?'

'We found this on his person.' The man approached the table and set down a strange-looking object that Cortés had never seen before. It was made from clay and obsidian, in the shape of a star. The light from the fire wasn't bright enough for him to make out the intricate carvings in the clay in the centre of the object, but the light bounced off the fragments of obsidian that spread menacingly out to make the star shape.

'What is this?' he asked.

'We're not sure. But it took a lot of effort to take it from him. He was loathed to part with it.' The Nahua man's eyes widened at seeing the object being handed to Cortés. The Spaniard noted this and smirked. He enjoyed the feeling of having the upper hand over others. Despite not knowing the full details at this point, he knew the man wanted this object, and it was now his. Such was the thrill of conquering new lands. He picked it up carefully, watching the prisoner's eyes follow it, and touched the sharp edge of the obsidian, cutting his finger and drawing blood. What a fascinating weapon. He wondered how it must have been used.

'Marina,' he said, looking to the soldiers. 'Where is she?'

'I'll request her presence,' the second soldier replied.

Moments later, Doña Marina was by his side. She flinched when she saw the state the young Aztec warrior was in. While clearly a high-ranking warrior in the Aztec ranks, he couldn't have been older than twenty-three. Cortés gave her permission to speak with the prisoner, to ascertain as much as possible about the jewel and gold that had been transported out of the city.

'The man calls himself ocēlōtl,' she said at last. 'It means Jaguar Warrior. He is an elite soldier, despite his years.'

'Then I suppose I should congratulate him,' Cortés sneered. 'Where did they take it?' His impatience to learn the whereabouts of the treasure cut through.

'He didn't tell me,' she said.

'A pity. Perhaps he needs some persuading.' Cortés walked over to the table and picked up a short dagger. The two Spanish soldiers instantly grabbed the Nahua man's arms, pinning him down. He began to struggle and called out in frustration as Cortés felt the weight of the blade in his hand. The light from the fire glinted off the edge of the sharpened steel. The native warrior could sense the end approaching. He was trained not to fear death, but there was a primal survival instinct taking hold which he could not control.

With one last effort, the man forced upwards with all his strength, tilting his head to the side to catch one of the soldiers in the face with the back of his skull. He heard the crunch of bone as the motion broke the soldier's nose, and the Spaniard reeled backwards, holding his face in agony. Before the second soldier could react, the Nahua man swung an uppercut with his bound hands, catching him with force on the chin. He then sprang to his feet, picking up the star-shaped object in both hands and tossing it into the fire. He shouted something in Nahuatl in the direction of Cortés and spat at him. By this point the soldiers had regained their composure and restrained him once more, using more force than before to hold him down.

Cortés was surprised by the sudden brash act, although his expression did not show it. He wiped the spit that had caught his face, and in the next moment slammed the dagger down onto the table, point facing down. The tip of the blade penetrated the wood, leaving it standing upright. He then walked over to Doña Marina and whispered in her ear to ask what the man had said to him. She replied, telling him that he had cursed him in the name of the gods, and declared that he would never find the Heart of the Jaguar now. This last part caused a shadow of a smile to etch itself onto his face. The jewel had a name. They wouldn't have given a name to any old gem; the local informants to the soldiers weren't lying. Wherever the rest of the Aztec warriors went with the late king's treasure, they were almost certainly carrying with them a special gem of particular worth. He took the dagger off the table and hunted around in the fire for the star-shaped object that had been thrown there, using the tip of the blade as a fire poker. He found what he was looking for and flicked it out onto the ground, letting it cool on the cold stone floor. It appeared to be undamaged, which was unsurprising as the clay and obsidian were unlikely to succumb to damage from extreme heat over such a short period. Then, he approached his prisoner with the dagger. The end of the blade still glowed orange from the fire. The Nahua man could feel its heat and almost hear the crackle as Cortés hovered it over the top of his ear.

'Now,' he said, addressing Doña Marina, but staring deep into the eyes of the warrior. 'Ask him again where the Heart of the Jaguar is being taken.'

ONE

Rain pitter-pattered on the window as Ted Mendez stirred from his deep slumber. Just as the first few conscious thoughts began to form in his head, a sudden shooting pain took hold. He winced and let out a low groan. The pounding headache was an instant reminder of the evening spent drinking at The White Horse, a short walk from his place. This thought was quickly followed up by a clouded recollection of the events that had sparked the subsequent rapid consumption of pint after pint of beer to drown his sorrows.

It was a combination of a sudden burst of emotion evoked by the memory and his stomach's reaction to so much alcohol sloshing around his stomach that created the sudden onset of nausea. He lay still, his head face down into the pillow as he waited for the feeling to subside long enough for him to summon the strength to get up and make his way to the bathroom.

As his mind became more active, his memories of the previous evening came clearer into view, cruelly toying with him as he relived the whole thing again.

He was back in the pub, his hands wrapped around a pint of his favourite ale, while sat across from him was the most beautiful person he had ever laid eyes on. Julia. Golden hair tucked behind elfish ears, supple skin void of even the smallest blemish, curves in all the right places. But it was her eyes that held Ted's attention, captivating him as she spoke. They'd been good friends throughout their three undergraduate years at City University, right from the day they moved into their dormitories opposite each other. He'd been crazy about her since that first flash of a smile, the first time those big green eyes had twinkled at him.

Ted wasn't what people would describe as 'classically handsome'. He'd experienced a fair amount of online dating vicariously through his friends, and he'd taken note of the number of women who cited 'tall, dark and handsome' as their ideal match in their profile. Beauty is in the eye of the beholder, but at least his brown hair got him part-way there. At below average height and above-average weight, he'd come to terms with the idea that he didn't fit the mould. People would also seek a match who was confident, fun-loving, yet ambitious and career-driven, while not taking themselves too seriously. Ted didn't like the idea of trying to appeal to someone who was holding out for a unicorn. But the real reason Ted had never given it a try was because he was completely and utterly infatuated with Julia.

She was telling him about her plans to go travelling after graduating. She didn't know what she wanted to do; she'd become disillusioned with psychology and only decided to finish the degree because she'd already come so far. If only she'd felt this way in first year, she'd have a chance to change her field of study and have something she cared about lined up for when she finished. Still, she could always rely on her parents to keep her afloat for a year while she did some soul searching in Vietnam, or Peru, or wherever it was she said she was going.

'I don't know what I'm going to do either,' Ted had replied. 'Maybe I can come with you?'

Julia burst into laughter. 'Oh, come off it, Teddy. You'll be the editor of The Guardian before you know it. At least one of us needs to put their degree to good use.' Despite introducing himself as Ted when they first met, Julia had insisted on calling him Teddy since. Ordinarily, he would hate such a pet name; it reeked of upper-class whimsy. But for some reason, he didn't mind it coming from her.

She stuck her tongue out playfully. 'Besides, you wouldn't want to be a third wheel all year.'

That's when it hit him, the realisation smashing into him like a freight train. The cogs starting whirring around his brain, thoughts scrambling as he quickly pieced together what she meant.

'Third wheel?' was all he could say.

'Yes, silly. Richard's coming with me. It was all his idea, actually.'

Richard? That slick, pompous, stein-chugging, gap-year-gloating arsehole. He'd already wasted a year of his life gallivanting from one continent to another, experiencing life off the beaten track like every other tourist. He'd spent the vast majority of his university life handing out pearls of wisdom akin to the scrawlings of a note inside a fortune cookie, pretending to be one with the locals of every culture. He was as cultured as a microwaveable lasagne. Ted hated Richard.

'I didn't realise you two were—' a frog caught in his throat as he couldn't finish his sentence. It was if his body refused to speak the words, as though only saying them would make it true.

Julia laughed once more. 'You knew we were dating, right? I swear I told you.'

For the first time since they'd sat down, Ted took his gaze from her eyes and stared deep into the drink in front of him. Julia had mentioned Richard before, but she hadn't been specific. Ted felt stupid to have not seen it sooner. In hindsight, it made complete sense. But that didn't make it any easier to swallow. The beer was much easier, and Ted took a long swig from his glass before placing it back on the table with a little too much force.

'Figures,' he mumbled.

The evening had spiralled from then on. He had only looked up once from his glass to note the surprise on her face when she realised there was more to Ted's dislike of her relationship with Richard than just his dislike of Richard.

'Wait,' she said. 'You thought you and I—'

'It's fine,' Ted cut her off, her words only driving the blade further through his heart. 'I never expected you to feel the same way.' He went back to staring deep into his beer, as though by avoiding eye contact the embarrassment would go away.

Six pints and a poor night's sleep later and here he was, hungover to hell with no recollection of how he had got home. At least the nausea had subsided, for now.

He mustered enough strength to paw at his bedside table, eventually finding his phone. It lit up like a beacon in his face and he squinted while his blurred vision tried to adjust. The nausea came back almost instantly when he read the display. It was 10:34. He also had five missed calls and three unread messages, all from his best friend, Carl. He saw the most recent one first.

Where are you? Seminar starts in 5.

The nausea overcame him and he just about managed to spring out of bed and make it to the bathroom before being sick. When he'd finished retching the headache pounded harder than ever, but his stomach felt better. The message from Carl was received nine minutes ago, which meant he was already late. Again.

The lecturers told them from day one that it was completely up to them how many lectures and seminars they attended. It was their own future they were throwing away. Ted always took that as a free pass to miss the ones he didn't feel like going to. But the end of his degree was looming, and he was suddenly very afraid of what life would hold for him if he failed.

He scrolled back through his messages to read them chronologically. Two more from Carl, received last night.

Dude, what happened to you?

Lucky for you the film was worth seeing twice.

Shit. He was meant to be seeing a film with him last night. The latest Star Wars episode. They'd been looking forward to this one for ages. But instead, he'd stood him up when Julia had asked him to meet up to share her 'good news'. Ted knew he needed to find some way to make this up to him.

**

He made it to the seminar ten minutes before the end. He'd nearly thrown up again on the tube ride in, and his dishevelled appearance and messy hair gave away the precise reason for his tardiness. But he'd made it. And crucially, he'd made it in time to hand in his latest assignment, the deadline of which the lecturer had clearly stated to be this seminar. She hadn't specified which part of the seminar.

His late entrance was noted by everyone in the room, who seemed to find great amusement in watching his long walk of shame to the empty seat Carl had saved next to him. Ted stared at the floor the whole way, and the walk seemed to last forever. Trust Carl to pick the seat furthest from the door.

Carl took a long look at Ted. 'You look like hell.'

'I don't want to talk about it,' Ted replied.

Carl smiled to himself. 'I didn't ask.'

The seminar was over quickly, and the class began shuffling out the door, one by one handing in their assignments to the lecturer. Ted could never understand why the university insisted on receiving hard copies of each assignment when so many other establishments were completely digital. It always seemed like a waste of paper. Even as a journalism student, he didn't like the fact that newspapers still existed in their dated, paper form. People were so stuck in their ways that they refused to get with the times and adapt as technology made the articles they'd read so much more accessible, not to mention convenient. You could get every scoop, every thought piece, every crossword puzzle you could possibly want on your phone. He was contemplating this, not for the first time, when he found himself the last person in the room, still sitting at his desk, staring at the printout of his take on the decline of cinema. He'd tried to take an objective view, but truth be told he couldn't be happier about the state of the industry. The cinema was expensive and it was far easier and cost-efficient to stream movies nowadays. He struggled to see why the people he interviewed for the article had clung to the cinema experience, almost with a sense of grieving. He'd put it down to nostalgia.

The Aztec Secret

'Mr Mendez?' Hilary, the most lenient of his tutors throughout his degree, stood expectantly at the door. Ted's eyes shot up from his work and to her folded arms, then fell on Carl who was standing in the doorway.

'I'm gonna grab a coffee,' Carl said. 'I'll get you a bacon sarnie.'

'Legend,' Ted replied as he made his way across the room. He addressed Hilary with an apologetic smile. 'I'm sorry for being late.'

'Don't apologise to me, Theodore. It's up to you how much you want to get out of your education.' He found himself wincing at hearing his given name. Theodore was just so formal; it didn't sound right referring to him. He'd always preferred Ted, insisted on it.

Ted handed over the assignment and gave another sheepish smile. He turned for the door, his mind already on the bacon sandwich that would curb his hangover.

'Theodore,' Hilary called.

He spun around. 'Is something wrong? The deadline was today, wasn't it?'

'Yes, yes,' she replied. 'It's nothing like that. It's just, is everything alright?'

Ted looked uneasy, so she began to ease off the gas. 'It's just, attendance aside, you haven't seemed all that committed to this class. What are your plans after you graduate?'

'Why do you ask?' Ted asked defensively. His stomach growled as his body urged to be away from the conversation.

'It's part of my duty as your tutor to take an interest in your career aspirations,' she replied candidly. 'You have one more term before you're out in the world, taking your first step on the career ladder. I've just had your notes come through from Professor Rowe and I couldn't help but notice you don't have a single bit of work experience listed here. Is that a mistake?'

Professor Rowe was Ted's previous supervisor, who Ted had seen once all year, purely because it was mandatory to have one meeting and Ted didn't see the point in having more than that. She had advised meeting with him more frequently, to set up side projects and work experience opportunities to pad out his CV to include more than a sole stint behind the student union bar. But Ted hadn't got around to it. She'd transferred him to Hilary in hopes of encouraging him to put more thought into it. A sneaky tactic, as a change in supervisor forced another mandatory meeting. It was an uncomfortable conversation and one that Ted knew he'd have to address sooner or later. He just hadn't expected it to be here, now, while he was hungover and would rather be literally anywhere else. It made sense, he supposed. Julia was seeing someone else, he was barely passing his classes, he was feeling rougher than rough, and now he was having to face his lack of career prospects head on. Maybe this is where he hit rock bottom. Now was as good a time as any.

'I hadn't really given it much thought,' he said.

'Well, start,' she retorted. 'You won't always have someone to gift you something like this.'

Ted arched his eyebrow. 'What do you mean?'

Hilary shuffled through her papers and handed one to him. It was a printout of an email exchange between Hilary and a man named Jasper.

'What is this?' he asked.

'I've been given an opportunity to send one of my best students with Professor Thornton on a field trip to Mexico. Apparently, there's been a big Aztec discovery in Mexico City, and the university wants to write a feature on it for the website.

'The university website? Nobody reads that.'

'Well, I think Professor Thornton has some pull with some reputable Archaeology journals. That might be part of it. Either way, it's newsworthy stuff. Professor Thornton is really excited about it. He's funding part of the trip himself.'

'I'm far from your best student,' Ted said. 'Why me?'

'This would be a great experience for you,' she replied. 'Get that CV of yours looking a bit sharper.'

'So, this is charity?' Ted saw the change in her face and retracted immediately. 'Sorry, I don't mean to be ungrateful. When is the field trip?'

He watched as her lips slowly spread across her face into a satisfied smile. 'The flight is tomorrow. You'd be there for just a few days.'

'Tomorrow? That's so soon. What would you do if I said no?'

'I've got a list of students who would be very interested in this opportunity. But I wanted you to have first refusal.'

Ted pondered it a moment. Today was the last day of term before the Easter break, over which final year students start to cram for their end of year exams. He'd be missing valuable study time for this, but what use was his degree if he went out into the world with no real journalism experience, competing with every other fresh-faced grad who would look infinitely better on paper? He wouldn't have a shot at getting an interview, let alone a job.

The painful memory of last night then cropped up out of nowhere; a cruel trick the mind often plays. Leaving the country could be just the thing to get his mind straight and give him some space away from the mundane day-to-day that would only cause him to mope around.

'Alright, I'm in,' he said. 'Tell Professor Thornton I would be delighted to accompany him on this trip. And thank you very much.'

TWO

Something in the air had changed later that day, as though Ted was living life with renewed vigour. It might have been the energy the bacon sandwich and strong coffee had given him, plus the disappearance of his headache, but the trip to Mexico had excited him more than he expected. Hilary had given him a lifeline, helping him get out of the rut he was sure to find himself in after his conversation with Julia the previous evening. It was the perfect distraction for him and the catalyst to get his career prospects out from the gutter. When his mind started to wander back to Julia, he busied himself with something productive.

The aspiring journalist in him thought it a good idea to do some research around the 'great discovery' that had been made in Mexico City. It must have been exciting to warrant Professor Thornton booking a last-minute trip across the Atlantic just to be a part of it. And had Hilary said he was funding part of it himself?

He started by Googling 'Mexico City history', discovering that the centre of the country's capital was once the ancient city of Tenochtitlan, home to the Aztecs until the 16th century. Ted wasn't much of a history buff, but he found it fascinating. In school he'd learnt a lot about English history: kings, queens, infamous figures such as Guy Fawkes and Jack the Ripper. But the curriculum hadn't stretched much outside of that, save for a few cases where continental European history became entwined with that of England; both world wars, for example. It was typical of the school he went to, only concerned with the subjects and events that were closest to home. Religious Education was another prime example of this; being a Church of England school, classes had focused solely on Christianity.

His online search quickly took him down the rabbit hole as he got lost in the Aztec world, learning about their culture and beliefs, deities, and sacrificial rituals. He then moved on to the biggest turning point in the Aztec civilisation, and ultimately the reason for their demise; the invasion by the Spanish conquistadors, led by a man named Hernán Cortés. It quickly consumed his afternoon. He trawled through page after page, following links from one article to another until he felt like he had a very basic grasp on the subject.

His next idea was to head to the British Museum, which he'd read displayed hundreds of Aztec objects. It would be a shame not to visit with it being so close. He logged off from the computer he was using and began to leave the study room.

'Any plans tonight?' Carl asked from the next computer along. Ted could tell he was itching to watch the film again. It must have been one hell of a movie to invoke two sittings in as many days.

'Let's take a rain check on Star Wars,' Ted suggested. 'It'll be something for me to look forward to when I'm back from the trip.'

Carl shook his head. 'No way, I can't hold it in that long! I need to talk to someone about it. I've been sitting here on the verge of exploding not being able to give away spoilers.'

'It's Friday,' said Ted. 'I'll be back from Mexico by next Wednesday. That's not long.'

'How can you be so calm about it? Isn't it eating you up inside not knowing what happens?'

'Kinda, but I've got a lot else on my mind. Why don't you take Steve?'

Carl rolled his eyes. 'Steve? He's a Trekkie and you know it. He'll just sit there yawning obnoxiously, pretending he doesn't like it. No way.'

'Sorry, I don't know what to say,' Ted shrugged.

'Come on, Ted. You owe me. You stood me up last night.'

'You'll get over it.'

'I was inconsolable,' Carl joked, sticking out his bottom lip in mock sadness.

'I'm sorry, I really am. And I'll make it up to you. But this trip could be the most important thing I do all year. I can't keep screwing around, I'll end up on the dole.'

'Look at you, thinking about your future. I like this new Ted,' Carl said. 'OK, how about this. You can make it up to me by telling me what you were doing last night.'

Ted said nothing.

A few moments went by before Carl made a frustrated sound. 'Fine, nerd. You swot up on your Mayan history of whatever and just let me know *when* you get bored and can't take it anymore. There's a showing at half nine.' He motioned to his screen, which was on a page displaying film listings for the local cinema.

Ted chuckled. 'We'll see.' He stood up and walked out. 'And it's Aztec, not Mayan.'

'Don't act like you know the difference!' Carl called after him as the door swung to and fro.

**

In his haste to get to the seminar on time that morning, Ted had forgotten to take his raincoat with him. He was paying for it now, as the rain hammered down outside the university. He squelched with every footstep as he ran to the bus shelter. He wasn't in a rush; he had a couple of hours until the British Museum closed. But the bad weather forced his hand and he sprinted across the road as the number thirty-eight bus came into view. Transport links in London were better than most places, and another bus would be there soon if he'd missed this one, but he wanted to avoid another few minutes waiting in the rain if possible. He scanned his travel card and took up a seat next to an elderly woman.

She looked him up and down, appraising the drenched figure who'd sat down beside her.

'Shame you didn't get on a stop earlier,' she said. 'You could have stood under my brolly with me.' She motioned to the small umbrella folded up neatly in her lap.

Ted smiled. What a sweet woman. When she'd started talking he'd prepared himself for a complaint that he'd somehow splashed water on her or disturbed her peace when there were other perfectly good seats available. Such was the typical response of so many Londoners to a stranger sitting in close proximity to them. London transport made it nigh on impossible to respect personal space, despite its inhabitants wanting nothing more than this on their daily commute.

'That's too bad,' Ted replied.

'Oh hell, what am I saying?' the elderly woman said. 'My brolly's probably too small to keep us both dry. I take it back.'

Ted laughed. 'I appreciate the thought, anyway.'

The woman stayed silent, staring ahead with a blank expression on her face, as though she was returning to the stoic norm she'd briefly broken. That was the end of that, then.

He was at Holborn before he knew it and pinged the button to alert the driver of his intention to get off at the next stop. He waited at the door for it to open, only to be brushed aside by a large man as the bus came to a halt. The man subsequently stopped dead to get out his phone the moment he hit the pavement, blocking the exit for the other passengers. Normal service had resumed.

Ted squeezed around and gave an audible tut for good measure. It was easy to get sucked into the aggressive mentality of the busy, impatient commuter, especially in bad weather. He caught himself before he said anything more and headed in the direction of the museum, plugging in his headphones and starting up one of his favourite playlists. He got lost in the music while the rain poured around him. On came a song from a band he'd seen live with Julia earlier that year. He cursed his luck that his attempt to soothe his mind had created such an unwanted segue back to her again. He fumbled around his pocket, blindly tapping for the skip button.

His foot slapped the ground in an abrupt stop as he made way for an onrushing cyclist, who was marauding around the corner at speed. His mind snapped back to his surroundings as the cyclist turned to shout abuse his way.

'Idiot!' came the burst of fury from the helmetless rider.

Ted gritted his teeth and stuck two fingers up in retaliation. He hadn't looked properly when crossing the road, but the commuter mentality had gotten the better of him this time. The cyclist turned away and didn't see his gesture, but it made Ted feel better.

**

The British Museum was as impressive as he remembered. He couldn't recall how long it had been since he was last there, but he quickly decided it had been too long. The tall pillars of its exterior exuded grandeur, instantly identifying itself as a place of great importance, beckoning him to discover the wonders that awaited inside. The Natural History Museum and Science Museum were arguably more popular, at least in Ted's friendship circles, but there was a certain charm to this repository that gave it such regal authority. The first national public museum in the world, it was as though the building knew what an impact it had made on making pieces of history accessible to all.

After his preliminary research of the Aztecs earlier that afternoon, he continued his education on the catalogue of the British Museum's website. But something had felt wrong, like he was missing something. Yes, it was efficient, practical even, to get the information he needed at the speed of a mouse click, safe in the warm and dry confines of the university study room. But it was then that Ted remembered why people came to museums. It just wasn't the same on a screen. Coming here and seeing the artefacts in person was so much more immersive, as if to touch them would instantly transport you back to the time from which they originated. It suddenly struck him that perhaps it was a similar situation with the cinema. He now better understood the opinions of those he'd interviewed who'd felt such a strong connection to the cinema experience. The sight of the Great Court, the sound of echoing voices chattering away in hushed tones, even the smell of the place. It all provoked an excitement within, at the possibility of discovering something amazing.

He found a map of the museum and took stock of where he was and where he wanted to go. He briefly considered taking a sweeping tour of the museum to see a few other galleries on the way but settled on the idea that he was only interested in one. Room 27: Mexico. He located it next to the stairway by the East corner. The room was fairly small, but who was he to judge it by its size.

The collection seemed to be even smaller, as the room was shared by many cultures that had inhabited Mexico between 2000 BC to 16th century AD. Aztec artefacts made up a small portion of this, and in fact, the room had apparently been designed to reflect the architecture of a Mayan temple. Ted remembered the throwaway comment Carl had shouted as he left the study room. He was right, he didn't know the slightest difference between Aztec, Mayan, or anything else in this room. If it weren't for the helpful display descriptions indicating their origin he might have looked in the wrong place. Still, he had been studying this for all of three hours.

His first impression of the collection had been that of slight disappointment, given that on the way to this part of the museum he'd walked by so many impressive looking statues, ornaments, and the like from other periods of time that stretched much further back than the Aztec era. Most of the Aztec artefacts seemed to be small pottery items, including many jugs and spindle-whorls. However, a few objects did catch Ted's eye, much in the way it would a child's. He found himself taking a keen interest in an obsidian arrowhead, and a strange-looking weapon made of wood, cotton and something shell-like. He read the description below, which labelled the item as a ceremonial *Atlatl*, or spear-thrower, used to hurl dart-like projectiles at the wielder's foe. For an instrument of war, it was intricately designed; gold in places with the body of a warrior carved along its neck.

He was also drawn to the items that had been carved into the shape of a face. He remembered how in one session down the pub Julia had told him about how humans are subconsciously drawn to faces because of our nature to seek out attractive mates. We study faces for familiarity and linger on those we either recognise or are attracted to. Which would explain why Ted always stared so intently at Julia. Of course, Ted wouldn't satisfy either of these criteria by looking at the small carved figurines in front of him, but they were intriguing, nonetheless.

There was one figurine he was fascinated by: a jadeite carving of an Aztec eagle warrior. Naturally, the warrior's helmet was in the shape of an eagle, creating an almost totem pole effect of face upon a face. Their eyes seemed to be closed, their hands together in a peaceful pose that put the character in stark contrast to the nature of their work. He studied the detail on the warrior's ears, where notable indents were carved, as though denoting piercings in the lobes.

'I like your style,' he mused.

**

Satisfied he'd learnt enough to make sense of the discovery on the Mexico trip, he called it a day and made his way home. He'd been on the bus back to his flat when his phone buzzed to alert him of a new email. It was from Professor Thornton. The subject line stood out immediately.

The Adventure of a Lifetime!!! was the caption. Ted thought the three exclamation points to be a tad excessive. Ted opened the email and began to read. He quickly decided that

Hilary's description of this man as 'very excited' hadn't done justice to his level of enthusiasm for the upcoming trip.

Theodore! (Or do you go by Ted?)

Hilary informed me of the excellent news that you have accepted my offer of accompanying me on this most epic of adventures. That is wonderful!

Wow, this guy wasn't messing around.

Firstly, thank you for taking time out of your Easter break to join me on this quest.

Quest? Ted was starting to wonder if this guy was for real.

This is a fantastic opportunity for us both. We will be part of one of the greatest discoveries to come out of the ruins of Tenochtitlan. I trust you've been brushing up on your 16th Century Mesoamerican history?

Yes, he had.

You will of course be the university's official reporter for this venture, which will give you the chance to dazzle prospective employers with your journalistic prowess.

Professor Thornton's enthusiasm shone through in the rest of the email, which also gave details of the flight number, what to pack, and a brief itinerary of the trip. They would spend the first day exploring the city at their leisure and recuperating from the long flight. Then he had scheduled a trip to a dig site and a museum on the second day, with a party planned on the third day before travelling home.

Ted scanned the email again. Nowhere had it said what the discovery was. Perhaps the professor had assumed Ted was as plugged into the latest archaeology news as he was. Ted closed the email and brought up Google on his phone. Searching for the discovery should have been his first port of call after accepting the offer, but he'd assumed the professor would fill him in on this. A quick search for the discovery yielded exactly the result he was looking for. A dig site in Mexico City, above the ruins of the old city of Tenochtitlan had uncovered a number of artefacts, including clay and obsidian objects that were being examined by specialists before they would be displayed in the Museo Nacional de Antropología (National Museum of Anthropology). But the focal point of the discovery was centred around a capsule that was believed to hold manuscripts written by Hernán Cortés. Why was this such a big deal?

Ted got home and started packing for the trip. He thought about texting Julia to let her know he would be away but then thought better of it. She probably hated him for the way he'd acted, and he was embarrassed at how she'd act now she knew how he felt about her.

He continued packing his clothes when another thought popped into his head. Professor Thornton had asked him in his email to reply with his passport details so he could check them both into the flight. Since the professor held Ted's ticket, he'd need to meet him at the baggage check-in before heading through security. He'd never met Professor Thornton before, so he'd need to know who to look out for. He Googled the guy's last name, finding a number of matches. But there was one that caught his eye. A middle-aged man, possibly in his late fifties or early sixties, with a bald head and thick grey beard with a styled moustache. He was the perfect physical manifestation of the eccentric email Ted had received earlier. Ted logged onto the university website and scoured through to the members of staff section, hoping to find a match. A few clicks later and there he was, this time sporting a tweed jacket. He couldn't have been more of a stereotype if he tried. Ted chuckled away to himself before getting an early night. This professor seemed passionate about his field, if not a little nutty. But he was probably a lot of fun. Ted was looking forward to this trip.

THREE

The engines roared as the plane tore down the runway, tilting back as it began to climb into the sky. Ted was pinned to the back of his seat, a bead of sweat forming at the top of his forehead while he closed his eyes and gripped the armrest. To say he was a nervous flyer (a term regularly bandied about in reference to aviophobia, which didn't even begin to do justice to its severity), was an understatement. The ascent reminded him of the few times he'd reluctantly ridden a rollercoaster. The slow cranking of the rails as he rose higher and higher to the apex, and inevitable plummet that followed. He had a vivid memory of screaming for someone to let him off, saying he'd made a big mistake. But the ride continued, and so too his screaming. That was a thirty second ride, this was an eleven-hour flight.

He started to feel trapped, and being wedged against the window didn't help that. He hastily started looking around for the nearest flight attendant. He'd been told time and time again; if they looked cool as a cucumber, everything is fine. Not that it helped him much.

Air travel had never prevented Ted from visiting parts of the world he wanted to see, but it was always the part of the holiday he dreaded. His parents would always count down the days until they jetted off to some faraway place. But for Ted the countdown his mum placed on the fridge simply served as a ticking time-bomb for the next time he'd be thirty-thousand feet in the air with no control of the situation. The only saving grace with this trip was that the countdown had started at one, and he hadn't had all that long for the anxiety to build up.

'You know, I used to be a nervous flyer too,' Professor Thornton gave him a big smile from the aisle seat. There was that phrase again, *nervous flyer*.

'Oh?' Ted replied, still pressed into the back of his seat.

'Yes,' the professor confirmed. 'It's all about statistics, you see.' He turned to address Ted more personally. 'You're far more likely to be in a car crash than for anything to go wrong up here.'

Somehow that didn't make Ted feel any better.

'Is that so?' he replied, trying to be polite while secretly wishing he would stop talking. His mind screamed with every ripple of air that moved the plane slightly from side to side.

'It'll get better once the plane reaches cruising altitude,' the professor reassured.

Cruising altitude? Who was this guy, some sort of hobbyist pilot? Ted just forced a half-smile in response.

'Anyway, we've got a long flight ahead of us,' the professor yawned. 'Best to try and get some sleep.'

Easier said than done, Ted thought.

The professor had been right, Ted did feel a little better once the plane had evened out at a higher altitude. The seatbelt sign switched off and the trolley made its way down the aisle as the cabin crew began offering drinks to passengers.

Ted breathed a sigh of relief. The ride was smooth now, but perhaps they'd have something strong for him to drink to get him through any unexpected turbulence along the way.

'Would you like something to drink, sir?' The pretty flight attendant batted her false eyelashes at Ted.

'Yes please. Err... I'll have a gin and tonic.' Ted hated gin and tonic, but instead of asking what alcohol they stocked he'd felt compelled to answer quickly by repeating the order of the previous passenger.

'Certainly,' she replied. 'And your friend?' She motioned to Professor Thornton who was fast asleep in the aisle.

'I'm not sure,' Ted replied. 'But I don't want to wake him, so let's get him a coke and hope for the best.' The two exchanged a smile as she poured out the drinks.

The trolley caught the professor's armrest on the way past, causing him to stir. Ted watched as the man slowly got his bearings, remembering where he was.

'Professor Thornton,' he started.

'I told you earlier, call me Jasper,' the professor replied. 'This isn't a classroom, we're business partners now.' He turned to Ted and saw the drinks on his tray. 'Ah! I see you have tremendous foresight. Gin and tonic is my favourite. Well done, sir.' He reached over and took the drink, folding down his own tray to pop it down on.

Ted pulled on the ring of the can of coke, opening it with a click and a fizz.

'Don't tell me you don't drink,' Jasper said, eyeing Ted's choice of beverage. 'Or are you saving yourself for some tequila later?' The raise of an eyebrow gave away a glimmer of cheekiness about the man.

'Actually, I could use a stiff drink,' Ted replied. Jasper wasted no time in hitting the button above their seats. The light went on with a satisfying tone, and moments later the pretty flight attendant was at his side.

'What's your poison?' Jasper asked.

Ted thought a moment. He usually just drank beer.

'Do you have any whiskey?' he asked, uncertainly. He'd never once drank whiskey, but it seemed like an appropriate choice for a stiff drink.

'Is Jack Daniels alright?' the woman replied.

'Perfect,' said Ted, not at all sure about his choice.

The plane wobbled slightly, momentarily disturbing the smoothness of the ride and reminding Ted where he was.

'Right. Down the hatch,' he announced, taking a big gulp of his drink. The sweet, woody taste of the whiskey cut through the familiar cola bubbles going crazy on his tongue. He swallowed and licked his lips, picking up the small bottle of Jack Daniels in his other hand. This was delicious.

Three drinks later and Ted was in much better spirits. He'd almost completely forgotten that he was thousands of feet in the air travelling at five-hundred miles an hour in an aluminium tube. The professor had asked Ted about his studies and ambitions after graduating, and Ted had shown genuine interest in the professor's work.

'Why did you choose to specialise in archaeology and anthropology?' Ted asked.

'Why ever not?' Jasper replied. 'It fascinates me to learn how other civilisations lived. The more we uncover about the past, the better our understanding of it. Our knowledge of history has so many gaps, and we fill a lot of them with guesswork. But history can be rewritten with just one piece of new information.' He paused and turned to Ted as if to let him in on a secret. 'Well, and I'm a sucker for a good adventure,' he smiled. He took a sip of his third gin and tonic.

The Aztec Secret

'Some people spend their lives chasing urban myths, with nothing to show for it. But every now and then something amazing happens, and a discovery is made in the most unlikely of places. Did you know that the remains of King Richard III were found under a carpark in Leicester?'

'I didn't,' admitted Ted.

'And the terracotta army guarding the tomb of Emperor Qin Shi Huang was discovered when a man tried to dig a well.'

'I don't know who that is.'

'Qin Shi Huang,' Jasper repeated. 'The Qin dynasty?' Ted's blank expression left him bemused. 'The first emperor of unified China?' he tried finally.

Ted shook his head. 'Sorry,'

The professor rolled his eyes, obviously disappointed.

'Still, it is fascinating,' Ted enthused. 'What a stroke of luck.'

'Not if he really wanted his well there,' Jasper chuckled.

It might have been the alcohol or the professor's infectious laugh, but Ted found himself joining in.

'So, how about you, professor?' Ted began. 'What are you hoping to discover in Mexico? El Dorado?'

Jasper let out a hearty guffaw, drawing the attention of the neighbouring passengers.

'El Dorado, he says!' He stroked his beard in contemplation, a slight glimmer in his eye. 'Now that would be something. But alas, I think we're getting into the realm of fantasy here.'

'Even so, we wouldn't have the slightest idea where to start looking,' said Ted.

'Or what to look for.'

Ted narrowed his eyes questioningly. 'What do you mean?'

The professor eyed Ted carefully. 'What is El Dorado?'

Ted was wary of the question, sensing some trickery at play.

'A city of gold,' he replied matter of fact. 'Like the Spanish were looking for.'

'Not just the Spanish,' Jasper corrected. 'Germans, English too. Hell, all of Europe wanted to find it. But who's to say it's a city? The legend of El Dorado supposedly started as a man, who covered himself with gold dust.'

'Huh,' was all Ted managed to say.

'Ever heard of Sir Walter Raleigh?'

'Yes.'

'He tried to find it, twice. Of course, he was unsuccessful on both occasions. He believed it to be a city called Manōa on the shores of Lake Parime. So, which is it? A man or a city?' The professor paused as if waiting for Ted to provide an answer.

'Was that rhetorical?' asked Ted.

The silver bearded man beside him smiled. 'As you can see, the myth has changed over time, become more exaggerated.'

'I guess the more people look for it, the more the appeal grows,' Ted suggested, almost philosophically. 'It's a bigger prize now.'

'Precisely.'

The two sat there a moment, pondering the topic.

'So, tell me really,' Ted brought the conversation back to his original question. 'Why are we going to Mexico?'

'I trust you've seen the news reports?'

'Of course. What kind of journalist would I be if I went into this blind? But forgive me in saying it doesn't add up for me,' he added.

'What doesn't?'

'The discovery. I mean, it sounds very exciting, but why would the university part-fund us going all the way there? Does this kind of thing happen often?'

'Not really,' the professor replied candidly. 'Academia is tough. Budgets are tight and field trips like this almost never happen. But if you spend as long as I do complaining to the system *about* the system, you sometimes get what you want.'

Ted raised an eyebrow curiously.

'There's a lot you don't know about the way universities are run,' he continued. 'Politics operate in the background and it's exhausting. We've had our differences, the board and me. But I work hard, and I deserve a reward for that. It doesn't matter how much of a contribution this trip makes to student applications, university rankings or whatever arbitrary figures they care about. I'm contributing to the uncovering of history, well, or at least commenting on it. I've made that case with them more times than I can count.'

'So, the squeaky wheel gets the oil?' Ted tried to find the moral to this story.

'Tell me, Ted. If your employer agreed to part-fund your next holiday on the basis you withheld your opposing views a while, what would you say?'

Ted smiled knowingly. 'They signed this off just to shut you up?'

The professor replied simply with a wink.

**

The inflight entertainment helped the rest of the journey go quickly, creating enough of a distraction for Ted to take his mind off where he was once the initial alcohol buzz had worn off and the professor had gone back to sleep. He had watched a couple of trashy action movies and a comedy he'd been meaning to watch but missed when it was showing in the cinema. All enjoyable flicks but nothing he'd write a raving review for. He saw the previous Star Wars film when scrolling through and felt a surge of excitement about the prospect of watching the new one with Carl when he got back home. That was something to look forward to.

It was early afternoon in Mexico City by the time they had gone through passport control and picked up their bags. But on their time, it was getting on to late evening.

'The key with jetlag is to stay up as long as you can, or you'll get out of sync and have a torrid time of it,' Jasper warned. 'I need you shipshape tomorrow morning.'

That reminded Ted that the visit to the dig site was tomorrow, and he'd barely started planning the questions he was going to ask in his interviews with the team that uncovered the newly found artefacts. Apparently, the workers took great pride in retelling stories of the moment they discovered something. They must have to retell it to a hundred different reporters. Ted would have found it tiresome.

Jasper hailed a cab to take them to their hotel. The driver took one look at the pair and asked Ted in Spanish where they were headed. Ted froze as he tried to decipher the quickly spoken words. His slightly tanned complexion and dark hair meant he was often mistaken for a local in Latin American or Mediterranean countries. He owed his looks to his grandfather, Felipe Mendez, who had moved to England from Argentina. His dad, who seemed to have inherited more genes on the maternal side, told him he looked more and more like his grandfather as he got older. Although he looked the part, the truth was Ted didn't speak much Spanish at all. His grandfather had passed away when his dad was young, and Ted's London-born grandmother hadn't spoken much

Spanish since Felipe had been so proficient in English. Thus, Ted had never learnt the language, aside from the basic phrases taught in secondary school.

Ted stared back at the driver, trying to think of even one word. He was exhausted from the journey.

'*Hotel Castropol, por favor,*' Jasper stepped in with a well-rehearsed phrase. '*Pino Suárez.*'

'*Sí, sí.*' The driver knew the place.

Ted lumped his suitcase in the boot and hopped into the back seat. The driver pulled away with gusto as they made their journey to the city centre. The world went by in a haze as the bright sunshine streamed through the window and the intermittent sound of car horns kept Ted from falling asleep. He caught himself marvelling at the great city. Having known nothing about the country's capital, save for the odd history titbit he'd learned over the last couple of days, he was blown away by it. The architecture was stunning in places, and the car passed a few extraordinary buildings on the way. Jasper pointed out the beautifully curved shiny building as Museo Soumaya. Not the museum they would be touring the next day. If the inside was half as impressive as the outside, they'd be missing out, Ted decided.

The car sped by a large billboard advertising one of the presidential candidates' slogans. Ted had heard that there was an election looming for the Mexican presidency, but he didn't know more than that fact. This billboard was one of many adverts he'd seen since landing. It seemed a bit closer to American levels of in-your-face tactics than those seen in Britain.

The cab rolled up outside their hotel. The traffic noise intensified as Ted opened the door and stepped out onto the street. Living in London got him used to the sounds of a busy city, to the point where he could almost tune it out. But there was something different about the noises of foreign cities. He couldn't tell if it was the change in pitch of the emergency vehicle sirens, or the chatter of an unfamiliar language around him, but he was instantly overwhelmed by the noise, as though his ears were adjusting to the new frequencies.

'*Gracias, muy amable,*' the driver said to Jasper as he counted the cash in his hand. Ted didn't understand the words, but he made sense of the interaction by the smile on the driver's face. The professor must have left a nice tip. '*¡Que tenga un buen día!*' the man called as he got back into his car.

'What does that mean?' Ted asked as the car pulled away.

'I think he told us to have a nice day,' Jasper replied. 'Don't worry, I don't think we'll be needing to use much Spanish while we're here. I like to give it a go where I can, but I only know the basics. Besides, most people we come across will speak good English, and if the people we interview don't, there'll be translators on hand.'

Ted was relieved, although a little ashamed. Given his heritage, he didn't want to come across as another lazy Englishman who couldn't be bothered to learn just a few basic phrases when travelling abroad. But the truth was he was exactly that. He made a mental note to take Spanish lessons in his spare time after graduating.

The hotel itself was nice and Ted was pleasantly surprised to be handed his own room key. He didn't mind sharing rooms with strangers; he'd spent plenty of nights staying in budget-friendly hostels before. But there was a difference between a twelve-bed dorm and sharing a twin room with just one other person he'd only met that day. Clearly Jasper had the sense to understand this too.

'Why don't you try and get some rest?' Jasper suggested as they waited for the lift to take them to their floor. 'Catch a few hours and we can get some grub later this evening.' The fatigued look on Ted's face made it obvious he wouldn't make it to a normal bedtime.

Ted yawned. The prospect of a soft bed was too good to turn down. 'Sounds great.'

He entered his room and instinctively turned the TV on. He enjoyed sampling the channels of different countries while he had the opportunity, to see how different they were from the ones back home. The news came on with what looked like a discussion around the upcoming election. Ted suddenly felt a wave of tiredness and decided against watching it. He fell asleep the moment his head hit the pillow.

**

The alarm on his phone went off at seven o'clock. Luckily, he'd remembered to bring the right travel charger, plug his phone into it and set an alarm before his head hit the pillow and he was dead to the world. It felt like the best sleep of his life, but he wanted more. He wiped the drool from the corner of his mouth and shuffled his way to the edge of the bed. He drank from the water bottle the room had provided, remembering the warning he'd read online about the risks of drinking tap water here. Better safe than sorry; getting a stomach bug would be far from ideal.

He was contemplating showering when he heard a knock at the door. Must have been Jasper checking in on him. He trudged sleepily across the room to open the door. To his surprise, it wasn't the professor who greeted him on the other side, but a young petite woman dressed in jeans and a black t-shirt featuring an iconic Nirvana logo.

'Hi,' she said. 'You must be Ted.'

'Uh, yeah,' Ted replied, eyeing her uncertainly.

She smiled at him, before extending a hand. 'I'm Quinn. Jasper said you'll be joining us on the field trip tomorrow.'

Joining us? As far as Ted was aware it was just the professor and him on this trip, and now this woman was insinuating he was the late arrival tagging along.

'Yes,' was all he managed in response, before quickly realising where he was. 'I'm sorry, I just woke up and I'm still a bit groggy. What did you say your name was again?'

Her smile started to recede, and her eyebrows narrowed.

'Quinn,' she repeated. 'I heard your alarm go off next door. Thin walls.'

'Oh, I see.'

'Jasper asked me to pick you up. He took a walk but said he'd meet us at the restaurant.'

'Oh,' Ted replied. 'Which restaurant?'

'It's not far, I'll walk you there.' Her eyes lowered as she assessed his outfit. 'I'll let you get dressed and then we can get going.'

A sudden pit formed in his stomach as Ted realised he was still in his boxers. 'Right,' he said. 'Gimme two minutes.' He hurriedly shut the door and ran to the bathroom to splash some water on his face. He caught a glimpse of his messy bedhead in the mirror and cursed under his breath. What a great first impression that must have been.

Quinn called after him from the corridor. 'And don't worry, I didn't hear any snoring.'

Ted hadn't worried about that until now.

He hastily brushed his teeth, aware Quinn was still waiting outside the door for him, and pulled on a pair of jeans. He cast another glance at his reflection in the mirror by the door and half-heartedly attempted to fix his hair. It made no impact.

'OK, I'm ready,' he said as he shut the door behind him. A sudden brainwave hit him, and he scrambled through his pockets for the room key.

'Are you OK?' Quinn watched his panicked dance curiously.

'Ah, crap,' Ted mumbled. 'I think I left the key inside.'

'You mean this key?' she asked, picking up a white card from the floor.

'Yes!' Ted breathed a sigh of relief, taking the card gratefully and putting in securely in his pocket. 'Thanks.'

The pair made their way towards the lift and Ted quickly experienced the awkward silence he always felt when meeting new people. He never knew what to say.

'So,' he began. 'When did you arrive?'

'This morning. It was the only flight cheap enough for the university to approve, but who am I to turn down a free trip?'

'You should tell Jasper that, he seems to enjoy that thread of conversation,' Ted suggested.

'Oh really?'

'Yeah, it came up once or twice on the way over.'

'Yes, you must have had a long flight,' said Quinn as the lift door pinged open. Ted pressed the button for lobby and the doors shuddered closed again.

'Eleven hours. How long was your flight?' he asked, trying not to make assumptions of her origin. While her accent was clearly American, or possibly Canadian, she was of East Asian descent.

'A little over 4 hours,' she replied. 'I flew in from New York.'

'I've always wanted to go there.'

'It's a great place. I grew up in LA, so the weather's colder than I like. But I really like the city.'

'I've always wanted to go to LA too.'

'Are you hoping for an invite?' Quinn raised an eyebrow at him.

'Oh, no, sorry,' Ted backtracked. 'It's just I've never been—'

'I'm just messing with you,' she laughed. 'You should see your face right now.'

The lift doors pinged open once more as they reached the ground floor.

'The restaurant's just around the corner,' she said, leading them outside and down the street.

FOUR

It was that perfect time of evening Ted had only experienced in warmer climates or on the occasional summer day in the UK. A light breeze welcomed the pair as they walked in the fading light of the setting sun. The restaurant, a fairly touristy-looking place serving traditional Mexican dishes, was a short five-minute walk away. The pair were seated at a booth the professor had reserved.

Ted had asked Quinn about her background: what LA was like to grow up in, how she ended up in New York. She mentioned that her grandparents had moved from Tokyo in the 50s. Growing up as a third-generation Asian-American, she felt like her upbringing was very similar to those of her school friends, with the added bonus of being taught Japanese from a young age and her parents having a wider repertoire of recipes come dinner time. She wanted her college experience to be something completely different than what she was used to, so enrolled at Columbia University.

'And you?' Quinn opened up the menu to peruse the drinks selection. 'Where are you from?'

'Isn't it obvious?' Ted replied.

'British,' she replied, matter of fact. 'Not too obvious meeting you, but Jasper on the other hand…' she trailed off and shrugged her shoulders.

'I know what you mean,' Ted smiled. 'He's quite, erm—'

'Eccentric?' Quinn chimed in. They both shared a laugh.

'Yes, he's quite a character,' Ted added.

'Yeah, he is. You don't sound like him though. Do you come from different regions?'

'Different region is one thing. But we're both from London, so it's not that. Social class comes into it, I guess. Where I'm from, Professor Thornton is considered posh. Well-to-do.'

'I can see that,' she agreed.

The waiter came over and took their drinks order. Ted reverted back to his predictable self and ordered a beer, convincing himself it was adventurous because it was a local beer.

'And your parents?' Quinn probed. 'Where are they from?'

'Both English,' he replied coyly.

Quinn's expression showed an element of surprise. 'That's interesting.'

'Why?'

'Your olive skin.'

'Maybe it's the Mexican sun?' he said, tongue in cheek.

'Nice try. You just flew in.' Quinn sat back in her seat, her shift in body language signalling her disappointment at his cagey response.

'My grandfather was Argentinian,' he added.

'That explains it.' She cocked her head to the side. 'So, you're third-generation English. What's the story there?'

Ted's phone buzzed and he pulled it from his pocket to check the notification preview. It was a text from Julia. He

The Aztec Secret

hurriedly opened it and read the long prose she'd written. She was clearly still angry with him, and signed off with a sentence that made Ted's blood boil.

Give Richard a try. You might find you have a lot in common.

A lot in common? Had she completely lost her mind?

'So,' said Quinn, snapping Ted from his thoughts and bringing him back into the room 'What's the story?'

'I'm from London. So are my parents. There's nothing much more to say,' Ted replied bluntly, putting his phone back in his pocket and taking a sip of beer.

Quinn frowned. It seemed unfair for her to divulge details of her upbringing and not have him do the same. 'What brought you on this fieldtrip?'

'That's a different question.'

'It's the question I'm asking now,' she said.

Ted stretched and looked around the restaurant to catch a glimpse of the food on the other patrons' tables. 'I dunno,' he replied dismissively. 'Free holiday. CV building.'

'CV?' she asked.

'Resume.'

'Right, sorry. Go on.'

'Interview a few people, write some garbage for the university website. Nothing more to say really,' he finished.

Quinn folded her arms. 'Wow.'

'Wow, what?' Ted enquired.

'I studied hard for this,' she said. 'They don't just offer an opportunity like this to any student.'

'Congratulations,' he said with an air of sarcasm, the annoyance of Julia's text message still fresh in his mind.

'This discovery could be one of the biggest finds in Mexico's history. Don't you feel honoured to be part of it?'

'You sound just like Jasper,' Ted snorted.

'What?' she was taken aback by his sudden attitude.

45

'You're both obsessed with this stupid 'discovery',' he used air quotes to accentuate his opinion of it. 'It's like you're expecting to uncover some kind of supernatural wonder. It's just some bits of clay and the scrawlings of a long-dead man. You've watched too many movies.'

'You arrogant jerk!' Quinn snapped. Her words pierced the air, hushing the neighbouring patrons who turned to see what had caused the commotion. What they saw appeared on the surface to be a lovers' feud. Quinn was red in the face, staring incredulously at the startled Ted, who had spilled some of his beer down himself.

The outburst caught Ted unaware, and he quickly felt ashamed and embarrassed as the pair became centre of attention.

'That was unfair, I'm sorry,' he said. 'I didn't mean that. I've just been going through some stuff.'

'I don't want to hear it,' she said, before suddenly standing up and plastering a huge smile on her face to greet Jasper, who had just entered the restaurant.

'What a lovely evening!' the professor exclaimed as he sat down beside Ted. 'I see you two have been well acquainted.' He took note of the drinks on the table. 'Ah! You've started without me.' He signalled to a nearby waiter to take his order.

Neither Quinn nor Ted responded.

'Everything OK here?' Jasper asked, reading the room.

'Yes, everything's fine,' Quinn lied. 'Ted was telling me how excited he was to be a part of this trip.' She gave Ted a piercing look. He'd spent less than an hour with this woman and she already hated him.

Jasper grinned. 'And so he should be.' He patted Ted enthusiastically on the back, then picked up the menu. 'So, what's good here?'

**

Ted devoured his enchilada mostly in silence, only chipping in on snippets of conversation when called upon. Jasper and Quinn were engrossed in a discussion on Mesoamerican history: the artefacts uncovered at the dig, cultural differences between the Mayans and the Aztecs, and more that Ted didn't feel qualified to contribute to. Every time Jasper asked him a question, Quinn would glare at him, probably imagining all the ways she wanted to kill him for being such an arse to her.

Her outburst had made him think about the way he'd acted. Not just what he'd said, but why he'd said it. She had been trying to take an interest in him and he'd put up a wall, countering her questions with senseless mockery. Perhaps subconsciously he was afraid she'd delve deep enough to learn his real motivation for being there: to escape his life. To get his mind off Julia. It was no use, that text message had brought it all crashing back.

The evening had been a blur from then on. Jasper had tried to get Ted involved in conversation, with limited success, and after paying the bill had agreed to call it a night.

Ted tossed and turned all night, his tiredness kept in check by his restless mind that was torturing him with flashbacks of his evening with Julia, and now the fresh wound of seeing the disgust in Quinn's eyes as he senselessly ridiculed her passion for history. His body ached for sleep, but his brain denied him; his punishment for being so unappreciative of the opportunities provided to him. Quinn had been right; he should feel honoured to be there. Not just to be a part of a discovery, however big or small it really turned out to be, but to be given a lifeline when his prospects were so poor.

He contemplated knocking on her door to apologise. She was only in the next room, after all. He got all the way to the corridor before thinking better of it. Perhaps she was still angry with him. Why wouldn't she be? Here he was, a complete stranger picking apart her interests like he didn't care for anything but his own prejudices. Was that the kind of man he was, or was that a momentary lapse of sanity while his obsession for Julia stripped away his good character? That was a thought for another day.

He was going to apologise to Quinn first thing in the morning, at breakfast, he decided. She had saved his blushes at dinner by not mentioning anything, but the professor would get wind of something sooner or later if he didn't own up to his mistakes. And how would he react if he learned that Ted had insulted his co-worker the first chance he got? He could kiss goodbye to any chance of a good reference, and this whole trip would have been a waste of time.

After more spiralling and wishing he could start this whole day again, flight and all, his mind eventually succumbed to tiredness and he drifted off to sleep.

**

Breakfast consisted of the usual continental options, plus a few Mexican items for those wanting to immerse themselves a bit more in the local culture. Ted went for the familiar choice, the enchilada from the night before still working its way through his system. His stomach rumbled before he took his first sip of coffee.

'A spot of stomach trouble?' Jasper asked, upon hearing the distress call from Ted's abdomen.

The Aztec Secret

'The food was delicious,' Ted assured, worried the professor would be offended by his choice of restaurant for them last night. 'I'm probably just not used to it.'

'What would a holiday be without a little case of the runs?' Jasper whispered, before letting out a hearty chuckle. Ted nearly spat his coffee out.

'Oh, it's not that bad yet, fortunately.'

'Well, count yourself lucky.'

Ted narrowed his eyes and stared at the assortment of food on his plate. That was a little too much information for this time of morning.

'I always get a funny stomach the first few days away,' Jasper continued, not seeming to care who could hear. He patted his belly gently. 'It seems to sort itself out though.'

'That's good,' said Ted, desperately trying to find a way to change the conversation. His distraction came in the form of Quinn, who had just sat down beside him with a yoghurt and selection of fruits.

'Hmm,' said Jasper, appraising her breakfast.

'What?' she asked, wondering what she'd done wrong.

'Where did you get that yoghurt from?'

'Over there,' she pointed. The professor got up straight away and headed in that direction.

Ted took his opportunity to speak to Quinn one-on-one.

'Look, Quinn, I'm really sorry for the way I spoke to you last night. I don't know what came over me.'

'It's fine,' she replied, not looking up as she dipped her spoon into the yoghurt.

'No, it's not. I want you to know that I really am sorry.'

'It's fine,' she repeated.

'The things I said. I didn't mean any of it,' he said.

'Ted,' she suddenly turned to face him. 'I don't know you, and you don't know me. You might be a stand-up guy. You might be a total jackass. But don't tell me you didn't mean the things you said. They came from somewhere, that's why you said them.'

Her words stunned Ted for a moment. Perhaps it was the directness with which she spoke. Ted had never met anyone that was able to cut through the bullshit with such ease. But she had a point.

'Well, I shouldn't have said it,' he replied. 'It was totally uncalled for. You didn't deserve that.'

'I appreciate that,' she turned back to her yoghurt. 'I'm not sorry for calling you an arrogant jerk.'

Ted smiled. 'Don't be. I am.'

Jasper came back to the table with two yoghurts, placing one in front of Ted before tucking into his own.

'Thought you could use this,' he said. 'Good for the old belly.'

'Thanks,' Ted replied. He caught a flash of a smile from Quinn, who hadn't looked up from the orange she was now peeling.

'Our taxi will be here in fifteen minutes,' the professor announced, after polishing off the last of his yoghurt. 'I'll meet you back at the lobby in ten.'

The taxi was a little later than advertised, but more than made up the time en route to the dig site. Ted scrawled the last few questions he was planning on asking in his interviews on a memo on his phone.

Quinn leaned over. 'You actually look like you know what you're doing.'

'Are you surprised?' Ted inquired.

'A little.'

Ted noticed that she'd changed outfit since breakfast. 'What was wrong with the band t-shirt?' he asked.

'Oh, that? I was wearing that yesterday. I'm not going to wear it twice in two days. I like to look like I've washed in the last twenty-four hours. Presentation is everything, you know.'

Ted did know. Although his dress sense rarely strayed from casual, he was very self-conscious of his appearance. Which was why he'd been so mortified at being caught in his boxers with a bad case of bedhead on his first meeting with Quinn.

To his surprise, while Professor Thornton was sporting his usual tweed jacket and smart trousers, Quinn had opted for a casual look of jeans and a plaid shirt over a white t-shirt. Perhaps archaeology nerds came in all shapes and sizes after all.

'I've never understood this,' Quinn prodded Ted's phone.

'It's a mobile phone,' Ted replied sarcastically. 'Like a computer, but really small, and you can ring people on it, and—'

'No, not that,' she scowled. 'I mean, is it any easier typing on that than writing on a notepad?'

'Well, I mean, it's OK. But it means I can record the whole interview, so I don't miss anything. Plus, notepads are a waste of paper. We've developed a lot since then, so why rely on old ways of doing things when there's a solution that doesn't cause deforestation?'

'Ah, so you're a hippy,' Quinn teased.

'Not a hippy, it's just a fact. Don't you watch the news?'

'It was a joke.'

The taxi driver slammed on the brakes, lurching the pair forward in their seats. A string of Spanish abuse was then hurled at the car that had almost t-boned them at a junction, along with incessant horn blowing.

'You two alright back there?' Jasper asked concernedly.

'Yeah, we're OK,' Quinn replied.

'Lovely city for commuting, don't you think?'

The car drove on and resumed its journey well over the speed limit.

'So, I guess you're one of those e-book readers, too?' Quinn turned back to Ted.

'As a matter of fact, I am.'

'Let me guess, paperbacks are a waste of paper?'

'Correct.'

'But it's not the same, is it?' she countered. 'I mean, yeah, I get that saving the trees is a good idea, but don't you love the feeling of finishing a book and looking back at the mass of pages you've read? Reflecting on the journey you've been on with the characters. It feels so much more satisfying than an e-book when you can feel the weight of your achievement in your hands.'

'Huh,' was all Ted managed to say. 'I guess I hadn't thought about it like that.'

'Well, maybe we can finally agree on something,' she smiled.

For the first time that morning, Ted felt as though he could redeem himself from his horrible first impression. He was starting to look forward to the day ahead.

The dig site looked like nothing more than a construction site. What was reported as a major Aztec temple and a ceremonial ball court looked to Ted like heaps of rubble with layers of cobbled stones. He was lacking the imagination that Jasper and Quinn shared, as they speculated on how it must have looked in 16th Century Mexico. They seemed so enthusiastic about the spectacle, as though this were their Disneyland. Tape cordoned off areas the public weren't given access to, and people in hard hats walked around busily. Jasper sorted out their press passes and filled them in on who

The Aztec Secret

they would talk to and what time they were able to do so. It seemed there were a few other reporters in the mix, and timings were crucial if everyone was to get what they needed.

It was time for Ted to ask his questions, and he introduced himself with a handshake.

'Hi, I'm Ted. Thanks for giving up your time to talk to us.'

'*Encantada de conocerte,*' the woman replied. The speech was too fast and fluid for Ted to pick up, and he bumbled straight on to his first question.

'So, I've been told you were the one who discovered the scroll containing the manuscripts from Hernán Cortés. Can you recall the moment for us?'

'*Lo siento,*' the woman replied, followed by a string of words Ted couldn't comprehend. He then read the puzzled look on her face and got everything he needed to know. She didn't speak much English. He started to panic as the interview began to crumble around him. He'd been assured he wouldn't need to speak much Spanish. Again, he felt like a typical ignorant English tourist. Suddenly, a short bald man wearing thick-lensed spectacles came rushing over, apologising profusely in both English and Spanish. He informed Ted that he was the translator for these interviews and had been running late. Ted breathed a huge sigh of relief.

Ten minutes later, Ted was listening back to the interview on his phone to ensure the audio quality was good enough for him to be able to transcribe later. Quinn had finished taking photos of the dig site. Ted hadn't asked if they were for a report or for her personal collection, but both seemed equally probable scenarios.

'Isn't this great?' she enthused. Ted put his phone away.

'Yes, it is something,' he replied.

Quinn saw right through him. 'You sound delighted to be here.'

'It's just all dirt and rubble to me,' he admitted.

'Use your imagination, Ted,' she said, standing beside him to guide his vision with her outstretched hand. She pointed to the indents in the stone that cascaded down in layers. 'This was once an Aztec temple. They say it was dedicated to the wind god Ehecatl-Quetzalcoatl. You can tell because of the shape. It's cylindrical.'

'I've heard of Quetzalcoatl before,' said Ted. 'He's the feathered serpent.'

'Yes!' Quinn was excited by Ted's knowledge. 'So you know a few things after all.'

'Hey, I did some research,' he protested. 'So, what's that other name for? Ear-cattle or something?'

She snorted loudly. 'Ehecatl,' she corrected. 'It means wind god. Ehecatl is a pre-Columbian deity, but it's often considered the same as Quetzalcoatl, hence why sometimes the two as paired together.'

'That sounds confusing.'

'I guess,' she admitted. 'Quetzalcoatl is the classical Nahuatl name, which was the language used by the Aztecs. I usually just use that one.'

'So,' Ted said, looking at the temple ruins. 'What happened here in 16th Century Mexico?' He pulled his phone from his pocket and tapped on the record button.

'Is this an interview?' Quinn asked.

'An exclusive,' Ted replied. 'With the famous archaeologist, and all-round nerd, Miss…' he realised he didn't know her last name, and waited for her to chime in.

'Miyata,' she played along, narrowing her eyes at his use of the word 'nerd'. 'Back in 16th Century Mexico, before they were wiped out by the invasion of the Spanish, led by Hernán

Cortés, this was an important ceremonial space for the Aztec people.'

'Interesting,' Ted put on a funny voice in his part as the interviewer. 'Please, Miss Miyata. Tell me more.'

'Temples like these were used for numerous rituals, which often included human sacrifices.'

Ted broke character for a moment. 'Wait, are you serious? That's horrible.'

'Yes, it was,' she continued. 'But it was a big part of their culture, providing offerings to the gods.'

'Gruesome. So, Miss Miyata. When do you imagine this impressive structure was first built?'

'An interesting question,' she replied. 'The original white stucco is still visible in some places, and experts believe it was built during the reign of Ahuizotl, between 1486 and 1502, predecessor to Moctezuma II.'

Their faux interview was interrupted as Jasper had finished making the rounds, thanking those who had organised their time at the site. It was time to leave.

FIVE

Ramón Andrés Villacrés, Governor of the Mexican state of Coahuila, composed himself as he prepared to enter the room. He lifted his head while straightening his tie, taking a moment to reflect on the progress he'd made to get to this point. He'd worked his way up the ladder over years of careful planning and tactical moves. He was far from the ideal politician; for all of Mexico's efforts to reduce its role in politics, corruption still existed in places. Ramón had walked the line throughout his career, often swaying over to more illegitimate means to get what he wanted. He believed that everyone had a price, and so far it had worked in his favour. He'd been Governor of Coahuila for six months now; a role which brought him the power to make impactful decisions that could affect not just his state, but the country as a whole. He now had the opportunity to play his hand at the biggest table in the game. This meeting would be crucial in deciding the part he played in the upcoming election.

He knocked on the door and a voice from inside asked him to enter. He took a deep breath as he turned the doorknob and stepped inside. General Secretary Alina Cicerón, fellow Institutional Revolutionary Party member and second in command to the President, awaited behind her large solid oak desk. The nation's flag draped behind her, creating an image of authority and a possible glimpse into the future of the party's leadership. At thirty-eight, she was one of the youngest people to hold that position in the party's history. A few years her senior, Ramón immediately felt the familiar sting of jealousy and bitterness that came when he was face to face with someone younger and more authoritative than him. It was a flaw of his character he'd never learned to overcome.

She looked up from the papers on her desk. 'Good afternoon, Governor Villacrés.'

'Good afternoon,' he replied. 'Thank you for making time for a meeting with me.'

'Are you well?' she gestured for him to take a seat opposite her.

'Yes, very well, thank you. And yourself?'

'Very well, if not in need of another coffee.'

'It is a busy period,' Ramón smiled.

'Would you like a drink?'

'Please. I too feel the need for a caffeine boost. A coffee would be nice.'

Alina punched in a couple of buttons on the conference phone on her desk. The line clicked and a voice came on the other side. She asked the person on the other end to bring them two coffees.

'So, Governor Villacrés,' she said. 'How are you liking your new role? Do you feel like you've had time to settle into it?'

'It is an honour,' he replied. 'I'm enjoying it very much, but I'm still learning a few things.'

'Some people say we never stop learning.'

'Wise words, indeed.'

Ramón lapped up the small talk. It settled any nerves he'd felt before entering the room and gave him time to consider how he wanted to approach the meeting. Experience had taught him that it wasn't always what you said that mattered, but the way you dressed it up. However, he knew Alina wouldn't play into his hands as easily as most.

The door opened and a young woman entered, carrying a tray with a jug of hot coffee and two empty cups. She poured the drinks and offered sugar and milk. Ramón took both and thanked her warmly.

'What can I help you with?' Alina got to the point, stirring her drink as she spoke.

'My apologies, General Secretary. You must have a thousand things to consider today. But a most interesting opportunity has come our way. Please allow me to elaborate.'

Alina narrowed her eyes appraisingly, her face showing a mix of intrigue and suspicion.

'Go on.'

'You might have seen the news about the remains of a new Aztec temple that was discovered in the city.'

'What of it?'

'There were a number of artefacts dug up as part of the excavation. They were given to the National Museum of Anthropology to be displayed for the public. But there are people interested in these artefacts.' He paused for effect, as though to pique her interest or watch her visibly sit forward in her seat. But her expression remained the same and her body language was closed. 'There's one person in particular who is very interested in them. He collects objects of historical significance all around the world, for his personal collection. Somewhat of a hobbyist with a lot of money.'

The Aztec Secret

'What is it you came to ask me?' Alina was growing tired of him dancing around the topic. Ramón took a moment to compose himself. He always had more success in these meetings when he had the time to weave his story first. He would have to use all of his experience to get the outcome he wanted. He had a tactic up his sleeve that worked on most.

'You've seen the polls,' he said. 'MORENA are growing in popularity. At the rate they're going they'll be our number one opposition by the time the vote comes.' *Movimiento Regeneración Nacional*, or the National Regeneration Movement, were a recently established left-wing party that openly supported ethnic, religious, cultural and sexual diversity. Their policies to oppose monopolisation of the mass media and the privatisation of a large petroleum company, as well as to provide better treatment of the indigenous peoples proved extremely popular. It was no secret that all other parties were worried about their presence in the upcoming election.

'Get to the point, Governor,' Alina was getting impatient and didn't appreciate his scaremongering tactics. Ramón complied.

'This artefact collector I mentioned. He wants to offer us a lot of money, which can really help us in our campaign.'

'We have money. Money is not the issue.'

'He also has access to some of the best private investigators in the business. They can find dirt on anybody. Literally *anybody*.' Ramón emphasised his point by speaking slowly and clearly.

Alina caught his drift instantly and quelled the notion there and then. 'That's not what we do. We're not Americans; we don't publicly drag our opponent through the mud and hope it turns the voters against them.'

'This is politics,' said Ramón. 'It happens all the time.'

'Governor Villacrés, it seems you and I have a different understanding of the word 'politics'. While I am part of this campaign, this is not how we do things.'

Ramón paused a moment. This was not going the way he had hoped. Had he pitched this idea to any number of others in the party, he'd have at least expected them to consider it. There were one or two he knew would have pitched the idea to him had they have been contacted instead of him. However, he still had another card to play.

'Consider we win the election, as we expect to do. This man has contacts who have a lot of influence with one of the major Cartels on the border. Do not underestimate the demand for drugs in America. It is a very lucrative business. Cocaine, methamphetamine, you name it. We can make a lot of money working with these Cartels.'

'Cartels? Have you lost your mind?' Alina snapped. 'Tell me this is some sort of joke, Governor. We cannot be seen to be cooperating with the Cartels, let alone profiting from them. The world already thinks we're a corrupt nation. What progress have we made if we do this and prove them right?'

Ramón was taken aback by her response. She was foolish to think this was how things worked. How had she got to where she was now without greasing a few palms? She obviously wasn't understanding the full benefit of this opportunity. It was too good for the party to pass up. If only she would see the big picture like he could. He considered his next move carefully; it was critical to the success of this meeting. He couldn't walk away with nothing.

'Think of it from this point of view,' he suggested, trying a new angle. 'We give them freedom to move their goods in bigger volumes, and they keep a low profile. We don't have any conflict with them, and drug related violence begins to decrease. We let the Americans get high and keep the conflict

The Aztec Secret

in their country.' He paused as he noted the dour look on the General Secretary's face. He quickly segued into a point she might buy into. This wasn't the first time he'd had to talk his way towards getting what he wanted. He'd done his homework and planned to pique her curiosity with a common interest.

'Fatalities as a result of the drug war are at the highest levels ever.' Ramón knew this was an issue on the General Secretary's radar. 'When the public sees this drop, they'll think we're making a real difference. The next election will be easy.'

He set his empty coffee cup back on the tray and folded his arms. He'd made his point. The benefits were clear to see. Politics was a dirty game, but ultimately it was a game he knew how to win at. Alina set her cup down and leaned forward in her seat, lowering her voice to little more than a whisper.

'Working with the Cartels is suicide,' she said sternly. 'We cannot trust them. And I am insulted that you would consider for one second that I would put our entire party's reputation on the line by working with them.'

'General Secretary, I would have contingencies in place if ever—'

'And don't think I don't know the real reason you're proposing this,' she interrupted. 'As Governor of a border state, you should be building bridges between our nations. The relationship between Coahuila and Texas is fragile and in need of constant care. We have worked hard for years to improve relations between us.'

'Alina, please,' Ramón tried to protest once more, the desperation cutting through in his voice.

'Do not test me, Governor.' Alina's stare lingered for a moment. It was an intimidating power play that made Ramón's blood boil. He recognised his own tactics when he saw it, but being on the receiving end was something he wasn't used to. She picked her cup up once more for another sip, leaning back in her chair satisfied he'd got the message. 'Given the stress of this period, I shall put this down to a temporary lapse of sanity. But if I hear another mention of this, I shall be requesting your dismissal.' She motioned towards the door with her hand.

Ramón was furious. He had outlined the benefits of this arrangement clearly. This was a critical time for the party, with MORENA gaining traction in the polls. Anything they could do to secure their future should be grabbed with both hands, not dismissed. He stood up and left the room without a word, slamming the door behind him like a petulant child. The General Secretary's assistant was taken by surprise at his abrupt and violent exit, but he stormed off down the corridor before she had a chance to comment on the matter.

He exited the building and made his way to the carpark. He mashed the button on his key as he approached the car, the luxurious black saloon greeting him with a chirping noise and a flash of lights. He sat inside and shut the door, the noise shut off from the outside and the sudden silence isolating him with nothing but the aggressive panting of his breath. He sat still a moment in the leather seat to let what had just happened sink in. Another rush of fury quickly overwhelmed him, and he let his anger out on the dashboard, punching it twice in frustration. The force knocked a button on his stereo and the muffled noise of talking crackled through the FM channel. He cursed aloud, but decided to let the radio play as a mild distraction. Today he had achieved nothing, other than lowering the General Secretary's opinion of him. He was now going to be a watched man, and every decision he made in his position as Governor of Coahuila would be scrutinised. He needed something to take the edge off before working out his next move. He popped open the glove box and retrieved a pack of cigarettes. He didn't bother winding down the window more than just a crack before lighting up and drawing in a long puff. He allowed the smoke to sit in his lungs a while before letting it out his nostrils.

They wouldn't get a better deal than this. All they had to do was give this collector a few old bits of clay. They had museums full of the stuff. They shouldn't care so much about the past; the past was dead. They should be concerned with the future. Deals like this were necessary to survive. He had no doubt that other parties would be doing the same to maximise the success of their campaigns. He wondered if the General Secretary had any idea how politics in Mexico was supposed to be run. He let the cigarette burn down before he wound the electric window down so he could flick the butt outside. Turning his attention to the long journey home, he plunged the key into the ignition and started up the engine. He started reversing out of the bay when something compelled him to slam on the brakes. He lifted the handbrake and shut the car off. Enough was enough. He couldn't stand by and let this opportunity slip through the party's fingers. Pulling the phone from his pocket, Ramón checked his contacts for the number and hit dial. He put the phone to his ear as the dialing tone sounded.

'Governor Villacrés,' the recipient was expecting his call. The voice sounded deep and distorted. 'How did the meeting go?'

'Very well,' Ramón lied, trying hard to give off optimism in his voice. 'We discussed it at length, and I'm pleased to say that I now have permission from the General Secretary herself to agree to this.'

'Excellent. So we have a deal?'

'We have a deal.'

'And she agreed to my terms?'

'Yes. You will be granted unrestricted access to excavate anywhere in Mexico, at your leisure. If your work affects any nearby buildings, I'll see to it that you receive permission to proceed.'

'And the artefacts recovered in Mexico City this month?'

'You will have those too, plus a team of men to help you with your excavations.'

'Excellent news. I will make the arrangements on my side. Best of luck in the upcoming election, Governor. I have a feeling this will be a very successful year for you all.'

SIX

Jasper could barely contain his excitement as they approached the National Museum of Anthropology. The most visited museum in Mexico, it was busy with tourists and there was a buzz about the place. The feeling on entering the building was altogether different from the British Museum; no pillars to exude grandeur here. Yet the large concrete slabs making up the architecture, mixed with the exotic greenery leading up to the building gave off an adventurous impression.

The trio had stopped by The Monolith of Tlāloc and asked some passers-by to take a photo, in front of where the great sign for the museum greets its guests. Ted returned the favour for the cheery couple, and received an unexpected compliment from Quinn for his photography skills. She'd been peering over his shoulder to evaluate the frame as he took a few snaps on the stranger's smartphone. Judging from the weighty Canon DSLR camera she'd had slung over her shoulder all day, Ted made the assumption that she knew a little more about these things than he did.

'So, what's the plan?' Ted asked as they entered the impressive building. 'We find the exhibition containing the new artefacts, take some notes and then grab some food?'

'What's the rush, my boy?' Jasper patted his shoulder. 'You're in one of the most fascinating museums in the world. Explore. Take in the sights.'

'Maybe you'll learn something,' Quinn said.

'Hey, I know plenty,' replied Ted.

An elderly gentleman and a middle-aged woman walked over from the main desk and greeted the professor. The man was dressed in a grey suit, with a distinct bald patch in the middle of his short grey hair. The woman wore a beige dress suit that came down to her knees and wore her dark brunette hair in a bun. It was her who spoke first as they approached and took Ted completely by surprise with a British accent as she greeted Jasper.

'Quinn, Ted, this is Lillian Pembroke,' Jasper gestured towards the woman. 'And Evan Anderson,' pointing now at the man in the grey suit. 'They are both very well respected in the world of Archaeology and Anthropology.'

'Much like yourself,' Quinn piped up. However, her attempt at brown-nosing fell flat as an awkward silence followed.

'Yes, quite,' Evan said sarcastically at last, as though dismissing Quinn's claim. 'Professor Thornton might have told you about some of our work?'

Ted noticed Jasper wince as the man spoke. That told him everything he needed to know about the dynamic between the two.

'A pleasure to meet you both,' Lillian shook each of their hands.

'Likewise. I suppose you're both colleagues of Professor Thornton?' Ted asked.

The Aztec Secret

'Not directly, although we have crossed paths a few times before,' Evan said. 'I'm head of my department at UCL. Lillian here used to work at Oxford, but she has since retired from academia. But us anthropologists are always in tune with our peer's achievements,' he paused to glance at Jasper. 'Or lack thereof.'

'That's enough, Evan,' Lillian cut in. Jasper said nothing, but was red in the face with anger.

'Here for the new Aztec collection?' Ted asked, breaking the silence.

'Naturally,' Lillian replied candidly. 'It is most exquisite.'

Exquisite? Ted tilted his head at her choice of adjective. It was a word used more often for brightly coloured jewels than lumps of old clay that had just been dug up from the ground.

'We've just come from the place they dug them up,' Ted added. 'The people who found the artefacts seemed very proud.'

'Yes, yes, I can imagine,' she replied. Jasper was still locking eyes with the grey-suited man next to her, and the atmosphere between the two parties started to become unsettling.

'We're very excited to see it,' Quinn chirped.

'Well, we mustn't keep you then,' Lillian said. 'It is worth the journey, I can assure you.'

The pair nodded as they bid the group farewell and walked away towards the exit. But after a few moments there was a scuffing sound on the floor as Lillian turned quickly on her heel.

'Oh, Professor Thornton? I almost forgot. How rude of me.'

'Yes?' Jasper replied.

'A few of us are having dinner in town tonight if you and your students would like to join us?'

'Of course, we'd be delighted,' he forced a smile. They watched as the pair exited the building for good. Jasper waited until they were out of sight before storming off into the first exhibition.

'What the hell was that about?' asked Ted when he caught up with him.

'That bloody arsehole,' the professor replied, perhaps a little louder than he'd intended. A passer-by stopped to look at him, startled by the outburst, before hurrying along to another part of the room.

'Yeah, I got that impression,' said Ted. 'What's his deal?'

'Evan's always thought himself a hot-shot. Always thinks he's better than everyone else.'

'I got that impression too.'

'You know,' Jasper continued. 'Not once have I been to a conference or archaeology social without him boasting about his accomplishments and rubbing it in my face.'

Before answering, Ted took a moment to imagine what an absolute hoot an archaeology social must have been.

'Don't listen to him,' Quinn reassured. 'It takes a lot to make a good professor. So what if his name is attached to this paper or that discovery? He's a jerk.'

Ted was acutely aware that Quinn didn't seem to use that word lightly, as though she saved it only for those who really deserved it. Him and Professor Anderson.

'Hilary raved about you too. She said everyone loves taking your class,' Ted lied.

'Is that so?' Jasper asked.

Ted nodded.

The museum became more spectacular as they discovered more of it. It wasn't just the items within this repository that grabbed Ted's attention, but the architecture surrounding it. He was blown away by the colossal Olmec stone heads which

The Aztec Secret

were unlike anything he'd ever seen, but what really captured his attention was the stone umbrella-esque structure in the courtyard. The massive roof stretched out by an unbelievable distance, to say it was held up by a single stone pillar. The pillar itself was ornate with interesting carvings and jets of water spraying from all directions. It looked almost like a giant toadstool in a rainforest. Ted took a rare snap on his phone.

They finally made their way to the exhibition that held the new artefacts. The room was windowless and dark, lit up by a few bulbs scattered around the ceiling and walls. There were a good few more people gathered here than in the last room. Ted chuckled to himself at the irony of how people were excited by new things, despite these 'new' things being five-hundreds years old.

'What's so funny?' Quinn asked.

'It's nothing,' Ted played it down. 'You'd lower your opinion of me if I told you.'

'My opinion of you is pretty low as it is,' she quipped.

Jasper was checking his phone and was taken by surprise as Ted tapped him on the shoulder.

'This is it, professor,' said Ted. 'The moment you've been waiting for.'

The professor locked his phone and put it back into his pocket. 'Yes, yes. How exciting!' He hesitated on entering the room. 'Err, Ted. I'm still having a little stomach trouble. Appears that bio yoghurt didn't do the trick after all. Can you excuse me a moment while I go to the bathroom?'

'OK,' Ted replied. 'We'll be here.'

The room was full of interesting Aztec objects, holding a much larger collection than the British Museum. It made sense, given this was their home. Plus, what would a Mexican anthropology museum be without a fair share of items from its own ancient civilisations?

The focal point of the room was in the centre, where a large glass display held a number of interesting objects. One was clearly a weapon of some kind; a long club-like item made primarily of wood, with shards of obsidian fixed along its edges, resembling the spine of a stegosaurus from the Jurassic period running along each side. The label next to the item read *Macuahuitl*. Ted remembered reading about this in his preliminary research at the university. Used by both Eagle and Jaguar Warriors, the Aztec elite fighting forces, these weapons would be used in both war and in ceremonial settings. The warriors would attempt to wound their foe, without killing them, so they could capture them and use them later in sacrificial rituals. The macuahuitl would be swung hard to deliver a devastating blow, and the obsidian edges would cut and tear at the skin when the wielder made contact.

Ted took great pride in recalling everything he knew about it to Quinn. Her face depicted the look of someone who was both impressed and disgusted at his knowledge.

'Trust you boys to learn everything there is to know about weaponry. Do you know what this is?' she tested him, pointing at the next item in the display. It was a star-shaped object, roughly the size of a hand. The points of the star appeared to be made of obsidian, with solid clay compacted in the middle, surrounding both the top and bottom sides. The sign next to the piece seemed to be fairly descriptive. The translation of obsidian was similar to English, and instantly recognisable.

'It just looks like a star made from clay and obsidian,' Ted guessed.

'Very good,' she replied. 'The sign actually says something along those lines. Are you sure you don't know Spanish?'

'Positive,' he said. 'Why doesn't it have a name like this one?' he pointed back to the macuahuitl.

'Perhaps they don't know what it was for. That happens a lot. If a museum has an artefact that they don't know the purpose of, the labels tend to be quite visually descriptive.'

'What do you think it was for?'

'Me?'

'Yeah, you.'

'I dunno,' she tucked her hair behind her ear and a smile crept over her face as she thought about it. Ted could see she enjoyed conversations like this. He noticed how attractive it was to see her in her element. 'It could be a weapon, like a throwing star?' she suggested.

'What, like a ninja?' Ted laughed.

'Or...' she thought some more. 'It could be related to the sun god, Tonatiuh. It's in the shape of the sun, with its rays coming out the side like that,' she motioned towards the jagged obsidian edges. 'Tonatiuh was a patron of warriors, so it would make sense for them to pair the two together. Maybe that was their guess, even if they don't know for sure.'

A man brushed past Ted, knocking him into Quinn and sending her tumbling to the deck. Her camera case went flying, and the other small bag she was carrying opened, the contents spilling onto the floor.

'I'm so sorry,' Ted tried to help her up. 'Are you alright?'

'Yeah, I'm fine. And this time you don't need to apologise, it wasn't your fault.'

The man who had knocked into him was walking briskly off towards the exit. Ted noticed he was one of the museum's security guards. The man looked back at Ted before he hurried out of the room.

'That was rude,' he said. 'He didn't even say sorry.' He helped Quinn to her feet and started to retrieve her possessions from the floor. He picked up a set of keys with various keyrings on it. One in particular piqued his interest.

'What is this? A torch?' It appeared to be a small penlight.

'Oh, that's a UV light,' she replied, matter of fact.

'UV light?' he repeated.

'Yes, it's also a UV pen.' She took it from him and showed him by taking the lid off.

'Why do you need that on your keys?' He gave her a strange look. 'Do you need to use it often?'

She shrugged her shoulders. 'No, it's just something I found and thought was pretty cool.'

'You're so weird.'

'So are you,' she countered, putting the keys back into her bag and zipping it shut. Ted sensed her annoyance of him starting to grow and ceased his mocking.

'So,' he said, returning focus on the artefacts in the display. 'Where are these letters that were written by Hernán Cortés? They were supposed to be here too.'

'I think Jasper mentioned that they're still being looked over by experts. They probably have them locked away someplace safe until they're ready for display.'

The lights suddenly went out, leaving the room in complete darkness. A woman yelped in surprise and there were a few murmurs about the place. A moment went by before there was a loud crashing sound, immediately following by the sound of the alarm being triggered. The noise was shrill, ringing in their ears. Mild panic started to take hold of a few people as the loud noise and lack of visibility brought unnerving insecurity. Ted felt someone push past him, but it was too dark to see who it was.

A couple of minutes went by before the lights went back on and security personnel began to swarm into the room, shouting commands in Spanish.

The Aztec Secret

'Are you alright?' Ted asked to Quinn. They had both crouched down in the darkness, as if the lower position would shield them from any potential danger.

'What?' she shouted, not able to hear him above the persistent ringing of the alarm. The security team pushed their way through to the centre of the room, muttered a few words to each other and sped out the exit.

'I said are you alri—' Ted stopped mid-sentence as he watched the security team leave, and then caught a glimpse of what had them so worried. The glass protecting the display they'd been looking at moments earlier had been smashed, and the strange star-shaped artefact was now missing.

Quinn followed Ted's gaze and her eyes widened at the sight.

'Oh my God,' she gasped. 'It's been stolen!'

Ted surveyed the rest of the display. The star was the only item missing. Everything else, the macuahuitl included, remained where it was.

A loud voice suddenly echoed around the room as a man carrying a megaphone informed everyone, first in Spanish and then English that the museum was in lockdown, but to remain calm and leave the room. It was now a crime scene and the police were on the way. People instantly started pouring out of the room.

'We should find Jasper,' Quinn suggested. 'We don't want to get separated from him.'

'Agreed.'

They left the room and looked at the nearest map of the museum for guidance.

'I think he was in the bathroom,' Ted remembered. 'I'll see if I can find him.' The alarm was still sounding loudly, even more so as they got closer to one of the ringing bells above the doorways. Ted covered his ears as he made his way to the restrooms, following signs for *baño*. That was some of the limited Spanish he did know, same as any tourist. He entered the gents and called out for the professor, but there was no answer. He called again, louder this time, but still nothing.

'He's not there,' he said on his return.

'Where did he go?' Quinn wondered aloud.

As if on cue, Ted caught a glimpse of a tweed jacket through a crowd of people coming out of another room. The figure separated from the group, heading down another corridor. Ted and Quinn followed and as they were clear of the crowd, they could see him more clearly. It was unmistakably him.

'Jasper, over here,' Ted called, but it seemed the professor couldn't hear above the noise of the alarm.

'Professor?' Quinn shouted. Still no answer, and the distance between them was growing.

'Where is he going?' asked Ted.

'How the hell should I know?' Quinn marched on in pursuit. Ted took one last look at the stream of people heading in the other direction, before following her.

They rushed down one corridor into another. The professor was a fair distance away now, having broken into a run. He barged into an emergency exit door, sending it swinging open. With the alarm already going off there was no risk of causing a scene in doing so. He seemed in a real hurry, and as Quinn called again after him his head turned quickly in their direction, revealing a worried expression on his face. Something wasn't right.

The pair reached the door and looked out into the brightness of the outside. Before they could see which way the professor had gone, voices shouted from further up the corridor, the way they'd just come. They turned to look back, but there was no one there yet. The voices got louder and the sound of running footsteps could be heard coming their way.

'Shit,' Ted started to panic. 'Someone must have seen us. They're gonna think we're up to something.' His mind spiralled as he desperately tried to come up with some sort of excuse as to why they were standing in the opening of an emergency door that had been slammed open in the midst of a lockdown. How he planned on translating that with his horrendous Spanish he had no idea.

Suddenly, a hand grabbed Ted by the back of his shirt, pulling him outside. He spun around to find Jasper staring him in the face.

'Quickly!' Jasper shouted. 'Follow me.' He led them around the side of the building.

'What's going on?' Ted asked as they hurried.

'No time to explain.'

A black van was parked on the road outside the museum and as they neared the sliding door opened and the professor jumped in. He signalled for Ted and Quinn to follow.

'Come on, what are you waiting for?'

The windows were tinted on all sides, making it impossible to see who else was in the vehicle. The sound of sirens could be heard in the distance.

'I'll explain everything. Just get in!' the professor pleaded. Quinn jumped into the van, quickly followed by Ted. The door shut behind them and the tyres screeched on the asphalt road as the vehicle lurched and drove away.

SEVEN

The van careened around a corner, sending them tumbling in the back. The back of the van was empty for the most part with benches along each side, except for the part covering the sliding door. Ted was just getting his bearings and managed to sit down, while Quinn and Jasper sat opposite. The benches at least had custom seatbelts fitted and Ted grabbed his and strapped himself in. The belt was tight around his waist and he couldn't figure out how to slacken it. This was one of those moments he wished he hadn't avoided the gym most of his life.

In the panic of getting into the van and speeding away from a crime scene, he had only just noticed there was another person already in the van when they got in. The Hispanic man sat next to Ted hadn't said a word. He was wearing the same uniform as the security guards in the museum. It was then that Ted recognised him as the man who had knocked him into Quinn in the exhibition earlier.

'Jasper, what's going on? Who is this?' he asked.

The professor didn't say anything right away.

'This looks really bad,' Quinn looked equally confused. 'Professor, after you left us, there was a robbery. Someone took one of the new Aztec artefacts. Us leaving like we did—' she started to get breathless as the panic showed in her voice. 'They're going to think it was us.'

'You said you'd explain, so explain,' Ted insisted.

'Alright, alright,' Jasper gave in. 'You were never meant to be involved in this.' He turned to the man sat next to Ted. 'This is Carlos. He was hired to pose as an employee at the museum to give us our window of opportunity.'

'What are you talking about?'

Carlos pulled something out from behind him and held it casually before them. To their horror, sat idly in his hand was the star-shaped object that had been taken from the museum.

'Oh my God,' Quinn gasped. 'You're criminals!' She thought for a moment about the repercussions of what they had done. 'We're criminals.'

'Woah, woah, woah,' Ted's brain started to go into overdrive. '*We* are not criminals. We didn't have any part in this.'

'And you weren't meant to,' said Jasper. 'You weren't supposed to follow me. I tried to protect you. If you'd have just stopped—'

'Tried to protect us? Are you serious?' Ted could feel the anger building inside. 'Professor, explain everything right now, because none of this makes any sense.'

The van veered around another corner, causing Carlos to jolt forward in his seat. The artefact jumped in his hand, almost falling to the floor before he caught it again.

'Careful with that!' shouted Jasper.

'Professor?' Quinn brought the attention swiftly back to him. The look in her eye told him he wasn't getting away without an explanation.

He let out a long sigh. 'Look, before I tell you everything, you have to know I didn't mean for this to happen. You weren't supposed to be involved.' Ted and Quinn glared at him, understandingly unsympathetic given the situation.

'I've spent my whole life in academia,' he continued. 'And I've got nothing to show for it. Sure, I've written papers on this and that, but nothing that's really got people talking. Every sabbatical I've taken has turned out to be a waste of time. Field work has yielded nothing to me, yet my peers have managed to find something worth shouting about. And that idiot Evan lords it over me every opportunity he gets. He thinks I'm a crock, but I'm not. I'll show him. I'll uncover the biggest secret in Mesoamerican history, and then we'll see who's a crock.'

'You keep saying that,' Ted interjected. 'Both of you, actually.' He turned to Quinn. 'You've both said that this could be the one of the biggest discoveries in Mexico's history. Why is it so significant? We don't even know what it is.' He pointed at the object in Carlos' possession.

Quinn chimed in. 'It's not that he's talking about. It's the parchment. You remember the woman you interviewed earlier who found them? She read some of the contents before it was sent away for full examination by experts.'

'Yes,' Ted remembered. 'She told everyone what she'd read, and it's been posted online too. It was just a letter written by Hernán Cortés. Why is that significant?'

'Because it was addressed to King Charles V. Until now we only knew of five letters he wrote to the King during his conquest. The letter mentioned a treasure of unparalleled power.'

'Come on, he was a conquistador,' Ted was having none of it. 'They were obsessed with gold and jewels. That's why people spent so long looking for El Dorado. It's a myth.'

'Yes,' Jasper agreed. 'El Dorado probably doesn't exist, but I wouldn't be so sure about this.'

'Oh come on. A 'treasure of unparalleled power'?' he recited, using air quotes for effect. 'So you think there's a pile of jewels lying around in some undiscovered temple in Mexico?'

'Not a pile of jewels. Just one,' Jasper corrected. 'There are records in various writings that mention a ritual the Aztec Jaguar Warriors would go through to become initiated into their role. They were said to have touched a sacred stone, known as the *Heart of the Jaguar*, which would give them strength in their fights to come.'

'A sacred stone?' Ted was unconvinced. 'I'm not buying it.'

'Of course, it didn't actually give them some sort of unnatural power. It was just a ritual. The Florentine codex notes that the Aztecs would frequently use entheogenic plants during these ceremonies, which were powerful psychoactive substances. The warriors might have thought they were gaining powers from the stone, but in reality it was just a ritual to boost their courage in battle.'

'So they were high as a kite?'

'Yes.'

'But that still doesn't explain why Cortés calls it a treasure of unparalleled power.'

'Well, to the Spanish conquistadors, wealth was power. If it was a precious stone, it was perhaps a large fragment of Turquoise or something else bright and shiny that was indigenous in this part of the world. It would have made any man rich. For Cortés to write about it this way, it must have been greater than any single gem he'd seen.'

It wasn't completely implausible for such a precious stone to exist and for a conquistador to have mentioned it in writing. Their greed for gold was notorious, so if that was anything to go by the prospect of something worth more than a chest full of gold would have certainly been noteworthy. Ted considered what he had heard. Why Cortés was telling the King of the Holy Roman Empire about the jewel, who was thousands of miles across the sea, remained to be seen.

The van began to slow down, taking more measured angles into each corner, as though it was reaching its destination, wherever that was. They'd been driving just a few minutes, albeit at high speed, so they couldn't have gone far.

'Where are we going?' asked Ted.

'He booked a safe place for us to hide out.' Jasper replied.

'He? Who's he?' Quinn chimed in.

'The man who organised this whole thing. I don't know his real name; he signed off his email as *Sigma*. He was very secretive about the whole thing. He contacted me out of the blue, paid for the trip and hired Carlos and the others.'

'Well that doesn't sound dodgy at all,' said Ted sarcastically. 'Hang on, the others?' he wondered aloud as the vehicle came to a stop and the engine died. He'd barely considered the driver's role in all of this. Both the driver's side and passenger side doors at the front of the van slammed shut. The sliding door at the side then opened, and Ted found himself staring at a slim man with dark hair that had been slicked back, a pointed nose and an ugly soul patch under his bottom lip. He was wearing a black t-shirt that showed off his tattoo sleeves on either arm. A lit cigarette hung from his mouth, smoke starting to blow into the van. He looked at Ted, and then Quinn, seemingly surprised at their presence. He then turned his attention to Jasper with a long and cold stare.

'It was a mistake,' Jasper protested before the man spoke. The tone of his voice and the uneasy atmosphere that was

The Aztec Secret

quickly building gave away the dynamic between the two. The professor clearly wasn't the one in charge here.

'Mistakes lead to jail,' the man replied coldly. 'How?'

'They saw me leaving. I tried to lose them, but they followed me. By the time I got to the exit, they'd drawn the attention of security. I couldn't just leave them there.'

The man looked annoyed, his right eye twitching. He let out a frustrated noise and slammed the side of the van with his fist. He glared at Ted and Quinn, as though assessing by their looks how much their presence had disrupted his plans. 'Get out.'

Ted was the first to leave the van. As he stepped down he noticed the handgun tucked into the back of the man's trousers. He caught Quinn's eye as she stepped down, sharing a worried look. Upon taking in their surroundings, it was obvious that they were in a garage of some kind, a little way out of the city centre. There were workbenches along the sides with various tools and car parts strewn about. The entrance was wide enough for a single car, which was just about all that could fit in the area.

The driver had made his way around the side of the van and leaned against it as he lit a cigarette. Like Carlos and the other man, he looked like a local. But unlike Carlos and the other man, he was of stocky build and tall; probably around six foot three. He too had a handgun tucked into his trousers.

'Eduardo,' the man with the tattoo sleeves addressed the stocky man. '*La puerta.*' It was spoken like a command. It seemed as though this guy was in charge of everyone here. Eduardo complied and pulled down the shutter door, closing them in and securing it with a padlock at the bottom.

'Come,' he said to the group, pointing to a doorway leading into a small dark office. He allowed Ted and the others to walk ahead of him. Ted flicked the light switch on entering the room. It looked like a typical small business owner's office. Filing cabinets lined one wall and there was a small desk against the other. Jasper entered the room behind Carlos, who placed the star-shaped artefact on the desk.

'Before we get to work, I need to reassure my students,' Jasper said. The tattoo sleeved man nodded, permitting him to proceed. 'Quinn, Ted, these men are here to work with me. You don't need to fear them. This is Lucho,' he pointed at tattoo sleeve. 'Eduardo,' now pointing at the larger man. 'And you've already met Carlos. They're armed for *our* safety, but it's just a precaution. We don't want any attention from the authorities, and they are under strict instructions by Sigma that violence of any kind is a last resort.' The three Hispanic men remained silent. 'We can stay safely hidden here until we figure out what's next.'

Ted and Quinn didn't say a word. Ted was still staring at the handgun sticking out of Lucho's waistband. He'd seen a gun before, but only strapped to the belt of a police officer in a foreign airport somewhere in Europe. Then it had just been part of the uniform and it had made him feel safer in its presence. Seeing one protruding so casually from this stranger's civilian attire gave it a whole different look. It was a sobering experience; the gun seemed so much more dangerous in this setting. He kept watching it, as though he needed to keep an eye on it, lest it go off. Lucho caught him staring at it, which made him uneasy too.

'Problem?' he narrowed his eyes.

'Don't worry, they're harmless,' replied Jasper.

'He is looking at this,' Lucho pulled the gun from his back and held it up.

'For God's sake,' Jasper pleaded. 'Don't wave that thing around in here.' Lucho maintained eye contact with Ted while he slowly tucked the gun back into his waistband, as though sending him a message. Ted read it loud and clear.

'Professor, what are we doing here?' Quinn broke the tension by changing the subject. 'What was your plan after the museum?'

'Sigma believes the jewel Cortés wrote about exists, and he wants me to find it.'

'OK,' she replied. 'If it does exist, why not go through the proper channels? Let the experts look over the letter and offer to work with them to find it. Why all the secrecy, and why steal this?' She pointed at the artefact on the desk. 'We don't even know what it is.'

'That's not all we took,' Jasper smiled. He reached inside his tweed jacket and slowly retrieved a black plastic cylindrical tube, holding it carefully in both hands. There was a cap on one end that presumably came off to allow the insertion and removal of the contents of the tube.

Quinn gasped at the sight of it, knowing instantly what was inside. So many questions entered her mind, most prominently how he had managed to find and then take it. The tube was presumably something the professor had taken into the museum, ready to transfer the manuscript into to keep it safe and smuggle it out. Plastic tubing like this was an invention that came about long after the days of the conquistadors. For the manuscript to still be intact it was likely found in a secure wooden container of some kind.

'How did you—? Where did you—?' she struggled to find the words.

'I had some help from my inside man, Carlos. But a magician never reveals his secrets,' replied Jasper smugly. That sent Quinn over the edge.

'This is all a game to you, isn't it?' she said, exasperated. 'Do you realise how serious this is? We could be wanted all over Mexico City!'

'Of course I do,' he retorted. 'You know I tried to keep you both out of this.'

'Just don't joke about it like what you did wasn't a criminal offense. And you still didn't answer my question. Why are you doing this secretively?'

'Because he wants the glory,' said Ted candidly. 'He's so embittered about Professor Anderson. He said it himself, he wants to prove him wrong by chasing a fairy-tale.'

'It's real, I assure you,' Jasper objected.

'No. What's real is the crime you committed. There'll be a Mexican jail cell with our names on it.'

'It won't be like that, I promise. We'll find somewhere to drop you both off and you can go home without incident.'

'*¡Eso es suficiente!*' Lucho's limited patience had worn thin, the switch to his native tongue emphasising his frustration. 'They go nowhere.'

'Their faces are all over the museum CCTV,' Carlos chimed in, his accent less thick than Lucho's. 'You send them back to the airport, they'll be arrested on site, and it'll take the police five minutes to get the truth out of them. How long do you think it'll take them to catch up to us then?'

Ted knew he was right, but the way the man said it put a weight in the pit of his stomach. A wave of nausea began to wash over him as the realisation dawned that there was no way out. Just a few days ago he was in the safety of his London bubble, living a normal life. Yes, he'd been shunned by a woman he had been infatuated with, who had zero romantic interest in him. But at least he had Carl. And Star Wars. What he would give to go back in time and turn down the opportunity Hilary had kept him behind at the end of class for. A simple no would have allowed him to coast effortlessly along in his safe, familiar life. Now here he was, surrounded by a collection of strangers he'd known for as little as a few minutes to a couple of days, being told by a gun-wielding stranger that he was an accessory to a theft, and there was no way back. Time stood still as the feeling of dread set in. He watched Jasper take the cap off the tube containing the manuscript, tipping it so the rolled-up parchment started to slide out into his awaiting hand. The professor appeared to be taking great care with the letter, but as he caught it his fingers creased the edges ever so slightly. Ted saw Quinn cover her mouth to stifle a gasp. Something so fragile as this was usually handled with extreme care by experts with gloves, tweezers and an almost surgical-like precision. Yet here the professor was with his bare hands in the office of a run-down car service garage. The professor set aside the empty tube and placed the parchment carefully on the desk.

'We need to use something as a paperweight,' he declared. Ted looked at Quinn, knowing full well that exerting pressure on the five-hundred-year-old manuscript could cause it to tear. Carlos began to sort through a drawer, finding a hole punch, a stapler and a box of staples filled enough to satisfy the required weight. He placed them on the table and let the professor ease the parchment open. His hands were shaking as he slowly unravelled the page. He placed the hole punch over the corner, and relaxed his grip on the other side of the page as the weight came down on it. A wave of relief came over him at seeing the parchment remain intact. The stapler went on another corner, and the professor then rolled the rest of the manuscript down to reveal the rest of the letter, until the squiggle of an ink signature could be seen.

'Hernán Cortés,' he breathed.

'So it's true,' Carlos chimed in. 'I thought the bitch was lying.'

'Why would she lie? They'd find out when they examined it at the museum.'

'You'd be surprised what some people do for a slice of fame,' he replied.

Jasper placed the box of staples on the bottom of the parchment, the corners curling up, but not obscuring any of the text written on the page.

'What does it say?' Ted asked.

'I don't read Spanish well,' he replied. 'One of you better read it out loud.'

Carlos volunteered and began to study the scrawled handwriting. 'It's impossible,' he said. 'There's a reason why there are experts for this.' He began to walk away from the desk when Jasper grabbed him by the wrist.

'You have to try,' he hissed.

Carlos looked at the hand grasping him, and then at Lucho, as if asking for permission for something. Lucho shook his head and muttered something in Spanish. Carlos pulled his arm away and went back to the desk, pulling an irked expression. He looked once more at the manuscript, studying the thin black text that was ink-stained into the parchment. The handwriting was so unique that it was difficult to make out each word. Experts must have spent hours trying to unpick the patterns. How the woman who found it had managed to make sense of it was anyone's guess.

'I'm sorry,' he said. 'It must be written in old Spanish.'

'It can't be,' Quinn piped up. 'The Old Castilian version of Spanish was phased out in the 15th Century. This is from the 16th Century. He must have been using contemporary Spanish.'

The Aztec Secret

Ted looked at her in astonishment, wondering how a student could know so much about a topic. It was as though her understanding of the subject was on a par with that of the professor, who had been working his whole life on gaining such knowledge. Was this the level of investment people typically put into their degrees? If that were true, what the hell was Ted doing with his life?

'Yes, she's right,' said Jasper.

'I can take a look if you like?' Quinn offered. The glint in her eye gave away her excitement at the prospect.

'Of course, I don't see why not.' The professor looked at Carlos. 'If you wouldn't mind?' Carlos looked happy to be relieved of his duty and stepped back. Evidently the sense of desperation Jasper had emitted when urging Carlos to help translate the manuscript had been transferred to Quinn the moment he saw her as a better option. She seemed to get this vibe too as she approached the desk nervously.

'My Spanish is pretty good,' she said. 'And we studied his other letters to Charles V one semester,' she quickly followed up, emphasising the value she was adding against the Mexicans in the room. 'I've seen his handwriting before in screenshots, but I'm not promising anything.' She looked at the words on the page and began to decipher the first part of the first word, looking for intricacies in the way the letters were formed. Carlos had scanned the entire page, trying to find a word or phrase he recognised, which immediately set him down the wrong path as he hadn't got to grips with the way Cortés shaped each letter in the alphabet. The way Quinn worked was more akin to the way Alan Turing and his team had worked on cracking the enigma code; identifying individual letters so that she could quickly see them further down the document. The more frequently appearing shapes were likely vowels. She took a long time working through the first few words, and there was a long silence as her mind worked through the puzzle in front of her.

'Well?' Carlos asked impatiently. Despite wanting to get things moving along, there was a part of him that wanted her to fail, if only to justify his own failure at the same task. Jasper shushed him.

'I think I can make out the first few words,' she said at last, the excitement building in her voice. The task seemed to be almost exhilarating for her. As in the museum, Ted saw a different side to her he hadn't fully appreciated. It was an attractive trait. And she spoke a foreign language? Quinn continued to surprise him.

The pieces of the puzzle seemed to come together more quickly from then on, and twenty minutes later she'd deciphered most of the manuscript. A phenomenal feat, despite the fact there was only roughly a couple of hundred words on the page. She pulled her notepad from her backpack and began to scribble a rough translation of the letter, before reading it aloud to the room. The letter began by addressing the king. Cortés hoped that the contents that followed would please him and go some way to proving his dedication to the crown and the pardoning of the charges he believed were unfairly placed against him.

'What's he talking about?' asked Ted.

'When Cortés sailed from Cuba to Mexico, he did so against the orders of Diego Velazquez de Cuellar; his superior and Governor of New Spain,' Jasper replied. 'The expedition was cancelled but Cortés went anyway. Velazquez didn't take this well. He was charged with mutiny and shunned by the crown. As Quinn well knows, his other letters to Charles V asked for the king to acknowledge his successes instead of punishing him for disobeying orders.'

Quinn nodded in agreement. She continued with her translation, which went on to talk about the development that had led him to write to the king.

After taking control of Tenochtitlan, Cortés had gotten wind of a number of the recently deceased Aztec king's elite warriors fleeing the city with the king's most precious treasures; treasures that had been previously unknown to the Spanish.

She paused as she validated a word with Carlos, who nodded in acceptance of her correct translation. She went on to echo the line that the woman at the dig site had picked out, where Cortés had written about the 'treasure of unparalleled power'. Cortés promised to find this rare jewel and send it to the king as an offering. His letter ended by sharing progress of this task. He had captured and interrogated one of the warriors, who had revealed that the treasure was taken to the ends of the empire. The warrior had an unusual weapon on his person; a thick clay tool with sharp obsidian edges. The warrior had unsuccessfully attempted to destroy it, giving away its importance in locating the treasure. Cortés had sent his most trusted companion, Pedro de Alvarado, south in pursuit of it.

Upon finishing reading this aloud, Quinn looked at the star-shaped object sitting on the desk next to the manuscript. It seemed the first clue to finding this rare artefact was already in their possession.

EIGHT

Ted was staring at the star-shaped artefact on the desk, contemplating its significance. A few moments had gone by since Quinn had finished reading her rough translation of the manuscript aloud, and the room had been stunned by the mention of the very object they had taken from the museum. It seemed far too fortuitous for it to have happened this way.

'How did you know?' he asked in Jasper's direction.

'I didn't,' he replied candidly. 'Sigma instructed us to take anything found in the dig. He didn't say why, but now I'm thinking he knew something we didn't.'

'But we still don't know what it is. If Sigma knew, why didn't he tell you?'

The professor thought about it a moment, scratching his beard. 'I suppose he would have done. Which means he doesn't know what it is either. Perhaps he didn't know it was significant, just that there was a chance it could be.'

Ted frowned at the response. The whole thing stank. But the professor was right; if Sigma had known what the artefact was for, he surely would have told them, unless he didn't trust them with that information.

'So, what now? You tell him Cortés wrote about the existence of a priceless jewel, you got the artefact that's meant to give a clue on where to find it, and figure out how to deliver it to him?'

'No, no,' Jasper shook his head. 'He wants *us* to find it. That was the deal.'

'How are we supposed to find it from that?' Ted pointed at the manuscript on the table. It was hardly a treasure map with a clear 'x marks the spot' in the centre. All they had to go on was the knowledge that the star-shaped object was in some way linked to the jewel. There was clearly a large piece missing from this puzzle.

'I don't know,' said Jasper dejectedly.

'You find it, old man,' Lucho piped up. His presence had almost been forgotten as he lurked in the corner of the office by the doorway. He was scraping the wooden doorframe with his fingernail like a restless child with a nervous habit. It was evident that patience wasn't this man's strong suit. His English wasn't perfect, but the message didn't lose any of its intended menace. He looked at Carlos and snapped his fingers, before issuing a command in Spanish. He then looked the professor in the eye. 'That's why you're here.'

Ted got the feeling this was already a rocky relationship. Jasper was obviously no more than a resource to Lucho, and one that was worth nothing to him when idle. Carlos left the room and went back to the van, before returning a few moments later with a laptop.

'I can only work with what I've got,' Jasper protested.

'Then work,' Lucho sneered.

The laptop was placed forcefully in Jasper's hands, who stared at it incredulously. 'I don't even know where to start.'

'Not my problem,' replied Lucho. He pulled a lighter and a packet of cigarettes from his pocket and left the room with Carlos. He'd barely left the room before lighting up and blowing a cloud of smoke which lingered with the strong smell of tobacco. Eduardo was left in the office, presumably to keep an eye on them. He seemed completely indifferent about having to carry out this duty. He repositioned himself to be closer to the door, leaning against the wall with his hands folded like a bored teacher waiting for their class to finish a long exam.

Quinn was already carefully repositioning the Cortés manuscript to make room for the laptop on the desk. Jasper brought it over, opened the lid and powered it on.

'What are we supposed to do with this?' Ted asked as the computer went through the slow booting-up process.

'I guess we try and find anything we can that gives us more information about this artefact,' Quinn suggested.

'It's a good place to start,' Jasper agreed, sitting down at the desk and taking the lead on the task. He opened up a browser and hit something in the search bar. A notice appeared informing him that there was no internet connection. Ted explained how the small dongle hanging out the side of the laptop was their internet source and they simply needed to set up the connection. It took a while for the professor to understand the process.

'My computer is usually connected automatically,' he said. 'I don't understand these doo-dahs.'

Their search for the star-shaped artefact yielded nothing. They tried searching for Aztec obsidian weaponry, and then for star-shaped clay objects in the Mesoamerican period, but still nothing. They moved on instead to a deep dive into Hernán Cortés and his life after the conquest of Mexico. Ted learned that he'd moved back to Spain at one point in his life and was actually granted honours by the king. However, it seemed Cortés still did not feel as though his reward was enough. He died embittered in his early sixties, with no reference to any treasures he had failed to locate.

Next, on Quinn's suggestion, they looked into Cortés' children, who would have been the recipient of anything left by their father after his death. It was said that his children were left with riches in his will, but there was nothing else to go on. One child in particular was of interest to the trio: Martín Cortés, Hernán Cortés' illegitimate first-born son. He was the product of Cortés' relationship with Doña Marina, also referred to as '*La Malinche*'; his personal cultural interpreter and concubine during his conquest of Mexico. He was legitimised in 1529, and it was written in multiple sources that Martín was Cortés' favourite child. The reason for this wasn't understood by the trio until they read of a note that was left for Martín upon his father's death. They found a transcription of the note in a Mexican historical library database and began to take in the contents. To their disappointment, Cortés had not talked about the jewel or any such treasures in his note, but rather talked of his love for Martín's mother, Doña Marina, and how he had loved her more than any other. He recounted an old song she would sing in her native tongue. At his request, she translated it to Spanish so he could appreciate it as well.

Quinn copied the lyrics into a blank document and translated them line by line from Spanish to English. It translated roughly as:

Passing swift, this fleeting life
Your path is set, you must go
When the eagle soars, the jaguar roars
Your heart is offered, your body is done

And they take your spirit to the temple
Where the serpent sings, and the gods will cry
For eternity, they cry

Ted couldn't say they'd learnt nothing in their furious searching on the web, as they'd uncovered a part of Hernán Cortés they didn't know existed. They'd delved into his personal life, learning of his achievements, grudges and regrets. There also seemed to be a serious disconnect between what constituted a song in the 16th Century to now. Being two languages removed might have something to do with that, but Ted had to admit the poem-esque writing about death, presumably in regard to human sacrifice, was creepy. Although fascinating, their research had found nothing that could help them pin down where the treasure could be.

Moving on, they tried searching for Pedro de Alvarado; the man Cortés had sent after the Aztec Jaguar Warriors. Perhaps he had written something down that gave insight into where he had tracked them to.

'How would he have tracked them, anyway?' Ted asked. 'I mean, they must have had a good head-start on him and his men. If they really took the jewel to the ends of the empire, like the manuscript says, they couldn't have tracked them that far.'

'They probably had hunting dogs that followed their scent,' Jasper suggested. This response was satisfactory enough for Ted, who pulled a face to show that what the professor had said was valid. After more searching and running down more rabbit holes, the research into Alvarado bore no fruit.

A door slammed from over by the van and the sound of footsteps echoed through the garage. Lucho and Carlos were returning from their lengthy absence to check on the progress they'd made. Eduardo moved aside to let them through the door.

'So?' Lucho said on entering the room.

'What did you expect?' Jasper threw his hands up apologetically. 'We're trying to uncover a five-hundred-year-old secret. If it were that easy, don't you think someone would have found it by now?'

Lucho's face dropped and his eyebrow furrowed. He began picking at the loose wood chippings of the doorframe. The sound of a siren sounded somewhere in the distance. It began to build in volume as the vehicle it belonged to grew closer. Ted felt sick with worry as his mind spiralled at the prospect of Mexican prison if they were discovered with the stolen items in this garage. Eventually the siren began to die down as the vehicle headed in a different direction.

'We're out of time,' Lucho broke the silence in the room. 'Get in the van.'

The trio by the desk stared at him in disbelief. Out of time? What did that mean? Had they simply given up? Or had the professor proven himself useless, and therefore dispensable?

'Where are we going?' asked Quinn.

'Get in the van,' he repeated.

'You didn't answer my question,' Quinn stood firm. Her courage in the face of an armed stranger with questionable temperament surprised Ted, who didn't dare do anything more than watch the scenario play out.

'Where are we going?' she asked again.

Lucho gritted his teeth, visibly frustrated by the lack of obedience to his initial command. He muttered something to Carlos in Spanish, who responded for him.

'He told Sigma what the manuscript said and about the artefact. The jewel was taken to the ends of the Aztec empire. That means it is somewhere near the Guatemalan border.'

'That's a huge area,' she laughed in disbelief. 'You can't search the whole border. Besides, where the Aztec empire ended, and the Mayan empire began is unclear.'

'Well, your professor failed to find a more accurate point. So, we go along the border,' Carlos said.

Lucho pulled his pistol from behind his back. His hand gripped it hard, but he didn't point it in a specific direction; the action of drawing it alone intended to put an end to any further comments. It worked, as Quinn ceased her protestations.

Jasper collected the artefact and carefully rolled the manuscript back into the plastic tube, popping the cap on securely. Lucho made sure he was the last to leave the office to see them out, following closely behind so they went directly to the van. Ted could almost feel the man breathing down his neck, he was so close. On entering the back of the van and taking his seat, he watched the pointy-nosed man tuck the gun behind his back once more. He sure loved to wave that thing around. Ted wondered how proficient he was at using it. The frequency with which he drew the weapon was akin to a child playing with a new toy. They say that most kitchen accidents are the result of people misusing sharp knives they're not skilled at using, and if this logic applied to firearms this guy might be an accident waiting to happen.

The engine started up and Eduardo unlocked the shutter door, hoisting it up to allow the van to pass him. The driver, presumably Carlos this time, as Lucho could be heard shouting instructions out the passenger side window, waited for him to lock the door behind them. The door to the back remained open, the van perched in the middle of the road with its rear wheels mounting the edge of the kerb. Ted could see all the way down the quiet street. He watched as another car turned in from a crossroad a hundred yards away. He had no idea where they were, but the noise from outside suggested they were still in a built-up area. He considered checking his phone and flicking on his maps app, but he didn't want to give the impression he was doing something he shouldn't be. He caught that thought and hung onto it a moment. He wasn't doing something he shouldn't be. He was essentially a hostage in this situation, being kept against his will. The Mexican gunmen had tried to scare them into staying, for fear of being arrested as an accessory to the museum robbery, but Ted and Quinn had done nothing wrong. He'd taken note of the van's licence plate number. If he managed to escape now, he could explain everything to the police and help them track down the vehicle to free Quinn. Jasper would have to explain his part in all this, but at this point Ted didn't care. The important thing was that he and Quinn were innocent, and if he was quick he could put an end to this nonsense now.

With renewed hope growing inside him, a flash of courage came over him and he leapt out of the van and set off as fast as he could down the street. The car that had turned into the street passed him just as Lucho began to shout and bang his hand on the body of the van's door to get Eduardo's attention. Ted was by no means physically fit, but he noticed that Eduardo was the stockiest of the three Mexicans. The man's muscle-to-fat ratio was far better than Ted's, but he figured he had the best chance against him in a footrace.

Ted had waited for the car to grow near enough that Lucho wouldn't be able to casually flash his gun in his direction, being careful to not wait too long and risk Eduardo finishing locking the door and cutting off his route to freedom. His gamble worked, and he didn't hear any gunshots. He didn't hear much else, aside from the panting of his breath and the thumping heartbeat in his ears. The running motion immediately brought back unwanted memories of physical education class at school and cross-country in the pouring rain. His pace was much quicker this time, as it wasn't a mandatory sporting event he had to endure; his life could well depend on this. After fifty yards or so he hazarded a quick glance back to the van to assess the level of threat behind him. He saw Quinn and Jasper hanging out the doorway he'd just exploded out of like a horse champing at the bit in the starting blocks at race day. Their faces told an expression of surprise and concern at his sudden departure. He then saw Lucho going crazy from inside the front of the van, shouting furiously in Spanish at Eduardo, who had abandoned the lock on the shutter door to chase Ted down. Seeing the brute of a man gaining on him gave Ted a burst of acceleration he didn't know he had in him. His legs pumped hard as the adrenaline carried him. He had barely reached the crossroad when he heard the shrieking of tyres on the asphalt road behind him, knowing instantly what it meant. Looking in every direction, he decided to take the road to the left at the crossing, without the slightest idea of where it led.

The noise of activity in the distance indicated that there were people not too far away. He hoped for a crowd he could get lost in, or at least passers-by he could call to for help. But on reaching the crossroad and darting left he realised, to his dismay, that there were no other cars nearby. He kept on running, gasping for breath as his lack of fitness quickly caught up with him. He was still running on adrenaline, but he knew as soon as it wore off, he'd be toast. There was still no sign of anyone to call to, but luckily he'd managed to build up enough of a gap that Eduardo hadn't reached the corner yet. He assessed his options and decided that hiding would be better than running. There was an alleyway to his right which took him around the row of buildings the garage was connected to. If he could lose Eduardo in there, he'd have a chance, as the van wouldn't be able to follow him. He cut into the alley just in time to hear the screech of tyres as the van rounded the corner at speed. He didn't turn to see if they'd spotted him on their way past, but the vehicle tore down the road, completely bypassing the alleyway.

The alleyway was a bit of a maze, the path leading this way and that. He couldn't hear Eduardo behind him, but perhaps he had more sense than Lucho and was adopting a stealthier approach to hunt him down. Not knowing how far away he was served as added panic for Ted, who nearly tripped when looking over his shoulder at full speed. A dog barked from the other side of a fence, which immediately made Ted think of the hunting dogs Pedro de Alvarado had likely used to pursue the Aztec warriors. It evoked a strange sense of symmetry to this moment, except Ted wasn't hiding any treasure or secrets. He was just a terrified nobody who had been accidentally caught up in something and now couldn't escape it. If only they hadn't gone after the professor in the museum. He'd known something was up, but he hadn't had time to think. It was all Quinn's fault. If she hadn't run on ahead, he might not have followed. But then she'd still be in this mess and Ted would have no idea how to help her.

The winding alleyway straightened out, and another road loomed about twenty feet ahead. Ted made for the opening when the sound of a roaring engine grew near. He stopped in his tracks, hoping the van might pass by before Eduardo caught up to him. The engine grew louder before Ted saw the van drive past. He thought he had earned a slice of luck, but suddenly the van broke hard and made a sharp U-turn back towards him. He backtracked into the alleyway, before a panting Eduardo came into view behind him. The van pulled into the opening and Lucho stepped out. He was trapped. Ted cried out in desperation, looking for a way out. But there was no escape. Standing between Eduardo and Lucho, his spiralling mind set about deciding which of the two he had a better chance of barrelling his way past. Eduardo's frame took up more of the narrow passage; he was unlikely to succeed there. But then Lucho looked furious. Ted could see the crazed look in his eyes; this man wanted to kill him just for the brief inconvenience he'd caused. The gap closed and Ted was out of options. He watched as Lucho drew his gun. Ted's lungs were burning from the running, his body defeated as he knew there was no option but to accept his fate. Lucho paused for a moment, which seemed to last a lifetime, before swinging his arm wildly in a flash of fury. Then there was nothing but darkness.

NINE

Alexandra Rodgers was propping up the small bar next to the hotel she'd checked into not two hours earlier. The shores of Guatemala had kept her entertained for only a few days, and she had quickly grown bored of lying on the beach with nothing to do. Snorkelling, sea-kayaking, jet-skiing; she'd done it all and had quickly run out of activities to keep her mind occupied. Perhaps she wasn't like everyone else, who seemed perfectly content to spend a week frying in the sun while reading a trashy novel. Or, perhaps she just didn't want to be there. The free bar in the all-inclusive resort had often been too good to turn down, no matter what time of day. The alcohol numbed her, which provided a temporary relief from the feelings of guilt and failure that were lingering in her mind like a parasite. But she had noted the judging glances from the same few couples and families who passed her on their way to the beach in the mornings. It had been enough for her to decide she needed a change of scenery, so she headed inland to a quiet place on the outskirts of the jungle. This small place had little of interest, and the small hotel was the largest building in the village. So once again she found herself sitting on a barstool, her only company the owner of the lone bar in this derelict corner of the world. The bar itself was nothing more than an old wooden shack that sat on the main road leading through the quiet village. A few sets of cheap plastic table and chairs were strewn about on the deck, but it was hard to imagine that they were all required at one time. Perhaps Sunday evening didn't have the same atmosphere as Friday or Saturday.

Her phone buzzed in her pocket. She contemplated not checking the notification, but eventually curiosity got the better of her. She pulled the phone out and lifted it to eye level. The screen lit up, revealing a message from Joel. The first part of his text showed on her lock screen.

Alex, it's not your fault.

She winced as the resurgence of guilt rushed up from the pit of her stomach to her throat. Not her fault? Of course it was her fault. Joel almost died because of her. She put the phone face down on the bar and distracted herself with a sip of cocktail.

A dog barked somewhere down the street and a voice called after it. She watched as the scrawny canine bounded up the road in the direction of the bar. The voice belonged to a child of around eight or nine years old. Where her parents were was anyone's guess. The little girl chased after the dog with a rope leash in her hands, and the scene quickly became clear. The mischievous runaway raced past the bar, pausing momentarily to look at Alex. Its tail wagged and its tongue lolled out while it panted excitedly. After deciding Alex wasn't going to provide either food or attention, it went on its way, just evading the grasp of the girl who had almost caught up.

'Don't worry,' the bartender laughed. 'The dog always finds his way home.'

The Aztec Secret

Alex smiled politely, taking another sip of her drink. She noticed that the bartender was eyeing her cautiously. She was getting through her drinks quickly and was onto her third in an hour, but she was by no means the heaviest drinker he must have seen pass through his bar. Maybe he was more used to a different type of patron; young backpackers off on adventures in loud groups, pounding beers and giggling over nothing. Or perhaps old men who liked to spout fabricated stories of a better time to anyone who'd listen. But here she was, the lost version of an almost forty-year-old woman with no spouse, no kids and nothing but regret swimming around in her head. The man stood there, idly drying glasses with a rag. She'd hardly said a word to him, save for a few requests for a refill in broken Spanish. He was probably just bored.

'What troubles you?' he asked, in much better English than she could ever hope to reciprocate in his native language.

'I'm sorry?' she feigned ignorance, forcing a smile out of politeness.

He smiled back and cocked his head to one side, not falling for the bluff. 'In my experience, people only come here for two reasons: to make mistakes, or to forget the ones they made yesterday.'

She pondered on his words for a moment. The word *mistakes* struck a chord with her. Suddenly, the memory she'd tried so hard to repress came flooding back. The cold musty air of the warehouse, the sound of gunshots and sirens roaring in her head. The crackle of radio as she desperately called out for assistance.

She snapped back to reality, pushing the pain away. 'That's awfully deep,' she said, acknowledging what the bartender had said. 'You should write poetry.'

'Poetry is for girls,' the man retorted. Alex shifted her body in her seat and subconsciously closed herself off from him. The moment could be used to perfectly encapsulate her dating life back home. The perfect gentleman would tick all the right boxes, charm her with his playful conversation, and then drive the train clean off the tracks with a wildly sexist, racist or otherwise inappropriate comment. One time her Caucasian date had used the term 'you people' when asking a question about her African heritage. Usually she would make her excuses and call time on the encounter, but this time felt different. It might have been the strong cocktails starting to kick in, but she couldn't hold her tongue and began to speak before she was fully aware of what she was saying.

'Name a famous poet,' she said.

The bartender was back to wiping glasses. 'Sorry?'

'Tell me the name of a famous poet,' she challenged, raising one eyebrow as she prepared to lure the man into her trap.

'A famous poet?' he asked.

'Yes, the first one that comes to mind.'

He thought for a moment. 'Shakespeare.'

'Good choice. How about another one?'

The man looked uncomfortable. 'Er, Alejandro Aura.'

'Interesting,' Alex smirked.

'I don't understand,' the man said.

'They're both men. So much for poetry being for girls.' She took a sip of her cocktail, satisfied that she'd made her point. The man seemed taken aback, a look of embarrassment on his face. Luckily for him, the girl returned with her dog. She had clearly managed to catch up to the pooch as she was gleefully holding the end of the leash in her hand, the other end securely fastened to the dog's collar. The bartender waved at the girl.

'*¡Felicidades!*' he called. The girl beamed at him. '*Celebremos juntos,*' he said, ushering her over. She made her way to the bar and tied the dog's leash to one of the legs of Alex's stool, before hopping on the one next to her. The bartender pulled a bottle of cola from the cool fridge and removed the cap. The drink fizzed and gave off a cool mist as the carbon dioxide bubbles escaped the glass. The little girl's eyes widened as she gratefully took a sip, letting out an exaggerated exhale in satisfaction.

'*Gracias,*' she said.

'*De nada.*'

The man walked around the side of the bar with a metal dish filled with water, which he set down at the foot of Alex's stool for the dog to drink from. The sound of its tongue lapping up the liquid quickly followed. Alex was rather fond of dogs and could never pass up an opportunity to fuss one. She bent down to tussle the fur on its back and pat its head. It stopped drinking momentarily to look at her, its tongue still hanging out its mouth as it panted hot air in her direction.

'What a sweet dog,' she said. 'What's his name?'

'Hector,' the man said. 'He belongs to my neighbours. Martina takes very good care of him,' he motioned towards the girl to her left.

'I can see that,' she replied, giving a warm smile. Martina, seemingly not an English speaker, said nothing, but smiled back, nonetheless. Alex couldn't work out if this was a regular occurrence; the bartender offering his neighbour's child a free soft drink as a gesture of goodwill. But it was a timely distraction from the awkward atmosphere that had quickly built between the pair before the girl's arrival. Martina said something quickly in Spanish that Alex's tourist-level grasp on the language couldn't comprehend. The man nodded and handed her the remote to a tiny box-like TV that was hoisted up in the corner of the bar. Alex hadn't noticed it until it flicked on and responded to Martina's inputs. She surfed through the channels, tapping the button as the numbers in the corner of the screen went up in steady increments each time. The numbers eventually reset, and she realised she was going through channels she'd seen already. Disappointed that there was nothing of interest to her, the girl placed the remote back on the bar and went back to her drink.

The TV was left on a Mexican news channel. They were so close to the border here the TV set must have been picking up programs from both countries. The faint sound of sirens came again, and for a moment Alex thought she was going crazy. The memory she had tried so hard to escape was manifesting itself in real life. But then she looked up at the monitor and saw the flashing lights of a police vehicle outside an impressive looking building. A reporter was positioned between the car and the camera, telling the story of what was going on to the viewers. Alex watched as two individuals in police uniforms walked past in the background. At a glance, one looked almost like Joel. Another memory hit her, and this time she couldn't escape. The moment she met Joel; her first day on the job.

Joining the police had been a drastic career change for her at thirty-seven, when middle-management in an office hadn't felt right anymore. Granted, police work still required its fair share of pencil pushing, but there was plenty of field work and Alex finally felt like she was making a difference in the world. In a busy city like Detroit, there was always something; the work of the police was never done. She loved her work, and with no family at home to look after she didn't mind spending almost all her time thinking about it.

She'd been partnered with Joel from day one, two years ago. He was much younger than her, but far more

The Aztec Secret

experienced. They'd formed a good partnership; they shared the same sense of humour, and despite her junior role on the team, Joel had quickly recognised Alex's aptitude for this line of work and treated her with due respect. She couldn't have asked for a better deal. Hell, she could have ended up with Frank or one of the other idiots who lauded their years of service over the new recruits. The thought of having to fetch coffee for those bozos every day made her shiver. Joel understood Alex's drive to move up the ranks as quickly as she could. She was open with him from the start. She wanted to make detective one day, and she was keen to learn as much from him as she could. Years of hard work stood in her way, but she was confident she could prove herself if she showed proactivity on the job. But there is a fine line between proactivity and overzealous stupidity, and last week she had found herself on the wrong side it. And what had it cost? Her badge, firearm, a two-week suspension, and her partner in hospital with a gunshot wound.

She watched the screen with interest, despite not understanding what was going on. The news ticker ran across the bottom of the screen with updates on the story, but it didn't help as it was all in Spanish.

'What's happening?' she asked the bartender, pointing to the TV.

'They say something was stolen from a museum in Mexico City.'

She nodded in acknowledgement and continued watching, now invested in the story. The scene changed to an interview with a representative of the museum, who was giving more information to the reporter. Alongside the interview, a photo was displayed on the screen, showing one of the items that was stolen. It looked like a hexagon made from clay, with jagged edges coming out of each side to make the shape of a star.

'This is what was taken?' she asked. The man shrugged his shoulders, evidently not as interested in this as she was. 'It must be worth a lot of money,' she surmised.

Martina drank the last of her cola and jumped down from the high bar stool. The dog leapt up from its prone position next to Alex and wagged its tail excitedly. Untying the leash from Alex's stool, Martina gave her another smile, before running off with the dog bounding along beside her.

'*Gracias. ¡Adios!*' she called over her shoulder to the bartender.

The news had changed to another story, and from what Alex could tell it was related to an upcoming election. The word *elección* was a dead giveaway. She thought it was strange how some words can be so similar across languages, and others so different. It made learning languages in school so confusing. She hadn't studied linguistics in any great detail, but she did remember watching an interesting TED talk about similarities between languages. She couldn't remember the application, but it was fascinating learning about cognates; words that share a common etymological origin. Often words that originated from Latin would keep a similar translation. These cognates would make learning a new language in school seem attainable. *Fantástico* would translate easily as *fantastic*, which is easy to remember. But just as she would get to grips with it, language would send a curve ball at her with something like *ananas*; Spanish for *pineapple*. In fact, the majority of Latin originating languages use *ananas*. It was only English that went off piste with pineapple. She had once heard that English was one of the most difficult second languages to learn, and she now had even more respect for those she came across in this part of the world who spoke

The Aztec Secret

English so fluently. Even in this tiny village in the middle of the jungles of Guatemala, the bartender spoke better English than she had ever spoken Spanish.

'Excuse me,' the bartender distracted her from her thoughts. 'Would you like another drink?'

Alex studied the empty glass in front of her. She'd been slurping from the straw without realising. These cocktails just went down so easy. She was starting to feel the effects of the previous three drinks and instinctively felt as though it was time to turn in. But she was on vacation; she had nothing to get up early for the next day.

'Sure, why not?' she replied.

As the man took her empty glass away and started mixing up a fresh daiquiri batch, she realised that she had nothing to get up for at all tomorrow. She'd journeyed inland for a change of scenery, hoping she'd find something to keep her mind occupied. She'd come to Guatemala on a recommendation from a friend, who had experienced what she had described to her as the most relaxing time of her life when she visited the coast. In hindsight Alex should have known better than to try and replicate that. More of an adrenaline junkie than her friend anyway, a two-week suspension from the police force for exhibiting reckless behaviour and poor judgement that could have cost her partner's life wasn't exactly the perfect precursor to a relaxing experience.

'What did you mean earlier, about people making mistakes?' she asked, ignoring her earlier dislike of the man. After all, he may have been the only soul for miles who was able to keep her occupied and away from stewing on the future on her career, and the way her colleagues would look at her when she returned. Not to mention what she would say to Joel. She still hadn't read his text in full.

The man looked up from making the drink with a quizzical expression.

'You said people only come here to make mistakes, or forget about the ones they made yesterday,' she clarified. 'Do you mean here,' she gestured to the bar. 'Or Guatemala?'

'Here, of course,' the man smiled. 'Guatemala is a beautiful country. It could never be a mistake to visit.' He handed her the freshly made daiquiri. 'Please forgive my intrusion,' he added. 'But you look troubled.'

'So you said.' Her walls were starting to go up, but the alcohol had loosened her a little. She let him say what he wanted to say.

'Sometimes you go to the church to confess, or to seek help with problems. But I find that the best advice comes with a drink.' He poured himself a glass and clinked it against Alex's.

'Cheers, as you say,' he said.

'What do you say?'

'*¡Salud!*' he replied.

'*¡Salud!*' she repeated, raising her glass.

TEN

A dim light came in and out of view as Ted slowly regained consciousness. His first thoughts started forming and he immediately felt lost. The feeling was akin to waking up after a long sleep in an unfamiliar setting, like the first day of a holiday away from home. He opened his eyes a fraction, but they didn't yet have the strength to open fully. They quickly closed again as he began to stir from his slumber. Moments went by as his eyes struggled to adjust to the light, opening and closing like the wings of a butterfly. Although he couldn't see well, his ears had been working just fine, hearing a high-pitched sound that seemed to carry on and on like white noise. The sound seemed to have been with him long before he woke. He recalled a low thumping sound that increased in frequency, but he didn't know if that had just been a dream.

Eventually he was able to hold his eyes open long enough to focus his vision on his surroundings. He was lying on his side, on the floor of a vehicle of some kind.

The van.

That's when the sudden memory of the van pulling in front of the opening of the alleyway came flashing back. He remembered the look in Lucho's eye; the flash of fury as the gun in his hand came crashing down. The headache kicked in instantly as Ted came to. The thumping sound could well have been his throbbing head. He reached up with a shaky hand and felt the lump on top of his skull. The bastard had knocked him out cold.

From his prone position, his eyes darted this way and that. He caught a glimpse of Eduardo sitting on a long bench opposite him, next to Jasper, who had a sombre look on his face. Ted grunted in pain as the headache worsened.

'He's awake!' Quinn's voice cut through the white noise. She seemed close. Before he knew it, she was in his immediate line of vision. 'Ted, can you hear me?' She was shouting so he could hear.

'Uh… ye…' he struggled to say.

'He needs water,' she announced, rummaging in her backpack from her seat next to him. 'Can you sit up?'

Ted responded by repositioning his body in a way that allowed him to sit upright. The action made him feel woozy and sick.

'Take it easy,' Jasper called from the other side. 'You took a pretty hefty blow to the head. You've been out a while.'

Ted looked at the professor curiously. 'How long?' he replied, as Quinn handed a bottle of water to him. He noticed that Eduardo hadn't acknowledged his presence. The man's arms were folded, and he stared straight ahead at a fixed point. He had a walkie-talkie in one hand, which he used briefly to mutter a quick line of Spanish into.

'A few hours,' said Jasper.

Ted unscrewed the cap from the bottle and took a quick sip. The water was warm, but welcome. He paused a moment

The Aztec Secret

and looked at the bench Jasper and Eduardo were sat on. It seemed different to before. The whole inside of the van seemed different, the more he looked at it. It was then that his stomach turned as he felt something akin to a sudden drop in altitude. It brought back the horrible sensation of being on a plane during turbulence. His mind began thinking more clearly, putting the pieces together. It was then that he noticed the gaping hole in the side of the vehicle, and the sky outside that. The thumping sound he'd heard in his sleep, the constant white noise since; it all suddenly made sense. His fear was confirmed when the machine banked forward and Ted caught a glimpse of the treetops a few-hundred feet below. He dropped the water bottle and clung onto the bench. This wasn't the van. They were in a helicopter.

From what Ted could tell, it wasn't a typical small chopper for taking tourists on tours over the Mexican landscape. The gaping hole in the side and less-than plush interior told him this was closer to a military-style bird, like the Black Hawks he'd seen in war movies. How the hell had they managed to commandeer one of these?

The upturned bottle spilled over the deck. Quinn leaned over and grabbed it to salvage the rest of the contents. Ted noticed she had to really stretch to reach it, and then noticed the seatbelt strapping her into the bench. It was a short relief to look down and see a similar belt holding him in place. The belt had dug into his side as he lay unconscious, but he hadn't noticed until now and the pain in his head more than outweighed any other feeling.

'Where the hell are we?' he asked.

'Somewhere over Southern Mexico,' replied Jasper. 'Take it easy, OK?' He could sense Ted's panic, and there was activity in the front of the helicopter. Presumably Lucho had been alerted to his waking up. After his escape attempt, the

Mexicans must have been wary of him pulling another stunt that could further disrupt their plans. After looking out the side of the helicopter at the ground hundreds of feet below, Ted was too afraid to move, let alone try anything like that. Escape at this height would be suicide. He noticed that there was a bundle of yellow backpacks on the floor, strew about and seemingly unsecured. They were likely parachutes and, counterintuitively, the presence of these safety devices didn't give Ted much relief.

A crackling static sound emanated from the walkie-talkie in Eduardo's hand. Lucho's distorted voice came muffled through the speaker. Even if he had understood Spanish, Ted probably wouldn't have made out what was said. Eduardo squeezed the push-to-talk button on his receiver and responded with a single word to acknowledge the request. Ted understood that plain enough; *sí*. Eduardo then signalled to Ted to get his attention, before uncovering a dust sheet on the bench next to him to reveal an assault rifle. Ted's eye widened at the sight of the thing. He recognised the model from a video game he'd played many times with Carl; AK-47, aka Kalashnikov. The twisted grimace on Eduardo's face told Ted he'd got the reaction he was hoping for. Lucho turned in his seat in the cockpit and shouted something to draw Ted's attention towards him. The noise from the helicopter blades rotating at 258 RPM masked anything he was saying, but he made his point by pointing vigorously at the assault rifle. He then made a motion with his fingers towards his eyes to let Ted know he was being watched. He got the message loud and clear; don't try anything or you get shot to pieces. Ted wondered how sincere these threats were. Lucho was clearly unhinged and wasn't afraid to cause harm where he had the opportunity. Knocking Ted out cold with the butt of his pistol was a prime example. However, shooting him dead was on a different level altogether. If he were expendable, wouldn't he be dead already? Whether there was any substance to the threats or not, Ted was far too afraid to test their nerve.

The helicopter began to descend and Lucho began pointing at things in the distance. Carlos nodded and tilted the big bird in that direction. Through the forest of trees below there was a small clearing with the faint signs of light grey stone protruding from the earth. As they got closer Ted could see that one structure looked like a pyramid.

'Where are we?' he called to Jasper, as if he was involved enough in the Mexicans' plan to know that much.

'Somewhere over Southern Mexico,' he replied.

Ted reached into his jeans pocket for his phone. The seatbelt around his lap was tight, but he managed to ease the device out and into his hand. The screen lit up on lifting it, greeting him with his home screen and the time, which read 18:12. The day felt like it was moving on quickly, partially due to the hours Ted had missed while he was unconscious. The sun was getting low, but there were still another couple of hours before it set. Ted's stomach rumbled as he realised he hadn't eaten since breakfast. Would his captors feed him? It was clear he was effectively a hostage at this point, but surely they were humane enough to allow him to eat. Perhaps they only needed to keep him and Quinn with them and away from the authorities long enough to find what they were looking for. After that they could all go on their merry way. As the helicopter was getting close to the ground, Ted hoped they'd find it here. This could all be over soon.

Unlocking his phone with his fingerprint, he tapped on the maps app to get an idea of where they were. The app loaded and his GPS kicked in. The signal was weak, but enough to work with, and after a few moments of watching the progress wheel spin, Ted saw the map load with a sea of green and scattered light grey markings. The display showed a number of landmarks in the near vicinity, all depicted with the rook symbol from the board game chess, representing historical monuments of some description. One read *Temple of the Inscriptions*, and another *Templo del Sol*. The map was zoomed in too far for Ted to get a clear sense of where they were, so he pinched the screen repeatedly to zoom out far enough to make sense of the journey they'd made. They were now on the edge of the Mexican/Guatemalan border, in an area called Chiapas, some 850km from Mexico City.

Eduardo caught Ted looking at his phone and suddenly became very animated, shouting profusely in his direction. Ted realised that the man couldn't see what he was doing and had probably assumed he was using the phone to call for help. He turned the device around so that Eduardo could see the map on the screen.

'I just wanted to see where we are,' he called above the noise of the rotors. Eduardo seemed to calm a bit, but the expression painted on his face was one of suspicion. Ted had obviously labelled himself as a troublemaker with his recent actions. If they were that worried, it was a wonder they hadn't taken his phone from him.

The wheels touched the grass in the clearing as the hum of the engine began to die down. The blades rotated more slowly and soon it was easier to talk without having to shout. Ted was relieved to be back on solid ground, and immediately unbuckled his seatbelt to release the pressure from his abdomen. The last few minutes of the flight had started to take its toll on his bladder, and he felt as though it were about to burst.

'No,' said Eduardo, noticing Ted's urgency to free himself from the confines of the aircraft.

'But I really need to—'

'No,' Eduardo said in a much stronger tone.

The passengers watched as Carlos flicked a few switches around the cockpit, shutting off the helicopter. The flight had certainly been smooth, at least for the part Ted had been awake for, and the landing was textbook. Sigma had clearly done his research when recruiting this group of mercenaries. It was some foresight on his part to include a skilled pilot, on the chance they needed to travel to another part of the country to locate the treasure he was after.

Ted pleaded with Eduardo as his bladder started to take hold of his emotions. 'Please, just let me go over there,' he pointed to the bushes fifty yards away. 'I'll be quick.'

Eduardo grunted and then waved his hand dismissively. Ted took that as a yes and jumped down from the chopper with a thud, his knees buckling slightly. He then jogged over to the brush to seek a modest level of privacy and relieve himself.

Finishing his business and zipping up the fly on his jeans, he looked back over his shoulder at the helicopter to see the others climbing down. The rotors of the aircraft had slowed almost to a stop, and Lucho was barking orders in Spanish at Carlos. Crucially, nobody was looking in Ted's direction. They were much more complacent than he'd given them credit for, to let him go off by himself. He wasn't going to let the opportunity pass. He would wait for a second more, just to check they didn't look his way, and then he would make a break for it.

'*Terminado?*' Eduardo's voice came from Ted's blind spot over his other shoulder. He spun around in surprise to see the big man looming a few feet away. Clearly it was he who was complacent, as he'd miscounted the number of people by the helicopter. Eduardo looked agitated, supposedly wondering what was taking Ted so long.

'Er, yeah. I'm done,' he replied as he trudged back towards the group. Lucho was already leading them to the ruins of one of the great stone pyramids, eager to get on with their task. The site was full of archaeological wonders, and they'd been clearly labelled on the maps app on Ted's phone. It was a wonder this place wasn't crawling with tourists. Ted unlocked his phone and looked again at the map of the area, tapping on the marker for *Temple of the Inscriptions* to find more information about it. He noticed that it was part of a larger site called Palenque, which had closed to visitors almost two hours prior to their arrival. The Mexicans couldn't have planned it any better; they still had some daylight to work with and the freedom to poke around without raising suspicion. Ted continued to read up on the area he found himself in, and something immediately stood out to him. He caught up with the others to share what he'd learnt.

'Jasper,' Lucho was standing at the foot of the pyramid, ushering the professor over. 'Come.'

'Guys,' Ted said as he reached the pair. 'They're looking in the wrong place. These aren't Aztec ruins, they're Mayan.'

'That's what we're trying to tell him,' Quinn gestured towards Lucho. 'He's got this hare-brained idea that the jewel is in a temple along the Aztec/Mayan border.'

'Why?'

'Because of what the letter said, about the treasure being taken to the ends of the empire.'

'But that could mean anything. What if it was in the other direction, towards America?'

'No, Cortés wrote that he sent Alvarado south in pursuit of it, remember?'

Ted hadn't remembered. 'It's still not enough to go on. It could be anywhere for a hundred miles.'

'Try telling him that,' said Quinn, pointing at Lucho, who had begun climbing the steps of the pyramid, passing a *no entry* sign. The sign labelled the pyramid as the *Temple of the Red Queen*. Lucho was quickly climbing the heights of the impressive structure, presumably to investigate the tomb inside. It was unclear why he'd picked this monument to begin his search; it was likely he was going to attempt to make his way through them all before the end of the day.

'Go,' Carlos said to the rest of the group, indicating that they follow Lucho up the stairs. The plan might originally have been to split up in situations like this, to cover more ground and locate the jewel more quickly. However, now they had two more unexpected guests to keep an eye on, that was no longer feasible.

'Don't you think that if it were in there, it would have been found already?' Quinn questioned.

'The boss says go,' came the stubborn reply.

'This is ridiculous,' she muttered under her breath.

'I'll try and talk to him,' Jasper said, as they started climbing the steps.

'No offense, Professor, but I don't think you're going to do much good,' said Ted. 'He's insane, and look at where we are. If he was ever going to listen to you, do you think we'd be here?'

Jasper frowned. He seemed hurt by that, but he couldn't deny that what Ted had said was true.

Walking up the old stone steps to the top of the temple was a surreal experience. Ignoring the sign forbidding entry had made Ted feel on edge, as though breaking that rule had somehow heightened his wanted status among the Mexican authorities. He had only seen ruins like this in movies or video games, in which the protagonist would be a physically fit, attractive badass who would shoot their way from temple to temple, dancing up the steps two a time, before evading elaborate booby traps to steal a valuable treasure from deep within. The reality was a seriously unfit slob who was barely managing to climb the steps without taking a break along the way. As for intense firefights and booby traps, luckily those were just fantasy.

Upon reaching the top, he looked back to the rest of the site. There was a good view from up there, and with it he was able to appreciate how much of the past had been preserved in this beautiful part of the world. The helicopter, a juxtaposed item of modern technology among the surrounding faded grey architecture of history, sat idly in the middle of the clearing. There must have been at least twelve other structures he could spot from where he was stood. The quietness of the place, long after the busy tourist hours, gave the place a sense of tranquillity. The weather was calm, with a light breeze blowing through the air, as though the spirits of the dead that were buried here were dancing about playfully. Ted suddenly felt shameful that he and his companions were disturbing their rest.

Lucho was already marching back up the steps when Ted made his way down. He pushed past him without apology, muttering something in an annoyed tone under his breath. Descending the steps into the tomb, Ted quickly realised why Lucho had left so quickly. The place was completely empty. Presumably everything that was found here on its initial discovery years ago was taken away for study. Unsurprisingly, there was no sarcophagus full of treasure, or a skeleton of a long-dead royal waiting for them on this occasion.

'I don't know what he was expecting,' Quinn said. 'He's like a bull in a china shop. Running around without any real plan.'

'The boss told him to search the temples. So we search the temples,' replied Carlos. It seemed he wasn't privy to the plan either, if there was one.

'Does he really think it's going to just be lying around in one?'

'He has the key,' Carlos replied, pointing to the artefact Lucho was carrying in his hand. 'Sigma says it will unlock the way to the jewel.'

'That's a big leap,' said Ted. 'We can't just assume that's what the object is for.' He watched Lucho reach the top of the steps, and then turned his attention back to Carlos. 'So, he's walking around looking for a star-shaped lock?'

'He's deluded,' said Jasper. 'Firstly, these are Mayan temples. Secondly, if the Aztec warriors *did* hide the jewel in a Mayan temple, again extremely unlikely, does Sigma think there will be an obvious star-shaped lock sitting there in plain sight for us to find? These places are well documented. Excavators have been in here to clear everything out. It's a tourist attraction for goodness sake!'

Carlos didn't reply. He just pointed back up the stairs for them to follow Lucho outside.

Ted could tell it was going to be a long evening. There were at least twelve more temples in this site alone. He wondered how many of them they'd have to get through before they came up with a new plan.

ELEVEN

An hour went by as Lucho led the group from temple to temple, finding nothing that so much as hinted towards the treasure Cortés had written about. The sun was setting, and the light was quickly fading, making their journey from one temple to another more difficult as the site did not have lights to guide them between each one. Lucho was getting more and more frustrated with every dead end. Even he was starting to wonder what the point of their aimless searching was. On their way down the steps of the eleventh temple, Jasper let out a howl and lost his footing. He tumbled a couple of feet and landed hard on his backside.

'Jasper! Are you alright?' Ted clambered up the steps to tend to the professor. Quinn was already on the scene, offering a hand to help him to his feet.

'Get up.' Lucho's voice came from the bottom of the steps.

'He's hurt,' Ted shouted back. Quinn attempted to pull the professor up, but he cried out as he tried to steady his legs and sat down again, a pained expression on his face.

The Aztec Secret

'Let go, it's no use,' he said, every word an effort as the pain started to swell.

'What is it?' she asked.

'My ankle. I think I've twisted it.'

'Ted, we're going to have to carry him together,' she said. Ted was two steps ahead of her, sitting down alongside Jasper to allow him to put his arm around his shoulder. With a count to three, followed by a grunt and a struggle, they hoisted him up and helped him slowly down the first step. Looking downhill, there must have been twenty more steps to go.

Eventually, with a few more shouts of pain, the professor had descended the last step and was at the bottom. Ted noted the look of annoyance on Lucho's face at the hold-up. The pointy-nosed man muttered something under his breath and began marching off towards the next temple.

'What are you doing? Can't you see he's injured?' said Quinn. Lucho carried on ahead without turning around. 'We need to go back to the helicopter and assess his foot,' she said stubbornly. Lucho let out an annoyed noise. He turned to see Jasper sitting on the bottom step, his leg outstretched to rest his injured ankle. He then pointed at Carlos and Eduardo, issuing commands in Spanish. He walked on towards the final temple while the other two Mexicans signalled for them to follow them the other way, in the direction of the helicopter.

'Charming bunch, aren't they?' said Ted sarcastically, acknowledging the lack of help offered by either of them.

**

Jasper winced as he took his shoe off. He rubbed his foot and his ankle throbbed. 'I don't think it's broken,' he said. 'Just feels like I've twisted it. A sprain at worst.'

'Still bad enough that you can't walk though, which isn't good,' Ted replied. 'We should get you to a hospital to get it looked over.'

'No hospital,' Eduardo grunted.

Ted stared at the man uneasily, wondering how these hired goons could lack even basic human empathy. The professor was clearly in pain and there was not one shred of compassion shown by any of them. Lucho was the driving force behind the trio, leading them onwards at any cost, but despite their slightly better temperament, the others were no better. Only one thing seemed to matter to them: finishing their task and reaching payday as quickly as possible.

'How much is he paying you?' Ted asked.

Carlos looked taken aback by the sudden question. 'What?'

'Sigma. How much is he paying you?' he repeated.

'Sixty-million peso,' Carlos replied. 'Only if we find the jewel.'

Ted was gobsmacked. Sixty million! Sigma was loaded. No wonder the Mexican trio were so hell-bent on finding the treasure.

'And you?' Ted looked at Jasper, almost accusatory. 'How much?'

'The same,' Jasper replied. 'Sixty-million, to be split between us.'

'That's insane,' Ted said. 'Who needs that much money?'

'It's not as much as you're thinking,' said Quinn. 'Sixty-million peso is probably about...' she pouted while she did the rough calculation in her head. 'Nearly three-million dollars, give or take. Split between the four of them, it's less than seven-hundred-and-fifty-thousand dollars each.'

'I mean, it's still a lot of money.'

The Aztec Secret

'Yes,' she agreed. 'Enough for some to become reckless.' She looked through the opening of the helicopter to see Lucho returning from the last temple. Unsurprisingly, aside from the star artefact, he was empty handed and a scowl was still on his face. He had his phone to his ear, and after a moment took it away and pressed the red button to end his call. He muttered a few words to Carlos before moving into the cockpit to start up the engine. Eduardo resumed his position on one of the benches, folding his arms as he took up his guard duties once more.

'What's the plan now?' Ted asked. Lucho didn't answer him and made for the passenger seat in the cockpit next to Carlos. He had barely glanced at the injured professor, much less asked how he was.

'They're going to find another site to explore,' replied Quinn.

'How do you— oh yeah,' Ted caught himself as the penny dropped. 'Spanish.'

Quinn sat close to Ted, while Jasper strapped himself in next to Eduardo. The engine started up and the tail rotor began to spin quickly. The big rotor on top started off much slower, and then picked up the pace to lift the helicopter into the air. Quinn leaned close to Ted and whispered in his ear, just above the noise of the aircraft.

'We're in trouble.'

The rotors quickly got louder and louder while she was speaking and Ted didn't catch anything else she said. The only part he managed to understand made him feel uneasy. Why were they in trouble? Was something wrong with the helicopter? He tried to keep calm and show his best poker face, so as not to alarm Eduardo, who although was not paying much attention to them, might have grown suspicious at their whispering. Ted came up with an alternative form of communication; one that he'd used in noisy nightclubs when he couldn't hear what his friends were saying. He pulled his phone out and started drafting a text message to no-one. He tilted the screen on the phone so Quinn could see what he'd written. She gave a half-smile in acknowledgement of his plan, before reading his message.

Let's talk on here.

They noticed that Eduardo was now looking in their direction, alerted by the phone screen lighting up in the growing darkness. The sun was setting, giving everything a beautiful pale orange tint, and the inside of the chopper was just dark enough for the phone to draw attention. Ted double-tapped his home button, bringing up the apps he hadn't yet closed. He then tapped on the maps app and turned the phone around.

'More ruins further north,' he shouted, cutting through the noise. Eduardo didn't seem to care. Carlos was already on his way somewhere and it wasn't his job to navigate. Ted went back to texting, handing the phone to Quinn. She took next to no time to tap out what she wanted to say.

Lucho isn't happy with Jasper. He told Carlos he's going to slow us down.

Ted took the phone back and wrote his reply.

So? They need him to find the jewel. They won't ditch him.

Quinn wrote again. *I dunno. Carlos told him to think about the twenty-million peso.*

Ted's eyes widened at the realisation of what she was implying. The maths didn't add up. They weren't planning on sharing the payment four ways, but three. What did that mean for Jasper? And them? If they somehow found the jewel and it was all over, Lucho and his men would have no more need of them. And if they didn't find it, would Lucho let them go their separate ways and risk them going straight to the police?

Should they hang around and wait for an opportunity to get away at the next site?

What do we do? he wrote back. Quinn's eyes fell on the pile of yellow backpacks next to her. Ted followed her gaze and could almost see the lightbulb appearing on top of her head. He put his hand firmly on her arm to get her attention. When she turned to face him, he shook his head. There was no way that was an option. They could find another way out that didn't involve plummeting to the earth.

I need to tell Jasper what they said, she tapped into the phone. Ted nodded and allowed her to text the professor's number. Moments later, Jasper's phone buzzed. The sound was lost among the white noise that had built up as the helicopter gained altitude. Carlos had brought the bird up high to survey a larger area. Eduardo hadn't noticed the text exchange, and Jasper pulled the phone from his jacket pocket, a look of surprise on his face as he saw who it was from. Ted watched the man's face drop on reading the text, his expression of worry mirroring exactly how he felt. The professor took in what Quinn had written and texted back, asking the same thing Ted had. What should they do? She responded by pointing very subtly at the parachutes. Jasper gave her an uncertain look, as though he too thought it a foolish idea.

Ted thought about what would happen when they reached the next site. There wasn't much opportunity to separate themselves from Lucho and his men last time. But it was getting late. Sooner or later they'd have to sleep, presumably with one staying awake in shifts to make sure there were no escapees. That would be the best chance they got.

Suddenly, the professor cried out and grabbed his injured foot. Eduardo looked over, surprised by the sudden outburst. Jasper howled in pain, shouting for Eduardo to find pain relief for him. Quinn took her opportunity, and her seatbelt was off the moment he started howling. She grabbed a backpack off the ground beside her and flung it at Ted, who sat there staring at it on his lap. She wriggled her own onto her back and secured the straps. Ted couldn't believe it. She was actually doing this. This was actually happening. His heart raced as he thought about what was about to happen. He fumbled with his backpack, getting it over one shoulder and trying to get it round the other side to hook his arm through the other strap. Quinn helped him, just as Eduardo had clocked on to what they were doing. The noise from the aircraft had masked the sound they were making, but when he looked up from the professor's foot he quickly realised he had been tricked. Ted had just clipped himself in round his waist as Eduardo desperately tried to unhook his seatbelt to stop them. Jasper reached over and slammed his hands into the big Mexican's stomach, preventing him from unbuckling the belt. Eduardo shouted and fought him off, pulling the professor's hands away with one strong hand, while trying to fight against the safety belt with the other. The shouting got the attention of Lucho and Carlos in the cockpit, who turned to see what the commotion was. Lucho looked from the struggle between Eduardo and Jasper to the two yellow backpacks that were standing on the other side. He roared in anger, knowing instantly what was happening, but knowing he was too far away to stop it.

'It's now or never, Ted!' Quinn yelled.

'I don't think I can,' Ted replied, utterly terrified as he looked out over the opening to the ground far below. Despite being so high up, Ted wondered if there was enough free fall time for the parachute to open.

'Yes you can.' Quinn saw Lucho fumble in the cockpit, searching for something. She looked at Jasper, who had just

The Aztec Secret

lost his fight with Eduardo. He didn't have a parachute. Her heart sank as she realised he wasn't going to come with them. Eduardo had released himself from his seat and would surely stop him.

'Go!' the professor shouted.

Lucho had found what he was looking for and took the safety off his gun.

'As soon as we're clear of the blades, pull the cord,' Quinn shouted, before pushing them both clear out of the helicopter.

Time seemed to slow down in the very moment their feet left the floor. It was as if they hovered in the air for just a second, before Ted looked up and saw the helicopter getting smaller and smaller. The wind instantly whistled past him, causing the skin on his face to pull upward through the g-force. He heard the whoosh of Quinn's parachute opening and remembered what she'd said a moment ago. He fumbled for the cord on the back of his pack, praying he could grab hold of it. He found it and gripped it tightly, pulling it with all his strength. The parachute opened, but for a moment nothing seemed to happen. The pilot chute shot out of the backpack the moment he pulled on the cord, but the main canopy hadn't fully opened out. His free fall continued while the suspension lines followed the pilot chute and the canopy waited for the right ripple in the air to force it out. The moment came suddenly as Ted felt his body jerk back. The canopy caught the air and unfolded in one swift motion, slowing his descent. The world was in much clearer focus now, and for as far as he could see there was nothing but dense rainforest with the outline of trees illuminated a pale orange against the glow of sunset.

Noticing that his hands were gripping tightly onto the shoulder straps of his backpack, he looked around at the suspension lines and then up at the inside of the canopy. It was then that he found the steering lines and hooked his hands around them. He tested them by gently pulling down on the left side and watched as he turned in a sweeping left arc. He then tried the right, and it worked as expected.

The ground was getting closer now, and Ted could see the details of each tree more clearly as he soared high above them. A popping sound came from somewhere above him, and then again shortly after. Quinn's parachute came into view, the speed at which she was travelling giving cause for concern. She swayed this way and that against the wind, almost as if she had lost control. Ted saw the culprit as she passed and sailed away below him. Her canopy was torn, a gaping hole lessening her air resistance drastically and causing her to lose altitude at an alarming rate. It was then that Ted heard the familiar noise of the helicopter blades. The chopper banked past him and hovered just above the tree line. Ted was just about to brace his dangling legs for impact with the tops of the trees when he saw a flash of light come from the opening of the helicopter. The popping sound came again, and Ted suddenly realised he was being shot at. His feet touched the tips of the leaves and the wind took him on a slalom course through the trees. He could see Quinn's parachute off in the distance, following a similar path, but his descent carried him below the treeline and he quickly lost sight of her again.

He pulled at the cord on the left side, and then the right as he frantically tried to avoid colliding with the tall trees. It was a wonder he hadn't hit one at full force yet. Hitting one at this speed with such little protection could be crippling. Inevitably, the canopy got caught on the top branches and his progress was stalled. The fabric tore as a sharp branch punched through it, but Ted was stuck, hanging there

The Aztec Secret

helplessly. He looked down at the ground below and estimated that he must still be a good twenty feet from the rainforest floor. A fall from that height was enough to cause serious injury. The helicopter was still hovering somewhere above, but he couldn't see it from his poor vantage point. The gunshots had stopped, which was both reassuring and unsettling at the same time. It could mean that they'd given up chasing the pair once they slipped through trees, or it could mean that they'd found their mark. Thinking of Quinn, he began to panic at the prospect that she could be dead. He tried to cast the thought aside and hope for the best. If she was still alive, she might be in trouble. They had a better chance of making it through wherever they were together.

Pushing his body forward and letting himself rock back again, he tried to build up some momentum in a pendulum motion. He swayed gently for a while, exerting as much energy as he could to swing back and forth. Soon he was swinging back far enough to almost touch the trunk of the tree with his foot. He repeated the process again and again until he could make meaningful contact with the trunk and push off again. As soon as he pushed off, the force caused the canopy to rip a bit more against the sharp branch. He went again and again, feeling the parachute give just a little bit more each time. Using both feet this time, he gave one last push. The canopy split and continued to tear down the fabric, until Ted felt it give way. The point at which Ted's weight forced the remaining part of the parachute to come down with him was when he was swinging back into the tree. He came tumbling down with a thud, smacking into the tree as he felt gravity take control of the situation. Digging his hands and feet into the trunk, he was able to slow his fall just enough to prevent knocking himself out as he hit the dirt. He cut his hands and tore his canvas shoes. Ruining a good pair of Converse was the last thing on his mind, however. While he'd managed to slow his fall, the ground approached quickly, and he hit it with a thud. The wind was knocked out of him and his hands stung from the friction against the bark of the tree. He lay in the dirt for a couple of minutes, catching his breath and coming to terms with the pain as the adrenaline started to leave his body. Eventually, he felt strong enough to get to his feet. On rising, he noticed that the helicopter noise was faint now. He was relieved to be away from the Mexicans, but he couldn't help wonder what this meant for Jasper. He had openly assisted their escape, battling with Eduardo to buy them enough time to ready their parachutes and jump. Would Lucho punish him for it? No, he thought. They still needed him to help locate the treasure. There was no point worrying about Jasper, there was nothing he could do. He needed to catch up to Quinn as quickly as he could. He made a mental note of where he'd last seen the top of her parachute disappear into the thick jungle and slowly trundled off after her.

TWELVE

Four drinks were enough for Alex to decide it was time to call it a night. She could handle her alcohol just fine, but the older she grew, the worse the hangovers seemed to become. Gone were the days of staying up all night drinking all manner of concoctions, before heading out to work the next morning as though nothing had happened. Luckily, the ice in her glass had watered down the drinks and, unlike the all-inclusive resort at the beach, the bartender had been careful with his measurements. After getting recommendations of which sights to see while she was here, she was content that there was enough to keep her occupied for another day or two. She would head further into the jungle and join a tour to visit one of the many collections of Mayan ruins that were scattered around the Guatemalan/Mexican border. Apparently, on the other side of the border were picturesque waterfalls that would be more beautiful than any she'd seen. It was an endorsement that encouraged her to add it to the itinerary. Besides, she had nothing else to do.

She set off down the street towards her hotel. The sunset cast an orange tint along the skyline, glowing between the gaps of dark silhouetted trees. Crickets chirped in the brush around the village, creating a blanket of sound that served as a constant reminder of how close she was to nature. Back home, the instruments playing the score to her evenings comprised of the constant hum of vehicles, car horns and the occasional shouts of the drunk patrons of the local bar. It was the kind of noise that grated on her the first few weeks she lived in Detroit, but she was now well used to. While an altogether more soothing sound, the unfamiliar noise from the crickets was sure to keep her up a while tonight.

The hotel was a small two-story building, with no more than six or seven rooms. Alex entered through the reception and made her way up the stairs to her rear-facing room. The whole village was situated atop a hill with views of the surrounding rainforest. She hadn't asked specifically for a room with a view but had gotten lucky and found herself staring out at what remained of the dying light as it disappeared behind the trees on the horizon. The prospect of venturing out into the jungle the next day was an exciting one. She wasn't ready for bed just yet, so she sat out on the balcony with a glass of water, kicked off her boots and put her feet up on the chair opposite. After a few minutes her eyes fell heavy and she began to drift off to sleep.

Dosing in and out of consciousness, a low humming sound drifted into her ears. She swatted at her head, thinking it was a mosquito buzzing around her ear. But it grew steadily louder and louder, until it drowned out the noise of the crickets. She woke up fully and placed the sound, seeing a helicopter coming into view just above the treeline. She'd heard one or two buzzing overhead earlier, but this one didn't belong to a tour company offering private excursions to wealthy holiday-goers. It looked military grade. Shortly after it appeared, Alex caught sight of a parachute drifting through the air. Perhaps the army were operating training drills in this area. The individual gliding through the air was too far away to make out, but they seemed to be landing right on top of the rainforest. The parachute swayed this way and that as the person operating it fell beneath the treeline and out of view. Suddenly, a flash of light emanated from the helicopter, followed by the loud crack of a gunshot. Alex jumped in surprise and a sinking feeling crept over her. This wasn't a training drill. She saw a figure hanging out the side of the opening in the helicopter with a handgun drawn. The shooter. Another flash came from the muzzle and another crack rippled through the air. The gunman appeared to be looking in the direction the parachute had gone moments earlier. From the limited light Alex could just about make out that he was wearing civilian attire; not military camouflage. Who were they? She thought again of the parachute that had glided haphazardly between the trees. Whoever was guiding it, they were in trouble. Instinctively, Alex reached for her radio, ready to call in the incident and request backup. But, realising it was missing, she remembered where she was.

The helicopter quickly banked and flew away. Soon the noise of the rotor died down to nothing more than a distant rumble. Alex took note of where she'd last seen the parachute, before bolting back inside, hurrying to pull on her boots. The noise of the crickets returned and seemed to be chirping louder now, as though screaming for help. Grabbing her room key, she left and locked the door behind her.

Her first port of call was to report the shooting to the hotel staff. They would be able to call emergency services quicker than she would with her poor Spanish. But the reception was empty and after dinging the bell that was sitting idly on the counter over and over, she resigned herself to that fact that there was no-one on duty. The street outside was deserted too. She'd have to do this alone.

A myriad of thoughts raced through her mind as she took off down the winding dirt road. Who was the gunman? Who were they shooting at? Why? Next came a question she answered before her mind could finish asking: why was she getting in the middle of it? She was a cop; this was what she did. She had no jurisdiction in this country, but jurisdiction went out the window when someone's life was in danger. She kept looking over her shoulder to check the location of the hotel, so she could keep herself moving in the right direction. It was easy to get lost, particularly as the light had all but faded to darkness. The road veered off to the left, away from the direction she needed to be heading in. She pulled her phone from her pocket and flicked on the torch function. The bright white light illuminated the edges of the forest in front of her. All she could see were trees behind more trees; it was impossible to see more than a few feet ahead. There was no way she could find her way through there.

**

The ground remained dry under Ted's feet as he ran as fast as his legs would carry him. The rainforest hadn't lived up to its name with such dry weather the last few days, which was fortunate as a muddier surface would have slowed him down. He tried hard not to think of the possibility of any number of spiders or snakes that could be lurking in the darkness, inches from where he was at any one time. He hadn't seen any yet, but he wasn't looking very hard in his haste. These animals called the rainforest their home and would be experts of camouflage. He'd learned in a documentary that snakes sensed vibrations through the ground and slithered away before

The Aztec Secret

people grew near, but Ted couldn't help but think there was one waiting to strike with every slap of his shoe on the dirt.

Using his phone as a torch, he pressed on, hoping he would catch sight of Quinn soon. He felt something brush his face as he bundled his way past a tree. He recoiled instinctively, not knowing what critter had just caught him unaware. He stopped and pointed his phone in its direction and noticed the familiar cord pulley setup. A wave of relief rushed over him as he realised what it was. Looking up, he saw the orange canopy caught on the tops of the trees. He moved his phone hand up and down, scanning the area with light in the same motion of an airport security employee using a handheld metal detector. The parachute was all here, but there was no sign of Quinn.

'Quinn!' he called into the darkness. There was no answer. Where could she have gone? The light on his phone died and he brought the device to his face just long enough to see the battery alert flash on the screen. Moments later the phone shut itself off completely.

'Unbelievable,' he cursed his bad luck.

A rustling noise came from behind him, and a dim light slowly illuminated the space around him. He spun around just in time to see a figure approach and yelped in panic as he realised it wasn't Quinn. The figure was too tall to be her.

'It's OK,' the person said. 'I'm here to help.'

Ted detected the accent. 'You're American?' His voice had calmed a bit, safe in the knowledge it wasn't Lucho or one of his men.

'Yes,' the figure grew closer, but Ted couldn't see them as the torch in their hand was shining right into his face.

'Do you mind?' he said, squinting at the bright light.

'Oh, sorry,' the figure lowered the light to his chest, and he could see the woman in front of him more clearly.

'I'm Alex,' she said.

'Ted.'

'Is everything alright, Ted? I saw the helicopter and heard gunshots from my hotel.'

'I'm fine,' he replied. 'But I'm looking for my friend. This was her parachute,' he pointed up at the canopy above them. 'Wait. What hotel?' Ted didn't think they was any sign of civilisation for miles.

'There's a village back this way,' she pointed back the way she had come. 'It's where I'm—'

They heard another voice somewhere nearby, causing Alex to pause mid-sentence.

'That's her,' Ted recognised her instantly. 'Quinn?' he called out.

'Over here,' came the reply. Her voice seemed strained, as though she were in pain. Alex led the way with her phone pointing out in front, illuminating the space ahead with its bright white light. They followed Quinn's voice fifty feet away from the parachute landing zone, finding her sitting with her back against a tree. She was cradling her right arm and there was a red blood trail running down to her elbow.

'She's hurt,' Alex declared, kneeling down next to Quinn. Ted had already read the situation and took a knee on the other side of her. 'Quinn, I'm Alex. Looks like you've had quite the fall.'

Quinn was gritting her teeth in pain. 'It stings so bad.'

Ted surveyed the blood seeping through the arm of her t-shirt. The fabric had been torn and was sticky from the blood. He then looked back at the blackness, towards where the parachute was. She'd travelled some distance before slumping down by this tree. If she'd been hurt by the fall it was a wonder she'd made it this far from where she landed. He then

The Aztec Secret

remembered the flash emanating from the helicopter and the loud crackling pop noise that had followed.

'It wasn't the fall,' he said. 'She's been shot.'

Alex narrowed her eyes, shining the light onto her arm. She then gave the phone to Ted and asked him to keep it pointed at the arm, while she rolled the sleeve up to Quinn's shoulder. Quinn winced.

'Sorry, I know it's painful,' Alex said sympathetically. She took the phone back off Ted and with her other hand pointed to the source of the oozing blood. 'There's no exit wound on the other side, and it doesn't look like the bullet is in there,' she said.

'How do you know?' asked Ted.

'I'm a cop. I've seen gunshot wounds before. If she was hit, it only grazed her arm on its way past. She's lucky.'

'I don't feel lucky,' Quinn said with a strained voice.

'It cut close enough to open up her arm though,' Alex continued, assessing the amount of blood she was losing. 'We need to get her to a hospital. Help me get her up.'

Ted leaned close to let Quinn put her uninjured arm around his neck. Together, they lifted her slowly. She yelped out in pain, and once they were all on their feet Alex started leading the way back towards the village.

'Wait,' Quinn said. 'My bag.'

Ted looked behind them and at the tree. Beside it was her backpack. Her camera was nowhere in sight. He slung one strap over his shoulder and they carried on. He'd break the news that her camera was gone when they'd got her to safety.

'See if there's something inside to help stop the bleeding,' Alex said. Ted unzipped the bag and rummaged around in the dark, eventually gripping onto fabric and pulling out the Nirvana t-shirt she had been wearing the day before.

'Sorry,' he said. 'I'll get you a new one.' They stopped so Ted could crudely wrap it around her arm. It helped a bit, but it wasn't the best solution.

It was slow going back to the village, but they eventually made it without incident. Quinn was really starting to feel the pain as the adrenaline had worn off. They sat her down on the floor outside the hotel.

'The people in the helicopter. Who were they?' Alex probed.

Ted and Quinn looked at each other, as if attempting to discuss telepathically whether they should tell Alex the full story. Ted quickly decided against it.

'I don't know,' he said.

Alex didn't seem convinced. 'So they just shot at you for no reason?'

Quinn groaned in pain, drawing attention back to her wound.

'Wait here and keep talking to her,' Alex said. 'I'm going to go inside and get something to wrap around the wound a bit better. Just until we get to the hospital.' She left and dashed inside to the reception. The lights were off inside, and it didn't look like there were any staff on hand to offer assistance. It didn't surprise Ted much; the place looked quite basic. Twenty-four-hour reception duty wasn't high up on the list of priorities for hotels of this size in such remote places.

'How are you feeling?' Ted knelt next to Quinn, looking concernedly at the wound.

'My arm feels like it's on fire.'

'I'm sorry,' he said.

'What for?' she asked. 'Are you sorry I pulled you out of a helicopter, or sorry a crazy Mexican criminal shot at me?'

'Uh, I dunno. Just sorry this is all happening.'

The Aztec Secret

'You've done nothing wrong.' She winced as the pain worsened. 'I hope Jasper is OK.'

'He'll be fine,' Ted reassured. 'They need him to find the treasure.' He tried to lower his voice, so they weren't overheard. Not that there was anyone nearby.

'But what if they find it? What will happen to Jasper then? Or what if they give up entirely? Neither scenario bodes well for him.'

'They won't give up. Lucho wants that money more than anything. Anyway, I think I've found a way to slow them down.' He reached into his back pocket and pulled out the star-shaped object. The softly lit pathway leading up the steps to the hotel bounced off its obsidian edges, illuminating it.

Quinn gasped. 'What are you doing with that?'

'I swiped it just before we jumped. Lucho was busy looking for his gun and left it lying around.'

'Why? You know they're going to be looking for us now, don't you?'

'I was trying to buy Jasper some time.'

'We could have been done with all this, Ted. Jasper got us into it, and I think he wanted us to escape. That's why he fought Eduardo, to buy us time.'

'So are you saying you don't care what happens to him now?'

'No,' Quinn sighed. She gritted her teeth as the pain intensified once more. 'God, imagine how bad it must feel if the bullet was in there.'

'You'd probably be unconscious from the shock,' said Ted. It didn't seem to reassure her one bit. He turned his attention back to the artefact in his hand.

'We should turn it over to the police,' Quinn said.

'I dunno,' Ted was unsure. 'What if Lucho was right? The police might be looking for us. If we go right to them we could be arrested.' He looked at her pained expression, and then at the blood-stained t-shirt that was lashed around her arm.

'I feel weak,' she said.

'You've lost a lot of blood. Let's get you to a hospital and we'll figure things out from there. Nothing else matters right now.'

'OK,' she smiled.

Alex came back through the reception door, holding a first aid kit. 'I found bandages,' she called. 'And a bottle of water for you both.' Ted hurriedly stuffed the artefact back into his pocket. In his haste he poked his skin with one of the obsidian edges. Luckily, the darkness seemed to conceal his actions and Alex didn't seem to notice.

Alex handed the water to Ted, who gratefully took a big sip. His headache from earlier had barely gone away, but with the adrenaline of the last hour he'd forgotten about it. Ted then poured some for Quinn while Alex worked the bandage onto her arm.

'That'll keep the bleeding under control until we get you to a doctor,' she announced. 'There's one a few miles away, according to my phone. I can drive us there.'

'You didn't call an ambulance?' Ted enquired. He was acutely aware that she'd referred to herself as a cop, and he felt uncomfortable in her presence with the stolen artefact on his person.

'It'll be quicker if I drive you straight there. My rental's just here.' She pointed to a run-down looking SUV a few yards away. She retrieved a set of keys from her pocket and pushed the unlock button. The car horn tooted and the lights blinked in response.

Another set of headlights illuminated the dark street and the vehicle stopped as the trio crossed the road. Noticing the wounded Quinn being helped across the road, the driver wound down his window and called out. 'You need the hospital?'

Alex squinted her eyes through the bright beams of the headlights and recognised the driver as the bartender from before. She gave a warm smile. 'Yes, she's been shot.'

The man's eyebrow furrowed in concern. 'Please,' he said. 'I can take them.'

Ted's heart nearly skipped a beat. This was the perfect opportunity to get away from the police officer. She was definitely American, so perhaps she was on vacation and had no jurisdiction here. But that didn't mean she couldn't turn them over to the local authorities. The longer they stayed with her, the more chance he had of blowing their cover and revealing the stolen artefact.

'I can take them, it's no problem,' Alex protested.

'Nonsense,' the man replied. 'I am visiting my friend in La Libertad. There is a hospital in San Benito; it is not far from there.'

Alex looked to the pair. 'Is that OK with you?' she asked.

Ted almost bit her hand off at the offer. 'Yes!' he said, a little overzealously. 'I mean, you're on vacation aren't you? We really appreciate your help, but you've done more than enough for us already.'

'Come,' the man said. 'Your friend needs medical attention.'

He was right, time was of the essence. 'Thank you so much,' Ted said, grabbing Quinn's backpack before opening the rear door of the man's car to help her safely in. He took his time going around the back of the vehicle to climb in the other side. While he was behind the rear bumper, he ducked down to carefully unzip the backpack and place the artefact securely inside.

'OK,' he said, waving goodbye to Alex. 'Let's go.'

THIRTEEN

Ramón was sitting down to have his evening meal with his family when the phone rang. The Governor rose from the table, ignoring the scowl his wife gave him as he absented himself from the dinner she'd spent an hour and a half preparing. He often took his work home with him and it had put a lot of strain on their relationship. He knew she would be having stern words with him later. He would remind her that it is a busy time with the upcoming election. This was a critical period in his career. Of course, he wouldn't divulge any details, choosing to keep his less-than-legitimate dealings to himself. Nobody could ever find out about that, not even his wife. Patricia wouldn't usually ask about the ins and outs of his work; she had learned over their years of marriage that although Ramón would bring work home with him, he didn't like to talk about it.

His latest deal was especially critical and it took someone with his vision and tenacity to make it happen. Politicians like General Secretary Cicerón were far too skittish of such bold plays for their own good. The party needed people with stronger stomachs for this kind of work. People like him. This was how things were done.

Psyching himself up for whatever conversation awaited him, he reassured himself that he had made the right choice. But as the landline rang louder as he left the dining room and eyed the receiver on the table in the hallway, a wave of anxiety washed over him. There was something eerie about this old technology. With his mobile, he would be able to see who was attempting to contact him flash up on the screen, giving prewarning of the possible conversation that could be about to take place. The old landline gave no clue as to who was calling or why. It was the fear of the unknown that made his heart race as he picked up the receiver and put it to his ear. His mind jumped to the worst-case scenario. Was it the General Secretary dismissing him after all?

'*¿Bueno?*'

There was a lot of background noise coming from the other end and there didn't seem to be anyone there.

'*¿Bueno?*' he repeated.

More static came through the receiver, before a man's voice was heard.

'There has been a complication.'

Ramón recognised the voice instantly. His eyes widened at the realisation. 'I told you not to call here,' he hissed.

'You were not answering the number you gave me.'

Ramón thought of the burner phone he had acquired for conversations like these. He wondered where he had left it. It was possible Patricia had moved it somewhere when they sat down for dinner. She hated distractions while they ate. Family time was important, but she did not understand the seriousness of the situation. The cogs in his brain whirred like an overheating computer fan. Where the hell was his phone?

'That is no excuse,' he replied to the man on the other end. 'You are not to call here again. This is my home.'

'We have bigger problems,' the man said dismissively.

'Ramón!' Patricia called from the dining room. He hastily covered the phone with his hand and grimaced. Not now.

'OK, tell me,' he hurried. 'Quickly.'

'The students have escaped. Shall we pursue them?'

'I don't care about the students,' Ramón said. 'Don't get side-tracked. Stick to the plan.'

'But sir—'

'Stick. To. The. Plan,' he said in a hushed, yet authoritative tone. There was a brief silence on the receiver.

'They have the artefact,' the voice said. 'Sigma said it was the key to finding it.'

Ramón almost broke the handset he was gripping it so tightly. A rage began to build up inside him. He had been assured these men were more than capable of getting the job done. How had he hired such amateurs?

'Find them,' he said. 'Clean up your mess. And do not call this number again.' With that, he hung up, slamming the phone down in frustration. He took a moment to compose himself by looking at his reflection in the window, opting not to reply to his wife's call. The light from the room reflected off the glass, revealing nothing but a faded version of himself staring out into the dark of the night. He realised his hands were shaking. Just a minute ago he was confident of the decision he'd made earlier that day. Truth be told, it was a decision he had made long before that. The pieces had been in place for a while; he had been waiting for the General Secretary to give the green light before he set things in motion. After her failure to acknowledge what was necessary to give the party a fighting chance in this election, he had taken it upon himself to give the go-ahead anyway.

'Ramón!' Patricia's voice came again from the other room. Ramón trudged back into the dining room and took his seat beside his ten-year-old daughter. Patricia gave him a questioning look from across the table.

'Sorry,' he said. 'I had to take care of some business. We won't be disturbed again.' He turned to his daughter, who was helping herself to the food her mother had beautifully presented in the middle of the table. 'So, did you do all of your chores today?'

'Yes,' she replied.

'Good.' He loaded up his plate with food and began to tuck in. 'And what did you do after that?'

'Adriana has her recital tomorrow,' Patricia reminded him.

'Ah yes, you have been practising?' he motioned to the piano tucked away in the corner of the room.

'When she is not watching television.'

'It's more interesting than piano,' Adriana said.

'I'm sure you will do brilliantly tomorrow,' Ramón smiled. 'If I close my eyes it could be Chopin himself.'

Adriana snorted and began to chuckle. 'I don't think so.'

'So, did you watch anything interesting on the television?' he changed the subject.

'She enjoys watching the news,' Patricia said, as though revealing new information to him. Frankly, this was new information to Ramón. He was so wrapped up in work he often neglected to witness the changes in his own daughter as she grew up.

'The news?' he replied, surprised. 'You are not watching cartoons anymore?'

'She hasn't watched cartoons for months,' Patricia gave him a cold, knowing stare.

'Something happened at a museum,' said Adriana. 'Someone stole an artefact right out of the display. A new one they just found.'

Ramón's stomach sank. The very mention of the event made him feel uneasy, as though by knowing about it his daughter was now swept up in the crime he had set in motion.

'I heard on the radio when I was driving. How strange.' He acted cool.

'I'm surprised they weren't caught,' Adriana said. 'The reporters say the museum was busy. It must be worth a lot of money for someone to take such a big risk like that.'

'Yes, I imagine so,' he replied.

'Do you think they'll catch the thief?' Adriana looked up at her father, which took him back to a time years earlier, when Adriana was at the age when kids ask questions about everything, when they believe that their mother and father are the greatest source of knowledge and wisdom in the world. It had been a while since she had asked such a question to Ramón. She was well versed in the technology of modern smartphones, able to find the answer to most questions using a search engine. But this was not a straightforward fact, thus the reason Adriana was asking him his opinion. There was something unnerving about this particular question. Not five minutes after returning from a phone call from a man he'd hired to steal the artefact, his daughter was now asking him if the person responsible would be brought to justice. If the authorities did catch up to them, it was sure to come back to him.

'I'm sure the police will do everything they can to find them,' he said.

**

Lucho let out an annoyed grunt as he heard the sound of the phone line being disconnected. The Governor had hung up on him. He hated taking orders at the best of times, but from a politician... He'd worked for a number of slimy individuals throughout his career, but politicians were the worst. They had a nasty habit of cutting you out of a deal at the last minute, once you've already done the hard work for them. And they were wealthy enough, or at least influential enough, to buy their way out of trouble. It had crossed his mind that should he and his men be caught by the police, Governor Villacrés would find a way to wriggle his way out of the line of fire. If the worst happened, Lucho would do everything in his power to ensure he took him down with him. He made sure to record their conversation, just in case it became a useful bargaining chip in the future. The police might be interested to learn which of their corrupt government officials had sanctioned the deal, with a reduced sentence as the carrot. Or, more likely, Villacrés would try and weasel out of the deal, keeping the reward for finding the Aztec jewel for himself. Lucho was not above blackmail. In fact, in the past it had served as a crucial tool for making a living.

He placed the phone into his pocket and turned from his position in the cockpit to face the back. Jasper was tightly strapped into the bench, his hands tied with flexicuffs behind his back. Whatever loose trust that had existed between him and the Mexican mercenaries had been lost completely after his stunt to assist the students' escape. He was being watched over closely by Eduardo.

The students were now the top priority, as they had foolishly taken the artefact with them. No official order had been given to eliminate them, but Lucho had been told to clean up the mess and the Governor hadn't specified how.

The Aztec Secret

Disposing of dead bodies was straightforward enough, but they were sure to be missed back home, and a murder investigation would surely follow. That could become more of a nuisance than it was worth. None of that had crossed his mind when he shot wildly at the pair as they parachuted down into the rainforest. And there was nothing to guarantee it would cross his mind again when he next saw them.

While the students needed to be found, the more immediate concern was the lack of fuel in the helicopter. The Governor, although holding the potential to stab them in the back once Sigma had paid him for finding the treasure, was proving resourceful while they remained allies. The plus side of working with someone with such authority. After receiving the phone call from Lucho earlier in the day to provide the information they'd learned from Cortés' letter, he had located a military base near the Mexican/Guatemalan border which could be used to refuel the helicopter. This was where they had landed.

The soldiers posted at the small base hadn't batted an eyelid at the new arrivals, who had remained in the helicopter, save for Carlos who had stepped out to get assistance refuelling the big bird. The Governor had pulled strings to make sure they were not disturbed. The last thing Lucho needed was for some nosey inexperienced recruit to find the professor handcuffed in the back and start asking questions. The sooner they got back in the air, the better.

Carlos returned to the cockpit and said something in Spanish to Lucho that Jasper didn't understand.

'You'll never find them, just let them go,' Jasper pleaded.

'Shut up,' Carlos snapped, as he began flicking switches and performing a routine of pre-flight checks. Lucho smirked. Here was an opportunity to teach the professor a lesson. He brought his smartphone from his pocket and switched on an app. The display switched to a map, similar in look to other geolocation apps. In the centre was a flickering white dot. He showed the screen to the professor, who eyed it curiously.

'What is this?' he asked.

Lucho was hoping for that response, so he could reveal his clever foresight. 'It is your student, professor,' he said matter of fact.

It took a moment for Jasper to process it, before he understood what was happening. 'You're tracking them? How?'

'After the fat one tried to escape the first time,' Carlos chimed in.

'Ted. His name is Ted,' Jasper scowled. 'Why can't you just let them go? I'll help you find the jewel.'

'They should not have stolen from me!' Lucho twisted his face in anger. Jasper wondered then whether the man's motivation was purely to retrieve the artefact, or an act of vengeance towards two civilians who had got one over on him. From what little he knew of Lucho, it was likely a mix of both.

The engine came to life and the whirring of the rotors began to build in intensity. Carlos looked at the phone screen Lucho was still holding outwards.

'It is not moving,' he noted, pointing at the flickering white dot in the centre of the picture.

'The last location,' Lucho replied. The fact that they were speaking in English gave Jasper the impression he was still involved in this conversation. He didn't feel the need to contribute anything though; he wasn't interested in helping them hunt down his students. Judging from what Lucho had said about it being the last location, it meant one of three things: Ted was dead already and his phone lay with him in the rainforest, he had lost his phone where he landed, or the

The Aztec Secret

phone had died and wasn't emitting a signal. He prayed that it was one of the latter two.

He set about trying to remember everything he could about the manuscript Quinn had roughly translated. Was there something they'd missed, a hidden clue perhaps, that could point their way to the jewel Cortés was after without the need for the artefact? Lucho was on a mission to find Ted and Quinn. He'd need to think quick if he wanted to protect them from his wrath.

He thought about what they knew already from Cortés' letter. The warrior Cortés had interrogated had attempted to destroy the star-shaped artefact, giving away its importance in locating the jewel. Cortés had also sent Pedro de Alvarado south in pursuit of it. Alvarado would have used hunting dogs to follow the scent of the Aztec warriors who carried the jewel, and thus he was sure to have tracked them down. That was the end of the clues from the manuscript, but there must have been something more. He thought about everything he knew about Alvarado and his role in the Spanish conquest of Central America. After taking control of Tenochtitlan, Cortés sent Alvarado south towards Soconusco and Guatemala, to continue their expedition to new lands. This initiative coincided nicely with chasing down the escaped Aztec warriors, and perhaps Cortés' motive for setting it in motion was less about the conquest of new lands and more about the retrieval of the peace offering he planned on gifting to the king of Spain.

As Cortés did to Charles V, Alvarado wrote letters back to Cortés to report on his progress through Soconusco and Guatemala, however these letters were lost. Jasper wondered if the conclusion of the jewel's location was reported there. He looked at Lucho, who was staring at his phone, fixating on the flickering dot on the map where Ted was, or had once been. The helicopter was airborne and they were quickly making their way back to the part of the rainforest where Ted and Quinn had escaped. He needed to act now.

'I've got it!' he exclaimed. He almost made Eduardo jump with the sudden burst of excitement. Lucho turned in his seat to address the animated professor.

'What?'

'I know how we can find the jewel,' he said. 'We don't need the artefact after all.'

'Really?' Lucho was intrigued. 'Explain.'

The professor leaned forward in his seat, closer to Lucho so he could hear him above the noise from the engine. 'History tells us that Cortés sent Alvarado south towards Guatemala. We didn't need this letter to tell us that.'

'So?'

'So, we've been thinking about this all wrong. We don't need to unpick everything Hernán Cortés said about his conquest of Mesoamerica. We need to see what Pedro de Alvarado wrote about it. He was the one who went after the jewel.'

Lucho looked at him curiously. 'Explain, old man.'

'We're wasting our time with this artefact. It won't get us closer to the treasure. We should stop somewhere we can spend a few hours researching any writings Alvarado had about his expedition to Guatemala. Maybe he learned more about its location on the way?'

Lucho looked to Eduardo, who gave him a shrugged response. He pondered what the professor was suggesting while scratching the small patch of facial hair under his bottom lip. Jasper waited anxiously for his response. The longer the pair looked at each other in silence, the more the professor's poker face began to break. Lucho smirked as he saw the cracks appear.

'Bullshit,' he declared. He said something in Spanish to Carlos, who maintained his course towards Ted's last known location.

He'd seen right through Jasper's bluff. The professor hoped that if his students were still alive, they had the sense to get far away from where they were.

Joe Topliffe

FOURTEEN

The drive to San Benito was bumpy, owed both to the pothole-filled dirt roads that led to the town and the speed at which their driver had taken them. Ted didn't blame the man. Someone had been shot; he'd clearly read the situation as an emergency. At least that was the vibe Ted had got from his erratic driving.

It had taken Ted three attempts to pass his driving test back home. The first time had been marked as a fail due to an accumulation of minor faults. The second was for mounting the kerb whilst making a three-point-turn. Mirror, signal, manoeuvre didn't seem to be as important here. Perhaps Ted was being a little harsh; the man was doing his best without a wing mirror. If this had been a fairly accurate example of the norm for driving in this part of the world, Ted felt as though he'd missed a trick. He should have learned to drive here. The test would have been a breeze, and it would have saved him an arm and a leg in examination fees.

The car had given off a foul smell of burning rubber, or perhaps that was the gearbox, and there was a constant loud squeaking noise as the suspension struggled to cope with the terrain. Ted was glad for it. Silence would have been worse as he would have been forced to talk with the driver. They'd exchanged pleasantries as they started the journey; Ted introducing himself and the driver likewise. His name was Sebastián and he owned a bar in the small village where Alex was staying. Ted thought he seemed like a nice enough guy, but he was glad the questions had stopped after he'd asked how his friend had ended up with a gunshot wound. Ted feigned ignorance, claiming that it had come from nowhere. No tourist excursion would involve parachuting from a helicopter, let alone at night, so he left that part out. It would only raise more questions. Instead, he said that it must have been an accident, and they hadn't seen the shooter. It was unlikely that Sebastián bought his story, but he hadn't asked any follow up questions and simply tore down the long roads until they reached the hospital.

As they drove into the outskirts of town, the car passed a farm with fields of low-growing crops. An old shack, presumably the farmer's house, whizzed by as the driver sped on toward the centre. Alongside the house was a tractor sitting outside a dilapidated shed of corrugated iron. Its red paintwork had chipped off for the most part, fitting in with the theme of its surroundings. In the blink of an eye as he passed the open shed, Ted thought he spotted the propeller of a small plane from within, poking out from underneath a large tarpaulin sheet.

San Benito was much larger than the village they'd come from, however the buildings looked the same. While the village had been hidden within a tiny pocket of the rainforest, this place sat on the edge of a large lake, giving it the feel of a coastal town.

The car passed an empty marketplace, presumably where stalls sold fresh fruit and vegetables during the day. The high-pitched buzz of Vespa engines could be heard whipping past the vehicle on its way through the centre of the town. The car pulled up outside the entrance of the hospital and Ted had his seatbelt off and the door open before it had come to a complete stop. He opened up the rear door to help Quinn out. She took his hand, and as he pulled to lift her from her seat he misjudged the amount of force needed and she lurched into him, bumping into his chest. She gasped as the sudden motion took her by surprise and they found themselves inches from each other, their noses almost touching. They maintained eye contact for a moment, before a voice came from the driver's seat.

'My friends,' Sebastián said. 'Your bag.'

Ted realised he'd left Quinn's backpack in the car, and darted back to retrieve it. Opening the zip, he took a peek inside to check that the star-shaped artefact was still safely tucked away. It was. He picked the bag up and slammed the door shut, shouting a hearty thank you as the car pulled away, leaving them alone again.

'Let's get you inside,' he said, relieved they were able to get this far. He swung the bag over his shoulder, forgetting it wasn't zipped shut. The artefact fell out and landed hard on the ground. Ted fumbled with the bag as he desperately picked up the artefact and hid it safely away again. Luckily it was still in one piece, although he noticed that fragments of clay had chipped away as it smashed the floor. Now wasn't the time to worry about that, however, and he zipped the backpack shut before helping Quinn through the double doors of the building.

The Aztec Secret

Ted had always hated hospitals. They were all the same; bright white lighting, long corridors, that distinct smell. On the rare occasions that he'd had to make appointments to see a specialist rather than his local GP back home, he was instantly transported back to his six-year-old self, visiting his sick grandmother before she passed. There were so many triggers in these buildings that evoked memories of sadness he'd rather not revisit. Hospitals were a place to heal, a place to recover, a place to save lives. But to six-year-old Ted it was the place that took his grandmother from him. There was a part of him that never recovered from that experience.

Waiting in the seating area by reception in hard plastic airport-style chairs was agony. Quinn had been seen to quickly, and it seemed as though everything was going to be alright. The nurse didn't seem overly concerned with the situation, despite the gruesome blood stain on the fabric that had been wrapped around the top of her bicep. They were used to seeing much worse, he supposed.

The people who worked there were heroes. It took a certain type of mental steel to work in a place like this. The very thought of being there for longer than an hour gave Ted an uneasy feeling, let alone caring for patients on long shifts with unparalleled resilience.

On top of his prior experiences coming back to haunt him, another thing that concerned Ted was the suspicious glances he'd received from the staff behind the counter. Gunshot wounds were cause for suspicion. Back home that would usually prompt a police investigation. Had the staff informed the authorities? Being interrogated by Mexican police would certainly lead to the exposure of the artefact in his possession. Why the hell had he taken it? They could both be high and dry had he left it behind. He considered throwing it away, but then if Lucho and his men were after them and found them without it, they'd surely kill them. Then something Carlos had said came in a sudden flashback. They must have been caught on CCTV in the museum, plus there were the security guards who caught them slipping out the back door. It wouldn't matter if they had the artefact or not; they would probably be stopped and questioned by police the moment they checked in at the airport.

Ted could feel his mind spiralling again, as a horrible feeling of impending doom set in. He tried to focus on positive thoughts instead of the potential of spending time in jail. If they turned themselves in, there was a chance the police would listen to the truth. Plus, having the artefact went some way to reclaiming the stolen items from the museum.

He decided he needed a distraction: checking in on his social media profiles, watching cat videos. Hell, he'd even take a video chat with Julia and Richard at this point. Anything to take his mind off of the trauma of the last day. Besides, there was nothing he could do while Quinn was being treated. He may as well have a moment to himself where he could fully detach himself, just for a while. He pulled his phone from his pocket and pressed the lock button. The screen remained black, reminding him the phone needed charging. He'd left his charger in the hotel room in Mexico City, along with most of his luggage. His backpack with the things he'd packed for their day out to the ruins and museum were still on the helicopter.

He looked down at Quinn's bag sitting between his legs. He tried his luck and zipped it open, before rummaging around inside. He immediately hit the artefact and removed it, setting it down on the seat next to him. The area was quiet, so he wasn't worried about anyone seeing it. Remembering the way the object had fallen out of the bag and hit the ground hard, he scanned the face of it for signs of damage. As he'd noticed earlier, shards of clay had been chipped away from the centre of the artefact. It was then that something caught his eye: an engraving of sorts, in the area where the clay had been chipped away. There were four symbols carved into it. The first was clearly a snake, with its mouth open, presumably about to strike. The second was a face, with wide eyes and a straight open mouth. The head was wearing a crown, with a band running along the base of it, and the points looking like flat-topped pyramids. The third symbol was more difficult to make out, but looked a bit like droplets of water. The fourth was the head of a cat. The detail on these small carvings was incredible. Ted couldn't hope to replicate it with a sharpened pencil on paper, and not only because he was terrible at drawing.

Ted couldn't believe it. All this time, there had been a clue as to the meaning of the artefact, concealed by layers of dirt that had built up over time, compacting on top of the object's core. But what did the symbols mean? He thought about researching the meaning of the symbols on his phone, but then remembered his predicament.

Moving his attention away from the artefact and returning to the bag, he continued his search. He eventually felt something that seemed promising. He gripped hold of it and pulled out a thick wire. He found one end; the pin that connected to his phone. Luckily it was the right type. So far so good. He then threaded the wire between his hands as he retrieved the other end from the bag. He hoped for a plug with a travel adapter tacked onto the end, but as the plug end came into view, his heart sank. All that was there was the American style two-pronged pin of the plug. No adapter.

'Shit,' he cursed under his breath.

He sat there a few minutes staring at a clock on the wall. The second hand ticked in sudden bursts of motion, as though the milliseconds between each movement didn't exist and time froze momentarily from one second to the next. He felt like he'd been watching it forever before it made a full circle and the minute hand twanged to the next dash along.

The high-pitched hum of a vacuum cleaner came from the corner of the room, as a member of staff began cleaning the floor by a row of empty seats. Ted watched it, void of anything better to do. And through his tired eyes something drew his attention. There were a pair of plug sockets raised just above floor level on the wall next to the vacuum cleaner. He studied the vacant one and looked at the two-pronged plug still in his hands.

Moving over to the other side of the room, he positioned himself in the seat next to the sockets and attempted to plug the charger into the socket. To his delight, it slotted in perfectly! Apparently Mexican plugs were the same as American. It was a trivial observation, but in his tired, delirious state he felt grateful for at least one thing to go his way. A light appeared on the phone's screen, indicating that the phone was charging. It was still too low on power to turn on, but Ted didn't care. With the small comfort of having a working phone, Ted's mind fell at ease for the first time in hours and his heavy eyes closed as he nodded off to sleep.

His head felt light and his vision was blurred as he floated down a corridor lined with fog. Everything was dull, as though the world had been painted in greyscale. He wasn't in control of his body, as though he were a passenger being carried through the never-ending corridor. He passed through one open set of double doors, and then another. Looked down at his feet, he suddenly realised he was sat in a wheelchair. He turned around to see who was pushing him, but there was nobody there. Instead, what he saw sent a

The Aztec Secret

feeling of dread deep within him. At the end of the hallway, back the way he'd come, was a menacing figure wearing a hood to mask his face. He was holding a gun in his hand and pointed it at Ted as he followed him. Ted turned back the other way and tried desperately to wheel faster down the corridor, but it was no use. He was moving in slow motion and his attacker was gaining on him. Seeing an open door leading to a room to his left, he leapt out of the wheelchair and landed in the opening. The fog on the floor dissipated and a bed appeared in front of him. He looked up and found himself staring into the face of his grandmother, who lay lifeless with her eyes closed. The sound of sirens rang through his head, getting louder and louder.

Ted jolted awake and found himself sat in the seat, his phone sitting on his lap with the cable still attached and plugged into the wall. The flashing lights of an ambulance were being emitted through the glass doors of the hospital entrance, and the siren faded as the emergency response team helped someone on a gurney out the back of the vehicle, before wheeling them through the building and around the corner.

It had been a bad dream. He hadn't dreamt about his grandmother since he was a child. Being in the hospital had brought to the surface a memory he thought he'd long since buried. He knew there was a part of him that had never fully recovered from the loss of his grandmother. Someone once told him that you never get over the death of a loved one, you just learn to live without them. He couldn't wait to leave this place.

He looked at his phone, which had charged up a fair way. He must have been asleep for an hour. He switched it on and waited to find signal. A thought hit him and he remembered the carvings on the artefact. He pulled it from the bag and opened up the camera app on his phone, snapping a pic of the symbols. He'd look them up later to see what they meant.

The phone had finally found signal and sent him a number of notifications. He swiped through them, dismissing most. But there was one that made him pause. A text message from his network. The preview of the message was clear as day.

Welcome to Guatemala! While you're here, you will be charged the following rates for data use…

Guatemala? Why was it welcoming him to Guatemala? He hurriedly opened up the maps app and waited for his location to update. The nearby area loaded and he pinched his finger and thumb on the screen to zoom further out. He saw the hospital, then the outline of San Benito, and finally he had a better sense of where in the world he was. They must have been more than sixty miles from the Mexican border. When Sebastián had mentioned going to see a friend in La Libertad, Ted had no idea where that was. He'd assumed that it, and San Benito, were towns in rural Mexico. He didn't remember crossing the border. He hadn't shown his passport to anyone. Then he remembered the helicopter flight and his escape with Quinn. They had been hovering above the border when they found the Mayan ruins. They must have landed on the Guatemalan side. He could add illegally entering a country to his list of criminal activities.

A woman behind the desk in reception called over to Ted in Spanish. He was caught off guard and completely missed what she had said. Not that it mattered as he didn't speak Spanish anyway. The woman looked at him as though he was deaf. This was obviously another occasion when his mildly Hispanic looks gave locals the wrong impression. His failure to learn the language of his grandfather let him down once more. He shrugged apologetically, before letting her know he

The Aztec Secret

didn't speak Spanish. She nodded understandingly and said in broken English, 'Your girlfriend OK.' She pointed down the corridor to the left, as though suggesting he follow it to find Quinn.

'Actually, she's not my—' Ted stopped himself before he finished his sentence. The details weren't important. What was important was that she was OK. He packed everything back into the backpack and set off in search of her room.

'*Ocho*,' the woman behind the desk called after him. Room eight. That at least was something he understood. He found the room quickly and sure enough there was Quinn, sat upright on the bed.

'How is it?' he asked, appraising the neat bandage covering her wound. He remembered the poor job he'd done of wrapping her t-shirt around it earlier.

'Not too bad,' she replied. 'They said I'll be fine.'

'I hope you have travel insurance,' Ted quipped. 'I'm not sure how much hospital fees are in Guatemala, but I doubt you want to pay for someone shooting you.'

'Guatemala?' she replied.

'Yeah,' he shrugged. 'I guess we must have landed this side of the border when you pushed me out of the helicopter.'

'Hey! I saved your life.'

'Is that what you call it?'

She looked at him with a playful smile and then a tear streamed down her face. 'I'm so scared, Ted.'

'Me too,' Ted replied. 'How did we get caught up in this?' Seeing the vulnerable look in her eyes prompted Ted's body to replicate the feeling. He'd tried his best to take everything in his stride: being bundled into the back of a van after the alarm at the museum, the gun pointed at him in the garage back in Mexico City, the chase down the back alleys, the look in Lucho's eyes as he knocked him unconscious, the escape out of the helicopter as the sound of gunshots chased his fall through the sky. Everything that had happened in the last twenty-four hours had been a new horrific experience that would have shaken Ted to his core on any given day. Having them happen one after another in the same day was something different altogether, and had taken its toll on his mental state.

He knelt beside the bed as his eyes welled up and his bottom lip trembled. He tried to fight back the tears, but they came anyway. As he wiped them away with one hand, he suddenly felt something brush his fingers on the other. Looking down, he saw Quinn's hand reaching out to his. He took it and their fingers intertwined. Her hand was a perfect fit in his, and the sensation felt comfortable, as though for a brief moment they had escaped the world and created a bubble that protected them from fear. Ted realised that he'd never felt like this before. He remembered one night at the cinema with Julia, how he'd brushed her hand, and how her fingers had twitched, before reaching into the bag of popcorn as the unexpected contact evoked a fight or flight response. Ted smiled at the memory, realising how foolish he'd been for so long.

As though responding to his facial expression, Quinn's hand squeezed tighter. He looked into her eyes, which sparkled through the tears. The way she was looking at him, in her most vulnerable state, as her fingers wrapped tightly around his, was the biggest connection Ted had felt with a woman. He couldn't explain the feeling, but it was as though he knew she trusted him completely. He reciprocated her hand squeeze, and she smiled back at him, seemingly feeling the same connection.

'What now?' he asked, his voice choked.

The Aztec Secret

She loosened her grip from his and their hands parted. 'The nurse said I'm free to go. I think it's time we go to the police.'

'You're right.' He stood up as Quinn started to shuffle towards the end of the bed. 'Oh, I almost forgot,' he said. 'I found something on the artefact.' He pulled the star-shaped object from the bag and showed Quinn the engravings that had been revealed. She took the object in her hands and stared incredulously at the shapes.

'They're so detailed,' she said.

'I thought the same. What do you think it means?'

She studied the symbols a moment, her face showing great concentration. 'The Aztecs' native tongue was Nahuatl, but it wasn't like a language that's widely spoken today. It was written down differently to how it was spoken, mostly using symbols like this.' She looked more closely at each one.

'That's a snake, right?' Ted chimed in, hoping to be of some use.

'Yes, in a way,' she replied. 'I think it's Quetzalcoatl.'

'Oh yeah, the feathered serpent,' Ted remembered. 'It looks angry. See how its mouth is open?'

Quinn nodded, moving onto the second symbol. 'This is an easy one. Tlāloc.'

'What?'

'Who,' she corrected. 'The god of rain. Well, water too.'

'That explains the water droplets next to him.'

'Yes.'

'And this last one? A cat?' Ted asked.

'Jaguar,' Quinn specified. 'The Jaguar was an important symbol in Aztec culture.'

'Oh, I knew that,' Ted kicked himself. 'The Jaguar Warriors maybe? Or the jewel, what was it called? The jaguar's heart?'

'Yes, the *Heart of the Jaguar*.'

'So, an angry serpent god, the god of rain, and a jaguar,' Ted tried to piece it together. 'This really isn't much to go on.'

A sudden commotion came from somewhere outside the room. Ted left the room and poked his head around the corner. He looked toward reception and his heart almost stopped. There, plain as day, was Eduardo. He was carrying the assault rifle that had been on the helicopter, which explained why he had caused such a ruckus with the staff. He didn't seem to be listening to whatever the staff were yelling at him, and stormed into the first room he saw. Ted bolted back inside and shut the door.

'We need to get out of here, right now.'

FIFTEEN

Ted hurried to zip the artefact into the backpack and haul it over his shoulders, worried that at any moment the Mexican mercenaries would come barging into the room.

'What is it?' Quinn asked, startled by Ted's sudden alarm.

'They found us,' he replied.

How had they tracked them down? Had they known they'd shot Quinn and searched every hospital within a twenty-mile radius? No, that couldn't be it. His head snapped into survival mode once more, and after such a short reprieve he found himself thrust into danger again.

He opened the door a crack and peered outside. There was no sign of Eduardo, but two of the doors at the far end of the corridor were open. The big brute was systematically making his way from one to the next, searching for them. Ted took stock of their options. If they made a break for it, they'd have a chance. They'd need to hope that there was a fire exit at the other end of the corridor. But there was no guarantee that Eduardo hadn't been ordered to shoot on sight now. He turned to face the room and quickly saw another option.

'The window,' he said. Quinn didn't waste any time and tried to slide the glass pane open. But it was no use, it wouldn't budge.

'It's locked shut,' she said desperately.

'Shit.' There was no alternative, they'd have to try the corridor. They waited by the door as Ted was about to crack it open again. But as he placed his hand on the handle, Eduardo's giant figure came into view through the door's glass panel. Luckily, he was facing away from them and burst into the room opposite. It was now or never.

As Eduardo entered the room, Ted opened the door and the pair bolted out and set off down the long corridor. They'd made it ten feet before Eduardo's voice shouted after them. They ignored him and continued running for their lives. Ted got a strange sense of déjà vu from the dream he'd had; being chased down a hospital corridor by an armed attacker. There was an emergency exit at the end of the corridor, as he had hoped. Eduardo fired the assault rifle into the air, smashing a light bulb on the ceiling and shattering glass just behind the pair. The noise was deafening, but they kept running until at last Ted drove all of his weight into the emergency door, setting off an alarm and almost sending him tumbling over as the door swung violently open. Then he felt an arm grab him, and before he knew it he was sent hurtling to the ground. The backpack, which had been over one shoulder, fell to his side, and a strong knee dug into his back, preventing him from getting back up.

'Enough!' Lucho spat, pointing his pistol directly into his face. It was a trap; they'd been waiting for them here. Ted looked to his left to see Quinn sprawled on the floor, clutching her injured arm. She was bleeding from her cheek. It was then he realised that Lucho had struck her. Eduardo picked her from the ground with ease and threw her over his shoulder like a disobedient child.

Lucho knelt beside Ted and his pointy nose came into full view. Ted grimaced as Carlos dug his knee harder into his back.

'*Idiota*,' Lucho hissed in his ear. He then said something Ted couldn't understand to Carlos, while Quinn kicked and screamed to get away from Eduardo. 'Today you are lucky. You leave with your life,' Lucho said to someone behind Ted. He realised it must have been Jasper. Turning his attention back to Ted, Lucho picked up the backpack and unzipped it, checking that the artefact was safely inside, before zipping it shut again and walking off. 'Don't follow, or she dies.'

Carlos took his weight from Ted's back and followed Lucho and Eduardo, who was still carrying a screaming Quinn towards a car. Ted coughed and wheezed, not having the strength to get to his feet.

'So they're just letting us go?' Ted just about managed to say, bemused as to why they were being left behind.

'She was right,' the professor said solemnly. 'Lucho was cutting me out of the deal. He said he only needed her now. Easier to keep an eye on one person over three.'

The professor hadn't exactly directed Lucho straight to the treasure, but what was he expecting? They didn't know if the jewel even existed, let alone where to find it. And now he had discarded Jasper in favour of Quinn? Ted thought back to the garage in Mexico City, how Quinn had been the one to translate the manuscript. Lucho was banking on her being able to piece together the rest.

The headlights flicked on as the battered old hatchback came to life. Quinn was still struggling to fight off Eduardo, who was sat next to her, pinning her back against the torn fabric of the rear seat with one strong arm. The tyres spun, kicking up a cloud of dust as the car tried to find traction, before lurching away. Ted had just about climbed to his feet, his back aching from the immense pressure that had been exerted on it, and watched in despair, completely helpless to stop them. The car rounded a corner with a squeal and the light disappeared, and eventually with it the sound of the engine.

'We have to go after them,' he said.

'No,' Jasper replied sternly. 'You heard Lucho. If we go after them, they'll kill her.'

'They always say that. That's just bad-guy speak.'

'Ted, I'm serious. Listen to me,' Jasper grabbed his shoulder and stared into his face. 'It's over. Let them go.'

'We can't just leave her!'

'We won't. I promise, we won't leave without her. But she's not in any danger right now unless we start acting rash. They need her, that's why they took her. She'll be OK as long as she leads them to the jewel.'

'And if she doesn't?'

Jasper paused uncomfortably.

'See, that's exactly why we can't leave her with them.' Ted began to hyperventilate. He felt utterly useless in this situation, with no plan of what to do next.

'They could have killed us, but they didn't,' Jasper reasoned. 'We have to believe they'll do the same for Quinn.'

'That's a big risk.'

'So is going after them.'

Ted let out a frustrated sound. This day was getting worse by the minute. He knew Jasper was right, but it didn't make him feel any better. He was furious with him for the danger he'd put them in. For once Ted had been excited about the prospect of actually doing something to move his career forward. And it had all been a lie. He wished they'd turned themselves into the police the first chance they got. If only he'd said something to the hospital staff, to let them know they could be in danger. Quinn would be safe, and he wouldn't have a mountain of guilt hanging over him.

He considered their options: they could go after them and risk Lucho killing them all, do nothing and hope Quinn miraculously leads him to a long-lost treasure that is only rumoured to exist, or they could seek help, either from the police or someone else. That came with its own problems too. The police could help with a kidnapping case, but would they buy the story and trust their word when they claimed innocence in their part in the museum robbery? Ted was a firm believer that the truth always came out, but the truth in this case was that Jasper was guilty. He looked to the street the car had disappeared down moments earlier. Locals that had heard the disturbance outside the hospital had gathered outside and were looking at the pair cautiously.

'You have to turn yourself in,' Ted said.

'What?' Jasper was aghast.

'It's the right thing to do.'

'Ted, I made a terrible mistake coming here, and an even bigger mistake bringing you both along with me. I promise, I'll admit to everything, but getting arrested now won't help us get her back.'

Ted could sense the remorse in his voice. He was clearly ashamed of what he'd done.

'Why did you bring us with you?' he asked. 'If you intended to ditch us at the museum, why bring us along at all?' He turned to address the professor, putting pressure on him with his body language.

Jasper said nothing and avoided making eye contact.

'You owe me the truth.'

Jasper sighed, knowing that what he was about to say would further mar Ted's opinion of him. 'It was the only way I could get approval from the university.'

It was the answer Ted had expected, but hearing it hurt all the same. 'You used us.'

'Yes. I'm sorry.'

A long silence followed. Ted felt as though nothing more needed to be said. Social situations like this had always made him feel uncomfortable, as though the apology gave the person in the wrong a sense of weakness, and he needed to reassure them that everything was OK to add balance to the equation. But something about the last day had given Ted a toughness he didn't have before. Coming face-to-face with death had a way of putting things into perspective. This wasn't like those other times when Carl had annoyed him about something trivial that he no longer remembered. This time someone who barely knew him had put his life in danger in a desperate attempt to raise his academic profile. He knew the professor's apology was genuine, but he wasn't in the mood to accept it. Not when the life of an innocent woman still hung in the balance.

Flashing lights emanated from around the corner, at the front entrance of the hospital. Ted thought it might have been an ambulance returning from an emergency, but then a pair of armed men in uniform made their way around the side of the building and approached them, one hand clutching the guns strapped to their belts. It seemed like the reception staff had called the police after all, most likely when Eduardo had barged into the building with an automatic rifle.

The officers called to them in Spanish. They seemed extremely wary, as though Ted and Jasper may also be armed.

'They went that way,' Ted said, waving his hands and pointing in the direction the car had left moments earlier. The officers called to them again, repeating what they'd said before. It was clear there was a breakdown in communication here.

'That way,' Ted gestured towards the road once more. The first officer shouted again, his hand firmly on the grip of his pistol, ready to remove it from its holster at a moment's notice.

'They think we're with them,' said Jasper, putting his hands in the air in surrender.

'With them? Can't they see we were just attacked?'

The second officer moved around behind Ted and grabbed his arm, pulling it down and twisting it. Ted let out a muffled groan as the sudden jerking motion took him by surprise. He then heard the faint crunching and clicking sound of handcuffs being tightened and felt the cold steel wrap around his wrist. His other arm was then yanked down and fastened next to the first. He eyed the man studying him carefully, hand not wavering from his gun. It suddenly dawned on him what was happening. They were being arrested.

After Jasper had been given the same treatment, they were shepherded to the police car that had been parked outside the front of the hospital. Jasper's ankle was still sore and had swollen, and he stumbled when led toward the vehicle. The moment he was bundled into the back seat was a reprieve from the pain. The pair peered out the windscreen as the two police officers got in. The lady from the reception was watching from the doorway, making sure they were escorted off the premises and the hospital could go back to normal once more.

**

The jail cell was dingy and there was an unpleasant smell coming from somewhere. This was a small, quiet town and crime was probably scaled down with the population. From what Ted could make out on being escorted to his cell, there were four or five other rooms of similar size. The door to each one was sturdy and didn't give any clues as to who, if anyone, were inside. Ted surmised that there were two possible reasons why he'd been lumped in the same cell as Jasper: either the place was overcrowded with criminals, or the authorities trusted them enough to let them share the space. They clearly looked unassuming enough that they weren't about to kill each other or plot to break themselves out. Yet they were in jail all the same, so there was something the authorities didn't trust about them.

The morning light poured in through the small opening at the top of the wall that masqueraded as a window. Horizontal and vertical bars made sure that the air came in, but the offenders didn't get out. The pair had slept a few hours, both exhausted by the events of the previous day. Ted couldn't stop thinking about Quinn, wondering where she was and hoping she was alright. But his body eventually succumbed to his fatigue and he was out for the count. A lot had happened since the last time he awoke to start a new day.

'How did he know we were here?' he wondered out loud.

Jasper was still in the process of waking up from his slumber on the hard bed. 'Hmm?'

'Lucho,' Ted clarified. 'We're miles from where we jumped.'

'Ah, I see,' Jasper had started to follow the conversation properly, the cogs of his brain whirring back into life. 'He bugged your phone.'

'What?'

'I don't know how. I struggle to understand how these modern-day gismos work.'

Ted couldn't believe it. He hadn't given the mercenaries enough credit. But that didn't explain why they'd taken so long to find him. If the phone had been bugged all along, why had it taken them until the hospital before they found them? The answer came to him with a sickening feeling. He remembered sitting in the waiting room, charging his phone before turning it on to get a bearing on where they were. Turning his phone on must have triggered the bug to send a beacon of his location straight to Lucho. If only he'd kept it off.

'So, what now?' he asked, hoping the professor had a plan.

'I don't know,' the professor admitted. 'We're going to have to figure that out.'

'Do you know where they're taking her? What happened after we left?'

'Lucho wanted to kill you both, but Carlos couldn't find somewhere safe to land and the helicopter was running out of fuel. We headed to a military base to refuel. Then a while later the tracker went off and next thing we knew we were landing in a small town in Guatemala.'

'Where's the helicopter?' Although helpless to do anything about it, Ted still wanted to have as much information as possible.

'They left it on the outskirts of town.'

'And the car?'

'Stolen. Some poor soul who was in the wrong place at the wrong time.'

Ted instinctively reached for his phone to check the time, but upon feeling his empty pocket remembered his belongings had been confiscated on arrival at the police station. Surely it was only a matter of time before someone came to interrogate them. There must be some rationale behind holding them in this cell without so much as a trial. But the longer they were in here, the further away Quinn could be. It had been hours already; they could be anywhere.

'How's your foot?' Ted asked.

Jasper rubbed his ankle, feeling the swelling all around the base of his foot. 'Not great. Hurts to walk on, but the pain isn't so bad when I'm resting it. I don't think anything's broken.'

The slit on the sturdy metal door opened with a sharp scrape and a pair of beady eyes stared inside. The figure mumbled something, before addressing the pair with a line of Spanish neither of them understood. The bolt on the door was then unlocked and it opened with a loud squeal that suggested the hinges hadn't been oiled for decades. A moment went by when the figure revealed himself as an officer. Not one of the pair that had arrested them the night before, this man was older. He stood beside the door and waited for them to move. Ted and Jasper hesitated, unsure what was happening.

'*Rápido!*' the officer called, signalling for the pair to vacate the cell. Jasper was the first to move, finally understanding what was happening. They were being set free. Ted gingerly put weight on his foot and limped to the doorway. For the brief time they were incarcerated, Ted had wondered how long they'd stay in there. As luck would have it, it wasn't half as long as he anticipated.

Another officer restored their belongings to them, and they left for the exit. No explanation or anything, it was a strange exchange. It was then that Ted recognised the face of the woman leaning against the entrance door.

Alex had her arms folded and a cautious look on her face. 'You have some explaining to do.'

SIXTEEN

Ted looked incredulously at Alex, wondering how in the world this was happening. How had she followed them and why? Had she bailed them out of jail?

'You can start by thanking me,' she said. 'If it weren't for me, you two would be in some serious shit.'

'Thank you,' replied Jasper. He eyed Ted, sensing the elephant in the room. 'Do you two know each other?'

'We met last night,' said Ted. 'She helped me find Quinn. When we saw she was in a bad way, Alex took us to a nearby village to get her patched up.'

'And then you two left as quickly as you could,' Alex finished, raising an eyebrow in suspicion.

'She'd been shot!'

'Yes, but her wound wasn't life-threatening, and I think you knew that,' Alex replied. 'There was another reason you couldn't wait to get away.'

'I don't know what you mean,' Ted played dumb. His mind raced back to when he'd been waiting outside the hotel for Alex to fetch bandages. Had she seen the artefact? Would she even know what it was? It had only gone missing from the

The Aztec Secret

museum a day ago, and it wasn't like the crown jewels had been taken from the Tower of London. How likely was it that the news of its disappearance had filtered its way into Guatemala? And for Alex to have heard about it in a village in the middle of nowhere? He tried to maintain an air of cool about himself.

'Thank you for bailing us out,' Jasper broke the awkward silence that had built up. 'But we really must be going. Our friend has been kidnapped and we don't know where they took her.'

Alex nodded knowingly. 'I saw them on my way into town. Were they the men from the helicopter?'

'Yes,' said Ted. Alex could sense that he was still wary of her.

'Let's go somewhere private so we can talk openly,' she glanced at the nearby policeman, who was just out of earshot of their conversation.

They headed outside and towards Alex's rental car in the small carpark. Ted had barely shut the door after climbing inside before he blurted out his next sentence. 'Where did they take her?'

Alex shook her head. 'First, I need to know everything.'

Ted sat uncomfortably in the back seat as Alex turned around to face him. Jasper was sat in the front passenger seat and gave Ted a look that told him to be careful. So much for wanting to turn himself in. Here he was sat next to a police officer, albeit not within her jurisdiction, and he was keeping his mouth shut.

'Alright,' he sighed, conceding that she was their best and only real option. He took out his phone, accessing the museum website and pulling up a photo of the star-shaped artefact. 'Do you recognise this?'

'Yes,' she said plainly. She confirmed Ted's fears by revealing she had seen it on the news. Ted then proceeded to tell her the full story; the university trip, the museum, Cortés' letter, the jewel, Sigma, everything. When he was done, he took a breath and waited for the response. The pair noted that she was processing this ludicrous story with extreme calm. There was only a flicker of concern on her face at the part where he'd mentioned his escape from the helicopter. Perhaps she was used to dealing with such extreme scenarios at work.

'OK,' Alex replied. 'My turn. I think your kidnappers are holed up in a house on the outskirts of San Benito. The helicopter was a dead giveaway; I doubt they have permission to leave it where they have. In any case, they're probably in one of the nearby houses. I saw two men having a smoke outside one of them.'

'What did they look like?'

'One was in the region of 6ft 4, muscular, probably around 220 lbs. The other shorter and leaner, wearing a black shirt with heavily tattooed arms. Both Hispanic.'

'Eduardo and Lucho,' Ted recognised their profiles instantly. 'It's definitely them.' Alex's description had been textbook cop. He'd never understood how police officers could estimate someone's height and weight with such close accuracy. Was that part of the training?

'We should tell the police what's going on,' said Alex.

'No, Lucho said he'd kill Quinn if we did.'

'Ted, I know it's scary, but if these men are armed, we're not going to be able to rescue her ourselves. I'm on vacation, I don't have my firearm with me. Plus, I'm Detroit police, I can't play cop here.' She intentionally left out the suspended part.

'You don't know this guy. He's dangerous.'

'He's right,' Jasper added. 'Lucho is unpredictable. If he gets wind that the police are on to him, he'll act rash. As long as he thinks he's safe, Quinn is safe. We should bide our time before we get the police involved.'

It felt strange being told what to do in a situation she had much more experience in, but Alex considered the argument. 'OK, let's do it your way, but as soon as—'

The sudden rumbling of an engine came; the familiar sound of the helicopter rotors whirring. The trio looked up to see the helicopter take off and fly over the town and away into the distance. They had already missed their chance to rescue Quinn.

**

The traffic on the motorway was backed up for a mile. The satnav informed Ramón that he still had half that distance to go before his turnoff. The morning commute to the office often consisted of sitting in traffic for far longer than he had the patience for. The gridlock gave him a moment to take a sneak peek at his phone. He opened the glove box and retrieved the burner phone he was using to keep in contact with the mercenaries he'd hired. One voicemail message awaited him. Lucho was the only one with this number; he must have news for him. He glanced at the traffic, which was still at a standstill, and punched in the command to play the message. The keys on the outdated phone fed back with loud irritating blip sounds with every press. He didn't remember mobile phones being this frustrating to use a decade ago when this model was at its height of popularity?

The message played as he held the mobile to his ear, casting a quick glance from side to side on the off chance he was sat next to a police car. All clear. Lucho's voice crackled through the speaker. He had found the students. Ramón breathed a sigh of relief. However, the next sentence brought his anxiety levels roaring up again. The idiot had let the professor go, with one of the students no less. Lucho had tried to justify it by claiming they weren't useful to the search. Ramón let out a frustrated grunt; he really had hired a bunch of amateurs. Did Lucho not realise the stupidity in his actions? He knew from previous phone conversations that Lucho had used force to make the professor cooperate, and that they were now being held against their will. The professor and his student would surely go to the police, which would expose Lucho and his men. Lucho would be questioned by police, and that rat would almost certainly give up Ramón's name. This wouldn't just be the end of his career; he could be facing serious jail time. He continued to listen to the rest of the message.

Lucho still had the other student as his guide, who was apparently more useful than the professor; the man Sigma had planted into this whole scenario for his credentials. He hoped Lucho knew what he was doing. The plan was falling apart at the seams. If he screwed this up, Sigma could pull out of the deal altogether. He couldn't allow that to happen.

This was supposed to be the start of his next big push in his career, not the end of it. He wasn't about to rot in some godforsaken prison because of the ineptitude of his subordinates. What would become of his family if he did? His wife would never forgive him. And Adriana? He dared not think.

Lucho ended his voicemail message with a promise to report back once they'd made more progress in their search. What was taking them so long? He'd understood this as a quick dig and retrieve job. Sigma had been sure that whatever was written in the manuscript found in Mexico City would

The Aztec Secret

lead them right to what he wanted. Ramón began to question Sigma's grasp on reality; there was very little evidence of this strange artefact ever existing.

He stashed the phone back in the glove box. It made him feel a little more at ease knowing it was out of sight. Should someone see the phone lying next to his more up-to-date smartphone they wouldn't know it was a link to his criminal activities, even if it did raise suspicion. But as the old saying goes, out of sight, out of mind. Except this issue would play on his mind for the rest of the day.

Finally, his lane of traffic rolled up to the slip road of his exit and he turned in at the first opportunity, squeezing past the car in front of him before the new lane had fully opened up. Work would take his mind off the mess he had got himself in. The quicker he got to the office, the better.

Fifteen minutes later, he was reversing into his usual parking spot. It was as though this was just another day. He strolled casually into the foyer, greeting the porter who opened the door for him. They exchanged brief pleasantries before Ramón was in the lift going up to the seventh floor. It was when the lift doors pinged open that things began to change. A woman greeted him before he'd exited the lift.

'*Buenos dias, Señor Villacrés.*'

Ramón eyed the woman carefully, not recognising her. '*Buenos dias,*' he replied. The woman was middle-aged, wearing a business suit and a stern expression. She had a laptop bag slung over one shoulder. An awkward moment passed, both parties waiting for the other to speak. Ramón looked around the room, noticing the strange atmosphere about the place. 'What's going on?'

'Señor Villacrés,' another voice came from a desk outside an office. His office. María, his PA, rushed out of her seat to greet him. 'This is Gabriela, from Auditoria Superior de la Federación (ASF). I sent you an email about her visit.'

'Apologies if I'm early,' Gabriela extended a hand. 'I wasn't sure what time you'd be here.'

Ramón shook her hand. 'Traffic,' he replied. The comment was intended more as an excuse than an apology for his tardiness. He looked to María, whose eyes were wide, giving off an anxious vibe. She was young and fairly new to the job, so perhaps she was afraid he'd be upset about being surprised with this meeting. But the look she gave him told him there was something not right here.

'Will you please excuse me for a moment?' he tried to buy himself some time to get a handle on the situation. 'I must use the restroom before we talk.' He gestured towards his office. 'María will show you to my office and get you a drink. I won't be a moment.' Gabriela seemed content with this and followed his PA to the room. Ramón wasted no time getting into the restroom and pulling his smartphone from his pocket. He unlocked it with his thumbprint and opened the email app. Sure enough, he had an email from María, received two hours prior. Ramón had been so preoccupied with other business that he hadn't checked his work email since the previous evening. He read the email, his heart rate beginning to climb as he digested the information. Just as he suspected, the General Secretary had ordered an official investigation into his work. This day was quickly spinning out of control.

This was the first time he had been subject to an investigation of this nature, and it shook him to his core. If Lucho didn't land him in prison, this certainly would. He needed to find a way out of this. If the ASF found evidence of some of the underhanded deals he'd conducted over the years, Alina Cicerón would make sure he was in handcuffs by the end of the day. He'd slipped up having the meeting with her

The Aztec Secret

the previous day. In hindsight, he never should have scheduled it. He triggered the motion sensor on the sink and ran his hands under the water. He dabbed the top of his forehead where it was starting to sweat, the cold water cooling him down and getting his head in the game. First thing's first, he needed to at least appear like an innocent man for this meeting.

Ramón entered his office to see Gabriela sitting patiently at one end of his desk. He made his way past her and to his seat just as María brought through a coffee for him. She placed it delicately beside his keyboard. Gabriela had already finished the glass of water in front of her, and the subtle glance at her watch was telling enough that she was keen to get things moving. Ramón spotted an opportunity.

'I'm so sorry to keep you waiting,' he said. 'Do you have a lot of other meetings today?'

'It's no bother,' Gabriela replied. 'I have plenty of time.'

'Perfect,' he flashed a grin and reached for his mug. 'So, how can I help you?' He took a sip of the hot coffee and lazily put it back down on the edge of his desk.

'As I'm sure you've been informed already, I've been sent by the ASF to conduct an audit of this office. It's a routine audit, nothing to worry about.'

Ramón's hand twitched. They both knew this wasn't a routine investigation. He maintained an air of confidence, sitting upright and trying hard not to give away any obvious signs of worry. 'I see. What kind of things will you be auditing?'

'Finances, transactions, contracts, that sort of thing,' she replied. 'Any business that has been conducted from this office, we just need to take a look to ensure everything is OK.' By 'OK', she meant above board. Ramón was a shrewd businessman, but he was sloppy in the admin department.

There would certainly be an audit trail of some of the less-than-legitimate transactions in his inbox alone. Previously, his superiors had been well aware of some of these deals and didn't bat an eyelid. There was an unspoken agreement between them that was always respected. If it benefitted the party and never made its way into the public eye, it was OK. Nobody had ever formally approved it, but the mutual understanding was clear. He had done a good job of keeping everything under wraps and had never needed to cover his tracks. Until now.

'I'm more than happy to help facilitate anything you need,' he lied. 'But this is the first time I've heard of such an audit. Are they conducted regularly?'

Gabriela gave a wry smile. 'Every couple of years, usually. Like I said, it's standard practice and nothing to worry about. We don't like to create tension in the office, so we organise them directly with the Governor of each state. It rarely filters down from there.' She looked him dead in the eye. 'I understand you've only been at this post for six months, is that correct?'

Ramón nodded. She was good. 'Well then, how can I be of service?'

Gabriela retrieved a document from her laptop bag and handed it across the desk. Ramón took it and scanned the front page. 'It's just the official paperwork I have to provide to put the audit on record,' she said. 'Everything we need is detailed there.'

Ramón scanned the contents. Access to emails, files, phone call records, everything. He couldn't refuse; that was as useful as painting 'guilty' on his forehead. He would need to get creative to get through this unscathed. He took another sip of his coffee and pulled a bitter face. 'I think María forgot to add sugar.' He picked up the landline phone and punched a number on speed dial. Within seconds of making his request his PA came back into the office with a surprised, yet apologetic look on her face.

'Sorry, Señor Villacrés, I thought I had—'

Ramón seized his opportunity. As she rounded the side of his desk, he knocked the mug, sending hot coffee everywhere. It seeped into his keyboard and, more importantly, the desktop computer. María gasped as her blouse was sprayed with specks of the brown liquid. That would leave a stain. Ramón jumped up and cursed in false anger. It was a cheap move, and one Gabriela probably saw right through, but it achieved his goal. He'd be able to stall for a while longer.

'I'm so sorry!' María was mortified. She rushed out of the office, returning seconds later with a box of tissues. She began to blot the spilt coffee in an attempt to rectify the situation.

'It's OK, it was an honest mistake,' Ramón took advantage of his PA's fear of him and promptly pinned the blame on her. 'My apologies, Gabriela. My assistant is new.' Gabriela looked at him in disbelief and Ramón could imagine exactly what she thought of him in that moment. 'I will need my tech team to look at my computer,' he continued. 'I'm afraid I will be useless in your investigation until I have it working.'

'On the contrary,' Gabriela retorted. 'I don't wish to take up any more of your time, Governor. I should be able to find everything I need via your server. I will speak with your IT team about accessing this remotely.' She gave him a knowing smile, like a chess player moving her queen in line with his king. 'It will save you the trouble.' She didn't enjoy putting innocent people under undue stress, which made her job difficult some days. However, there were times when she would discover a rat in an organisation, and from this discussion alone she had the feeling she'd discovered the rat king standing in front of her. She had no doubt there was something amiss here and it wouldn't take her long to find out Ramón was guilty of all manner of sins. She would enjoy putting him behind bars, even just to give María the opportunity to have a better boss.

She stood up to leave. Pausing at the doorway, she left a stinging imprint on the Governor of Coahuila. 'I'll be in touch, Governor. Have a lovely day.' She then turned to María. 'Thank you for the drink.'

Ramón watched her leave, once again feeling powerless. The moment she disappeared as the lift doors closed behind her, his mind began scrambling for his next move. If he were to cover his tracks, he would need to start right away. Emails and documents could be destroyed, but would there still be a trace on the server? And the finances wouldn't add up if some transactions weren't accounted for. He would need to create false accounts and backdate them without raising suspicion. For this he'd need help, but luckily for Ramón he knew just who to call.

SEVENTEEN

The rental car pulled up outside the collection of buildings where the helicopter had been resting minutes earlier. Quinn and her captors were long gone, leaving the others with no clue as to where they were headed. Alex had acted instantly on seeing the helicopter fly overhead, turning the engine on and slamming the car into gear to race to the hideout that had just been vacated. If they were going to find any clue as to where they were going, it would be there.

'We need to be on our guard,' she said as she eyed the building. 'One of them might still be here.'

'I doubt it,' replied Jasper. 'From what I know of Lucho, he goes full steam ahead at the first sign of a lead. They only came here for Quinn. They aren't coming back.'

'What makes you so sure?'

'Lucho had enough of me. I failed to locate the treasure, so he discarded me and took her instead.'

'Will she have better luck?'

'Finding a jewel that's been lost for over five-hundred years? And that's even if it really does exist.'

'You're sceptical?'

'Trust me, I more than anyone would love it to be true. But I'm a realist,' Jasper said.

Alex was still eyeing the building, working an angle on how they'd enter. 'Well, we won't know for sure until we go inside. If someone is still there, we could be in trouble.'

She pointed out the building she'd spotted the Mexican mercenaries smoking outside, and they approached the entrance cautiously. The door was open a crack, just enough for Alex to peer inside. The inside was dark, as though the place had no windows to let the light through. An uneasy feeling grew inside her; this had all the makings of an ambush.

She pushed the door open in stages, bit by bit getting a sense of the room inside. The interior looked akin to a small warehouse, possibly used to store materials at one time. She couldn't hazard a guess as to what for; her knowledge of the history of trade in the local area was zero. As the door opened fully and let more light through, she could see that the place was abandoned.

'You think she found where the treasure is then?' Ted asked.

Alex raised an eyebrow. 'I thought you just said it's been lost for five-hundred years? Professor, if someone of your experience had no luck locating this jewel of yours, how would a student simply discover it?'

'She is an extraordinary young woman,' Jasper countered. 'For her inexperience in years, she more than matches me in her knowledge of Mesoamerican culture and history.'

'That may be, but it's a bit of a stretch to go from history buff to discovering an ancient artefact.'

'You're right, it's not just about history,' Ted interjected. 'Maybe she solved the problem. It's like one of those escape rooms. You find the clues, solve the riddles and escape. It's not necessarily a knowledge thing, it's a mindset. A knack for solving puzzles.'

'Expert treasure hunter now, are we?'

'That's not what I'm saying.'

'So, you think she found it?' Alex asked. The question seemed genuine.

'That, or she's been forced to make a decision and taken a guess,' said Jasper. 'Either way, we need to find out where they've taken her soon.'

The trio spread out and searched the warehouse. The place was mostly an empty room, save for a few leftover crates and boxes from whatever it was last used for.

'Why did you come after us?' Ted asked.

'Aren't you glad I did?' she teased.

'Of course, that's not what I meant.'

'I know what you meant. And I think you know the answer. You seemed quite keen to hide that artefact you have in your bag and while I was brushing my teeth this morning it suddenly clicked that it was the same one I'd seen on the news.'

'So, you came to turn us in?'

'I don't know,' she said. 'I thought I should at least find out why you had it. The detective in me.' She felt a sense of longing with that addition. The detective in her? Was she kidding herself? The way her career was going, that was nothing more than a pipedream. She was lucky to still be on the force.

'And now?' Jasper added, eager to know where they stood with her.

'I haven't decided,' she replied plainly.

Ted and Jasper shared an uneasy look, before busying themselves with their search of the warehouse. They searched for another ten minutes, finding no evidence left behind by the Mexican captors. Ted had pinned his hopes on there being at least something for them to go on. Any clue would be better than nothing. He started to get agitated.

'We're going to have to solve it ourselves,' he said. 'But I don't even know where to begin.'

Something kicked off Ted's shoe and skittered across the dark floor. It rested in the stream of light that poured through the doorway. A flash of metal caught his eye and he recognised the outline of a keyring. Holding it up in his hand, he noticed that the item dangling from it belonged to Quinn.

'It's hers,' he announced. The UV pen light he'd teased her about in the museum. It must have fallen off her set of keys. This confirmed beyond any doubt that she had been there. He held it for a while, as though either studying the detail on it, or wondering what to do with it. To the untrained eye the pen looked like something that would belong in a ten-year-old's pencil case. But Ted had recognised the white dot on the other end, from which a UV light would emanate once switched on. He'd had one of these pens when he was a child, back when he and his friends would leave secret messages for each other on top of the desks at school. It was fool proof; the messages left no visible trace, and they'd shine the light on them when the teacher had their back turned to the whiteboard.

'Well, if we catch up to her you can return it,' said Jasper.

It was in that moment that a thought struck Ted like a bolt of lightning. He studied the end of the object. The pen lid had been removed. Someone had used it while they were here. Someone who didn't want their message to be seen in the light of day. Quinn.

He turned it around in his hand and twisted the two ends to turn on the UV light. It came on to reveal a dim purple

The Aztec Secret

glow on the ground immediately in front of him. He got down on all fours, scanning the floor with the light. Nothing there.

Alex and Jasper were wondering what on earth he was doing, but quickly cottoned on when he turned on the spot and they saw the ring of purple light.

'Over there,' Alex was one step ahead. She pointed to the corner of the room furthest from the door. Ted nodded and sprang up, before racing over to the area. There was a cluster of muddy footprints there, signifying a location of high traffic.

'Where in particular?'

'Against the wall, I would say,' Alex suggested. He shone the light onto the wall a foot off the ground. Still nothing. He moved the pen around from left to right, but couldn't see any writing. The light glowed in such a concentrated spot that it would take ages to scan the entire place.

Suddenly, Jasper was looking over his shoulder. 'Hang on,' he said, gesturing for Ted to hand the pen over to him. He didn't wait long before snatching it from his hands anyway. 'If she wrote on the wall, she'd have had to have been facing it. Whoever was watching her would have seen her writing. To do it inconspicuously, she'd have had to have been sitting down in a normal position. Which would restrict her writing arm to—' he paused as he pointed the light onto the floor. 'There.'

The trio looked in astonishment at the small white letter that had been revealed. Jasper shone the UV light slowly over the letters to reveal the message in its entirety. The handwriting was appalling, probably owed to the fact that Quinn had needed to scribble the message without looking at what she was doing, so as not to raise suspicion. There were just two words scrawled onto the floor.

Misol Há

Ted stared at the words with a perplexed look on his face. 'I don't understand,' he said. He turned to Jasper for help. He too looked confused.

Alex read the words out loud, and then again, as though the sound might conjure up recognition. 'It does ring a bell actually,' she said. 'But I can't place it.'

It then occurred to Ted that he could search the phrase on his phone. He had one bar of signal, which was good enough, but the slow connection served to add an element of frustration into the mix. He waited for the search result to load, the little spinning wheel promising progress while the page remained blank.

'That's right!' Alex found her eureka moment as the right memory was suddenly triggered. 'It was something the bartender had said. He was giving me a list of attractions I should visit. It's—'

'A waterfall,' Ted finished for her. The page had finally loaded on his phone and he was looking at a photo of a picturesque waterfall tumbling into a pool. He pulled up the location on the map app. 'It's not far from the Mayan ruins we were at yesterday.'

'So that's where they're headed?' Alex asked. 'Why?'

The answer came to Ted the moment the question left her lips. Two strings of memories became entwined in his brain, and the result was an understanding he didn't have before as he found new meaning to old information. Something clicked and he remembered the engravings on the star-shaped artefact. Quinn had recognised one as Quetzalcoatl, the feathered serpent, and another as Tlāloc, the god of rain. Then he remembered the song that Doña Marina would sing, and Cortés had mentioned in one of his notes to his son.

The Aztec Secret

Passing swift, this fleeting life
Your path is set, you must go
When the eagle soars, the jaguar roars
Your heart is offered, your body is done
And they take your spirit to the temple
Where the serpent sings, and the gods will cry
For eternity, they cry

'Where the gods cry for eternity,' he mumbled to himself.

'From the song?' Jasper remembered, intrigued.

'Yes,' he showed them the photo of the artefact's inscriptions on his phone, focusing on Tlāloc and the water droplets. 'It's a waterfall.'

'My God,' said Jasper. It was clear that this connection had rejuvenated his desire to pursue the jewel. 'So, you're saying it was under our nose the whole time?'

'Not just ours,' Ted smiled. 'It was right under Cortés' nose too.'

Jasper's eyes widened. The hunt was back on.

'Can somebody tell me what's going on?' Alex interjected.

'Cortés wrote a letter to his illegitimate son, Martín, and spoke of the boy's mother, Doña Marina. She was his interpreter and concubine during his invasion and occupancy of Mexico, right?' Ted looked to Jasper for validation and was met with a nod. 'He spoke fondly of her in his letter and recalled a song she would sing, parts of which translate roughly to taking your heart to the place where the serpent sings, and the gods cry for eternity.'

'The Heart of the Jaguar,' said Jasper.

Alex folded her arms, unconvinced.

'When Moctezuma II knew the Spaniards meant to overthrow him and their old way of life, he ordered his soldiers to hide his most prized jewel, so at least Cortés would never have that. Cortés' letter to Charles V mentioned that his men had pursued them south to the ends of the empire to recover it. We know from history that his right-hand man, Alvarado, was sent south anyway to continue their conquest of Central America. It's fitting that the Aztec Jaguar Warriors would choose a waterfall for the jewel's final resting place. A symbol of the death of the empire.'

'Why this waterfall, though? There are plenty of them in Mexico.'

'Geographically, Chiapas is roughly where the Aztec empire ended, and the Mayan empire began. It's true, it might not be the exact one though. If we're even on the right lines looking for one to begin with,' he added.

'In any case,' said Ted. 'That waterfall is where Quinn is leading Lucho and the others. We have to follow them.'

'Yes, you're right,' Alex agreed. 'We can't get side-tracked with this. Getting your friend back is what's important.'

Ted flicked back to the map app on the phone and began pinching his thumb and index finger to zoom out. He let out a deep sigh as the reality of the situation was setting in. 'It's three-hundred kilometres away from here. It'll take us forever to get there.'

Silence fell upon the trio. The distinctive noise of a rasping moped engine came suddenly, as a boy no older than fourteen rounded the corner at speed and flew past them on the dirt road. The boy's hands gripped the handlebars tightly as the suspension worked hard against the potholes on the uneven road surface. The noise unsettled a flock of birds who were taking shade in a tree. They scattered and flew off together in the opposite direction the boy had come from.

'Unless…' Alex had an idea.

'Unless what?'

'We don't take the car.'

EIGHTEEN

'Are you sure you can actually fly this thing?' Jasper asked apprehensively.

Like Ted, Alex had spotted the nose of the small prop plane poking out of the open corrugated iron hut on her way into San Benito that morning.

'We'll find out soon enough,' she replied, throwing the tarpaulin off one of the wings.

'That doesn't make me feel better.'

'It wasn't meant to.'

The little plane had seen better days. Ted could only wonder how long it had laid dormant in its corrugated iron shed. The shed itself was rusted to hell and the worn shell of the plane didn't inspire confidence in its ability to transport them safely. The bright yellow paintwork was chipped in places and the seams where the metal sheets met had the brown stains of rust appearing. The propeller was intact at least.

'How old is this thing?' Ted asked, the uneasiness in his voice echoing Jasper's concern that this might not be a good idea.

'1940s, I guess,' Alex replied candidly. 'It's a Piper something-or-other, American made. Can't see the model number.'

'Is that good?'

'It's not anything. It's just what it is.'

'OK.' At this point the age and condition of the plane would be much more of a factor in its performance than the reputation of the manufacturer. But he felt obliged to ask the question anyway. 'You seem to know a lot about it,' he added.

'My grandparents owned a farm. Every year they'd use a crop duster to fertilise the fields. He'd often take me for a spin and showed me how it works.'

'So, you've flown something like this before?'

'Sort of, yes.'

'Sort of?'

'I always had my grandpa there. I've not flown alone.'

Ted couldn't help but let out an involuntary gulp. Alex was fixed on the plane, assessing it for signs of obvious damage. She then took a quick look in the cockpit and let out a frustrated curse.

'We're not going to get far without the keys.' She shifted her focus to the workbench on the left side of the open shed. Various tools were haphazardly strewn about, but there was no sign of the key. Ted joined the hunt and bent down to look in case it had fallen below the workbench.

'Huh,' he said, finding something promising. 'This might be it.' He pulled a small lockbox from the ground and placed it on the bench. It had a padlock keeping it shut which required a combination to open. Four digits, each possibly being from 0-9. Ted did some quick mental maths, remembering the little information he had retained from school. Ten to the power of four. 'Ten-thousand possible combinations.'

The Aztec Secret

'Hmm.' Alex looked at the wooden box a moment, as if contemplating what the combination could be. She then reached over to the other side of the workbench and took up a sturdy looking wrench. After a quick exchange of glances with Ted, who proceeded to back away to give her room, she bashed the lock hanging from the box as hard as she could. A mighty clanging sound came as metal struck metal with ferocious force. The flimsy lock dented on one side but remained attached to the box. She hit it again, and again, until a ping rang out as the lock flew a couple of feet, narrowly missing Ted and landing on the floor.

'I suppose you're not much fun in escape rooms,' he said.

'What?'

'Never mind.'

Alex opened the lid of the lockbox, and sure enough the key lay inside. 'Bingo,' she said victoriously.

'Should we really be taking this?' Jasper asked. 'Assuming it does fly. This is theft.' His answer came from Ted this time, in the form of a stern look. The priority was getting Quinn back, whatever the cost. Compared to some of the crimes they'd already been involved in over the last two days, commandeering a neglected aircraft was fairly low on the scale. Besides, there was nobody around. The farmhouse neighbouring the shed showed no sign of activity. It was theirs for the taking, whether or not it was right to take it.

'Help me wheel it out,' Alex said. As Jasper and Ted moved to take up their position behind each wing, Alex removed the chocks from either side of the wheels. 'OK, now.' They began to push, and after a little give, the tyres moved, and the plane began to inch forward. After a few feet the tip of the plane had left the shade of the dilapidated shed. Sunlight streamed into Ted's eyes as the wings slowly entered the open air. It was a strange moment, pushing this old bird out for a venture. With every creak, it was as though the old plane were waking up from a long sleep.

Alex reached into the cockpit and turned the steering wheel. The plane squeaked as it tried to fight years of stiffness. It responded and the plane began to pivot. They kept turning until it was facing in the direction of the field. This was as good a runway as they could hope for. The crops lining the field were below wing height and there was a gap between two rows just wider than the cockpit to run through. It would be a tight squeeze, but the terrain was flat enough that they'd pick up enough speed to take off. The wooden fence at the other end, however, was a little too close for comfort. Ted wasn't sure if Alex had calculated the distance correctly, but she seemed determined to try it.

Ted looked inside at the seating arrangements. He noticed an issue straight away. 'There's only two seats.'

'I know,' Alex replied. 'You two are going to have to get comfortable.'

Comfortable was not the word Ted would have chosen. He looked closer at the back seat of the tiny prop plane. Neither he nor the professor had the slightest of frames, and even if they did there was no chance of sitting side-by-side in this case. The alternative of one on top on another was the only plausible solution, but that was far from a comfortable option. Ted looked at Jasper and imagined having to sit on his lap for the duration of the flight. He suddenly had a flash back to a memory he'd long forgotten; he was five years old again and in the queue at the local village hall to sit on Santa's lap. He recalled the apprehension and awkwardness as he was made to sit on the knee of a stranger while his mother took photos with a wide smile. Perhaps it was the professor's vague similarity to the iconic character that had brought it on, with

The Aztec Secret

his grey beard and rounded belly, but Ted decided he'd avoid revisiting that moment at all costs.

'I'll go first,' he said firmly, climbing in head first. He pulled his weight over the side and toppled into the rear seat. Jasper hauled himself over next, taking a longer and more careful approach to ease himself in on top of Ted. As he let go of the side, Ted felt the full weight of the man on his thighs and abdomen. The sudden pressure on his bladder made him realise he needed to pee. He'd have to wait until they landed now.

Alex hopped into the front seat effortlessly and shut the cockpit behind her. The sound from outside was suddenly shut off as they were cocooned inside, and the moment brought everyone's attention to what was about to come. The anticipation was palpable as Alex kissed the key for luck, before inserting it into the ignition and turning. The engine started and the plane whirred into life, like a confused and groggy patient waking up from a long coma. The controls were clunky, but they responded to Alex's commands. The propeller began to spin.

'Somebody better get their phone out to guide me,' Alex called, turning her head to the side so they could hear.

'On it,' Ted replied. He moved his arm as best he could round to his side to pat his pocket, searching for the rectangular lump in his jeans that gave away the phone's location. He prodded around until he felt it stuck under Jasper. 'Erm, can't get to it right now,' he said.

Jasper cottoned on to the situation and retrieved his own phone from the inside of his tweed jacket pocket. 'Here,' he passed the phone to Ted.

Ted was surprised by the professor's smartphone. It wasn't the latest model, but recent enough to be juxtaposed to the man who owned it. 'Nice phone, professor.'

'My daughter got it for me,' Jasper said. 'She likes to text me on that 'what's happening' app. Said I should be better at my GIF game. I don't know what that means.'

Ted cherished the man's misremembering of the app's name. He tilted it toward his face and the screen lit up, greeting him with harsh blue light. It wanted his thumbprint. Ted opted instead for the passcode. Better he knew that in case he needed to unlock it again.

'Passcode?' he asked.

'1, 2, 3, 4,' came the reply.

'1, 2, 3, 4?' Ted repeated. 'You can remember intricate details of the invasion of Mesoamerica in the 16th Century, but you can't remember a four-digit number sequence more complicated than 1, 2, 3, 4?'

The professor didn't respond.

The plane lurched forward and made its way to the entrance of the field. Alex fought hard against it to steady it on a straight path. 'This thing's got a mind of its own!' she exclaimed as they began to pick up speed.

The terrain has appeared flat at first, but the plane was bobbling and rattling away. Ted's backside became numb from the vibration. He looked out the side of the cockpit to see the world race by. He already missed solid ground and they hadn't taken off yet. He'd almost forgotten about the fence at the end of the field that was rapidly closing in on them. Alex had clocked it and was leaning back in her chair, pulling the yoke down in an attempt to raise the bird in time to clear it. The rattling grew louder still and Ted could see the fence line snaking its way from the other edge of the field into view. They were almost out of runway. With one last effort, Alex slammed her foot against the dashboard and pulled hard on the yoke. The wheels left the ground and the plane tilted

The Aztec Secret

back. It gained just enough altitude for the tyres to clear the fence, and they were airborne. Alex let out a shriek of delight.

'You two OK back there?' she asked, the adrenaline rush still strong. There was a murmur from the back seat. 'Great,' she said, guiding the plane as smoothly as she could over a cluster of trees.

**

The white noise of the helicopter was the only sound that accompanied them on their journey, which seemed to be lasting a lifetime. The three mercenaries were certainly business-first in their approach. No banter shared; no comment given on the lush scenery that passed by below. Quinn sat back in her seat, watched intently by Eduardo on the other side of the cargo hold. His stare rarely left her and she could feel his eyes burning through her as if he were a hungry animal observing its prey. The remaining parachutes had been safely stowed away on the other end of the helicopter. No more mistakes and no chance of escape this time. Lucho's orders had been clear. Do not take your eyes off her. Perhaps Eduardo had taken the command a little too literally, but there was a lot at stake. Just a few more hours and they could have what they came for.

Lucho cut a frustrated figure as he grunted and hung up the phone that had gone to voicemail. Governor Villacrés had made it clear. No messages, no traces of any kind. But Lucho didn't like to be kept waiting. If the Governor couldn't answer his phone, he would have to be the one to deal with the consequences. He punched in a concise message into the outdated SMS function and hit send. The stuttered animation of an envelope flying off into the distance played on loop until the display changed to confirm it had been sent. He then turned to Carlos to mutter something in Spanish. Quinn couldn't work out what he was saying above the noise of the rotors. The interaction was subtle, but more noteworthy than any that had happened since they left San Benito. Eduardo's attention was finally pulled away to see Carlos pointing to somewhere in the distance.

'Are we there?' Quinn called. The two up front gave no response. She looked to Eduardo for an answer, but he wasn't in the mood to give one either.

The helicopter banked around to the right and, out of the opening, the treeline of the Mexican rainforest appeared below. She caught a glimpse of the waterfall tucked between the lush tropical vegetation. Even at this height it looked colossal. The white water cascaded down in three streams into the pool below, a vague mist appearing at the bottom from the force of the water. It was strange watching it without sound.

Carlos found a clearing just wide enough for a safe landing a quarter of a mile walk from the waterfall. The place was busy, as was expected for a normal morning at a major tourist attraction. The sudden appearance of a military chopper had drawn a lot of attention, but Lucho wasn't interested in a covert entrance. Carlos switched off the engine and the rotors died down, replaced by the gradual building of water tumbling into the pool from over a hundred feet high. Eduardo picked up the assault rifle in readiness. Lucho hissed something in Spanish and the big man put it down again. The exchange was pretty clear; whilst their entrance didn't go unnoticed, this was a densely populated area. Strolling into the place with an AK-47 wasn't the smartest move if they wanted to keep the police away. Lucho secured his pistol behind his back, ensuring the back of his t-shirt nestled over the top to

The Aztec Secret

conceal it. Eduardo was relegated to backpack carrying duty. With that, it was time to go.

Despite arriving unannounced and leaving a small aircraft without permission, they weren't given the time of day when they arrived at the site. They entered on the tail end of a tour, but the guide didn't question their sudden appearance. Either they knew not to ask questions they didn't want the answer to, or they were too preoccupied to notice them tagging along.

The moment she saw the waterfall the way it was meant to be seen, from the bottom looking up, Quinn was lost for words. The tour guide began to shout in English and then Spanish, reciting their scripted commentary over the roar of the water. The sight was even more majestic from this viewpoint. As she looked up at the white sheets of water pouring down from the top, she sensed what everyone else felt when they came here. When she'd looked up the waterfall online, the photos gave away its beauty. But it wasn't until you experienced it in person - the sound and the spray of misted water as you reached the edge of the pool - that you appreciated it in full. The whole atmosphere that this natural beauty created in its little corner of the rainforest evoked a deep respect for Mother Nature. She opened the camera bag she had slung over one shoulder. She had left it on the helicopter before her parachute escape with Ted. Lucho had allowed her to take it with them, if only to add detail to their guise as tourists in this place. She switched the DSLR on and peered through the lens to snap a shot of the majestic scene. If she managed to get out of this situation, she would make damn sure she got some souvenirs to make it worthwhile. The top of her arm twinged and she almost dropped the camera. The flesh wound was still painful. She tried once more to look into the lens. Isolating herself through the view of the camera lens, she looked at the waterfall and remembered part of the song Cortés had quoted in the letter to his son: the whole reason she had brought them here.

Where the serpent sings, and the gods will cry
For eternity, they cry

It made her wonder what the Aztec warriors thought of this place. Did they know it to be the marvel of nature it was, or did they think it was actually the water god, Tlāloc, manifested in the form of an endless stream of tears? She played around with the aperture and exposure a while until she got the shot she wanted. She'd edit it when she got home. *If* she got home.

A strong hand gripped her non-injured shoulder, startling her. She turned to see the towering Eduardo looming over her. He gestured towards the waterfall and the path leading up to the cave behind it. While the waterfall was the focal point of this attraction, Quinn had a hunch that the Aztec warriors would have hidden the jewel inside the cave. Tour groups were entering the cave one at a time, but it seemed there was constant foot traffic entering and exiting throughout the day. They wouldn't be able to snoop around too much before someone grew suspicious.

A group had just returned from the cave and were heading back towards the pool for a quick swim before continuing their tour, quite possibly to the Mayan ruins at Palenque. The group they had tagged onto the back of were next to see the caves. Lucho muttered something to Carlos, who nodded and approached the tour guide. Lucho led the others up the path to the cave, as Carlos shook the guide's hand, exchanging a roll of notes in the process. A short exchange followed and the guide's eyes lit up as he made a quick judgement of the amount of cash that'd been handed

The Aztec Secret

his way. He accepted the offer and made an announcement to his group that they would be taking an extended break before entering the caves. This would buy Lucho and co time to explore undisturbed.

Walking behind the waterfall alone brought a feeling of adventure and discovery, as though they were taking a look behind the scenes. Water sprayed in Quinn's face, causing her to squint until they entered the cave behind. Upon entering, she quickly realised that the cave behind the waterfall was actually a cluster of winding tunnels. The jewel wouldn't be in plain sight, meaning there was likely some tunnelling to do before they reached its hiding place. But which tunnel was the right one? Lucho pulled out a torch and flicked it on, shining it from one wall up to the ceiling and then over to the wall opposite. There were no obvious clues, not that they could expect any.

'Perhaps we should spread out, cover more ground,' Quinn suggested.

Lucho didn't drop his attention from the walls of the cave. 'No,' he replied. 'No more mistakes.' He knew that splitting up would give her a better chance of escape if she could somehow get Eduardo to drop his guard. They moved deeper into the cave, the noise of the waterfall dying down as they rounded a corner.

Ten minutes later, they had explored every tunnel. There was still nothing of note that gave away even the faintest evidence of Aztec activity here. No carvings on the walls, no small openings to explore. Despite being deep into Mayan territory, there wasn't even evidence of their civilisation here. It had been a long shot anyway.

'Where now?' Lucho looked to Quinn for directions. She shrugged her shoulders, much to Lucho's frustration. 'You said it is here,' he said expectantly.

'If it were that easy, don't you think someone would have found it already?' she countered. 'There are tourists coming in and out of these caves every day.'

'Where then?' Lucho asked impatiently.

'I don't know.' She could sense his growing impatience and sought to play on it. But she was walking a very thin line and would need to be careful. Every minute she wasted brought her closer to expendable status, but it would buy Ted and Jasper more time to catch up to them. She hoped they'd got the police involved by now.

'Perhaps we should check each one again, in case we missed something?'

Lucho pondered her suggestion a moment, scratching the little patch of hair under his bottom lip. 'OK,' he agreed. Quinn exhaled deeply, relieved that she'd bought herself a little more time. Suddenly, the clicking sound of metal echoed around the cave as Lucho cocked his gun, loading a bullet into the chamber. He levelled the gun right at her, and Quinn's face went white as a ghost. 'But we don't leave without the jewel.'

Lucho was insane to still think this wild goose chase would yield treasure, but the message was clear. If she didn't lead them to an ancient artefact which was quite likely the work of fiction, she was going to die. She began to tremble as the reality of the situation sunk in.

They retraced their steps, going from cave to cave. Once again, they found nothing. Stalagmites protruded from the floor and the widest cavern had long stalactites hanging from the ceiling. Still, nothing that gave away anything other than the cave's natural formation. Approaching a cluster of rocks, Quinn disturbed a critter which scrabbled away. She jolted at the unexpected movement. She was not usually one to be phased by insects, but to say the fear of death had put her on edge was a severe understatement.

Finally, they reached the tunnel furthest from the opening by the waterfall. Quinn began to sob, knowing this was the end of the line. She desperately looked around the cave, hoping to find something, anything. But her hopes quickly faded as it was as empty as the last time they looked. She began to hyperventilate, anticipating what was to come. Lucho had his gun drawn and ready and she could sense that a part of the crazed man had been hoping for this outcome. She placed her back flat against the wall and watched as Lucho approached, Eduardo and Carlos on either side of him. She closed her eyes, not wanting to stare down the barrel again. Before he brought the gun up, a cold tingling raced through her. Could this be her soul leaving her body in its final moments of life? The tingling came stronger, lifting the hairs on her arms. She recognised the feeling as a cool breeze. The breeze intensified and a faint noise bounced around the walls of the cave. It started as a quiet whistling but soon grew to a louder, more distinct howl. The wind swept in from outside and enveloped the interior of the cave in sound. This corner of the series of tunnels seemed to have the best acoustics for it. Quinn's eyes widened as she realised the significance of what was happening.

'Listen!' She got the attention of the mercenaries, who stopped in their tracks to hear the noise.

Lucho and Eduardo exchanged confused glances, but Carlos was one step ahead of them. He remembered what she had told them when pointing out Misol-Há as a potential resting place of the jewel; the excerpt from the letter.

'Where the serpent sings, and the gods will cry,' Carlos recited. 'Quetzalcoatl, the winged serpent.'

'The god of wind,' added Quinn.

Carlos scanned the rock face behind Quinn with his torch. 'This is the place.'

NINETEEN

María sheepishly poked her head around the corner of Ramón's office. 'Señor Villacrés, I'm going to take my lunch break now.' The Governor sat quietly behind his desk, where he'd been since the meeting with the woman from the ASF. He didn't so much as look up to acknowledge her. The narrowed eyes and furrowed brow that made up his usual sullen concentration face was replaced by a glazed look, as though his mind were a million miles away. María was wary of repeating herself, afraid her boss might snap. She'd been working with him just long enough to recognise the signs that he didn't want to be disturbed. But the look on his face gave her an inkling that this time it was different.

'Is everything OK?'

Ramón looked up at her with wide eyes, as though snapped awake from a dream. 'Yes, of course. Be back in an hour.'

María forced a polite smile and left. The blunt offhand comment on her timekeeping was in keeping with his usual belittling nature, but she knew something wasn't right. And

Ramón could sense it too. He knew full well that María was suspicious. Of what, he was sure she had no idea. But there was enough nervous energy emanating from her that he could smell it. Better he kept her in the dark. One would argue that he didn't want to implicate her and was trying to protect her if things went south. But the truth was something altogether different. Ramón simply didn't trust her. This feeling was completely unwarranted, as she'd proven herself to be more than trustworthy in the time they'd worked together. But he suspected her moral compass pointed a lot truer than his, and with such information, people could be unpredictable. That was one stress he could do without.

He heard the tapping of her heels enter the lift and the doors close behind her. It wasn't until then that he reached into his desk drawer for the burner phone. Immediately after the meeting with Gabriela, he'd called his former boss, Miguel. Now retired, Miguel spent most of his time sipping tequila in the sunshine of his beach house in Riviera Maya. But he was always happy to field the odd call to impart wisdom on his old protégé. Most of that wisdom came in the form of negotiation tactics and playing the system. But when Ramón had called his old boss, Miguel's wife had answered. Miguel had gone fishing and would be back at lunch. Ramón had declined to provide a number on which he could call back. Any ties back to a phone he would throw away by the end of the week would be dangerous; something Miguel had taught him.

He went back to his previously dialled numbers and pushed the button to redial. He'd set up the phone to mark all outgoing calls as withheld. Someone who knew what they were doing would still be able to trace it back, but the chances of that happening were slim.

The phone rang on a while before the receiver clicked on.

'¿Bueno?'

'Miguel,' Ramón cut to the chase. 'I need your help.' He leaned to one side to get a view of the corridor outside his office, as though checking for eavesdroppers.

'Give me the details,' Miguel understood the urgency and forgave the lack of pleasantry.

He quietly caught Miguel up on the situation. After he finished, there was a long pause, and for a moment Ramón thought the line may have been interrupted. After a few more moments of uncertainty, Miguel's voice crackled through the receiver.

'Write down this number,' he instructed.

'Hang on,' Ramón fumbled around his desk for a pen. He eventually found it on the floor; remnants of the destruction he'd caused when he knocked the coffee over. 'OK.' He listened intently and scribbled the digits down on the back of a receipt.

The ten-second silence had been all the time Miguel needed to offer a solution. Five years into retirement, it was if he had never stopped working. Ramón had a hunch he never really had.

'I have a contact who can work with you to create false accounts,' Miguel continued. 'Call that number. She will fix your problem.'

'She?' Ramón couldn't prevent his deep-rooted sexism from escaping in his surprised tone.

'She is the best in the business,' Miguel replied. 'You need to provide her with details of every deal you've made that would be flagged up in the investigation. She will delete these records and replace them with legitimate transactions, backdated. The books will stay balanced.'

'You're sure of this?'

'It is not the first time I've done this,' said Miguel.

Ramón had no choice but to trust his judgement. 'How do I address her?'

'No names. No trail. She is a professional, you understand?'

'I understand,' Ramón bit his lip. He remembered why he didn't call Miguel for anything more than business. The only man more condescending than himself was the man who made him this way.

'I'll tell her to expect your call,' Miguel said. 'Just give her the information she asks for and that's it.'

'And what about payment?'

'I will deal with this. But you will owe me a favour.'

A favour. Miguel's way of letting him know he still had power over him, even from retirement. The man was devious, yet a shrewd businessman.

'No need. I can pay for this myself,' Ramón negotiated.

'No trail,' Miguel reminded him. 'It would look suspicious if a transaction of this nature arose on the day you were told your department was under investigation.'

Ramón contorted his face, realising he had him right where he wanted him. A favour. Ramón pondered how this would come back to haunt him in the future. It could be years from now and Miguel probably didn't yet know what form this would take. But if he knew Miguel, when the time came it would hit more than just his wallet. Still, better than being jailed before the week was out.

'Fine,' he conceded.

His other phone lit up on the desk. The sudden light was distracting, and he instinctively glanced at the display to see the preview of the message that had flashed up. It was his wife reminding him of Adriana's piano recital that evening. His heart sank; he'd forgotten. He'd been so preoccupied with the stress of the last couple of days.

The Aztec Secret

'So, it's settled,' said Miguel. 'I'll make the arrangements.' Ramón didn't reply.

There was no way he could leave the office early enough to make it. He had years' worth of illegal transactions to cover up. He knew well that the ASF wouldn't be satisfied with only the records of his current posting as Governor of Coahuila. They'd go as far back as possible to find something on him. He would need to be one step ahead of them, but it would be a huge undertaking.

'You had better call that number I gave you,' Miguel prompted, satisfied he had what he wanted and eager to get back to his afternoon in the sun.

Patricia would kill him if he missed the recital. Their marriage was already on the rocks and had been for some time. There were a number of contributing factors: working late and on weekends, missing family dinners, not to mention the woman he'd spent the night with two years ago. She'd forgiven him, with time, but he knew she'd never truly got over that. How could she?

He did want to be a better father, sure. A better husband, too. But his family didn't understand the importance of his work. Granted, not every day was a crisis, but he was working toward something big. The party needed to win the election. Nothing else mattered.

'Ramón!' The voice came through strong on the receiver.

'I'm here,' he replied, shaken by the sudden noise. He searched his short-term memory for the words Miguel had last spoken while he was lost in thought. He recovered them and initiated the end of the conversation. 'I'll call her right away.'

Miguel put the phone down before he had a chance to. It was petty, but the move was yet another power play by his old mentor.

There was a knock at the door and María returned with two polystyrene containers. He couldn't see what was inside, but there was steam coming out the top and the smell was enticing. She placed one on the end of his desk.

'I thought you might be hungry,' she said, leaving the room with her portion. Ramón was still holding the burner phone in his hand. He looked at the origin of the aroma and saw that it was mole poblano mixed with what looked like pulled chicken. María had left him a plastic fork and a tortilla to dip into it. He tucked into the food, momentarily losing himself in the rich and spicy flavour. Good food had a way of distracting him from whatever was on his mind. Whatever ate away at him would disappear for a moment while he ate away at something delicious. It was a wonder he'd missed so many homecooked meals in favour of work; his wife was an excellent cook.

Mopping up the remnants of sauce with the tortilla, he sat a moment to savour the taste in his mouth. The moment was a brief reprieve, but it was time to get back to work. He washed the rest down with a glass of water, as though he were cleansing both his palate and his mind to get back into work mode. He picked the burner phone back up from the desk and began to dial the number Miguel had given him. But a thought hit him unexpectedly. He made his way to the doorway addressed María, who was on the phone.

'Gracias,' he said quietly, so as not to disturb her conversation. She caught his eye and beamed a warm smile. Ramón returned to his desk with renewed energy and continued punching in the numbers on the phone. Perhaps his wife had been on to something when she told him food was good for the soul.

His thumb had barely left the green call button before a voice came from the other end of the line.

The Aztec Secret

'*¿Bueno?*' the woman said. Her voice sounded bored, as though the call was already an inconvenience. Perhaps she was doing something on her phone when the incoming call popped up on the screen.

'Miguel gave me this number.' Ramón paused, wondering if he'd already said too much by using Miguel's name. There was a brief silence on the other end, which only added to his growing worry.

'Are you on a secure line?' the woman asked.

'I don't know,' Ramón said candidly.

The woman made a sound that Ramón recognised as an annoyed exhale. Miguel had said nothing about a secure line. While making him feel stupid, the fact she'd mentioned it inspired confidence that she knew what she was doing. Another short pause followed.

'OK, tell me what you need,' she said at last. Either she had got over her need for a secure line, or she had taken steps to ensure it was the way she wanted it. Ramón didn't know if that were even possible. He began to brief the mysterious woman on the situation, as he had done with Miguel. Although this time he was a bit more cryptic and chose his words very carefully. He trusted Miguel's judgement in this woman's ability to fix his problem, but he didn't trust her with the details of it. Not that it mattered; she'd learn as much as she wanted to soon enough after he followed her instructions to grant her remote access to the systems he used. 'Untraceable' was the word she'd used when he expressed concern at allowing an unknown into the government archives. He hoped it was as advertised, or this act alone would land him in prison.

Twenty minutes later and the call was over. The woman was satisfied she had everything she needed to complete the job and reiterated that if Miguel had set this up, payment was taken care of. Ramón wondered how often his former boss requested the services of this woman. Regardless, he finally felt at ease that he could get one monkey off his back. Now all that was left was to ensure the idiots he'd hired delivered the goods he'd promised to Sigma.

TWENTY

Ted's legs had gone numb from the weight of Jasper sitting precariously on his lap. The flight had been one of the most uncomfortable experiences of his life, and he was grateful to feel the slow descent as they reached their destination. After a nerve-wracking takeoff, the flight had been surprisingly smooth, considering this was the first time Alex had flown solo. Nevertheless, Ted hated being in the air and longed to return to solid ground.

There was activity from the front seat as Alex turned to the pair. 'I see the waterfall.'

'About bloody time.' Jasper was clearly feeling no different from Ted in this situation.

'Any sign of Quinn?' Ted enquired. 'Do you see the helicopter?'

'No, but it's hard to get a full view from this height. Better we find somewhere to land and take it from there.'

Ted couldn't agree more.

Alex banked the small plane around to the right, guiding it in wide circles as it gradually dropped in altitude. Ted caught a brief glimpse of the waterfall, but before he could take in the full scene the sun bounced off the aircraft canopy and into his eyes. It was a beautifully clear day, but as was typical with British tourists visiting more exotic countries than home, the bright sunlight quickly became something to shy away from. Added to the fact that there were three bodies in an enclosed space only built for two, it was baking hot inside the cockpit.

Alex found a clearing to land in and the wheels bounced off the ground before the small craft rumbled to a stop. Ted breathed a huge sigh of relief. Alex had barely popped open the canopy before Jasper clambered out. Ted helped to push him over the top, before watching him tumble to the ground. Jasper let out an audible groan of pain as he hit the deck.

'Your ankle OK?' Alex hopped effortlessly from the plane to see to him.

'I'm OK,' he replied, getting slowly back to his feet. He was moving more freely than the previous day, and he was convinced that his injury was nothing more than a twisted ankle, or at worst a sprain. Nothing he couldn't overcome, but it was still swollen and painful enough to slow his movement.

Ted sat for a moment inside the cockpit, allowing the blood to flow through his legs once more. He had been wracked with guilt ever since he had just stood by and watched Lucho and his men take Quinn away. But at that moment his desire to put things right was overridden by his lack of mobility from the waist down. A bead of sweat dripped from his hair into his lap as he leaned over to rub some life back into his thighs. The cool air from outside was welcome, but Ted knew it wouldn't be long before he was feeling hot and bothered again. The weather had been gorgeous since they arrived in Mexico, and it must now have been reaching almost thirty degrees Celsius. For someone used to much cooler temperatures and the frequent rain showers in April, these were difficult conditions to cope with.

The Aztec Secret

Alex appraised the pair, wondering how on earth these two had got so mixed up in all this. They had their work cut out if they were going to find a way to catch up to Quinn and get away unscathed. What was their plan exactly? Did she expect she would incapacitate three armed men by herself? Was it time to get the police involved? Her training told her that it was the smartest move. If this were happening back home, she would want the police on it in a flash. But for some reason, she was hesitant to do so. She started to wonder if she was trying to play the hero in an attempt to win back the trust of her colleagues. There was an innocent person's life at stake here; she couldn't lose sight of that. Joel had nearly lost his life because of her. What if Quinn lost hers because she didn't do the smart thing sooner? But what if in getting the police involved she actually alerted Lucho to the fact they were being tailed? Judging from Ted's account, this man was a loose cannon. Perhaps her instincts were right, and they would find an opening to rescue Quinn without raising suspicion.

Upon reaching the entrance to the waterfall it was clear that Lucho had raised suspicion all on his own. There was a large gathering of tourists chattering animatedly to each other, staring at the waterfall. As the trio grew nearer, they realised it wasn't the waterfall that had captured their attention, but the cave behind.

'Why does everyone seem panicked?' Ted asked.

A woman rushed over and began speaking to him in fast Spanish. He didn't understand a single word she said, but her tone was urgent.

'Uh, *inglés, por favor*?' he said, hoping his weak grasp of the language would trigger the right response. Luckily for him, her English was a hell of a lot better than his Spanish.

'The waterfall is closed. There is an emergency. Please,' she gestured back the way they had come.

Panic rose within Ted as he heard the words. He looked at the cave and immediately thought of Quinn. 'What happened?'

'There was an explosion. It is not safe.'

Ted's face went white. His head began to spin as he feared the worst.

Alex stepped into the conversation. 'Were there people inside?'

'Please, you cannot go in. The police are on their way.'

'Was there anyone inside when it happened?' she repeated.

'Please, you must leave.'

'She could be in there!' Ted panicked.

'Ted,' Jasper grabbed him by the arm in an attempt to calm him down, but Ted resisted. Without thinking, Ted barged his way past the woman and made his way up the path behind the waterfall. The woman called after him in vain. He ran as fast as he could up the incline and into the cave entrance. The spray from the waterfall cooled his red-hot face, but he barely registered the sensation as his mind was fixed on the situation at hand.

Entering the darkness, he pulled his phone from his pocket and switched on the torch function, illuminating the space a few feet in front of him. He charged blindly into the network of tunnels, shouting for Quinn as he went. The route through the darkness twisted and turned, and the further he went the more his panic grew. His breath became short and laboured, but he persevered. Eventually, he reached a dead end and stopped with his hands on his knees to catch his breath. Where had the explosion happened? Perhaps she was buried under a pile of rubble. He looked around to see any sign of disturbance, but there was nothing obvious.

Eventually, he heard the sound of echoing voices following him. Alex had caught up to him.

'What the hell were you thinking?' she called as she spotted him.

'There's no sign of her.' Ted ignored the question. He panted hard as his lack of fitness had presented itself to him once again.

'Ted, we need to go. It's not safe here,' she pleaded. It was unclear where the explosion had occurred, and there was no telling how much damage it had caused. They were at risk of being crushed if there was a cave-in.

'I'm not leaving until we find her.' Ted wasn't giving up. He took off further into the darkness, the light from his phone waving this way and that. 'Quinn!' he called out over and over. But it was to no avail. There was no sign of her.

Against her better judgement, Alex raced after him. The adrenaline started to kick in as the danger intensified with every step deeper into the cave. She chased after the torchlight, which seemed to dance like a firefly at midnight as Ted pumped his arms to run faster. They rounded another corner and suddenly something rumbled above their heads. A stalactite dropped from the ceiling, missing Ted by no more than a foot. Alex skidded to a halt as the sharp rock smashed into the ground just in front of her.

'Ted!' she called, her voice wavering with fear. 'We have to go, right now!'

He ignored her and carried on running. She had no choice but to follow; there was no way she was leaving him alone. Another small cluster of rocks trickled down the wall of the cave. The place had been unsettled from the explosion, and the pounding of their footsteps was making it worse.

A lone bat flew over Alex's head. She felt the whoosh of air as the animal nearly clipped the top of her hair, and instinctively ducked after the fact. 'Ted!' she cried, the light dimmer now as he increased the distance between them. She stumbled over a stalagmite protruding awkwardly from the ground, stubbing her toe painfully. Putting her hand out to stop her fall, she scraped her palm across a rock. Alex cursed aloud as she got back to her feet and set off after the fading light.

It didn't take long for her to catch up with Ted, who had stopped by a mound of rubble at the far end of the cavern. He was stood motionless, staring at the pile of rocks. He knew full well that this was the origin of the blast. If Quinn was here when it happened, she wouldn't have stood a chance. There was still no sign of her, but the rocks had piled up quite high.

Before he could say anything, Alex grabbed him by the arm and pulled him back. The sudden strong motion took him by surprise and before he knew what was happening, he was being forced back the way they had come.

'We have to look for her,' he protested.

Alex's grip on his arm didn't relax. 'It's over, Ted. She's gone.'

**

Fifteen minutes later, the police had arrived. They had cordoned off the entrance to the cave with a roll of barricade tape and shepherded the public well away from the waterfall. Ted stood among the quickly growing crowd of tourists. Clearly, the guides giving tours later in the day hadn't been forewarned of the site's temporary closure. The place was filling with more and more confused-looking holiday-goers, all muttering to each other, asking the same questions to their guides.

The Aztec Secret

Ted watched the entrance like a hawk with a solemn look on his face. It was as though by keeping a close eye on it, things might be different, and Quinn would come waltzing out at any moment. The reality of what must have happened hadn't set in yet. But the facts remained. Quinn had led them to this cave, and there was little doubt she had been in there around the time the explosion happened. Ted couldn't shake the sight of the rocks piled up high from his mind. He would be a fool not to believe she was under there somewhere.

He felt empty. As he had watched her being dragged away by those despicable mercenaries outside the hospital he knew there was a good chance he'd never see her again. To think that her life would end this way was tragic. If only he could go back in time a few days and warn her not to get on the plane to Mexico. But life didn't work like that. Hindsight was a beautiful thing, and yet so cruel. All this for a wild goose chase to find a pointless artefact that probably didn't exist. He wanted to feel angry, but that wasn't the feeling that was building inside him. It was a growing void; a pale state of nothingness that was slowly pulling him in. He didn't know Quinn very well, not to mention he'd only met her two days ago, but experiencing this whirlwind together had created a bond between them. Had Quinn felt it too? He may never know.

The police hadn't been inside the cave to assess the damage, as the risk of cave-in was still high. The tour guide that had tried in vain to prevent Ted and Alex from entering the cave was talking with an officer. She kept glancing in their direction when talking with him. Perhaps she thought the pair had something to do with it. Alex hadn't said a thing to Ted since dragging him out of the cave. He would thank her later for potentially saving his life but now didn't seem the time.

A big hand clutched Ted's shoulder unexpectedly. He flinched and spun around to see the professor staring at him with wide eyes.

'They got away.'

Ted spun to face him. 'What?' He focused on the man's blushed cheeks, while the words he'd heard evoked a reaction inside Ted's brain. It was as though Jasper had plunged into the void to pull him out.

'Quinn. Lucho and the others too.'

Ted's heart jumped into his mouth. The unexpected glimmer of hope. A thousand thoughts entered his mind, and he suddenly became aware of the sounds of the environment around him again. 'How can you be sure?'

'I just spoke with a Welsh couple in that tour group over there,' he turned to point into the crowd. Ted couldn't help but feel the reference to their nationality was superfluous, but he was too giddy to care. 'They had just arrived when the blast went off. They saw three men and a woman return from the cave sometime after. I asked about them, and they definitely fit the description.'

A wave of relief rushed over Ted. 'Thank God!'

Alex put her arm around Ted, sharing his glee with a squeeze of his shoulder. 'Any idea where they went?' she asked.

'I don't know,' Jasper replied. 'They saw a helicopter take off shortly after they exited the cave.'

'So, they found what they were looking for?' Alex suggested.

'A more likely scenario is they didn't, and they've gone somewhere else in hopes of finding it there. There are plenty of other waterfalls in this part of the world.'

'Then she's still not safe.'

'What makes you think she's safe if they find it?' Ted challenged. 'Lucho has no incentive to let her go safely. He wouldn't risk her heading straight to the police with their names and descriptions.'

'This is ridiculous,' said Alex. 'Either way, we need to tell the police now. We should have done it long ago.'

'Are you sure?' asked Jasper. 'Lucho is unstable.'

'Which is exactly why we need to call this in.'

Ted looked back at the waterfall. There was something about being in the cave that had got him thinking. The explosion wouldn't have just happened. It was almost certainly caused by Lucho and his men. But why? Was there something he hadn't seen that they had? He had been too panicked to pay much attention to what was in the cave besides a lack of Quinn.

'We have to go back in,' he said.

'No way. It's too dangerous,' Alex replied sternly.

'I'm going back in,' Ted declared. 'We have to know what went on in there.'

'Ted, there's nothing in there,' said Jasper. The professor's expression was apologetic, knowing it wasn't what he wanted to hear. 'Quinn is buying us time, that's all. She's leading Lucho from one place to the next, hoping we've been smart enough to have the police waiting for him at one of them.'

Ted scowled. He was probably right. But he had to know for sure. He looked around to the police officer who was now getting statements from the public. The Welsh couple Jasper had pointed out earlier were speaking with their tour guide, who was acting as a translator between themselves and the officer. If he was going to do it, now was the time.

'I need someone to cause a distraction,' he said.

Alex gave him a disapproving look.

'I'm serious about this,' he said. 'Please. Give me ten minutes. I'll be careful.'

'You can't just say you'll be careful. That's not how it works.'

'I'll watch out for him,' Jasper offered.

'Oh really?' Alex appraised him sceptically, noting his sudden change of allegiance in this ridiculous debate. 'And who's going to watch out for you?' she gestured to his injured ankle.

'Ten minutes,' Ted pleaded.

Alex shook her head and let out a loud sigh. 'You have exactly ten minutes. Then I'm going to drag you out again. You hear me?'

'Loud and clear,' Ted replied. 'Just give us a window so we don't attract unwanted attention.'

'I'll think of something,' she replied.

Ted and Jasper began walking to the edge of the crowd to slip away. Alex looked around for inspiration. She spotted a line of minivans parked up on the narrow dirt track leading away from the site. Moving behind one of them, she picked up a large rock from the ground, crouched down, and checked she wasn't in sight of anyone. Then, with a wide arc, she threw the rock towards the van at the very end of the line, furthest from the crowd. It connected with the roof of the vehicle with a loud thud, bouncing away with the momentum her throw had generated. The sudden irritating combination of a wailing alarm and regular bursts of a tooting horn went off. The startled crowd looked to the minivan to see its lights flashing on and off, and the police officer left his conversation to investigate. It was the perfect distraction Ted had been looking for, and he and Jasper wasted no time in navigating the path up behind the waterfall.

TWENTY-ONE

Ted strode up the pathway to the point where he was closer to the rockface than the water that poured down from overhead. Turning back the way he'd come, he looked beyond the lagging professor to watch for any sign that their advance had been noticed. The distraction Alex created had worked wonders; a small crowd had gathered around the vehicle, its lights still flashing and the horn still beeping. Ted could see the tour guide who had previously advised them to leave the area furiously pointing a set of keys at the minivan, trying to kill the alarm. Most importantly, the police officer was facing away from the waterfall. The success of the plan hinged on this very detail. So far so good.

The cooling spray of the water greeted Ted on entry to the cave. He wiped his brow and peered in, his other hand rummaging for his phone in his pocket. He got hold of it and pressed his thumb against the home button, waiting a brief moment for the scanner to validate his thumbprint and unlock the device. Jasper had just caught up and did the same on his phone. Soon they both had their torch apps on and the whole cavern was lit up in bright white light.

'What are we looking for?' Jasper asked curiously.

'The far corner, at the end of the tunnel,' Ted was flicking his torch between the entrance of two tunnels. He eventually settled on the one to the left. 'This way.'

A few minutes later the pair were stood in front of the pile of rocks that were left by the explosion. The sound of the wind whistled through the cave, and the hairs on Ted's arm stood on end.

'Let's be quick,' said Jasper. 'It's already too dangerous being here.'

'Give me a minute,' Ted replied. He moved closer to the rubble, scanning it from top to bottom with the torchlight. Nothing but rocks, until something caught his eye to the right. A tingly feeling ran down his spine and his heart started to beat a little faster when he saw a small gap behind the rubble. He hadn't been close enough to see it the first time around, and the gap couldn't have been more than a few feet wide; just large enough for someone to squeeze through. Quinn was sure to have been through there. He imagined Lucho ordering her through at gunpoint.

'Incredible,' Jasper had seen it too, shining his light on the area to get a better view. The pair shared a knowing look. The professor had doubted him, but they were both glad Ted had trusted his instincts. Ted tried not to get too ahead of himself; all they had gained from this was evidence of a hole in the rockface. There were a lot of dots to join up before it led to anything significant.

'How did she know?' asked Jasper.

'The wind,' Ted replied as if the answer was obvious. 'Where the serpent sings, and the gods cry for eternity. The waterfall is where the gods cry for eternity. This,' he paused and listened to the wind whistling through the cave. 'This is the point in the cave where the wind is loudest.'

'Where the serpent sings.' A smile grew on Jasper's face. The boyish excitement he had felt at the prospect of finding an ancient lost relic had rekindled inside him once more. 'Incredible.'

Ted handed his phone to Jasper as he needed both hands to climb over the rubble and squeeze through the gap. Jasper shone both torches into the void as Ted's legs disappeared into it, followed by the rest of him. A moment went by, and then a hand came back through and gestured for the phone. Jasper handed them both back to Ted and began to hoist himself through the gap.

After regaining his composure on the other side, he saw something that nearly took his breath away. Ted had both phones pointed further ahead, illuminating a long pathway that snaked around to the right. He had already begun walking, eager to investigate where it led. The professor could barely contain his excitement. His heart skipped a beat as it dawned on him that they may have just stepped onto a path that before today hadn't been walked for hundreds of years.

He followed closely behind Ted and retrieved his phone to spread the light around as much as possible. The place was completely pitch black but for the blue light from their small screens and the white glow from the makeshift camera flash torches. Noting the distinct lack of stalactites hanging down from the cave ceiling, he shone his torch over the area with curiosity. The ceiling appeared higher at the point of entry.

'Jasper?' Ted asked as they rounded the first corner.

'Yes?'

'How much battery do you have?'

The professor studied the display on his device. '30%.'

'OK. Let's be quick. That'll soon drain with these lights on.' Ted's own phone was warming up from the prolonged heavy power use.

'Fascinating how the pathway was completely sealed off,' Jasper thought aloud. 'The wall must have been created from rock in the ceiling. Perhaps it was already partially blocked off, but there's been a change from the natural formation of it.' He thought some more as he stopped to consider the likely scenarios. 'It's odd.'

'What is?' Ted replied.

'I didn't think the Aztecs had the knowledge to use gunpowder this way, especially in such high quantities.'

'You think it was blasted shut?'

'Perhaps, yes. But the Aztecs didn't use gunpowder. Far too advanced for such a primitive civilisation. When Cortés brought the Spanish across from Cuba, the canons they used was something the natives had never seen or heard. They thought it was some kind of dark magic.'

'They'd have a fit if they saw us with these then,' Ted waved his smartphone around.

The professor chuckled. The excitement of what was happening had lightened his mood enough to enjoy a moment of relief.

'Maybe they were really strong?' Ted joked. 'Just placed the rocks there after they—' He lost his footing as the floor suddenly gave way. Jasper was just close enough to be able to grab his arm before Ted fell into the large square hole in the ground.

'Shit!' Ted shouted. The professor had reacted just in time, keeping him just teetering on the edge. After he regained his balance, the pair looked down into the shaft below. Shining their phones into it, what they saw could only be described as something straight out of an Indiana Jones movie. Ten feet below at the bottom of the shaft were a series of sharp stalagmites protruding menacingly from the ground. Something caught the light between two spikes, reflecting it

The Aztec Secret

back into their eyes. Ted bent down to peer closer into the hole.

'What is it?'

Jasper gasped. 'It— it can't be.'

'Can't be what?' Ted pressed.

'That's a helmet.'

'Helmet?'

'Yes, unmistakably,' said Jasper. 'By the shape of it, it can't be anything other than a Spanish soldier's.'

'That's crazy,' Ted was gobsmacked. 'Are you sure?'

'Of course I'm sure! I've been studying this since before you were born,' he said indignantly. 'The round base, the pointed rim protruding upward at each end. The ridge running across the top is a dead giveaway.'

'So, the Spanish were here after all?' Ted deduced.

'It seems so. Most likely Alvarado's men. There is so much of his journey south to the Mayan territories that wasn't documented. The general agreed canon is that he was sent south to continue the conquest into Guatemala.'

'You think there was an ulterior motive? Following the jewel?'

The professor nodded. 'This could confirm it.'

'The existence of the jewel?' Ted could sense the professor was trying hard to cling to any possibility of a worthwhile discovery. 'That's a stretch.'

'Yes, quite right. But we could have evidence that Cortés sent his right-hand man in pursuit of it.'

Ted looked down at the rusted helmet. 'He could have sent Alvarado on a wild goose chase. Another El Dorado, like you said.'

'Perhaps.'

Ted navigated cautiously around the side of the square hole in the ground. 'Be careful,' he said, pausing to check his footing. 'Do not fall in there.'

'You don't have to tell me,' Jasper replied, waiting for Ted to make it safely past before following in his footsteps. He hesitated a moment, staring down at the ominous-looking stalagmites. There was no sign of a skeleton strewn about the bottom of the pit, so whoever had lost their helmet five-hundred years ago had been lucky. Unless their body had been recovered and taken away for proper burial. A lump caught in his throat at the thought and he moved on with added haste.

The narrow tunnel snaked around another bend, and then Ted noticed the walls on either side of him began to veer off as the pathway opened up. He shined the light onto the left, then the right, realising that they had just entered a larger cavern. It was then that Ted turned his attention to the ground ahead. Something had distracted him just long enough to steal his gaze. The pathway ahead opened up to rows of stone slabs. There was a light dusting of rubble covering them, but there was a hint of unmistakable colour trying to escape from underneath. He approached the centre slab of the first row, bent down, and reached forward, running his hand across the surface. His eyes grew wide as he saw the dull red-painted symbol revealed underneath.

'Astonishing,' Jasper gasped from behind him. The pair stood a moment, trying to make sense of the strange artwork.

'I didn't know the Aztecs were into graffiti,' said Ted playfully. 'What does it mean?' He stood up and shined his phone light around. Immediately to the left of the slab was another square with a light dusting of debris. Again, it was painted in faint dark red. He didn't need to brush away the dirt to make out the symbol drawn on it. He recognised it from the artefact.

The Aztec Secret

'Tlāloc,' the professor said before he could recall the name. Ted shined a light directly to the right of the middle slab, revealing a square-shaped hole in the ground, similar to that of the pit he had almost fallen into moments earlier. Again, at the bottom were a number of sharp-looking stalagmites sticking out of the ground. No helmet at the bottom this time. Beyond that were two more square slabs, with other symbols painted onto them.

Ted eyed the first slab he'd come to more carefully. 'It's a jaguar,' he said. He then moved cautiously over to shine the light on the right-most two on the other side of the hole. 'The serpent,' he recognised the figure of Quetzalcoatl. The last one he didn't recognise. 'What is this?' He illuminated the slab and the professor came closer to inspect. The image was faint but appeared to be the face of a woman with an elaborate headdress.

'Interesting,' Jasper muttered. His attention moved away from the symbol and back across the other slabs from right to left. Ted kept his phone trained on the last one.

'What is this one?' he asked again. But Jasper said nothing. 'Professor?' he turned and shined the light in his direction, impatiently seeking an answer.

'For the love of God, Ted,' Jasper squinted in the light. 'Give me a moment.' He blinked repeatedly as his eyes readjusted to the dark, and focused his light source on the painting of the jaguar. He then skipped slowly from slab to slab, over and over again. Suddenly, the professor flicked back from the last slab to the gap between the middle set.

Ted watched the man's face as the moment of realisation happened. Jasper made the connection between what was in front of him and his vast knowledge of Aztec history.

'Five suns,' he said.
'What?' Ted asked, confused.

'The creation myth. This is how the Aztecs believed the world was created. There were four cycles of creation and destruction, represented by five suns.'

'That doesn't add up,' replied Ted. 'Do you mean five cycles?'

'No, the fifth sun has not been destroyed yet. We are living in the world of the fifth sun now.'

'Oh.'

'You see, the sun was very important to the Aztecs. It was a prominent part of their worship, their sacrificial rituals.'

'What do these pictures have to do with it?' Ted asked, trying to hurry along the history lesson.

'These are the five suns. The first sun was Tezcatlipoca. It took me a while to find the pattern because he is not depicted by any of the pictures. But then I realised that he has been represented by the jaguar.'

'But he wasn't a jaguar?'

'No. When the sun was knocked from the sky by Quetzalcoatl, Tezcatlipoca became angry and commanded his jaguars eat all the people.'

'What? Are you serious?'

'So the legend goes.'

'That's brutal.'

Jasper turned his attention to the second slab. 'Then we come to the second sun, Quetzalcoatl.'

'The feathered serpent, I remember,' Ted said proudly.

The professor nodded approvingly. 'Then on the right, we have Tlāloc, the third sun, and on the very far end, the fourth sun, Chalchiuhtlicue.'

'Chalchi what now?'

'Chalchiuhtlicue. The goddess of water, rivers, seas…'

'But I thought Tlāloc was the god of water?' Ted questioned.

'There's a lot of crossover. It gets confusing.'

'You're telling me.'

'I hadn't recognised her at first,' Jasper continued. 'There are only a few depictions of her in existence. There are a few statues of her, but the only painting that looks like this one is in the Codex Borgia that's kept at the Apostolic Library in the Vatican.'

'You've been there?'

'No, I saw a scanned copy online.'

'Well, then why would you mention the library specifically?'

The professor looked at Ted with a blank expression. Ted decided to move the conversation on. He looked at the four slabs with concern. 'And the fifth sun?'

'I think it has been removed. Or perhaps broke away.' Jasper gestured to the hole in the ground in the middle of the row of slabs.

'And that's today's sun?'

'Correct.'

Ted looked down into the spiked pit revealed by the missing middle slab. 'Do you think Alvarado's men made it this far?'

'Only one way to find out,' the professor said. 'One of us needs to get to the other side.'

'You mean me?' Ted raised an eyebrow.

'You don't expect me to try it in my condition?' Jasper used the injury card to great effect.

'Shit,' Ted cursed under his breath. He eyed the slab representing the first sun: the jaguar. 'I suppose I cross via this one?'

'That's what I'm thinking. In order of the suns.'

Ted took a deep breath and placed a tentative foot over the slab. His heart was racing as he fought his instinct not to put weight on the slab in case it gave way beneath him. After a few seconds of hesitation, he found enough courage to put his foot down on top of the slab. It held. He lifted his trailing leg and placed it on the slab too. He could now see the second row of slabs behind the first more clearly. He breathed a huge sigh of relief and called back to Jasper. 'I have to say, I was about ready to expect poison darts to come at me from the walls.'

The professor chuckled, but a sudden sound cut his laughter short. A deep rumbling from within the cavern began to grow in intensity. Ted froze on the spot, kneeling down as though anticipating a poison dart to come flying over his head after all.

The noise turned from a deep rumbling to the more defined sound of footsteps coming from the tunnel leading to their location.

'Someone's coming,' Jasper hissed. There was nowhere to hide, and their limited options quickly ran out as the footsteps thumped and echoed around the cavern. Jasper watched the entrance for the arrival of what was sure to be the police to arrest them for trespassing. Then came the voice. Alex's voice.

'Ted? Jasper?'

'Alex!' Ted called.

A light emerged from the tunnel, revealing Alex holding a pen-sized torch. 'Thank God I keep this flashlight on my keyring,' she said. 'My phone died halfway down.'

'What are you doing here?' Jasper asked.

'I said you had ten minutes before I dragged you out. So here I am, ready to drag your asses out. And don't think I won't.'

'Wait,' Jasper protested. 'Don't you realise where you are? We're in a part of the cave that hasn't been explored for maybe hundreds of years.'

The Aztec Secret

'Lucho blew a hole in the side of the cave wall, which revealed this old tunnel,' added Ted. 'You've got to see this, it's incredible.'

Alex stepped forward and scanned the rows of large square slabs. For a tiny device, her torch was bright and allowed them to see further into the cave and a few rows further back. 'What is all this?'

'Five suns. The story of creation according to Aztec legend,' said Jasper. 'It's a puzzle.'

Alex looked sceptically at him. 'This is not a movie, this is serious. We need to get out of here before there's a cave-in. Look, if we don't get out in the next five minutes, the police are going to come and get us themselves. I made a bargain with them. I told them about Lucho, and about Quinn. It was the only way I could convince them to let me come after you.'

'You're turning us in? I can't believe this!' Ted scowled.

'I'm not turning you in. I'm getting us help. We need the police if we're going to have a hope of getting your friend back.'

Ted ignored her, turning his attention back to the next row of slabs. He brushed away the layer of dust and debris from the one immediately ahead of him. The goddess of water. Ted couldn't remember the name, but he knew it wasn't the next one in the sequence. He reached over to the next slab and wiped the surface, although only to confirm his suspicion about the shape outline he could already make out. The serpent. He drew a sharp intake of breath and took a big step from the first plate to the second. The slab remained solid as he put all his weight on it. Two down, three to go.

'What is he doing?' Alex asked.

'He's taking the plates in order of the suns, according to the myth,' Jasper replied candidly.

'Is that really necessary? I highly doubt this place is booby-trapped. That kind of thing doesn't exist.'

'Tell that to the explorers who discovered Tutankhamun's tomb.'

'What?'

'Some of them died afterwards. They call it the mummy's curse.'

'Stop that,' she said. Being this far into the cave had made her uneasy enough. 'Ted. If you're intent on checking it out over there, hurry up. They'll be here any minute.'

'Yep, got it,' Ted replied plainly. This sudden urgency was completely unwelcome. He took a look at the slabs ahead of him. 'What's next?'

'Tlāloc,' Jasper called back.

Right, Ted thought. The water god. He located the picture he was looking for, right in front of him. He put one foot out and stepped down hard on the plate ahead. As his weight shifted onto his front foot, the plate cracked and gave way, sending the whole thing crashing into the pit below. Ted found himself off balance and falling into the void. Alex and Jasper let out a despairing cry as they watched him tumble. Ted saw the sharp stalagmites reveal themselves as the plate completely crumbled away, inviting him to his death. At the last moment, his brain switched into survival mode and his body instinctively swivelled ninety degrees. He stuck an arm out, his fingertips grasping desperately at the hard edge of the slab he'd just hopped off. They made contact and he held on with one hand for dear life. His legs dangled as he looked down, knowing his grip wouldn't be strong enough to hold him long. It was only a matter of time before he would succumb to gravity. Twisting his body, he swung his right arm over and latched a second hand onto the plate, kicking at the wall of the pit in an attempt to get a foothold onto something.

The Aztec Secret

Something clasped itself around his forearm and then the elbow of his other arm. Alex's face appeared over the edge of the pit and her face strained as she tried to heave him up. He summoned as much strength as he could muster and together they managed to pull him back onto the plate.

'Jesus!' Ted panted, sweat running down his face. 'Thank you.'

'Don't mention it,' Alex sat back on the plate with her hands pressed against the cold stone.

'Are you alright?' Jasper called across the cave.

'Yeah, I'm fine,' said Ted. 'Just a bit shook up.'

'You're lucky Alex has a sharp mind. She remembered the moves you'd made over the first two when she flew over to you. Never seen someone move so fast. What happened?'

Ted cast his mind back to the moment he stepped on the plate. It was then that his error dawned on him. 'I picked wrong. Those water gods are too similar.'

'Tlāloc is next,' Jasper reminded.

'I know,' Ted bit his lip. He took a few moments to compose himself, before standing up once more and scanning the next row for the Tlāloc drawing. To his left was a drawing of the sun, presumably the fifth and current sun. To the right of that was the space vacated by the water goddess, Chalchiuhtlicue. Then was the jaguar, and after that was unmistakably Tlāloc. The serpent was the furthest right.

'I'm going to have to jump to make that,' Ted said. This just got better and better.

'I'll do it,' Alex suggested.

'No, please. I need to do it. You don't even want to be down here.'

She gave a half-smile in response. He was right, she didn't.

Ted eyed up the jump. He studied the drawing on the destination slab to confirm it was definitely the right one. Then he took a step back and gave himself a short run-up before launching himself into the air in a leap of faith. He landed hard on the plate, the large square slab of rock causing a layer of dust to lift off all around. But crucially, it held firm. Ted exhaled deeply.

The next two in the sequence were much easier to navigate and required Ted to just step diagonally each time. He reached the end and took stock of where he'd come from, and the options available to him now. There wasn't much of anything on this side of the cave, save for a narrow tunnel leading off to the right. He placed his hand on the wall to steady himself while stepping off the last slab. The wall was damp, and he immediately took it away. He'd always hated having wet hands. His biggest pet peeve at home was washing his hands only to remember that he'd just put all his towels in the washing machine. He wiped his hand on his shirt and studied the entryway to the narrow tunnel. The air here had changed. The deepest parts of the cave had a stuffy feel, as though no fresh air had gotten in for years. But the air felt lighter and cooler here.

He disappeared inside the tunnel and followed it around, twisting and turning like a maze until finally, he reached an alcove. A faint stream of light shone through from the ceiling in three or four diagonal beams, gently illuminating the small space. Ted moved his phone light around, confirming what he was seeing.

'It's a dead-end,' he called back to the others, who were still within earshot.

'Are you sure?' Jasper replied. This couldn't have all been for nothing.

'Pretty sure.'

The Aztec Secret

The air was definitely easier to breathe here. Ted looked up and noticed the ceiling was much higher than any other part of the cave. The shape of the alcove was much clearer looking straight up. It looked almost like half of a well, conjoined to the rest of the cave. He didn't remember seeing any signs of a well on the surface. He could hear the gushing of the waterfall in the distance. Perhaps this was deeper in the forest.

He scanned the alcove for a sign. Anything. He moved his phone light in a deliberate motion, akin to that of a window cleaner. He'd seen a crime scene investigation unit on a TV show move a blacklight like this to cover all areas. Starting on one side of the alcove wall, he moved his phone fluidly over the bumpy surface. He wasn't sure what he was looking for. Another message from Quinn? A map with a giant letter X with arrows pointing to it from all around? Then he found it. Carved into the wall was a trio of symbols. They were difficult to see at first glance, but unmistakably man-made. He shined the light closer and studied them one-by-one. A sun, a crescent moon, and the feathered serpent.

TWENTY-TWO

The whir of the helicopter had once again become background noise as Quinn sat anxiously on one of the uncomfortable seats of the big bird. Eduardo accompanied her immediately to her right, blocking her path to the opening. It was a precaution Lucho had insisted on.

Rain pitter-pattered on the window as a layer of grey mist settled on the horizon. The weather had taken a sharp turn since they took off from the waterfall. Lucho was busy on his phone, calling out instructions to Carlos. A little bit of rain wouldn't deter him from his goal. Not when he was so close.

He would occasionally turn back to leer at Quinn, as though checking she was still there. She felt a shiver run down her spine every time he swivelled his head around. The man's stare was haunting, and his eyes lingered just a little too long on each occasion. It was the kind of menacing look that indicated either a deep hatred of her or some perverted attraction. Both possibilities made her feel sick.

Lucho's phone screen lit up and buzzed in his hands. He ignored the withheld number notice on the display, instinctively pressing the green receiver button and taking off his headset as he jammed the phone tightly against his ear.

'*¿Diga?*' he shouted above the noise of the rotor. The directness of the way he'd said it let on that this was the person he'd been talking with earlier. It was more than likely his employer. He listened for a few moments before turning back to look at Quinn. He continued to listen, as though the person on the other end of the phone was talking about her. He eyed her carefully, and then looked back up front. '*Si,*' he acknowledged the information he was being given. Another long pause while he gritted his teeth. He clearly wasn't happy with what he'd learned. Quinn wondered if Lucho was the kind of person who was ever happy.

Next to her, Eduardo let out a loud yawn. A sudden wave of rancid coffee breath attacked her nostrils. She screwed up her nose and sat back in her seat, burying her face into her loosely buttoned shirt. Closing her eyes, Quinn tried to think of happy thoughts. Her parents. Her childhood home. Her friends. Quiet nights in watching trashy movies. Banoffee pie. The soft purring of the fluffy cat that would greet her at the end of the road on the way to class. What she wouldn't give to be back home, back to normality. If she tried hard enough, she might wake from this nightmare and be safe and sound back in the soft single bed of her shared apartment. Hell, she'd take waking up to find she was in the middle of an exam she hadn't prepared for. Funny how a recurring bad dream had become a preferable scenario to reality.

The harsh bite of Lucho's voice came once again, muttering the odd sound to let whoever was on the other end of the phone know he was still listening. After a minute he took the phone from his ear and hit the end call button. Replacing the headset he'd taken off moments before, he issued a command to Carlos, who simply nodded in response, keeping them on course. Clearly, they still had faith in her assumption of where the treasure had been hidden.

The symbols on the wall of the cave were obvious. One look at that and she was sure the professor would see it as plainly as she had. She just hoped that the pair had somehow found the old warehouse in San Benito. It had taken her ages to write that message with the UV pen. For starters, she was writing blind, keeping her eyes facing forward to avoid drawing attention from Lucho and his men. Then she had to write it from right to left and upside down. If by some miracle Ted had found it and deciphered her scribblings, following her this far would be a breeze. With his crude use of explosives in a confined space, Lucho had given away the entrance to the tunnel to anyone within a mile radius. Once Ted and the professor arrived at the waterfall, it would be an easy task following the trail of destruction he'd left behind.

'Eduardo,' Quinn addressed the tired man next to her. His heavy eyes settled on her. 'Can I please have my phone for just a moment?'

He grumbled something under his breath and turned away, dismissing her request.

'You can watch what I do,' she pressed. 'I promise I won't try anything. I just need to let Ted and Jasper know I'm OK. I won't tell them where we are or where we're headed.'

The big mercenary said nothing.

'Please,' she pleaded. 'I need them to know I'm safe. They should know I'm helping you willingly and that I can meet them after we go our separate ways.' She was fishing for reassurance of what would happen to her once the jewel was found. *If* the jewel was found. She didn't trust Lucho one bit, but perhaps Eduardo had more of a moral code.

'No phone,' he said.

The Aztec Secret

She gritted her teeth, frustrated. Talking to Eduardo was like talking to a brick wall. Even the other two Mexicans couldn't get more than a few words from him when they spoke in Spanish.

The rain hammered down heavier on the glass and a gust of wind blew from the side. Carlos fought hard to steer the bird against it, putting heavy pressure on the cyclic pitch control stick to compensate for the blustery gale. But the erratic nature of the wind made this difficult, and as the wind died down momentarily before the next gust the helicopter would jolt violently to the right before Carlos had time to adjust his steering.

Quinn let out an involuntary scream when one such jolt bumped her from her seat. Her seatbelt dutifully kept her in place, creating a feeling akin to dropping suddenly on a rollercoaster. Eduardo shouted something into the cockpit, his voice panicked. Lucho ignored him and continued to point out the direction of travel to Carlos.

The sky had turned dark as the storm picked up. A flash of lightning emanated from somewhere in the distance. A couple of seconds went by before the rumble of thunder sounded.

Eduardo shouted again, louder this time. Lucho turned his head, revealing his crazed wide eyes.

'*¡No!*' he replied. '*Estamos tan cerca.*'

Another protest came, this time from Carlos. Quinn couldn't understand the quick Spanish that was exchanged, but the sentiment was clear as day. Everyone but Lucho could see it was far too dangerous for them to be flying through this storm. Lucho shouted in retaliation and pointed ahead, urging Carlos on. His pilot stayed on course as another flash of lightning appeared in the distance. The rumble of thunder came sooner this time and the anxious energy in the group grew.

The thick layer of mist and hammering rain made it almost impossible for Carlos to see where he was going. A strong gust of wind pushed the big metal bird to the side and Carlos fought once more to keep the helicopter steady. He decided enough was enough and lowered the collective pitch control to start their descent. Regardless of Lucho's commands, he was putting them all in danger by carrying on. Waiting for the storm to clear was better than crashing to their death following a lightning strike or engine failure. The way he saw it, if the jewel had been undiscovered for hundreds of years, it could wait a few hours more. They were the only ones who knew of its existence. As they gradually lost altitude, the sky cleared, and Carlos was able to see the ground below. He searched for a safe place to land, eventually settling on a field.

Lucho turned to his pilot, a look of shock and anger on his face as he reacted to this subordination. He shouted a command at him, which was ignored. Through gritted teeth, Lucho reached for the collective pitch control, grabbing it tightly and yanking it in a desperate attempt to change their course. Carlos had to react quickly as the helicopter lurched back, forcing him into the back of his seat. Warning sounds came from the computer and a red light started blinking at the controls. Suddenly, a bulky arm came from behind the pair and wrapped tightly around Lucho, forcing him back and away from the controls. Eduardo had unbuckled himself from his seat and flung himself to the cockpit to restrain the crazed man. Lucho let out a frustrated guttural sound as he tried in vain to free himself from Eduardo's grasp. Carlos regained control and steadied them once more.

As the helicopter descended at a more controlled rate, the ground getting closer and closer, Quinn let out a long exhale. She hadn't realised just how long she'd been holding her breath. Lucho had become still, accepting the fact that he would not be able to escape Eduardo's hold. Nevertheless, the maddened expression on his face hadn't gone away. Quinn could tell there would be an explosion of anger once the helicopter had landed, but as they descended the relative silence created a brief moment of respite. The rain had almost become a peaceful sound now that safety was within reach. Quinn shut her eyes and imagined being back home, sitting in her room on a spring Sunday morning, listening as the water droplets tapped away at the window.

The altimeter counted down, and even Carlos breathed a sigh of relief as they hovered just a hundred feet from the ground, a height still capable of causing trouble should something go wrong, but relative to dodging lightning strikes in a thick layer of mist it felt as though they were out of the woods now.

The landing skids touched down onto the grass and judging by the slight tilt the big bird was at, Quinn realised they'd landed on uneven terrain. Still, she couldn't fault Carlos' skill, not to mention composure, in bringing them down safely. The pilot busied himself in the cockpit, flicking switches as the engine powered down and the heavy whump of the main rotor began to slow. The chopper seemed stable, even if they were parked on the bottom of a slight incline. Quinn unbuckled her seatbelt and studied her new environment, shuffling to the seat Eduardo had previously occupied to get a better view of the outside. To her surprise, nobody had tried to restrain her and she was allowed the freedom to move about. Carlos was too busy with his post-flight checks and Eduardo was still positioned behind Lucho's seat, his right arm wrapped around the man's torso and his left holding the back of the headrest for leverage.

Quinn took a look outside at their surroundings. What had looked like a small field from a few hundred feet in the air was actually a clearing between two sides of thick jungle foliage. The dense greenery on either side was juxtaposed by the vast emptiness between. Quinn spotted wide tree stumps protruding from the ground just ahead; evidence of deforestation. She placed one hand on the roof of the cabin and peered out at the rain-soaked terrain. Hundreds more stumps were scattered for a mile. The place had an eerie feel, as though she had just stepped into a graveyard. What had once been the home of any number of animals had been reduced to nothing more than this. The issue was of no surprise to her; it was common knowledge that the world had lost the vast majority of its virgin rainforests. Knowing about it was one thing, but seeing it in person was different. Witnessing humanity's greed in such a stark view highlighted just how we really are the worst of all species. She could continue to separate her recycling, refuse to buy fresh fruit and vegetables wrapped in plastic, share posts on social media about climate change and humanity's contribution to the extinction of numerous species. But was any of it making a difference? Quinn took a moment to let the view sink in.

The silence was momentarily broken by the distant call of a howler monkey. Snapping out of her existential crisis, she felt a hand touch her shoulder. Carlos had finished his post-flight checks and was alerting her to the fact that Eduardo had just released Lucho from the confines of his seat. The pointy-faced man was sitting still, his headset on as he stared out the front of the cockpit. Quinn took up her position on the seat she'd vacated moments earlier to avoid angering him further.

The Aztec Secret

Carlos and Eduardo seemed pretty relaxed about the activity of their hostage, but the same could not be said of Lucho.

The pilot and the big brute sat near the opening, taking the opportunity to light up a cigarette. The rain had forced them further inside than they would usually sit to have a smoke, and the wind pushed the toxic air in Quinn's direction. She coughed as the second-hand smoke entered her nostrils and filled her lungs. She shot a disgusted look in their direction, but the pair didn't show any acknowledgement of her discomfort.

The rain wasn't letting up, hammering aggressively on the window. The sporadic gusts of wind would cause the droplets to blow sideways, spraying the inside. Lightning flashed through the grey haze of sky. Quinn waited for the thunder, but it didn't come for more than seven seconds. At least the storm was on the move. Unfortunately for them, it was headed in the direction they needed to travel, so they'd only catch up with it should they take off and continue their journey.

Through the pitter-patter, which eventually became background noise, she heard the faint sound of a dialling tone coming from the cockpit. Lucho was still sitting there quietly, now with his burner phone pressed against his ear. The chirping dial tone stopped abruptly and a calm woman's voice came through, speaking quick Spanish. Lucho mashed the end call button. It must have gone to voicemail. He let out a loud cry, throwing the phone to the ground. Lucky for him, it was a very old model and built like a brick. Had that been a new smartphone it probably would have shattered into a thousand pieces. Instead, it bounced up from the floor, hitting the inner wall of the helicopter before settling at his feet.

A switch had flicked in Lucho's brain and he suddenly became very animated, pointing at Carlos and Eduardo and launching a barrage of abuse their way. This seemed like the Lucho Quinn had come to know over the last couple of days: a constant undercurrent of Jack Russell-esque aggression that would erupt without warning. He had been embarrassed by the way his subordinates had undermined him, and he was made to feel powerless in a situation he desperately wanted to control. Now he'd shown weakness, he was set on putting things right. The pair looked up momentarily but didn't seem too phased by the outburst. They knew there was nothing to be done about the situation. Stopping to wait for the storm to clear was the sensible decision. Lucho would have to come to terms with it in his own time. Carlos took another drag from his cigarette, ignoring him.

Lucho could feel the wheels starting to come off, and he was becoming all the more frustrated as a result. He clutched his handgun and studied the pair of insubordinates with wide eyes, fighting his desire to reinstate superiority with the small logical part of his brain that remained. As much as he hated to admit it, he needed them. He punched the interior of the cockpit and relaxed back into his seat. This job just got more and more irritating. Most were simple hit jobs or kidnappings for ransom. He could usually find ways to cut corners when he wasn't so reliant on others. His employer had told him it would be simple. The professor would know the whereabouts of the jewel, and he just needed to ensure he got there quickly and without alerting the police. To find out the professor was incompetent was the first annoyance. Combining that with having to take orders from a slimy politician who wouldn't answer his phone, working with a team that didn't respect his authority, all while following the directions of a civilian who wasn't supposed to be part of the mission in the first place was a recipe for disaster. Just a little longer and he'd be done with this wretched assignment.

TWENTY-THREE

The tiny prop plane rattled through the air as it started its descent. Alex was at the controls once more, with Ted and the professor squashed into the back. The flight had been long and uncomfortable, requiring a stop for fuel. Alex determined that there must have been a leak in the fuel tank, as the gauge was once again dangerously close to empty.

Upon leaving the cave, the trio had been greeted by a disgruntled police officer, who told Ted in no uncertain terms how stupid his actions had been going in there, let alone staying for so long. The man emphasised that he was within his rights to arrest them on entering a cordoned off area alone. Ted didn't care one bit. Back home, such reprimand would have left him feeling guilty and ashamed, not to mention terrified of the consequences. But he was glad he did it. It led him further on the trail to finding Quinn, and that was all that mattered now.

The professor had been especially animated after Ted showed him the photo of the symbols on the cave wall he'd taken on his phone. He'd watched the eureka moment appear in his eyes. It had been right under their nose all along. They were headed for the site of Teotihuacán; a large collection of Mesoamerican pyramids just thirty miles northeast of Mexico City. The professor hadn't considered it as a possible resting place for the jewel since it was simply too obvious. The archaeological marvel was a UNESCO World Heritage site and one of the most visited attractions in Mexico. He had thought it impossible that such a well-explored place could contain an undiscovered treasure as significant as this. If the Aztec Jaguar Warriors wanted the jewel to remain hidden after the fall of Tenōchtitlan, why would they have hinted to its real resting place after doing such a fantastic job of sending the Spanish on a wild goose chase in the wrong direction? Perhaps in the hope that one day the Aztec culture would be rekindled? The carvings were unmistakably linked to Aztec culture, but there was no guarantee that an Aztec person had made them, and it was an even bigger stretch to suggest that this was evidence of the existence of the mysterious jewel that Hernán Cortés was hunting for. He accepted that with no further evidence, some things would always remain a mystery.

Alex had informed the officer of Quinn's kidnapping and the likely destination the captors were taking her to. Contrary to what Ted had thought, she had refrained from revealing any other details, namely their involvement with the stolen artefact. The officer had shown concern for Quinn's safety and made a call to his superior, who in turn had sent out an alert to a precinct in Mexico City. Alex was informed that there would be a team awaiting their arrival at Teotihuacán. Lucho and the others would be arrested on sight.

They had to stay at the local police station overnight due to a sudden storm that blew in and wouldn't let up. The weather hadn't predicted a drop of rain all week. Ted had joked that it was the curse of the treasure, now they were getting close. Jasper had eyed him carefully at that comment. It wasn't until the early hours of the next morning that the weather had finally improved.

As the plane slowly lost altitude, Alex called back to check in on her passengers. Ted gave a quick thumbs-up, not that she could see it. Soon this would all be over. Quinn would be safe, Lucho and his men would be locked up, and perhaps they'd be able to restore the stolen artefact to the museum without being charged with theft. Hell, after everything he'd been through, he'd take another short stint in jail if it meant everyone was safe and sound and the real bad guys were caught. As for wrapping up the mystery they'd been chasing all this time, he didn't care for it one bit. He couldn't deny that discovering the old tunnel, beating the trial of the stone slabs, and finding the carvings on the wall had ignited something within him. It had been quite the adventure. And to think of the stories he could tell once he got home. It beat anything else he'd ever experienced by a longshot. The more he thought about it, the more he questioned himself. Maybe he wasn't as content with the mundane as he thought.

He'd grown up on a staple diet of treasure hunters from the classics: Jim Hawkins and Bilbo Baggins, to the archaeologically focused: Indiana Jones and Lara Croft. But he had been content experiencing the thrill of their adventures through the medium of books, movies, video games. That was until now. For some reason, he couldn't help but smile when looking back at the last few days. It definitely wasn't the rush of narrowly avoiding death: instead of feeling alive after being inches from his demise, all he'd experienced was pure trauma. Perhaps it was the relief of knowing that it would soon be over; that the police could handle it from here on in, and Quinn would be safe? But there was something else, some underlying feeling he wasn't familiar with. Then he put his finger on it. Pride. A sense of self-worth, of feeling accomplished. He'd gone through the most harrowing of circumstances and come out the other side intact. He remembered bolting out of the van and trying to outrun armed hardened criminals in the backstreets of Mexico City. That was pretty ballsy. If he could survive this, he could do anything.

Ted, having begrudgingly agreed to sit on Jasper's lap for the second leg of the journey, was in a good position to peer out of the window. With a fear of flying, he'd always spent the last few minutes of flights staring out the window at the ground below. It seemed counterintuitive to face the source of his anxiety this way, but to Ted, it was oddly soothing. Watching the ground grow closer and closer; becoming low enough to follow individual cars on the roads outside the airport. It was the point where the plane would be in line with the tallest building around that made him breathe a sigh of relief, as though if anything went wrong now the fall wouldn't be that bad. The theory was founded on complete nonsense and there was a part of Ted that knew that. But for whatever reason, it worked as a coping mechanism, which was all he needed.

It was still the early hours of the morning and the sun hadn't yet come up. Ted strained to make out their surroundings, as there seemed to be nothing but vast darkness all around. The site of Teotihuacán was out in the middle of nowhere, miles from the nearest settlement. The plane dropped lower and lower until finally, the crest of a large pyramid entered his view. Craning his neck around, he caught a glimpse of another. There was still one he hadn't spotted; the professor had told them there were three. He twisted on the spot and looked out the other side and sure enough there it was. They were landing right amongst the trio.

'Hold onto something!' Alex shouted suddenly. The plane shuddered momentarily, reminding Ted that they weren't out of the woods just yet, there was still the landing to consider.

Ted looked around for something to hold onto, keen to avoid it being the professor. He opted for the headrest in front of him. He turned his head to the side and watched as they barrelled past one of the pyramids. The wheels bounced off the ground, causing him to hit the side of his head on the back of the headrest. A brief memory of the alleyway in the outskirts of Mexico City came flooding back. Lucho's gun arm raised high, bringing down the weight of the pistol butt onto his head. He winced at the thought, just as Alex slammed on the brakes. They could hear the wheels tearing up dirt as Alex tried desperately to keep them straight. Eventually, the speed slowed to a point where the steering wasn't fighting against Alex's every move and the plane came to a gentle stop. The makeshift runway had been long and wide enough for landing, but the surface was far from ideal for the wheels. The rubber sounded like it had been torn to bits and as they came to rest the plane became consumed by a cloud of dust.

A moment of silence passed as the trio recovered from the rough landing. Ted breathed a huge sigh of relief and vowed never to set foot in such a small aircraft again. It gave a little perspective to the comparatively smooth long-haul flights he'd feared before.

Alex switched off the engine and craned her head back to the others. 'All OK back there?'

'Positively splendid,' Jasper replied sarcastically. Ted could detect a hint of relief in his voice though.

Alex opened the door and one-by-one they clambered out of the tiny plane. Ted's foot met the dusty ground with eagerness, grateful as he was to be done with that flight. He looked back at the aircraft, appraising the damage dealt by the landing. The wheels had been shredded. He would be surprised if it ever took off again. He thought of the poor soul in San Benito who owned it, only for three disrespectful tourists to hijack and trash it. It was perhaps the longest joyride of all time. It certainly trumped that episode of that show he couldn't remember the name of where a car thief had taken a small hatchback and led a police chase from Edgware Road to Watford. But this hadn't been a joyride. It was an emergency, and there had been nothing joyous about the ride.

The dust had settled around them and the group began to really take in their surroundings. Dawn was breaking, the sun peeking out from the horizon. It painted the scene in beautiful orange, casting a shadow on one side of the impressive pyramid that towered in front of them. The military-grade helicopter that was sat idly some distance away confirmed they had interpreted the symbols from the cave the same way as Quinn. As they predicted, Lucho had made a beeline straight for it.

It was then that Ted noticed how eerily quiet it was. Sure, the site wasn't yet open to tourists, but he was also expecting a considerable amount of police activity on their arrival, seeing as the Mexico City police department had been tipped off to a kidnapping in this spot. There was no sign of this; not so much as a squad car. Alex had noticed it too.

'Where are they?'

'Maybe they haven't arrived yet?' the professor offered.

'No, that's not it,' she dismissed. 'The Guatemalan authorities contacted the Mexico City precinct yesterday. They should have been here waiting.'

'So, what are you saying?' Ted inquired. 'They didn't believe the message?'

'Or they didn't get it in the first place,' said Alex.

The Aztec Secret

Ted paused while he digested what she was implying. 'You think the Guatemalan police lied?'

Alex shook her head. 'I think whoever got the message the other side didn't pass it on.' She turned to Jasper and eyed him carefully. 'How much do you know about the person who hired the men who kidnapped Quinn? The man who funded your trip. What was his name? Sigma?'

Jasper took a step back and shrugged, getting a sense of accusation in her tone. 'Nothing really. The only interactions we had were over email, and he didn't give much away other than the details of the assignment and the people I would be working with. Are you seriously suggesting that there's corruption within the police?'

'Dirty cops aren't just from TV shows,' she replied plainly. 'I think your Sigma has more influence here than we realised.'

Ted's heart sunk. This was far from over.

'We need to call the police ourselves and get them out here,' he said. 'We're no use against three armed mercenaries without them.'

'On it,' Alex replied, picking her phone out from her pocket. The trio was thankful for being able to charge their phones at the police station they'd stayed at while waiting for the storm to clear. 'You want to wait here for them?' she asked before dialling the emergency number.

Ted studied the pyramid in front of them, and then the other two around them. Quinn was in one of these. But which one he had no clue.

'If we wait for them to return to the helicopter, it'll be too late. They'll have either found the jewel or given up looking. We need to find them while Quinn is still useful to them.'

'OK.' She gestured to each of the three pyramids in turn. 'Which way?' Her phone connected to the emergency switchboard and she turned away from the others to concentrate.

'So?' Ted turned to the professor, prompting him to offer guidance in this situation. 'Which pyramid?'

Jasper pursed his lips and twisted his face as he thought hard on the question. The pressure was firmly on him now, everyone was relying on his ability to find some connection between his knowledge of Aztec history and their surroundings. How was he supposed to know for sure?

He thought about the three pyramids in turn and what they represented. The feathered serpent Quetzalcoatl was the god of wind, air, and learning. When Cortés first appeared on the shores of Mexico in 1519 Emperor Moctezuma II believed it to be the return of the wind god. The deity had been key to much of the mystery surrounding the jewel so far, but was it more significant to the core beliefs that underpinned Aztec culture than the others? Jasper recalled a news story from 2014, about how thousands of sacred objects had been found in a tunnel underneath the Temple of Quetzalcoatl. Surely if the jewel had been laid to rest there, the archaeologists who had discovered this tunnel would have found it among the other artefacts?

The sun and moon represented the battle of light vs. darkness; something the Aztecs thought to be a constant power struggle throughout time. They believed the sun god Huītzilōpōchtli was in constant war against darkness and if the darkness won, the world would end. By offering blood, and often the beating hearts of sacrificed humans, the Aztec people believed they were feeding Huītzilōpōchtli, allowing the sun to continue its path across the sky and keeping the world going another day. The professor tried to understand the mindset of the warriors who fled the fallen city of Tenōchtitlan. These were people who had lost everything, invaded by strange foreigners who attempted to strip them of their culture. These were scared people, running from a force they didn't understand, fearful of their extinction. Perhaps bringing the jewel to this site was a last ditch attempt at honouring the sun with one final sacrifice? The Heart of the Jaguar, the last symbol of their religion, laid to rest inside the temple to the sun in the hope that the Aztec empire would not be lost forever.

Jasper then recalled another news story. After a heavy storm in 2003, an archaeologist with Mexico's National Institute of Anthropology and History found a sinkhole near the Temple of the Plumed Serpent, Quetzalcoatl. Upon later excavation with a ground-penetrating radar device, it was discovered that the sinkhole led to a tunnel that ran under the pyramid itself. It was rumoured that the remains of Aztec rulers had been laid to rest under the pyramid. Was it possible the Heart of the Jaguar had been placed here too?

Jasper's thoughts were broken as a sudden explosion boomed across the flat landscape. Startled, the trio looked in the direction the sound had come from: the Temple of the Moon.

TWENTY-FOUR

The plume of smoke would be seen for miles and the sound of the blast would have carried just as far. Alex had already called the police, but others within a mile radius would surely do the same. Receiving multiple calls about the same place might increase the impetus, and if the police weren't sure of the severity of the situation before, they sure as hell would be now. These were some of the thoughts rattling around Ted's mind as he raced over to the Temple of the Moon.

It was still early morning, but it was hot out and Ted could already feel a sweat coming on. The wide road he was running down had no protection from the sun. The straight road, around forty metres wide, had been pointed out as the *Avenue of the Dead* by Jasper on approach from the sky. He had explained that when the Aztecs found this place, they believed the flat-topped buildings running either side of the great road to be tombs, which is how it got its name.

The great temple, the second largest on the site, towered high above. A giant hill loomed large behind it, casting a shadow over the impressive structure. The professor hobbled

The Aztec Secret

along as fast as he could behind. Looking back to check on his progress, Ted could see the awe in Jasper's face. Despite the more pressing matter of a hostage situation to deal with, the man could not contain his amazement at the site. This place was like Disneyland to him.

Alex, clearly the fittest of the trio, was almost to the base of the temple. This part of the archaeological site was home to a cluster of smaller structures, which led up to the large temple. The plume of smoke, which was starting to dissipate, came from one of the smaller ones to the left. As they grew closer, she caught sight of Carlos, who was standing guard outside of the building. She darted to the left, moving out of the main pathway and tucking behind the ruins of another structure. Luckily for her, he had been looking the other way.

She stopped and turned to her companions, who were catching up to his position. Waving her arms, she tried to grab their attention. She pointed next to her, ushering them to get into cover. Ted got the message and moved off the wide pathway and alongside her. He was panting hard from the run. Alex put her finger to her lips, but Ted knew what was going on and wasn't planning on making a racket.

'There's a man with a gun standing outside the entrance to that place,' she whispered as Jasper finally regrouped with them.

'There should be three of them in total,' Ted replied. 'What's the plan?'

Alex thought a moment. 'We can't take them on until the police arrive. But we need to ensure your friend is safe.'

'OK, and how do we do that?'

Jasper suggested the solution before Alex had time to. 'We distract them. Buy some time keeping them on a wild goose chase.' He gave a knowing nod to Alex as if he had a plan for how to do that.

'Ted,' she said, 'Here's what I want you to—'

Before she could finish, she felt the cold steel of the barrel of a gun press against the back of her head. She watched the terror form on Ted and Jasper's faces, and felt a strange sensation, as though all her senses had suddenly faded, and she was being transported somewhere else. She heard the sound of her quickening heartbeat echoing in her inner ear. Now she was back in the cold, musty warehouse. The gunshots, the static of radio before she called for backup. Memories of her last day on the job flooded back like a recurring nightmare. She saw her partner, Joel. There was a hole in his uniform where the bullet had ripped through. Blood streamed down from the wound as the sirens began to wail. She could hear herself calling for backup on the radio in her squad car. What if backup didn't come this time? What if her conversation a few minutes ago had been with a corrupt officer; the same that had dealt with the Guatemalan police?

'Hands behind your head,' Carlos' voice pierced through, startling her. She complied, slowly bringing her hands up and over her head, interlocking her fingers as her palms rested on her hair. Ted and Jasper followed suit.

Carlos marched the trio around to the structure he had been guarding. It was a small courtyard with a building that wrapped around the sides. The stonework was damaged in places, but the intricate carvings could still be seen. There were so many buildings like this in the site of Teotihuacán, each carefully crafted with figures of various Mesoamerican deities. Ted spotted a carving of a cat's head on one wall, presumably signalling significance with the jaguar. Inside the entrance, Eduardo stood guard of the doorway with an assault rifle. Quinn was standing in the corner of the room, her arms folded, and her frame hunched. Lucho knelt next to a large hole in the ground; created moments ago by the explosion.

The Aztec Secret

Lining the walls around the room were the remains of murals. Some had been shattered as a result of the blast.

'What are you doing?' Jasper was furious. 'You're destroying everything!'

'Jasper!' Quinn recognised his voice instantly. Eduardo stepped aside and she saw the others enter the room. Her eyes widened and she smiled at Ted. She had wondered if she would ever see a friendly face again. She had left the clue to the waterfall in hopes Ted would remember their conversation at the museum about her novelty UV pen keyring. There was no way they would be here now if he hadn't found it.

Lucho signalled to Eduardo, and the big brute winded Jasper with a swift jab of the butt of his rifle to the old man's stomach.

'Hey!' Alex protested. 'Take it easy. We're unarmed.'

Lucho muttered something in Spanish to Carlos, who replied in English to Alex. 'Who are you?'

'Alex,' she said plainly.

Lucho stood up from his perch over the hole in the ground, one hand holding a pistol. The pointy-nosed man scratched the small patch of facial hair under his bottom lip.

'What are you doing here?' Carlos elaborated on his first question.

'We're just here to make sure she's OK.' Alex looked at Quinn, who understandably looked as confused to see her as the mercenaries. 'We'll cooperate. But we just needed to know she was safe.'

Lucho barked some more Spanish, this time not directed specifically at Carlos. He seemed just as tense and frustrated as ever.

'What are you doing?' Jasper asked Quinn.

'I suggested perhaps the Palace of the Jaguars could be a viable resting place for the jewel,' Quinn replied.

'So he's blowing a hole in the floor to see if it's directly underneath?' Jasper was dumbfounded by the mercenary's indifferent attitude towards the ancient artefacts adorning the room. It showed a complete lack of respect for the history of this place.

Quinn looked uncomfortable on the other side of the room. Granted, she had been held hostage for the better part of two days, but there was a distinct nervousness to her at that moment. She had led Lucho to this location, suggesting it could be the final part of this treasure hunt. If Lucho didn't find it underneath the Palace of the Jaguars, that could be the last straw; proving Quinn was no longer useful to him. They would all prove to be surplus to requirements if he thought they were out of ideas.

'Besides,' Jasper added. 'There's no way the jewel would be here.'

Lucho eyed him carefully. He brought his arm up slowly and trained the gun on the professor.

'You talk a lot,' he said through gritted teeth. 'Where is it?'

Jasper went pale as he stared down the barrel of the pistol. He still had his hands wrapped tightly behind his head, his white shirt soaked in sweat.

'The girl told us it would be here,' Carlos interjected. 'So, is she wrong?'

Jasper trod carefully. 'It was a good hypothesis to check here. There is no way we can know for sure, but there are only a few places it can be.' He gave a look to Quinn, pleading her to play along.

'The Heart of the Jaguar was sacred to the Jaguar Warriors who hid it,' Quinn piped up. 'This place has significance to them.'

'Yes,' Jasper agreed. 'They believed the jewel to be the source of their power in battle. And logically they could lay it to rest here.'

'But there's somewhere else it could be?' asked Quinn.

Lucho momentarily pointed the gun down and away from Jasper, rubbing the side of his head with his other hand. He muttered a few words in Spanish under his breath, the tone of his voice alluding to the fact that his patience was wearing thin. He gestured to Eduardo and spoke quickly. Eduardo nodded and pointed at Ted.

'*Teléfono*,' he demanded.

Ted looked confused for a moment, his brain searching through his limited Spanish vocabulary. It wasn't just the word that he struggled with, but the speed with which Eduardo had said it, and the low register of his voice.

'Your phone,' Quinn clarified.

Ted paused a moment, wondering why the man was demanding his phone. The first thing that came to mind was so that they didn't call the police. It probably wasn't a smart idea to reveal they had already done that. He slowly reached down to his pocket with his right hand, the other still behind his head. He reached in, pulled the phone out and handed it to Eduardo, who snatched it with a quick swipe. He then handed it to Lucho, who pressed the button on the side to illuminate the screen.

'*¿El pin?*' Lucho requested, not taking his eyes away from the screen. Eduardo looked at Ted, expectantly.

He didn't need this one translating. The number didn't come to mind immediately, as Ted had used his thumbprint to unlock the device since he'd got it. He hadn't had to use the passcode in months. What was it? He remembered wanting to use his debit card PIN, so it was easy to remember. But when setting it up, the device required six digits, not four. Then he remembered. He'd been with Carl at the time, and he had jokingly suggested picking some memorable numbers from a movie. But there was nothing with six digits that really stuck with Ted. The only thing he could think of was using his birthday, but although having the same PIN for his phone as his bank account seemed perfectly acceptable, he decided his own birthday wouldn't be secure enough. He went instead with the only other birthday that came to mind at the time. Julia's. 12th April 1999. Ted flinched at the thought that this was still his passcode.

'120499,' he said.

Lucho tapped the sequence in and the phone unlocked. After a short amount of swiping and tapping, he had found what he wanted. He took his burner phone from his pocket and checked it momentarily, before giving Ted's phone back to Eduardo who then returned it to Ted. Everyone looked confused. Why confiscate the phone and then just hand it back? Then Ted looked at the screen and found the clock app was up. A timer was counting down from an hour. It was currently at 59:50.

Lucho cocked his pistol with a loud click which echoed around the stone walls. 'I don't care which one,' he pointed to Quinn and Jasper in turn with the gun. 'Find it, NOW.'

**

Once Lucho was satisfied the jewel was not resting directly below the floor of the Palace of the Jaguars, he ordered the group outside. He allowed Quinn and Jasper to discuss the potential whereabouts of the treasure for a few minutes, at gunpoint. They both knew about the cavity in the sinkhole under the Pyramid of the Sun, and the tunnel underneath the Temple of Quetzalcoatl. The professor

The Aztec Secret

explained his theory of how the Pyramid of the Sun would be a fitting place for the jewel to be kept, as a last offering to the sun to keep the world from turning to darkness. While there were many deities in Aztec culture, the sun was the most significant. He explained that 'Teotihuacán' meant 'the place where men become gods', and with the sun being the most important to the Aztecs this would be as good a place as any to search. But the trouble was finding a way in. The space under the Pyramid of the Sun had been no more than a cavity from which a few items had been recovered.

Ted stood and watched, acutely aware of the time pressure Lucho had just placed on them. The message was clear; they had an hour to find the Heart of the Jaguar, or it was game over. He unlocked the phone and checked the countdown for the third or fourth time already. 56:34.

The format was akin to a large-scale escape room. Usually, this kind of time-sensitive activity would excite Ted and get him in a motivated, curious mood. But this wasn't a game, and all Ted felt now was raw fear.

'So, Temple of Quetzalcoatl it is,' Quinn announced. Her conversation with Jasper had come to an end, and they had made the decision to put all their eggs in that basket. Teotihuacán was a huge site; if they explored that area thoroughly enough they wouldn't have time to look elsewhere. Ted considered tampering with the timer. Pausing it a while, perhaps, or setting a new one later on. There was nothing stopping him from doing that while nobody was watching him. Would Lucho catch on? Would he realise if it had been significantly more than an hour? He remembered the burner phone Lucho had retrieved from his own pocket. He must have been checking the time, to account for any meddling on Ted's side.

The temple sat on the other side of the site, and it would take forever to get there. Lucho, clearly not intent on walking more than a mile down the Avenue of the Dead, ushered the group into the helicopter. The flight was short and tense, with the group held at gunpoint the whole time. Ultimately, it bought them more time to search at the other end, so Ted was grateful for that. A quick look at the countdown on the phone showed 40:23.

Upon leaving the helicopter, the sinkhole Jasper had described was just up ahead. The Temple of Quetzalcoatl sat just behind. On the outside of the pyramid, intricate carvings of two gods could be seen. They matched the carvings of the feathered serpent, Quetzalcoatl, and the water god, Tlāloc, that had been on the large stone slabs from inside the cave in Guatemala. The carvings ran in an alternating pattern across the sides of the pyramid. The significance struck Ted immediately, and he realised why Quinn and Jasper had settled on this pyramid. He recalled the excerpt from Cortés' letter to his son, Martín.

Passing swift, this fleeting life
Your path is set, you must go
When the eagle soars, the jaguar roars
Your heart is offered, your body is done
And they take your spirit to the temple
Where the serpent sings, and the gods will cry
For eternity, they cry

'Incredible,' Ted caught himself say. All the pieces of the puzzle were lining up. 'Your heart is offered' clearly represented the Heart of the Jaguar being taken to its final resting place, as an offering to the gods. The spirit of the Aztec culture, which was in jeopardy of being destroyed

The Aztec Secret

forever by the Spanish invaders, was taken to the temple where the serpent sings and the gods cry. The serpent god and the water god were both adorned across the side of this temple. This had to be it.

The group ignored the warning signs surrounding the cordoned-off area of the sinkhole and quickly lowered themselves in. If there was a risk of cave-in here, the stakes were too high for them to care. If they didn't find the jewel within the hour they would die anyway. Unless the police showed up before then.

Inside the sinkhole, a pathway of wooden boards had been laid out on the ground and fixed in place to allow easy passage through the tunnel. The way was dark, but the Mexican mercenaries spread themselves among the group with powerful torches to light the path ahead. The excavation from 2003 had delved deep into the ground, eventually ending up beneath the Temple of Quetzalcoatl. They walked along the tunnel cautiously for ten more minutes, before arriving at a junction of sorts. The excavation continued to the left and right, but both pathways led to dead ends. Further up the main route, the same occurred, this time the main tunnel coming to an end.

'Is this all of it?' Carlos asked.

'As far as the excavation went, yes,' Jasper replied.

'Perhaps we missed something?' Ted offered.

'If it were obvious, the original dig team would have found it,' said Quinn bluntly.

Tensions were running high and they were quickly running out of time. Ted made a quick check on how much time was left. 28:37.

'I suggest you find something that helps move this search on,' said Carlos. Easy for him to say, Ted thought, seeing as he wasn't the one with twenty-eight minutes to live.

'Let's split up and search in different areas. This is the place, I can feel it,' said Jasper. His tone wavered between enthusiastic and desperate.

Lucho took watch of Ted, with Carlos shadowing Quinn. Jasper and Alex stayed together, closely monitored by Eduardo. They ran the length of the tunnel looking for anything that could give a clue as to where the excavation team had missed something; possibly a burial chamber or a connecting tunnel to another unexplored part of the temple. The minutes ticked away as the group still found nothing. There was still no sign of the police, which worried them.

The countdown read 5:46. The end of the road was near.

Ted walked over to where Quinn was scanning the wall of the tunnel for signs of carvings or murals. This was a dire situation. He wondered what these poor souls had done to deserve this fate.

'I just wanted to say—' he began.

'Thank you,' she interjected.

'What for?'

'For going after me. I'm sorry that it brought you here though.'

Ted was taken aback. 'Of course. We couldn't just let you go alone.'

Quinn continued looking at the wall, determined to find anything that would prolong the inevitable.

'What I wanted to say,' Ted continued. 'Is that I'm sorry I was so rude to you, at the restaurant. You're clearly very passionate about this stuff,' he gestured to their surroundings. 'And I was a jerk for making fun of it.'

She turned to him. 'You already apologised for that.'

'Well, it seemed like something that needed two apologies.'

The Aztec Secret

She smiled and took his hand. Ted felt a sudden flush and his heart started beating out of his chest. His fingers tingled on contact with hers.

'I'm really glad I met you, Ted.'

He beamed at her. Everything he thought he knew about attraction had been blown out of the window. Nobody, not even Julia, had made him feel the way Quinn had just done with just a touch of the hand and a few words.

'Likewise. Even if the circumstances were utter shit,' he replied. The reality of the situation set in and her eyes began to well up. It was all Ted could do to not break down, or try a desperate dash for freedom. He knew it was of no use. He checked his phone once more. All he had was four minutes to hope for a miracle.

Jasper called over from the other end of the tunnel. 'Anything?'

'Nothing,' Quinn replied.

They regrouped at the deepest point of the tunnel. Lucho leant against the wall and tapped his foot against it restlessly.

'So,' Alex started, talking through something with Jasper. 'The excavation team stopped here, which goes directly underneath the temple?'

'Yes,' he replied.

'Why did they stop?'

'They needed more funding I think. These digs are expensive; a lot of people involved.'

'OK, so if they continued the dig, which direction would they have gone in?' asked Alex.

'My guess would be the path to the left. That's closest to the centre of the temple.'

The two continued their conversation as Quinn wandered back to the first crossroads in the tunnel, marshalled by Carlos. A moment later, she called for Ted. Lucho stayed to watch Jasper and Alex with Eduardo as Ted scampered over to find Quinn feeling the ground by the wall at the dead end.

'Look at this.' There was an excitement in her voice. She grabbed his hand and placed it on a pile of rubble on the floor.

'What is it?' he asked.

'This was a statue,' she said. 'Doesn't it look like it?'

Carlos shined his torch on the stone, revealing a carving on the side. What it used to be was unclear, nevertheless, Quinn was probably right.

'So is this just something the dig team left behind?' suggested Ted.

'Something they missed,' said Quinn. There was a glint in her eye. Ted had seen that look an hour ago, on Jasper's face, when they arrived at the site.

'Here,' she pointed to the wall at around head height. Carlos pointed the torch there. Quinn rubbed the wall with her hand, dusting away at the dirt that had built up. A triangular-shaped indent was revealed. She continued to brush away at it until it revealed another, coming out from the same point but at a different angle. After the third triangle, Ted cottoned on. He rummaged in the backpack Quinn had set on the ground and retrieved the star-shaped artefact. They shared a look as they realised the outline on the wall was a perfect match.

Suddenly, Ted's phone started buzzing and the melodic chiming of the alarm began to sound. Ted pulled it from his pocket and unlocked it with his thumb. The display flashed up, revealed the sickening 00:00 on the countdown.

TWENTY-FIVE

Lucho wasted no time in pointing the gun at Jasper's head. The professor couldn't help but let out a desperate whimper, his whole body trembling as he stared down the barrel. Lucho's expression exposed a sickening enjoyment, knowing that he would be the last thing this poor old man would see before his life was over.

'Wait!' Ted shouted. Lucho kept the gun trained on the professor, but the distraction kept him from pulling the trigger. 'We found something.'

Lucho let out a noise of frustration . The promise of progress had taken away his moment of violence, and the involuntary sound that escaped him indicated that he was disappointed by this, as though he had hoped they would fail.

'*Ven rápido,*' Carlos' voice came this time. Lucho gave the professor one last look, his eyebrows narrowing as though he was pondering whether to kill him anyway. Eventually, he tucked the pistol behind his back and took off down the tunnel to the others. Jasper had fallen to his knees, shivering with fear. Eduardo continued to watch over him and Alex as Lucho investigated what the fuss was about.

As Lucho arrived he found Ted standing next to a wall with the star-shaped artefact in his hand. Carlos was shining his light on the wall, where Quinn was brushing the dirt away to reveal an indent in the shape of the artefact. Lucho exchanged a few words with Carlos in Spanish, just as Quinn had finished what she was doing. Ted held the artefact over the indent and carefully placed it on top. Nothing happened.

'What are we looking at here, exactly?' he asked.

'I have no idea,' Quinn replied. 'But it has to mean something.'

'Maybe we're missing something,' Ted suggested. 'Perhaps it's another clue?'

'We don't have time for this,' Carlos hurried. 'You are delaying the inevitable.' He muttered something to Lucho, who reached for the pistol tucked behind his back.

Ted took the artefact away from the wall, studying the outline. He noticed that the points of the star on the artefact itself weren't even. He turned the object and rested it against the wall once more. Still, the outline didn't line up perfectly with the triangular points of the star. He repeated the process, turning it again and placing it back on the wall. This time the points lined up with the outline and fit snugly into the grooves. With a little pressure, the artefact pushed an inch further into the wall.

Ted paused in amazement and looked at Quinn, who had the same expression on her face. Even Lucho was mesmerised by what was happening and had stood motionless with the handgun hanging loosely in his grip. With his hand still pressed firmly on the clay middle portion of the artefact, Ted started to twist. The wall creaked from years of inactivity, but eventually, something gave way and the artefact pivoted clockwise. The ancient mechanism groaned and a part of the wall to the right of Ted started to give way. Ted twisted the object again until it locked into place. The wall continued to move, in response to Ted having initiated the unlocking procedure.

Quinn's eyes were wide, watching the unlikely events unfolding in front of her. The artefact wasn't just a symbolic object, or a vessel for a riddle, as they first thought. It was a key. A key that revealed a hidden passageway through the tunnels underneath the Temple of Quetzalcoatl. The wall to Ted's right moved slowly up into the ceiling with a loud cranking sound. Carlos shone his torch into the space that became a doorway, watching as the hidden tunnel came into view. The noise bounced off the walls in a sustained reverb until the stone wall locked into place at its highest point with a loud boom.

A moment of silence followed as the group took in the scene. Unable to move the star-shaped artefact any further, Ted took his hand slowly away from it. The device had been lodged into the carving of the wall and remained there. The moment had rendered him speechless. Had he really just witnessed an ancient artefact, stolen from a museum, open up a secret ancient door that had been undiscovered for hundreds of years? This was something that only happened in movies.

It was then that someone spoke for the first time in what felt like an age.

'Great heavens,' Jasper breathed. He had witnessed the last moments of the secret tunnel opening, having heard the screeching of the old door mechanism. A tear ran down his cheek; the residual effect of having been seconds away from losing his life, and now standing in front of what was certainly the pinnacle of his career. They had found what nobody had been able to find. This discovery alone trumped anything he or his peers had accomplished. But what kept his heart racing was the rekindled hope that it could in fact be true. All the stories indicated fantasy; another El Dorado. And yet all the signs pointed here: the note from Cortés, the song Doña Marina sang to their son, the symbols on the artefact, the carvings in the cave. It all pointed to this door, and what lay beyond.

Lucho stepped forward into the space behind the doorway. Pointing his torch out in front, he saw the tunnel carry on in a straight line before it disappeared into darkness once more. Unlike the excavation work before, it was wide enough for two people to walk side-by-side. The walls on either side felt smoother and the path had a feel of completeness to it. Whichever culture of people had dug this tunnel hundreds of years ago had spent a long time doing so. The place had an air of grandeur about it, as though it had been crafted for royalty. To call this a tunnel would be an injustice to the painstaking work that carved it from stone in such a way. It was more of a corridor, a passageway.

'Incredible,' Jasper said as he stepped through the doorway. 'Just look at this place.'

Alex entered next and stood by his side. 'What is it?'

'We're about to find out,' he grinned.

'I've never seen anything like that,' Alex said, gesturing to the door mechanism that the star-shaped artefact rested in.

'Yes, it is certainly unique. There are only a few accounts of door locks in Mesoamerican history, but nothing quite as sophisticated as this. They were round columns that were anchored to the corners of the door and jammed in place with sockets. They could be opened by anyone and replaced as they entered the room. This—' he looked back at the stone wall that had disappeared into the ceiling. 'This is a system of cranks and pulleys that lift heavy material and lock it into

The Aztec Secret

place. Like an iron gate on the other side of a castle drawbridge. Something like this here is astonishing.'

A musty smell lingered in Ted's nostrils as they ventured deeper into the passageway. Jasper had pointed out that the dead had been buried under these pyramids. The air felt stale having been contained underground in this passageway, sealed in by the hidden door, for centuries. Ted hoped that what he was smelling wasn't the lingering odour of death. The corridor went on for ages in a completely straight line. The only time Ted had experienced a similar feeling was when he took the train from London to Amsterdam on a weekend trip with Carl. Despite whizzing through the Channel Tunnel at high speed, it seemed to go on forever.

'Where is it taking us?' he asked, hoping Jasper or Quinn had a better sense of geography than him. Quinn took her small bag from over her shoulder and reached inside, retrieving the set of keys that had once had the UV pen attached. To Ted's surprise, she had another novelty keyring. At first glance, it looked like a bottle opener. But as Ted got a closer look he saw that the other end had a glass dome shape cut into it, with a set of letters and dash points in a circle. A red arrow pointed towards a dash point between S and E. It was a tiny compass.

'Does that even work?' Ted teased.

Quinn rolled her eyes. 'Just as well as the app on your phone, I'm sure.' She held up the set of keys until the compass/bottle opener combo was relatively level. She then pivoted on the spot, keeping the keyring steady as she lined up the red arrow with the north point. The direction lined up closely with the direction they were headed, albeit a little more to the east than true north. Jasper caught a glimpse of the compass points and tried to figure out their trajectory based on his knowledge of the tunnel layout earlier.

'The branch of the tunnel we found the hidden door in was headed north, going directly underneath the Temple of Quetzalcoatl.' His eyes lit up as he came to a realisation. 'If this path maintains its course, we'll end up directly underneath the Pyramid of the Sun!'

'How far?' Carlos asked impatiently.

'About half a mile in a straight line.'

**

The group quickened the pace a little as excitement had grown in Jasper. His ankle was giving him less trouble than before, but he still had a slight hobble in his walk. The discovery of the hidden door and passageway had rejuvenated his body, adrenaline coursing through his veins. They passed a number of strange clay artefacts that littered the ground: broken ornamental bowls and unusually shaped faces that had been intricately carved. Jasper stopped to pick one up, studying its warped features. Holding the ancient object in his hand, the whole situation felt surreal. He couldn't get over the fact that he was here, in this very moment, holding something so rare that nobody else alive had ever seen it. He'd dreamt of such a moment his whole career, and now that it was happening the sensation was overwhelming. Having been put through the wringer the last couple of days, particularly in the last hour, for a brief second it almost felt worth it.

He felt a strong shove in the back and fell to his knees, dropping the carved face onto the floor. It bounced on the surface, splitting in two.

'*Rápidamente!*' the harsh voice of Lucho followed. Jasper coughed as the force knocked the air from his lungs. He looked up to see Quinn and Ted being ushered on ahead of the trio of armed mercenaries. What had he been thinking?

The Aztec Secret

Those poor kids had been dragged into this mess and would be left traumatised if they got out of this alive. No discovery was worth this. The shattered artefact on the ground disappeared into darkness as the light from the Mexicans' torches moved further down the passageway. Jasper needed to hurry to avoid being left behind. There was no stopping Lucho now. He was hungry for his reward.

'Are you OK?' Alex helped him back to his feet.

'Yes, I'm fine. Keep going,' he reassured.

A few more minutes of walking followed when Eduardo's deep voice bounced off the walls of the passageway. '*Hace frío.*'

'Huh?' Ted asked, more as a reaction than a real question. It was rare for the big man to make any comment, and he'd almost forgotten what his voice sounded like. The sound had caught him off guard.

'It's getting colder,' Quinn clarified.

'Yeah, I feel it too,' said Ted, feeling the hairs on his arms stand on end.

Quinn glanced at her compass, verifying that the corridor had kept them on course for the Pyramid of the Sun. 'It's strange though. There's no change in the air here. We haven't descended at all either.'

Lucho, who was a few paces ahead, stopped suddenly. They had come to a junction, with two paths forking off in different directions. Both bent sharply and it was difficult to know which was the best one to reach the pyramid. Lucho turned to Quinn expectantly.

'Well?' Carlos prompted.

'Well, what?' Ted interjected. 'It's not like we've been here before.'

'Shut up,' Carlos raised a hand, cutting Ted off. He kept his eyes on Quinn and probed again. 'Which way to the pyramid?'

'I don't know,' Quinn replied candidly. 'As Ted said, nobody has been here before. We'll have to try both.'

Lucho gritted his teeth, dissatisfied with the outcome. Without asking for further guidance, he marched off down the path to the right. As they rounded the corner, the scenery changed quite drastically. What was previously a fairly open corridor with nothing of note except a few broken artefacts became a narrow passage with a lower ceiling. The path twisted and turned to the point where Ted couldn't see more than a few feet in front of him before a wall consumed his view. This part of the tunnel had a much more claustrophobic feel to it. Along each of the walls were long rectangular crevices cut horizontally into the stone.

'What is this place?' Ted asked. The cold, stale air created an eerie feel. 'Some kind of labyrinth?'

'Catacombs, more likely,' Jasper chimed in from the back of the group. 'Teotihuacán is full of tombs. A lot of people were buried here.'

'That's reassuring. So long as the dead don't come back to life,' said Ted.

'You've watched too many movies,' Quinn teased. Ted flinched at the comment, recognising it as his own. He remembered the dinner at the restaurant near the hotel.

'You jerk,' he replied tongue in cheek, recalling the response she had given him after saying that.

In single file, they shuffled through the maze of the catacombs. They arrived at a junction, where the path split four ways. Each time they carried on straight ahead, trying not to deviate from their northern trajectory. Quinn's compass kept them on track as they continued to pass the hollowed-out coffins carved into the walls. Eduardo curiously pointed his torch into one, shining the light into the crevice. Ted was walking just behind him and kept his head down. He could guess what was inside but would rather not see.

A final bend in the path led to a straight corridor that widened out. The pathway looked similar to that of the entrance past the secret door.

'It's still cold here,' said Ted.

'Fascinating,' Jasper replied.

'That it's cold?'

'The layout of this place. The people who once inhabited Teotihuacán thought the temples to be a place where the earth met the supernatural world. A point of ontological transition between the two plains.'

'So not that it's cold,' Ted muttered.

Jasper continued. 'It's eerie isn't it?' He turned to Ted. 'Perhaps what you're feeling isn't a chill, but the presence of cosmic energy?'

'Cosmic energy?' Ted wondered if he had heard that right. The professor gave him a look that indicated his comment was more tongue-in-cheek than Ted had understood. But the man was so eccentric it was sometimes difficult to tell when he was being serious.

The passageway continued on a little while before the light from Lucho's torch touched an archway. Moving closer, the picture became clearer and the group realised they had reached the end of the corridor and the entrance to another area. Stepping into the archway, a grand scene awaited them. The first thing Ted noticed was that the air felt crisper here. The ceilings were much higher than that of the passageway and the catacombs, and he felt a moment of peace from the claustrophobia he'd been subject to. A small crack in the ceiling sent a thin ray of light horizontally into the space, landing on a cuboid stone structure at the far end of the room. The beam of light was enough to get a sense of the scale of the area, but the details on the walls required the light from the mercenaries' torches to view properly. The sloped ceiling was evidence that they had made it to the Pyramid of the Sun. Spreading out across the room, the group managed to get a full sense of the geography of the place. Alongside the cuboid stone structure were three more, each tucked against the far wall, with equal spacing between them. They were arranged as though they were the focal point of the room, greeting those who entered through the single entryway. It was almost like a small court. The walls were lined with intricate murals.

'A burial chamber,' Jasper declared. 'These are sarcophagi.' He bent down next to one of the cuboid structures.

'Like in ancient Egypt?' Ted asked.

'Yes, only these people weren't mummified.'

'Some cultures in Mesoamerica were thought to bury their dead standing upright, rather than lying down,' Quinn chimed in. 'That would explain why the sarcophagi are stood vertically, not horizontally.'

'Where are the bodies?' asked Carlos.

Jasper studied the empty space inside the stone casings. 'Gone, it seems.'

Quinn gestured to Eduardo's torch. 'May I?'

The big brute looked at Lucho for approval. His boss nodded and he handed it over to Quinn. She wasted no time in scanning each of the other three sarcophagi for a clue. They were also empty. Something wasn't right.

'Where is the jewel?' Carlos cocked his head at the professor.

Jasper's heart sank. 'I think someone beat us to it.'

TWENTY-SIX

They looked at the empty sarcophagi, trying to work through the possibilities.

'Who has the jewel?' Carlos asked, his question tinged with anger. Lucho was pacing up and down the room, incensed by yet another dead end.

'How the hell would we know?' Ted countered. Carlos grabbed Ted by the collar and pinned him against the wall. His body slammed into a mural, chipping part of it away.

'Listen carefully,' Carlos barked. 'If we don't find it, we don't get paid, and you three finish the day inside those coffins,' he made a gesture towards the sarcophagi.

'Take it easy!' Alex intervened, trying to keep tempers from boiling over. Eduardo raised his rifle and pointed it at Alex, creating a stand-off.

'Hang on,' said Jasper. Carlos slackened his grip on Ted's collar and listened to the professor. 'As far as we know, there's no other way in here. The key to get through the door has Aztec inscriptions on it.'

'What are you saying?' asked Carlos.

'That key was only recently discovered, and since then it's been either in a museum or in our possession.'

'What about the corpses?' Carlos reminded. 'They've been moved.'

'Mutually exclusive events,' said Jasper. 'I think they were moved before the Heart of the Jaguar was brought here.'

'Or *when* it was brought here,' Quinn chimed in.

Alex was very aware that a gun was still trained at her head. 'Carlos, can you tell your friend to relax?' Carlos took his hands off Ted and backed away, gesturing for Eduardo to lower his weapon. Ted brushed himself down and distanced himself from Carlos.

'What do you mean?' he asked. 'Why would the Aztecs move their own dead? Wouldn't that be disrespectful?'

'Disrespectful, yes. But the dead may not have been Aztec,' Jasper explained. 'Teotihuacán was a living, breathing city long before the Aztecs discovered it. The founders of this place are not clear and there is much debate about it. The Florentine Codex attributed it to the Toltecs, but some scholars believe it was the Totonac people. The point is, some of these buildings go back to 200 BCE, long before the Aztecs.'

'So the Jaguar Warriors cleared out the corpses to claim the crypt as their own.' Quinn surmised.

Carlos considered the points laid out to him, before pressing with his original question. 'Who has the jewel?'

'Hard to say, but if someone did beat us to it, it was by hundreds of years,' said Jasper.

Lucho was still pacing the room, shining his torch in every nook and cranny as though he might stumble upon the jewel. Carlos watched the crazed man, before addressing Jasper once more.

The Aztec Secret

'If you don't find it, it's the end of the line for you. I may not be the one to put a bullet in you, but my boss won't hesitate.'

The warning didn't seem to be intended only to intimidate. The look in his eye indicated that Carlos wasn't as ruthless as his colleagues. Sure, his morals were questionable, but there was a feeling that if Lucho weren't in the picture he might let them walk free.

'Maybe it was Cortés?' said Ted.

The group eyed him suspiciously.

'I know it sounds far-fetched, but hear me out,' he continued. 'Wasn't it thought that Cortés had beef with his right-hand man, Pedro de Alvarado?'

'Beef?' Jasper looked confused.

'They had a problem with each other,' Quinn clarified.

'Yeah,' said Ted. 'Maybe Cortés knew to come here all along. Maybe he sent Alvarado on a wild goose chase as a distraction, so he could come here and take it.'

Quinn considered the theory. 'But the letter to King Charles stated that he would send the jewel to him as a peace offering, to clear his name. There's no record of it ever reaching him. Besides, isn't it coincidental that the wild goose chase would have pointed Alvarado in the right place anyway? His men didn't get far enough to see the carvings on the wall, but there was evidence that they had been in the cave.'

'I guess,' Ted conceded. 'It was just an idea.'

'But an idea we needed to rule out,' Quinn smiled, saving his blushes. 'I think there's a good chance the jewel is still here somewhere.'

'We have no choice but to look, anyway.' Ted was very aware that Lucho was close to giving up his basic search of the room.

Quinn bent down to examine the fragment of the mural that had chipped away from the wall when Ted had been thrust against it. She picked it up and studied the material. This mural wasn't like the ones that had lined the walls of the Palace of the Jaguars. These were shards of tile stuck to the wall, not stonework that had been painted on. The square-shaped tiles were equal in size and evenly distributed across the middle section of the wall, directly above where the sarcophagi stood upright. At first glance, it looked like a mosaic. But shining the torch onto each tile to study the patterns of colour, she realised that they were parts of the same image, like pieces of a jigsaw.

'Take a look at this,' she said, placing the tile back where it had been chipped away, holding it in place.

'What am I looking at?' asked Alex.

'The tiles, they're out of sync.'

Alex studied the tile Quinn was holding, and then the colours and patterns of the others sitting tight to the wall. It was then she spotted a blank space between two of the tiles and cottoned onto what Quinn was getting at.

'There,' she said, pointing to the space.

Quinn nodded enthusiastically. She put down the broken tile and moved over to the centre of the wall, between the middle two sarcophagi. Reaching up to the tile to the left of the empty space, she gently pulled the tile to the right. Sure enough, the tile didn't break, but instead slid sideways and took over the empty space, vacating the square area it had previously sat in. The tiles seemed to be set into grooves that could move about freely. This whole mural was a giant sorting puzzle.

'This just gets more and more surreal,' said Ted.

The group set about focusing all light from the torches onto the mural. Like any sliding tile puzzle, all they had to do was think logically and plan a few steps ahead to sort the painted tiles in order. Quinn seemed to have a knack for it and stood back from the wall to call the shots. Alex and Ted each took a side of the wall to control, carefully sliding the tiles into position.

'Ted, move that one right,' Quinn said, pointing to a tile. 'OK, now move that one up.' Alex dutifully carried out the request, moving the tile as instructed. Carlos held his torch steady on the wall to provide ample visibility, and even Lucho had quietly stopped his pacing to witness what was going on.

The image started to come together and before the last few tiles were in the correct position the group could tell what the picture was becoming. The tail, four legs, and a distinctive cat-like head revealed the outline of a jaguar. Ted completed the puzzle by dragging the top right tile over one step, leaving the empty space in the furthest top right corner. As the last tile clicked into place Ted braced himself for what was to come. A trap to be sprung, perhaps, loosing poison darts through the air at them? Or a boulder to come hurtling through the doorway? Everyone fell silent as the moment of anticipation came and went without anything happening.

'I'm not sure what I was expe—' Quinn wasn't able to finish her sentence as a loud rumble sounded, emanating from the sarcophagi. The tops of the stone caskets pinged open and more tiles fell to the floor with a smash. The rumbling sound continued as an object began to appear from the inside of the left-most sarcophagus. The object ascended slowly; the ancient mechanism responding to the correct ordering of the mural tiles. The object came into view and Lucho swung his torch around to see it more clearly. The light reflected off it in a dazzling glow, causing everyone in the room to squint suddenly.

Lucho could sense the treasure was within reach. He began to dart across the room towards the object when another emerged from the next sarcophagus along. Lucho stopped in his tracks as he watched the second reflective object come out from the top of the second casket. Then the third, and the fourth, until all four sarcophagi had identical-looking objects sprouting from their tops.

'It's not the jewel,' said Carlos, disappointed.

'No,' said Jasper, looking at his reflection in one of the objects. 'They're mirrors.' He approached one of the sarcophagi and took a closer look. The objects that had appeared on top were a plate of glass attached to long stems that protruded from the caskets.

'Remarkable,' he said, marvelling at this ingenious mechanism. 'This is unlike anything that's ever been seen from such an old civilisation.'

'This has to be a prank,' said Ted. 'This is like something from a video game. What next? A giant spider descends from the ceiling? A zombie hoard comes to attack us?'

'It's real, Ted,' Quinn replied. 'Just like the trial in the cave.'

'So what next? What significance do mirrors have in Aztec history?'

'None,' said Quinn, walking underneath the beam of light that came in from the crack in the side of the pyramid. 'I don't think this next part is reliant on anything but physics.'

As before, Alex followed her train of thought quickly and began to appraise the closest sarcophagus, looking for a way to remove the mirror from the top. Just before she began to pry the glass off the pole it sat on, she realised she was unsteady on her feet. Looking down, she noticed the ground was uneven, caused by the grooves that outlined the sides of the sarcophagus. She considered it a moment and then clicked her fingers towards Eduardo.

'Hey, you,' she said. 'Help me with this.'

Eduardo looked to Lucho again for approval. The pointy-nosed man scratched his soul patch and shrugged his shoulders, which was enough for Eduardo to agree to help. The big man moved in front of the sarcophagus Alex was stood next to and wrapped his arms around it. Alex indicated which way she wanted to move it, and he started to pull the heavy stone casket towards him. It moved slowly in response, running along the grooves Alex had noticed.

'Excellent!' Jasper enthused when he saw the plan that was being executed. The mirror on top of the sarcophagus was at just the right height to catch the beam of light coming into the room once the sarcophagus had been moved into the right spot in the centre of the room. Eduardo then moved around the back of the casket and pushed to gain more momentum. The stone coffin made a loud scraping sound as it moved along the grooves.

'Stop,' Alex instructed as it lined up perfectly with the beam of light. The moment the light touched the mirror it bounced off in a perfect stream to the corner of the room near the doorway.

'Of course, the Pyramid of the Sun. What a fitting tribute,' said Jasper.

'It's a good job we arrived during the day,' said Ted. Alex raised her eyebrows with an amused expression.

'Help me with this one,' Quinn said, pointing to the sarcophagus on the far side. The way the beam of light was headed, it seemed logical that this casket needed to be there to reflect the light somewhere else. The rules of this puzzle were quickly becoming clear.

Eduardo pushed the second sarcophagus the full length of the room until its mirror reflected the light to another part of the burial chamber. He repeated this process until the third mirror reflected the light back at the sarcophagus that was in the centre of the room. One more mirror sat atop the last sarcophagus, which hadn't been moved from its position at the end of the chamber by the jaguar mural.

'Something isn't right,' said Alex. 'If we move this to where the light is headed, the first mirror will be in the way.'

'We must have made a mistake,' said Quinn.

Ted studied the trajectory of the light after it bounced off the first mirror, assessing the tracks it crossed over before reaching the far side of the room.

'Here,' he said, walking over to the track between the first sarcophagus and the second. It was in line with the sarcophagus that hadn't yet been moved. 'This is where we went wrong.'

Eduardo wasted no time in dragging the stone casket along the track until he reached Ted's position. Ted moved out of the way so the big man could place it in the exact spot for the mirror to intercept the light beam. They noticed the way the angle of the static mirror changed the course of the light completely, meaning the other two sarcophagi would need to be adjusted accordingly.

'Nice work,' Quinn smiled, impressed.

The last great stone casket was pushed into position and the light was reflected upwards at an angle, landing on the jaguar mural. As the group looked to it, the familiar rumbling sound came again, stronger this time. It felt as though the whole chamber was shaking. Dirt fell from the walls as a giant unseen mechanism whirred into life. One by one, the tiles making up the jaguar fell from the wall and cracked on the

The Aztec Secret

floor as the rumbling continued. The group was stunned by the sudden activity and couldn't help but watch in awe.

The rumbling stopped around the edges of the chamber and became more focused on the wall immediately below where the mural had been. Suddenly, as they had witnessed with the secret door earlier, a part of the stone wall slowly started moving. A small doorway formed as the stonework moved backwards and rolled to the side, revealing a set of steps heading down into the darkness.

Lucho plucked his burner phone from his pocket and punched in the first number he had on speed dial. Despite being underground, the phone was able to catch one bar of signal. The dialling tone sounded for just two beats before the received clicked on.

'What took you so long?' the voice of Governor Ramón Villacrés hissed through.

'We had complications,' Lucho said plainly. 'I think we found it.'

A brief pause followed as static cut through the line. The weak signal was lost momentarily.

'Where—' more static followed.

'Sir?' Lucho battled with the poor reception.

'I can't hear you,' Ramón's voice crackled through the noise. 'Where are—' the static enveloped his voice, his words getting lost on their way through.

'Teotihuacán,' Lucho replied.

More static sounded, followed by silence.

'Sir?'

The static stopped, but there was no voice on the other end now.

'Governor!' Lucho shouted, trying to get through to his employer.

The voice came back. 'I told you never to use my na—' More crackling followed, cutting him off. Another short silence followed as Lucho listened for his employer's instructions. Eventually, Ramón came back through, much clearer this time. The signal had come back stronger, just long enough for Lucho to hear the plan.

'Sigma wants to collect personally. They'll meet you at Teotihuacán.' The receiver went dead and the line was cut off.

Lucho grunted and pocketed the phone, before racing off down the newly revealed steps. The rest of the group followed suit, bending down to enter through the doorway that could have been no taller than five and a half feet.

At the rear of the group, Ted entered last and made his way down the stone staircase, following who he thought was Alex. The torchbearers of the group had gone on ahead, leaving the rest to bumble their way along in the darkness. Upon reaching the bottom, Ted was able to see once more. Light from the torches hit the area the staircase led to from three sides, illuminating the space and giving Ted a good idea for the scale of it. The crypt had led to another chamber, smaller this time. Inside were a number of impressive artefacts. Ted could make out the glinted edges of a macuahuitl, which looked identical to the weapon he'd seen at the museum. The light from one of the torches bounced off the obsidian edges. A collection of bowls and other pottery rested in a pile to the side and Jasper was already inspecting a mural of what must have been another Aztec god.

'Tonatiuh,' said Quinn, recognising the figure depicted in the mural. 'God of the sun.'

The mural hadn't drawn the attention of the Mexican mercenaries, however, and Ted quickly learned why. Lucho's torch reflected off something that caught his eye in just the right way to make him squint and shield his face. Regaining his bearings, Ted saw what they were looking at. On a platform in the centre of the room was a small red stone, about the size of an apple. It sat idly on the stonework, as though it were beckoning someone to pick it up. Despite never seeing it before, Ted knew exactly what it was the instant he saw it. The Heart of the Jaguar.

TWENTY-SEVEN

Ted was completely transfixed by the jewel, as were the others. The colour and size of the thing made it clear how the stone had got its name. On first look, it seemed like a large shard of a ruby. But there was something else that made this jewel unlike anything he'd ever seen. There was an uncharacteristic quality to it he couldn't quite place. It wasn't the look of it, but more the feeling it gave him. It was as if the jewel was giving off some kind of aura, enticing him in like a siren luring sailors to shipwreck on rocky coasts. There was a power to this object.

'Magnificent,' said Jasper. The professor's voice was hushed to a whisper as he struggled to process his emotions. Ted didn't know if the old man was about to laugh or cry. He had spent his whole career wishing for a discovery like this. Mocked by his peers for his lack of achievement in the field, this was a feat far greater than anything they could even comprehend.

'It's really something,' Alex agreed. She managed to divert her gaze away from the rare jewel to watch their captors. She was very aware of the fact that they were disposable, now they had found what they were looking for.

'I wonder how much this thing is worth,' said Carlos. Despite being promised handsome pay for finding and delivering the jewel to their contractor, it was always a possibility that these crooks would go rogue. Carlos was smart enough to know the artefact would be worth more than ten times what he was being paid. But he was also smart enough to know that going against his contract could put a bounty on his head. No amount of money was worth being hunted for the rest of his life. 'It is the jewel we are looking for?' he turned to Quinn, acknowledging her as the source of authority over Jasper.

'Tonatiuh wasn't just the sun god, but the patron of warriors,' she replied, pointing to the mural. 'Jasper, didn't you say something about the Jaguar Warriors using the jewel as a ritual?'

'Yes,' he replied. 'They would touch the stone so it could pass on its power to them, to give them strength in their fights to come. Of course, there is an element of fantasy here; there were a lot of hallucinogens at play in these rituals.'

A faint droning noise could be heard, coming from back up the steps. Carlos recognised the noise instantly and rushed up the stone staircase to check it out. Hearing the noise more clearly through the gap in the pyramid's ceiling, he cursed under his breath and raced back to the others. He shouted something in Spanish to Lucho, who let out a frustrated noise.

The others heard the droning sound too and could just about recognise it as a siren.

'The police,' Alex said, suddenly realising that her call for help may have worked after all. They had taken their sweet time, but better late than never.

Lucho wasted no time and approached the platform. It would take the police time to find them all the way down here, but with only one escape route and their helicopter sitting suspiciously in the middle of the site, they needed to get out quickly before they were cut off.

It could have been a trick of the light, but the jewel itself seemed to be emitting a soft glow which lit up Lucho's face in red as he leaned over to pick it up. Reaching out with both hands, he scooped up the precious artefact. The moment his skin made contact with the jewel, a pulse of energy surged through him. A loud boom sounded, and a wave of deep red colour came out from the jewel and surrounded Lucho. It was almost like an electrical signal being pumped into him. His head titled back, a pained expression on his face, and his whole body shook uncontrollably. Ted watched on in horror as the contact with the sacred stone seemed to trigger a seizure. Lucho had the jewel gripped firmly in his hands.

'Lucho!' Eduardo called to his boss. Lucho didn't respond and kept holding onto the jewel. The aura from the sacred stone illuminated the room as the intensity of the energy seemed to grow. Lucho began to scream in agony as his body looked like it was being struck by lightning. A final boom sounded, and the room fell back into darkness. Lucho slumped over the platform, his body weak. His hands relaxed and the jewel tumbled out of his grasp, returning to its previous state.

Eduardo rushed over to his colleague. 'Lucho! Lucho?' He placed a hand on Lucho's shoulder, and as quick as a flash the pointy-faced man swivelled round and grabbed Eduardo by the throat. Lucho's eyes had turned bright red as the power of the Heart of the Jaguar swelled within him. Ted gasped as Lucho lifted Eduardo into the air, his outstretched hand clasped around the big man's throat. The juxtaposition of

Lucho's skinny frame lifting the full weight of the big brute was chilling. The professor had been wrong about the power of this jewel. It wasn't hallucinogens that had created the effect of the stone passing on power to those who touched it. What Ted was looking at was real.

Eduardo dropped the rifle he had been lazily carrying and grasped at the hand that had a tight hold of his throat. The big man's hands clawed at Lucho's fingers, trying desperately to free himself. He looked terrified as he stared at his boss, wondering why he was betraying him this way. Lucho stared right through Eduardo and tightened his grip further. The glossy look in his red eyes gave the man a possessed appearance. Eduardo closed his eyes and grimaced in pain, his body losing the fight as he struggled to breathe. His movements slowed and eventually all sign of life was gone. Lucho tossed his limp body across the room.

Without warning, Carlos leapt into action, wrapping the jewel in a piece of torn clothing before bolting up the stone steps. The fabric seemed to protect him from the effects of the stone, and he was able to get away cleanly. The others knew better than to hang around and chased after him. Ted just had enough guile to mop up the torch Lucho had dropped when he was transformed by the stone. Racing up the stone staircase, he tripped and fell, cutting his knee on the hard edge of a step. He winced in pain and let out a cry.

'Come on!' shouted Quinn, helping him to his feet.

By the time they had climbed the short set of steps to the burial chamber, Carlos had just disappeared out of sight into the passageway leading back to the Temple of Quetzalcoatl. Alex was hot on his trail, and without a torch, she was relying on keeping up with him to avoid getting lost in the darkness. Quinn and Ted quickly overtook Jasper, who hobbled along as fast as he could through the chamber. As they reached the doorway, a loud crash sounded from the way they had come. Taking a quick glance back at the stone set of stairs, Ted saw the red eyes of Lucho ascending the last couple of steps.

'Oh shit,' he cursed.

The adrenaline had kicked in and the group was running for their lives down the long passageway. Every few seconds there would be a loud clattering noise as Lucho pursued them. The crazed man had a supernatural level of strength as a result of the Heart of the Jaguar's power, but the effects of the energy transfer from the jewel seemed to have left him disoriented. His coordination was slightly off, which caused him to collide into the sides of the doorway. Each time he shunted into the wall it sent shockwaves through the passageway and debris fell from the ceiling further down the path. Ted was suddenly very aware of the possibility of a cave-in. Unlike the cave behind the waterfall, this place had been well tunnelled, and the well-crafted passageway had created the illusion for Ted that the place was structurally sound. As the dirt fell on his head, the fear intensified and he prayed for a clean getaway. He couldn't wait to be out in the open and breathe in the fresh air.

They flew down the passageway and into the catacombs. Alex followed the light from Carlos' torch, but by the time the other three reached the narrow passage the darkness had taken over once again.

'Which way?' said Ted, his voice panicked as they reached the first junction.

'Straight over,' said Quinn. 'Just keep going straight across each one.'

Forced to move through in single file due to the narrow passage, they were slowed by Jasper's limp. He hadn't fully recovered from it and he was starting to tire from the running. A crashing sound echoed through the catacombs behind

The Aztec Secret

them, reminding them that Lucho was close. Ted was worried that he would catch up to them before they even made it out of the catacombs. Then there was the long passageway to the Temple of Quetzalcoatl to contend with. At the speed Jasper was moving they were sitting ducks.

As they passed over the next junction, he stopped dead and shone his torch down the path to the right, considering something.

'Ted, what are you doing?' Quinn stopped just before following the curve of the path around a bend.

'He's going to catch up,' said Ted. 'We need to distract him.'

'How are we going to—' she saw the look on his face and knew he'd already figured that part out. His scared expression then told her what the plan was.

'No!' she protested. 'You can't do that.'

More crashing sounds came, louder this time. He was almost on them.

'There's no time,' Ted said. 'Get Jasper out of here. I'll catch up to you.'

She gave him a fearful look but seemingly agreed that there was no alternative. 'You better.' She disappeared around the bend in the path and Ted was left alone.

It didn't take long for Lucho to catch up. Ted had already started making tracks down the right-hand path and flashed his torch back at Lucho to grab his attention. The man turned to him, his fiery red eyes glowing in the dark and adding extra menace to his already intimidating appearance.

'Oh Jesus,' Ted said, already regretting his decision. Lucho spotted his target and began to take off after him. The plan was working, at least. This detour would hopefully buy Quinn and Jasper enough time to get safely out and in the company of the police. If he could lose Lucho through the maze of catacombs there was a chance he'd be able to join them.

The path twisted and turned in this middle section of the catacombs, and then Ted arrived at the next junction. There was no path leading straight on, only left and right. Without waiting to see how much distance he'd put between himself and Lucho, Ted made a snap decision and chose the left-hand route. He was panting hard now and the musty air he was breathing in made him feel sick. The claustrophobia was taking its toll too.

Another loud boom erupted through the catacombs and debris fell in chunks from the ceiling. A little further ahead, another T-junction came into view. Ted took the left path again, but a few feet ahead more debris started to tumble to the ground. The ceiling then completely gave way; he came to a grinding halt to avoid getting crushed under the huge slabs of stone that now blocked his path. He coughed and spluttered as the dust rose and filled his lungs. His progress had been halted and he would need to head back to the T-junction to take another route through the catacombs.

Lucho was almost at the T-junction himself, and Ted wouldn't have time to double back without bumping into him. He saw what the possessed man had done to Eduardo, a man twice his size. Coming into contact with him would be suicide. Hearing Lucho's grunts getting louder, he needed to act fast.

He wondered how on earth Lucho was managing to navigate through the dark tunnels. Had the power of the jewel heightened his other senses? Or more terrifyingly, given him the ability to see in the dark? Ted felt more and more like a victim in a monster movie.

Running was out of the question now, the only option was to hide. All around him were openings cut horizontally into the stonework, carved out for the dead to be laid to rest.

The Aztec Secret

He spotted one that looked easy enough to slide into. He pointed his torch into the crevice, hoping not to be greeted by a skeleton. Luckily for him, this one wasn't occupied. He lifted himself into the gap and shimmied his body deep into it. Lucho was at the junction now and there would be no escape if he spotted Ted. Lying flat on his back, his head turned away from the wall to keep an eye on the tunnel, he stayed as still as possible. It was only then that he remembered he hadn't switched off the torch. He reached for the button and flicked it, just as Lucho rounded the corner.

The moment the light went out Ted was plunged into darkness. He was completely blind while the torch was off. Relying only on his other senses, he started to become more in tune with his hearing. He noticed how heavily he was breathing and tried to steady it to avoid making noise. He was already breathing exclusively through his nose to help this, but with every inhale and exhale he expected Lucho to reach into the crevice and pull him out. Ted heard the man's footsteps come quickly towards him. The footsteps got louder, and dirt scraped off the wall right by where Ted lay as Lucho brushed past the crevice.

Lucho's breathing was heavy and his movement erratic, like a drunkard on his way home from the pub. The Heart of the Jaguar had really done a number on him and the effects were overwhelming. Jasper had said that the warriors would touch the jewel as part of a ritual. If a touch was all that was needed, what had this done to Lucho? The man had grabbed the rare artefact with both hands and held onto it for a long time. Was there such a thing as overdosing on this unexplained energy?

Lucho soon found the dead-end and made a frustrated noise. The crazed man knew that Ted had to have either taken the other path or was still around here somewhere. The fact that Lucho hadn't immediately run back down the tunnel made Ted's stomach drop. Did he know he was here?

Ted caught a glimpse of his bright red eyes as the man stumbled back along the path towards the junction. To his horror, Lucho stopped right by the crevice Ted was lying in. Ted held his breath, knowing one tiny sound could mean his death. The moment seemed to last a lifetime as Lucho lingered inches away. He heard his captor sniff the air like a predator tracking his prey. Another second went by as Ted closed his eyes and waited for the inevitable.

TWENTY-EIGHT

Minutes earlier, Alex had made it through the other end of the catacombs and was in hot pursuit of Carlos. She had never been the fastest runner, but her fitness levels were good. Good enough to smoke the idiots on the force who would continue to make the odd sexist remark at her. Showing them up in routine fitness exercises was always a strong motivator to keep in shape. But despite her strong stamina, Carlos had managed to put some distance between them. The man must have been a strong runner in his prime.

Escaping Lucho had been the first priority, but now the task had become stopping Carlos before he could get away with the jewel. It was obvious that the artefact contained great power, and it was vital that it didn't get into the wrong hands. Alex didn't know the full details of the deal to retrieve the sacred stone, but the shady nature of it made it pretty clear that Carlos, or whomever he worked for, was the wrong hands. The police would surely be outside, ready to assist her, but she couldn't take that for granted. It was up to her to protect and serve in this situation. She'd failed to protect in her last assignment; she wasn't going to let that happen again.

She stayed within a close enough distance to use the light from his torch as her guide to orient herself along the long passageway. She began to pant as her lungs worked overtime while she got her second wind. At this speed, the route through the subterranean corridor went by in a flash; the journey in had been so careful and considered in retrospect. She briefly thought of the others who were still much deeper in the tunnel. She saw what Lucho had done to Eduardo and made peace with leaving them by telling herself that there was nothing she could do to help them ward him off without a weapon. Besides, somebody had to see to it that Carlos didn't escape with the jewel.

The light from the torch suddenly dimmed as Carlos had reached the door the star-shaped artefact had opened and rounded the corner. Alex ran hard to catch up, feeling him slipping away from her grasp. After reaching the secret doorway she barrelled along the narrow walkway of the excavation site. Eventually, she saw daylight shining through from the entrance of the sinkhole. Carlos had ditched the torch on the floor and was climbing out. Alex launched herself at him, grabbing a hold of his shoe. He slipped as he tried to pull himself from the sinkhole and looked down to see the determined Alex. She had to stretch to keep hold of him, and with a swift kick, Carlos was able to free himself long enough to get a foothold in the earth. He scrabbled his way out onto the surface as Alex began her climb.

**

Ted opened his eyes and allowed himself a loud exhale. He had waited a good minute from the moment Lucho had disappeared further into the catacombs to start moving again. A noise had distracted him, and the crazed man had taken off in pursuit. Ted shimmied out from the crevice and dusted himself down. Reaching back inside, he felt for the torch, flicking on the switch as soon as he found it. As far as he could tell from the sound of Lucho's footsteps, the mercenary had taken the path at the right of the T-junction. Ted decided the best approach would be to double back. Perhaps he would find his way back to the point where he had veered off and separated from Quinn and Jasper. It was better than running around this maze with no sense of direction. He would have to take the risk of bumping into Lucho either way.

Turning the first corner, he immediately thought of Theseus and the Minotaur from Greek mythology. The situation certainly drew comparisons to that hero's adventure in the labyrinth. Lucho made a fitting monster in this maze-like arena, particularly in his current possessed form, but there were a few details that differentiated that scenario from this. Ted didn't have a ball of thread to help him find his way, and he was definitely no hero.

He pressed on, taking careful steps so as not to draw attention. He could hear a faint echo as Lucho crashed his way through the narrow catacombs, but as he rounded each bend Ted couldn't shake the feeling he would run straight into him. Eventually, he was able to retrace his steps back to the point where he'd left Quinn and Jasper. While most of the catacombs looked the same and he wasn't able to recognise the junction, he was pretty sure he'd reversed the turns he'd made at the previous junctions to make it back. Now he needed to turn right and ensure he kept a straight line through the rest of the intersections.

A distant rumble echoed through the tunnel; a constant reminder that Lucho was never far away.

'This better have been worth it,' he muttered to himself as he began to hurry. If Jasper still wasn't through the other side, this would all have been for nothing.

He could feel he was getting closer to the end now, and with each empty junction he picked up the pace, knowing the chance of colliding with Lucho was reduced. He followed the final bend around until he found himself at the opening to the grand passageway that headed back to the Temple of Quetzalcoatl. He breathed a sigh of relief as he saw no sign of Lucho. Setting off along the pathway, he shined his torch out in front. He couldn't see too far ahead of himself, even with the light source. The darkness swallowed it up after a few metres. His brisk walk switched to a jog, and then his heavy footsteps brought him into a run. He had a long way to go and the quicker he could cover it the better.

Another loud crash came, much closer this time. Startled, Ted swivelled round to see Lucho's fiery red eyes pierce through the darkness. While Ted had come from the right-side tunnel at the fork, Lucho had appeared from the left. It appeared that the catacombs were accessible from both sides, and Lucho had followed the maze around to this side while Ted had doubled back to take the other side. Lucho saw his target and gave chase. Ted wasted no time in picking up speed to a full-on sprint. He had made progress through the passageway before Lucho appeared, but he knew he was no sprinter. Or a long-distance runner, come to that. It wouldn't be long before Lucho closed the gap.

Clutching the torch in one hand like a baton in a relay race, he pumped his arms to generate as much force as he could. The light bounced up and down, affecting his vision, but he was just able to keep a straight course. Ted quickly felt a stitch develop in his side, but he pressed on, sure in the knowledge that his life depended on his ability to keep going.

The Aztec Secret

This wasn't the cross-country race at school; he couldn't just slow to a walk and wait for the pain to subside. He didn't dare look back to see how much distance there was between himself and Lucho. He knew he couldn't afford even the smallest error.

After what felt like a lifetime, he heard a familiar voice call out to him.

'Ted!' Quinn's voice echoed through the passageway.

'Quinn!' he called back, his voice hoarse as he struggled for breath. 'Close the door!'

Quinn tried to gauge how long she had before Ted made it safely through. She looked at the star-shaped artefact that was tightly wedged into the grooves of the wall, holding the door in the unlocked position. Once Ted was through, she could twist the key in the other direction to gradually lower the stone door. But Lucho was gaining ground on Ted, and there surely wouldn't be enough time.

'Now!' shouted Ted.

Quinn hesitated a moment, before grabbing the star-shaped artefact and yanking it from the wall. A loud scrape sounded as she freed it from its locked position, and the door mechanism whirred to life. The heavy stone door began to fall at an uncontrollable rate. Ted felt Lucho bearing down on him as he was just a few more steps from the doorway. He could hear the rattling of the door as it started to fall from the ceiling. He dropped the torch and launched himself at the opening. He just managed to slide through before it slammed shut, trapping Lucho inside. They could hear an angry roar come from the other side as Lucho slammed himself against the door. The heavy stonework held firm. It was over.

Ted wheezed as he recovered on the floor. He coughed and spluttered while the realisation sunk in; he was alive. He sat upright as he began to catch his breath, and was quickly interrupted by Quinn, who threw her arms around him.

'Thank God!' she said.

'I thought I was a goner,' Ted smiled. 'You timed the door to perfection.'

'I wouldn't put that down to anything more than luck.' She beamed at him, the pair revelling in the moment. After all the stress and danger of the past few days, they were finally safe. It may have been the rollercoaster of emotions they were feeling, but the way Quinn was looking at Ted he could have sworn she was waiting for him to kiss her.

'Ted, my boy!' Jasper interrupted the moment. Quinn relaxed her grip around Ted and stood up, tucking her hair behind her ear.

'It's good to see you again,' said Ted.

'Come now, enough dilly-dallying. We need to find the police and settle this,' Jasper told him.

That was the end of that then.

**

Emerging from the sinkhole, Alex was glad to feel a gentle breeze in the air. The stale smell of the tunnels had made her feel sick, and being out in the open once more was a welcome reprieve. She took a moment to breathe in the fresh air, her lungs thanking her for it. The break was brief but desperately needed as she had built up a sizable oxygen debt. It was at that moment that she saw Carlos scampering away from the Temple of Quetzalcoatl and towards the Avenue of the Dead.

This was far from over.

Making sense of her surroundings, she noticed that there was a distinct lack of police in the near vicinity. Just her luck.

The Aztec Secret

She could hear the sound of the sirens, but they were more distant now than they had been inside the Pyramid of the Sun. She picked herself up and made her way to the main path. Looking to her right, she saw the flashing lights of the police cars parked close to the Pyramid of the Sun. She waved to them and shouted in their direction, drawing the attention of one of the officers who quickly got inside their squad car and drove over to her.

By this time, Carlos was at the helicopter. The mercenary placed the wrapped jewel on the passenger seat of the cockpit and hastily started up the engine. A warning light flashed on the display and he cursed aloud when he realised what it meant. There was an engine malfunction. The big bird wasn't going anywhere soon.

A car horn sounded, and a plush black SUV rocked up alongside the helicopter. Carlos hopped out of the cockpit to get a closer look. The electric window of the passenger seat wound down to reveal a middle-aged woman. The driver alongside her was a stocky bald man, dressed in a black suit and sunglasses. He didn't take his eyes off the road ahead. Her bodyguard, he supposed.

'Do you have it?' the woman asked, her accent unmistakably British.

Carlos looked back at her with a perplexed expression. She had arrived completely out of the blue.

'The sacred stone,' she insisted. 'Governor Villacrés informed you I would be collecting in person.'

Carlos nodded and retrieved the jewel from the cockpit, keeping the clothing in his palms while he carefully unwrapped it. The woman's eyes widened as she saw the glimmer of red stone. As he wrapped it securely once more, the woman appraised the helicopter. 'I thought there were three of you?'

'You're Sigma?' he asked, confused.

'My identity is none of your concern.'

'My colleagues are dead,' he answered her original question.

'So be it,' she said. She heard the siren of the squad car drawing nearer. 'Get in the damn car.'

Carlos wasted no time in hopping into the back seat, the jewel sitting safely in his lap. The driver revved the engine and the vehicle lurched forward and made a sharp turn. The car drifted as the wheels spun up a cloud of dust until it completed its turn and the driver levelled out the steering wheel and floored the accelerator. The SUV took off with impressive speed as the scenery whizzed by the window. Carlos took a moment to look out the rear window and cursed when he saw the police car giving chase.

The moment the squad car had reached Alex she had hopped into the passenger seat and ordered the officer to follow the SUV. Her basic grasp of Spanish had got her that far, but luckily for her, the officer spoke fluent English and she was able to communicate the full story of what was going on as they tore after Carlos and his new companions.

The second squad car arrived outside the Temple of Quetzalcoatl just as Ted, Quinn, and Jasper had climbed out from the sinkhole. They flagged it down and spoke with the officer at the wheel.

'*¿Americano?*' the officer shouted out the window at Jasper.

'*Sí,*' Quinn answered for him, before informing the officer in Spanish that the criminal was getting away. A second officer was in the passenger seat and addressed them in English.

'You must stay here where it is safe. We'll send someone to take statements.'

The Aztec Secret

'Not a chance,' Jasper replied, pulling on the door handle and sliding into the back seat. Quinn gave Ted a funny look, and he shrugged his shoulders in response. The pair followed Jasper into the back of the car.

'I have to ask you to get out,' the officer said politely.
'There's no time. Follow them!' Jasper commanded. The officer sighed loudly and tapped his partner on the shoulder, who dutifully put his foot down. The driver revved the engine to the max before slamming the car into second gear. Jasper then began to fill the officers in on the details, starting with Carlos taking off with the jewel and working back from there.

TWENTY-NINE

Watching the world pass by in a blur, Alex was fixated on the SUV ahead of them. There was no way this criminal was getting away from her. She knew she didn't have any jurisdiction to arrest Carlos once she caught up with him, but at this point, she didn't care. They left the Avenue of the Dead and passed the visitor entrance to the site. Buses full of tourists sat stationary along the side of the road; the tour guides having received word that the site was temporarily closed while the police responded to a report of a kidnapping.

The squad car kept the SUV in view as it left the historical site and took off in a south-westerly direction. The SUV merged onto a dual carriageway and began to weave in and out of the traffic, making small gains as it tried to lose the squad car.

'Watch out!' Alex warned the officer of an oncoming car as they merged onto the road and nearly collided with it. The other car slammed on the brakes with a loud screech, the rubber tyres burning on the hot tarmac. What followed was a series of incensed honks of the horn from the disgruntled driver. The squad car continued on at full speed, its siren wailing as the traffic started to move out of its way.

'This never gets old,' Alex commented, watching as the cars ahead began to part like the red sea as the squad car straddled the dotted line of the lane separator.

The driver of the SUV maintained a stoic look as he guided the big vehicle in and out of the traffic. Looking in the rear-view mirror, he noticed the police catching up fast. He swerved sharply to the right and took the next exit into San Lorenzo Tlalmimilolpan. In the car behind, Alex didn't need to prompt the driver to make the exit. As soon as the SUV veered off, the officer slowed his speed to safely take the turning. Alex clutched the grab handle above her head as they made the sudden turn onto the slip road. Picking up the walkie-talkie that was strapped to the dashboard with a long coiled cable, the officer provided an update of their location to his partners. The traffic on the single lane road ahead had slowed to a stop in anticipation of the squad car's arrival. The SUV barrelled through, and seconds later Alex and the officer merged onto the road in pursuit.

Seeing the flashing lights of the police in his rear-view mirror once more, the driver of the SUV knew he wouldn't be able to lose them so easily. He waited for his opportunity and found it in the form of a dirt road that led out into nowhere. He shifted down gears and performed a slick handbrake turn off towards the dirt road. Releasing the handbrake once more, he floored the accelerator. Carlos nearly knocked his head against the window, deciding afterwards to put his seatbelt on. The jewel sat wrapped up on the seat next to him.

Now was time for part two of the SUV driver's plan. He knew his vehicle was much larger and hardier than the small hatchback squad car. As soon as the officer came into view, he slammed on the brakes. Carlos watched in horror through the back windshield as the squad car tried in vain to react quickly enough. Alex saw the red brake lights loom closer, almost in slow motion, before the impact. She leaned back in her seat and intensified her grip on the grab handle as the car smashed into the back of the SUV with a tremendous crunch.

Dazed and confused, she fought with the airbag that had caught her as her face fell forward. She turned to her side to see the officer was unconscious next to her, blood coming from his head. She pressed two fingers to his neck and found a pulse. Next thing she knew, the driver's side door of the SUV swung open and a stocky bald man in sunglasses and a black suit got out. She saw the flash of a pistol in his hand.

'Shit,' she breathed, searching for an exit route. The man approached the squad car cautiously, his gun now raised and trained on the driver's side. Alex fumbled for her seatbelt release button, finding it on the third attempt. The buckle snapped back and retracted into the side, freeing her. The man was almost to the front of the car now, and luckily for Alex, couldn't see through the cracked windshield. She looked to the officer's side for his weapon but found only an empty holster. Thinking fast, she pushed the airbag to one side and opened the glove box, finding the revolver inside.

The bald man saw the motionless officer's head resting in the airbag of the steering wheel and switched his attention to the passenger seat. Alex clicked the door open and lunged out, keeping low as the man fired a shot at head height. It grazed her shoulder and she cried out in pain as she fell to the ground outside the car.

The man fired two more shots through the back window, hoping to catch her if she moved towards the rear of the car. The glass shattered and fell on her head as she slumped against the bodywork. Her shoulder was bleeding, but luckily it was just a flesh wound. The bald man called out to her in

Spanish. The words were said so quickly she had no idea what he was saying. She didn't respond and instead peered underneath the car to get a sense of where the man was. She saw his feet moving back around the front of the vehicle. She brought her right hand to her chest, nursing the arm as best she could.

Sensing his moment to strike, the man hurried around the front of the squad car and to the passenger side. He rounded the corner and instinctively fired off another few shots. But Alex was no longer there. Suddenly, the sound of her revolver erupted from the back of the car as she fired three shots in retaliation. The bald man dropped to the deck; one of the bullets having found his neck. Alex fell back into cover and let out a long exhale. Lucky for her, she was left-handed.

The sirens of the second squad car could be heard and soon after it pulled up behind the first. Ted and Quinn leapt into action, attending to Alex's bloodied shoulder.

'I'm alright,' Alex said. 'Just be careful with—'

Another shot rang out, the bullet pinging off the bodywork of the squad car and narrowly missing the trio. The woman emerged from the front of the SUV, firing off another warning shot. The officers in the second squad car returned fire. The woman ducked out of the way, using the open door of the big car for cover. The officers split up, taking different routes to cut off the woman's exits. She was clutching the wrapped-up jewel in one hand and pointing her pistol at one of the officers with the other.

'Stay back!' she commanded.

The pinch manoeuvre was succeeding in overwhelming her. The danger was still very real, but there was no chance of her getting away. With no escape plan, the woman knew her options were to fight her way out or surrender. Seeing both officers training their gun on her, the latter option won out and she threw her weapon to the ground. An officer rushed over to subdue her while the second secured Carlos in the back of the SUV. He was just coming to his senses, having been knocked unconscious by the collision.

The others gathered around to help the police safely secure the jewel and call an ambulance. It was then that Jasper saw the woman being escorted to the second squad car, recognising her instantly as the former Oxford professor that was good friends with his bitter rival, Evan Anderson.

'Lillian?' he reeled in shock. What was she doing here?

'Hello, Jasper,' she said calmly. 'Looks like our plan didn't work out quite as we hoped, did it?' She winced as the officer tightened a set of cuffs to her wrists.

'Our plan?' Jasper was struggling to put the pieces together.

'You always were desperate for success. It's part of what made you such a perfect mule.' She looked at the dead bodyguard on the floor, and then to Carlos as he was being cuffed. 'Pity the goons he hired were so incompetent. We almost got away with it.' She gave a wry smile as she was helped into the back of the squad car.

It was then that it became clear to Jasper. 'You're Sigma?'

'Do keep up, dear,' she said, just as the door was slammed shut.

He couldn't believe it. All this time his employer had been one of his academic rivals. He had been so determined to prove them wrong about his lack of achievement, and yet she was the one who would profit from his discovery. He'd been such a fool.

A short while after, the ambulance arrived, along with another police officer. Alex was being seen to while the officer questioned her on the events. A forensic team took photos of the bald man, and Alex admitted to shooting him. The police were satisfied it had been self-defence, and the fact she had surrendered the revolver the moment the second squad car had arrived helped her case. Plus, she had three others who could testify to her role in the situation. Quinn sat alongside her in the back of the ambulance, taking large swigs of water from a bottle.

Jasper sat slumped against the crashed squad car, contemplating the mistakes he'd made and how foolish he'd been to accept this assignment. Ted walked over to check in on him.

'Is that who I think it is?' asked Ted, looking towards the woman sat in the back of the second squad car.

'Unfortunately, yes,' Jasper bowed his head in shame.

'What's she doing here?'

'She was the one who masterminded this whole thing. Hiring Lucho and the others, getting me involved. She used me like a pawn to get what she wanted.'

Ted put a reassuring hand on his shoulder. 'I'm sorry.'

Jasper gave Ted a concerned look, a tear forming in his eye. 'My boy, don't ever apologise to me. I'm the one who is sorry.'

Ted smiled. 'Just be grateful it all turned out alright.' He looked at Quinn, who passed the bottle of water to Alex while the paramedic bandaged her shoulder. 'We're going to have some explaining to do at the university, aren't we?'

'*I* will,' the professor clarified. 'You have your final exams to study for.'

Ted laughed. That was the last thing on his mind.

THIRTY

As the curtain came up and the introductory round of applause began for the school talent show, Ramón took a second to soak in the moment. He felt at ease, knowing that for once he had made it in time for Adriana's performance. Patricia was sat content next to him, rather than ferociously texting, wondering where the hell he was. He couldn't wait to see the look on his daughter's face when she spotted him in the audience. And he couldn't remember a prouder moment as a father than watching his little girl walk sheepishly on stage, before playing a gentle melody on piano in front of so many people. It brought a tear to his eye as he listened to the soft notes echo around the hall. She was so talented. He looked to his wife and shared a smile, making a silent vow to be better. He had gotten so wrapped up in his work he'd lost track of what really mattered. The last few days had been extra stressful, seeing the news of the arrest of the artefact collector, Lillian Pembroke, or as he knew her, Sigma. The moment the arrest had been reported, he feared he would become exposed too. But as the days passed and nothing

The Aztec Secret

happened, he breathed a sigh of relief. Now that this problem had been taken care of, he could get on with his life.

His phone buzzed in his pocket and he reached for it instinctively. As he retrieved it, he received a cold look from his wife. He knew that look. It warned him not to even think about it. He placed a reassuring hand on Patricia's knee; he wouldn't let work take him away this time. He would just take a quick peek at the preview of the email that had flashed up on his screen.

His stomach dropped as he saw that it was from General Secretary Cicerón. The email was just four words long, but the message was powerful enough to send his brain into overdrive.

It's over, Governor.

His whole body suddenly felt hot, like he had come down with a fever. The room started to spin as the sudden realisation dawned on him that it was over. Just like that, simply by reading three words, his whole world had changed. He knew exactly what the message alluded to. Somehow the General Secretary had discovered his lies. He thought of the auditors, then the conversation he'd had with Miguel. Somewhere along the line, his tracks hadn't been covered well enough. All of his illegitimate activity had been exposed; the agreement with Sigma, his transactions with the cartel, all of it. And now the General Secretary had been alerted to it.

He cursed loudly, drawing attention from both Patricia and the other parents around him.

'What is it?' his wife asked concernedly.

'I need to go,' he said.

'No,' she hissed. 'Your daughter is still playing.'

Ramón had stopped hearing the soft tones of the piano the moment he saw the email. He'd almost forgotten where he was.

Next thing he knew, the doors to the school hall opened and two police officers entered. They scanned the audience, just as Ramón started climbing over the people next to him to escape. They spotted him and began to chase, one flanking around the other side of the hall to cut him off. There was a loud commotion as Ramón forced his way through the narrow aisle of chairs, climbing over other parents and stepping on their feet. Adriana stopped playing and watched as her father darted towards the exit. She stood from her stool and watched as the officer blocked his path.

'Señor Villacrés, you need to come with us,' the man said, grabbing Ramón's arms and swinging him around so he could cuff him. Ramón yelled out in frustration before his eyes settled on Adriana. A tear rolled down his cheek as the officer began to read him his rights. He knew then that the next time he saw his daughter it would be from behind bars.

**

Ted sat at the desk of his room, taking a moment away from his laptop to stare out the window at the busy London streets below. It had been a week since he returned from Mexico, and life had just carried on as normal. Lectures were starting up again and he was into his last term of study before graduation. He'd learnt a lot about himself from his experience on the trip. Jumping out of helicopters definitely wasn't his cup of tea, nor was mixing with armed mercenaries. He had a newfound appreciation for quiet museums, where the most exciting thing to happen was the opening of a new exhibition.

Checking into his social feed, a photo popped up of Julia having dinner with Richard at a fancy nouveau cuisine restaurant. He couldn't help but smile at the scene, thinking how well suited they both were to that environment, and how out of place he would have felt had he been there instead of Richard. How things had changed since a couple of weeks ago. Scrolling down a bit further, an ad came up for a historical magazine subscription. The algorithm had slapped a label on Ted since his intensive research session on Aztec history before the trip to Mexico, and ever since he had been retargeted with ads like this. On another tab in his browser, he had left open a news story from a Mexican publisher. The page had been translated loosely by the browser, with the headline *Three Arrested in Museum Theft*. Ted scoffed at the title, knowing full well that the stolen artefact was just the tip of the iceberg in the crimes that had been committed.

The article went on to recount the details of the events, ending with the arrest of three individuals, who were each pictured below. The first was Lillian, who had a search warrant put on her house in London to reopen investigations into previous reports of stolen artefacts from years ago. As it turned out, artefact collecting was just a hobby for this businesswoman. Further reports into her criminal activity uncovered ties to an infamous Mexican cartel, along with a number of other organised crime factions across the globe.

The second person pictured was Carlos, who had charges of robbery and kidnapping against him. While the identity of the third individual was of no surprise, Ted was taken aback to see the mug shot of Lucho as he scrolled down. It seemed the effects of the Heart of the Jaguar had worn off, and the police must have arrested him on entering the secret door into the tunnels underneath the Temple of Quetzalcoatl. He too had similar charges, and after the testimony of Carlos, who no longer saw the point in remaining loyal to his boss, an additional charge of murder had been placed against him. He closed the page and sat back in his seat.

Joe Topliffe

It was just a few months until he graduated now, and he still wasn't sure what he wanted to do when his time at university ended and the rest of his life began. He wasn't completely turned off by journalism, so that seemed like the default for now. He'd added a small entry to his CV after the field trip to Mexico, which seemed understated alongside the paragraph he'd written about his part-time job tending bar at the student union. The actual journalism part of the trip had been overshadowed by the events that followed, but Ted remembered enjoying it. He couldn't tell if it was the interviewing and note-taking he'd enjoyed, or if it was the jokes he'd shared with Quinn that left a lasting impression on his memory. What he did know was that he'd not stopped thinking about her since they'd parted at the airport.

Glancing back to his social feed, he saw an update from Alex. A photo of her in a hospital room appeared. A man called Joel had been tagged in the photo. The pair smiled at the camera. Ted looked at the caption, which read 'Partners in crime'. He smiled, appreciating the good moments social media sometimes provided. It was nice how this medium allowed him insight into another person's life; a moment they wanted to share when others couldn't be there to appreciate it with them. The photo would give him a nice talking point the next time he spoke with Alex.

His laptop pinged another notification, and his video chat icon started flashing. It was Quinn. He checked the time; she was three minutes early.

He clicked the green answer button and watched as her face came up on the screen. She was wearing a white t-shirt under a zip-up hoodie, with a framed shot of a scenic mountain peak covering most of the backdrop of her dorm room. She'd done something with her hair, but Ted couldn't think what. He just noticed that it seemed different to before. Even through this pixelated view, she looked beautiful.

'You're keen,' he said.

'And how long were you sat watching your screen waiting for me to call?' she retorted with a smile.

She'd got him there. 'I was just walking by and saw it come up,' he lied.

'Right,' she raised an eyebrow playfully.

'How are you?'

She pondered the question. 'Not bad, considering.'

'Yeah,' said Ted, acknowledging the hidden meaning. 'I know.'

'So what happened with Jasper? Did he have the meeting already?'

After news broke of the museum robbery, kidnapping and shootout, with a well-known and respected former researcher being arrested for orchestrating it all, Jasper came clean to the university about his part in it. The authorities in Mexico had seen Jasper as a victim of the kidnapping and had decided against placing charges. Surprisingly, it seemed Lillian hadn't mentioned his name either. Perhaps the knowledge of having played him like a fiddle was enough satisfaction for her, knowing how much it would hurt him.

'He lost his job,' said Ted solemnly.

Quinn's face dropped. 'Oh, that's awful. How is he?'

'I saw him yesterday. He actually seemed fine,' said Ted.

'Really? That's odd. Wasn't this career everything to him?'

'Well that's just it,' Ted began to elaborate. 'He's getting toward retirement age. He said the adventure was a fitting end to his tenure. He knew what the verdict would likely be on the plane back from Mexico, and he told me then that he wasn't looking forward to going back to teaching. To be honest, he's lucky losing his job is the worst punishment he's receiving for getting two students kidnapped by terrorists.'

'Well, to Professor Thornton then,' Quinn raised a glass to the camera.

'To Professor Thornton,' Ted echoed, raising his refillable water bottle in response. 'What is that you're drinking? It looks…' he paused while he tried to find the right adjective. 'Green.'

'Kale smoothie,' she replied. 'It's super healthy.'

'That sounds disgusting,' Ted smirked.

'It is,' she laughed.

A short silence followed as Ted got lost in her eyes. 'There's something I've been meaning to ask you,' he remembered at last.

'What's that?'

'What's an archaeology social like?' he smiled devilishly.

'What?'

'Jasper mentioned it at the museum in Mexico when he was going on about Professor Anderson.'

'Well, I don't know what exciting activities they get up to, but for me, an archaeology social is just like any other. Drinking, making jokes, sometimes dancing.'

'Dancing?'

'Yeah. You know, something you do in a club sometimes,' Quinn said sarcastically.

'You go clubbing?'

'Sometimes. Ted, I know what you're thinking. A bunch of nerds meeting up in a museum for canapés, champagne, and high-brow conversation about ancient civilisations. We're students; we do what other students do.' She turned the conversation around on him. 'What is it you journalists get up to I wonder? Sitting in a library discussing your favourite

The Aztec Secret

newspapers, or perhaps you take it in turns to interview each other while someone records you on their phone?'

'Alright, alright, you've made your point,' Ted put his hands up in surrender. 'I was just wondering, that's all.'

'No, I still don't think you believe me,' said Quinn playfully. 'I'm just going to have to prove it to you.'

'And how would you do that?' asked Ted, intrigued.

'You'll have to come along to one, in the summer.'

'In New York?'

'No, the moon,' she stuck her tongue out in jest. 'But first, you need to show me around London. I've always wanted to go.'

'Are you inviting yourself?' Ted recalled their first interaction and how she had teased him about that.

'Well, luckily I don't need your permission to travel. But it would be handy to have a tour guide.'

Ted smiled. 'When are you thinking?'

'I already booked my tickets. I fly out right after graduation.'

Ted's heart swelled at the prospect of seeing her in person once more. 'It's a date then.'

She beamed back at him. 'It's a date.'

Joe Topliffe

Acknowledgements

Thank you for reading this novel! If you enjoyed the experience and would like to share it with others, please leave a review on Amazon, Goodreads or your book forum of choice. Your feedback means a lot to me.

A huge thank you for the encouragement I continue to receive from friends, family and colleagues. Finishing that first draft can be a long slog and your kind words motivate me to push on to reach the end.

But most importantly, the biggest thanks go to my wife, Hollie. Thank you for taking the time to review my work and provide such detailed and thought-provoking feedback. But most of all, thank you for being patient with me. Your love knows no bounds, and for that I am a very lucky man.

Printed by Amazon Italia Logistica S.r.l.
Torrazza Piemonte (TO), Italy